Cop vs. Killer

Detective Jack Murphy never met a cold case he couldn't crack. This one's been on ice for 37 years. The prime suspect in a decades-old unsolved murder is about to be named Evansville's next Chief of Police. The Mayor wants the top cop's name cleared—and that's why Murphy and his partner, Liddell Blanchard, are ordered to re-open the investigation. But when the victim's sister and mother are targeted for violence, troubling new questions arise. Is this the work of the same killer, or is someone else playing a deadly game? The answers lie buried in the past. But no one digs through the dirt like Jack Murphy . . .

"A jaw-dropping thriller that dares you to turn the page."
—**Gregg Olsen**

"A tornado of drama—you won't stop spinning till you've been spit out the other end. Rick Reed knows the dark side as only a real-life cop can, and his writing crackles with authenticity."
—**Shane Gericke**

"A winner of a debut novel... Reed is a master of describing graphic violence. Some of the crime scenes here will chill you to the bone."
—**Bookreporter.com**

Also by Rick Reed

The Jack Murphy Thrillers
The Cruelest Cut
The Coldest Fear
The Deepest Wound
The Highest Stakes
The Darkest Night
The Slowest Death
The Deadliest Sins

Nonfiction

Blood Trail **(with Steven Walker)**

The Cleanest Kill

A Jack Murphy Thriller

Rick Reed

LYRICAL UNDERGROUND
Kensington Publishing Corp.
www.kensingtonbooks.com

LYRICAL UNDERGROUND BOOKS are published by

Kensington Publishing Corp.
119 West 40th Street
New York, NY 10018

All Kensington titles, imprints, and distributed lines are available at special quantity discounts for bulk purchases for sales promotion, premiums, fund-raising, educational, or institutional use.

Special book excerpts or customized printings can also be created to fit specific needs. For details, write or phone the office of the Kensington Sales Manager: Kensington Publishing Corp., 119 West 40th Street, New York, NY 10018. Attn. Sales Department. Phone: 1-800-221-2647.

Lyrical Underground and Lyrical Underground logo Reg. US Pat. & TM Off.

First Electronic Edition: June 2019
ISBN-13: 978-1-5161-0458-1 (ebook)
ISBN-10: 1-5161-0458-7 (ebook)

First Print Edition: June 2019
ISBN-13: 978-1-5161-0459-8
ISBN-10: 1-5161-0459-5

Printed in the United States of America

This novel is dedicated to Amy Hollen, a good friend and my inspiration for this story. I hope you enjoy the story, Amy.

Chapter 1

Thirty-seven years ago

It was two days before Thanksgiving and the championship game. Maximillian Alexander Day, varsity wide receiver for the Rex Mundi Monarchs, stood behind the bleachers before practice. This weekend would be the playoff game against their rival, the Central Bears. While the rest of the team was in the locker room, checking equipment, gearing up, grunting and yelling inane slogans, he stood at the mouth of the tunnel, wearing his varsity jacket, well-worn blue jeans, and Western boots. The cheerleaders had taken the field. Practice could wait.

Max watched Ginger lead a cheer and his little Max was cheering right along with her. Ginger was the head cheerleader; Dick was the captain and quarterback of the team. Because of that, Dick thought Ginger was his property. Max hoped he got to play defense in tonight's practice, so he could knock that idea right out of Dick's head. He'd been warned by the coach a couple of times for using excessive force to sack his own quarterback, but it was funny. Dick never saw it coming. Truth was, Max didn't care who he creamed on the field. He didn't even care for sports. He just liked hitting people—hard—and he liked the varsity letter jacket. It was a chick magnet.

He was still dating two other girls but the girl he currently had his eye on was Ginger Purdie. Her copper-colored ringlets bounced around her shoulders and swept across perfect breasts as she led the cheers, urging them to victory. Max felt an urge too.

Part of his interest in her was that she would undoubtedly be queen of the prom. No surprise there. She was the prettiest girl in school. And of course, the king of the prom would be the quarterback of the varsity team: her longtime boyfriend, Richard Dick, aka Greased Lightning. Max was determined to change the buffoon's name to Greased Monkey because Ginger would slip right through the quarterback's hands and be picked off by defensive cornerback Mad Max.

The cheers ended. There was clapping and shouts and hoots from the bleachers above. Max stepped forward in time to watch Ginger bounce and jiggle and whip her curls around until she spotted him. She smiled at him and scurried off the field with every blue-blooded male's eyes following her, but she only flirted with Max. She ran to the sidelines and became part of the usual team enthusiasts. Max waited for her to turn around so he could motion her over. He would chat a few minutes and then change out for practice. When she saw him cut through Dick's offense like a knife through butter, she would see who the real man was.

The tunnel leading from the locker room to the field was right behind him, but Max wasn't worried about Greased Lightning. In fact, he hoped the arrogant asshole was watching Ginger as she brazenly flirted with him. He waved his arms over his head and Ginger turned. She stopped bouncing, her smile faded, and she pointed one of her pom-poms toward him. Max smiled and was motioning to her when something hard struck him in the back of the head. He fell to the ground, but he cushioned his fall with his hands and arms. He'd taken harder hits both on and off the field.

Max pushed himself up to his knees and saw Richard "Greased Lightning" Dick looming over him, helmet in one hand, the other hand bunched into a fist.

Dick was tall with blond hair combed into bangs down into his blue eyes, patrician features, perfect teeth, and always dressed preppy, not even wanting to soil his uniform. For a quarterback, he appeared less strong and solidly built than he did stringy and rangy. He had earned the name Greased Lightning because of his uncanny ability to hit the receiver with every pass while slipping through any defense. Max had watched him throw the ball away to avoid being tackled. And he never tried to run the ball. That made him a coward in Max's thinking.

"Better stay down, Max-e-pad," Dick said. "You and your sister have some lame ass names. Your mom must've been on drugs."

Carl Needham piped in. "Have you seen his mom? I wouldn't let my dog do her. She's a sow."

Carl and his pal Dennis hurled more insults, one grunting like a pig, the other repeatedly making motions like he was rooting in the mud. Needham hawked up a glob of snot and spat it on the ground beside Max.

You had your chance, Dick. Now it's my turn.

Max got to his feet, brushed some grit from the sleeves of his letter jacket, smiled, and deftly broke Dick's nose.

Only Dennis James made a move forward, but was halted by a shake of Max's head.

"Dennis, you're such a numbnuts. If you talk about my mother again I'll tear your head off and shit down your neck."

Max walked away without a challenge while Dick was bent over, hands covering his nose, blood running between his fingers and down the front of his red football jersey. A small crowd had gathered around, pretending sympathy and shock, while some in the crowd mocked Dick and danced around, hands over their own noses.

Max knew he'd be kicked off the team for punching Dick out and wouldn't be played in the championships. Hell, he'd be lucky if he wasn't kicked out of school. If that happened, his parents would ground him for the rest of the year and take away his one pleasure, his Camaro.

He was nearing the edge of the parking lot when he felt a strong hand grip his shoulder, pulling him around. He spun around and kicked Dick in the crotch. Dick fell to the ground. Squeaks like air leaking from a balloon came out of his mouth. Carl and Dennis stood with their mouths hanging open like dutiful minions and Dennis's hands went to his own genitals. Max stared at each of them, daring them to step up. They didn't move.

Max headed for his car. He would at least have one last night of freedom, knowing he'd be grounded for a month. He made it to his car, put his key in, and mimicked a sports commentator. "Oh my! The quarterback has been sacked! The quarterback is down, folks. Dick's dick and his nose are broken. The game is over. Score: Max, one; Greased Monkey, zero."

He unlocked the car and a hand grabbed his wrist. He instinctively ducked, turned, arm cocked, ready to trade punches when he recognized his sister.

"Are you going to hit me too?" Reina asked.

"Let go," he said and removed her hand.

"You can't leave, dummy," Reina said.

"Come on, sis. I'm going for a little ride to cool off. I'll give you a lift home."

Reina's arms crossed her chest. "You're going to be in big trouble. Mom and Dad are gonna kill you, Max. Why do you always do this?"

"Do what?" He sounded hurt. "You mean defend myself? Should I let him knock me down and make fun of me? Let them insult Mom? He had it coming and you know it."

"And *you* know what I mean, Maximillian Day," Reina said. She was seriously pissed. "You go back and talk to the coach. Maybe you won't be kicked off the team or out of school if you—"

Ginger Purdie interrupted her and caressed Max's face and shoved her ample breasts against him. "Are you okay, Max? Did he hurt you?"

Max grinned at her, keeping a cautious eye on Reina. "I'm not hurt, but thanks for asking. You'd better get back. The team needs you."

Pouting, Ginger said, "Don't *you* need me?"

Max laughed. "Of course. I'm fine. The team needs your particular talents to give them encouragement, babe. And I think Dick needs some TLC." He gave her a firm slap on the rear.

She giggled and bounced away, breasts jiggling, butt swaying, and all legs.

Reina said, "You'd better stay away from that one, Max. Mom won't approve and you're already going to be grounded for the rest of your life."

"Grounded works only if you get caught, Reina."

"Uh-oh!" She pointed across the parking lot, where Dick, Needham, and James were jogging toward them. Two or three other football players had joined them. "You can't fight all of them, Max. Get out of here." She moved off toward the approaching boys. "I'll slow them down," she said. "As usual."

"Thanks, sis," Max said, got in his car, fired up the Hemi engine, and threw a rooster tail of gravel and dirt behind as he accelerated out of the lot.

Max took back streets to Kratzville Road where he stopped, debating where he would go. Home was northwest. He could take Kleitz Road, but he didn't want to go home. He decided to go downtown, to the riverfront. He could sit in his car, watch the water, calm his mind, consider what he would do with all of his free time now.

His thoughts turned to Ginger. She was pretty, but he didn't really care for her. She was just a way to get at Dick and the rest of the "popular" kids. Snobs, every one. And he truly hated that smug asshole, Richard Dick. Punching him in the nose was worth missing the championship. Kicking him in the balls was priceless. He only wished Needham had stood up for his best buddy. Needham was smart not to go another round.

Max turned south on Kratzville Road. The back of his head was smarting and his fingers found a painful knot where the helmet had hit him. It hurt, but he smiled at the memory of Dick's nose exploding under his fist and the gurgling, wheezing sound after getting his crotch adjusted with a foot. "Bet you didn't expect that, Dick?"

He slowed for a red light approaching Gloria's Corral Club at Allens Lane. The normally bustling crowd was elsewhere on Sunday nights. It was dark-thirty and the streets were deserted.

He considered running the red light, but with his luck tonight, a cop would be sitting in the parking lot of the convenience store across the street, hankering to make his quota.

Headlights flashed in his rearview mirror. He recognized Dick's black Cadillac coming up fast. He let the car come up beside him in the right-turn lane and saw Dick at the wheel, nose still bleeding. Needham was in the passenger seat, leaning across Dick, giving him the bird while Dick laid on the horn. Dennis James was hanging out of the back-passenger window, hurling insults and threats, yelling for him to get out of the car.

Max ran the light, cut a sharp right across the front of Dick's Cadillac, and narrowly missed the left-quarter panel as he blew past and sped down Allens Lane. The Cadillac peeled out and made a sharp right to pursue. But the Caddy was a boat compared to the Camaro and swayed side to side before gaining purchase of the road. Dick stamped on the gas. The Caddy was fast, but it was no match for the Camaro.

Max slowed for the double railroad tracks, the double-dipper, and let the Caddy kiss his rear bumper before he braked hard and swerved left into the oncoming lane. His tires smoked as he skidded forward, coming to rest just before the first set of rails. The Caddy locked the brakes up and whizzed past just as he'd planned. He could see Dick's shocked expression before the Caddy went airborne over the first set of tracks, bottomed out on the lower set of railroad tracks, and went airborne a second time. Some of his classmates had gotten drunk one night and discovered the dangerous railroad crossing the hard way. Max had counted on Dick forgetting in the heat of the chase.

He watched the Caddy fly through the air, all four tires off the ground, bottom out a second time when it hit the asphalt. Sparks of hot metal shot from beneath the Caddy as it flattened out and slewed side to side before the right-side wheels dropped off the side of the road. Dick overcorrected and pulled sharply to the left. The Cadillac's right tires jumped the asphalt, throwing the car into a sideways slide and into a shallow ditch on the left side of the road.

Max slowly drove down the double-dipper and watched his pursuers clamber out of Dick's damaged car. He pumped a fist in the air, yelling, "Yeah! Who's your daddy? Whose mom is stupid now, ya buncha dicks?"

He turned the Camaro around and drove past them again. They threw rocks at him, but their aim was horrible. He made it back to Gloria's Corral Club and turned left. He'd had enough fun. He pulled into Locust Hill Cemetery to check out the front bumper of his car. Even crawling over the tracks at the double-dipper, his front end had scraped the pavement. He pulled to the back of the cemetery near a mausoleum, left the lights on, and got out. He was crouched down, checking the front bumper, when he saw a single headlight coming toward him.

Dick's Caddy screeched to a halt sideways, blocking him in. Max saw the front bumper of Dick's car was canted up into a lopsided grin, with one headlight missing. He laughed. That laugh was what started the fight.

* * * *

Car 35 cruised west on Diamond Avenue. Rookie officer Ted Mattingly had worked third shift, west sector for eleven months. He liked the hours, liked the job, and liked being out from under the glare of supervisors. He had a patrol routine and this was part of it: shining the car spotlight on the fronts of the few businesses, checking for signs of break-ins or drunks passed out on the parking lots. He made a circuit going north on First Avenue from Dunkin' Donuts, left on Diamond Avenue, and north on Kratzville. He decided to patrol tonight through Locust Hill Cemetery. Young couples sometimes parked behind the mausoleum to smoke dope and do other things. He could run them off and catch a nap. Working third shift and having two kids at home had really messed with his sleeping patterns.

He wouldn't normally care where people got naked, but there were reports lately of vandalism and break-ins to some of the vaults. Last week someone had started to dig up a grave. They dug two feet down and abandoned the project. That was the problem with kids today. They were too lazy to even finish the job of desecrating a grave. The crazy little bastards were probably doing black magic or summoning up demons in someone's basement with chicken bones.

He was just coming up on Kratzville Road when his radio crackled.

"Car 35. Suspicious circumstance. Locust Hill Cemetery," the dispatcher said.

Mattingly grabbed his microphone. "Car 35 enroute."

He stepped on the gas and turned north on Kratzville. The cemetery was less than a quarter-mile ahead just over the hill. He turned in and called dispatch. "Car 35 arriving on scene."

Mattingly saw the back of a red 1970s model Camaro SS with a wide white stripe painted front to back. It was parked in the middle of the cemetery drive with its headlights on. Mattingly flipped on his side spotlight and his takedown lights to illuminate the interior of the Camaro, but the windows were heavily tinted. The takedown lights caught a shape in the driver's seat that might have been a person. The driver didn't move, so he tapped his siren a few times. Still nothing. He hoped the guy wasn't passed out drunk. He'd just had his car cleaned by a jail trustee from the last go-around with a vomiting drunk.

Mattingly picked up the mic again. "Car 35."

"Car 35, go ahead with your traffic."

"Car 35. I'm in the back of the cemetery near the mausoleum. I've got a subject passed out in a red Camaro. Ten-twenty-eight on Indiana personalized plates." He gave the dispatcher the Camaro's license plate number. A 10-28 was police code for vehicle registration.

"Do you need backup?" dispatch asked.

Before he could answer, cars 32 and 37 advised they were enroute.

He considered giving them a signal 9, which meant he didn't need backup, but he knew they'd come anyway. He had just left Dunkin' Donuts on First Avenue before driving to the cemetery. He suspected he was being set up. This was some type of prank.

Mattingly kept an eye on the Camaro for any movement. Nothing. He flipped the high beam of his headlights on and off and tapped his siren several times. Still no movement.

He heard sirens in the near distance and the screaming of the big Ford Interceptor engines heading his way. He got out of his car, flashlight in one hand, model 10 Smith & Wesson .38 revolver in the other and eased up to the driver's side of the Camaro. Bits of matter mixed with blood coated the driver's window. It wasn't a prank. He tapped on the window with his flashlight and opened the driver's door.

"Jesus," Mattingly said and vomited on the Camaro, on the body, and down his uniform pants.

Chapter 2

Deputy Chief of Police Richard Dick was in full dress blues, sitting in his assigned vehicle, a Cadillac Escalade, scribbling notes on a yellow pad. His driver, Captain Dewey Duncan, was on vacation, so he had driven himself this morning. He wasn't comfortable with the idea that he might lose his driver when he was appointed Chief of Police. Marlin Pope, the current Chief, had never used a driver. Driving himself was a sign of weakness and would change when Dick took the reins of power.

He was parked in the lot of Rural King on the west side of Evansville, dreading what he was going to do. It needed to be done, and in person, but he was totally out of his element. Apologizing was not his forte. He went over his notes again. He picked up his iPhone with sweaty palms. He thought back to the night that had created this situation. It wasn't his fault. Things had totally gotten out of hand. He pinched the sides of his nose, remembering how it had bled all over his football uniform. He remembered the feeling of humiliation and that memory was so strong he could still feel the crunch of cartilage as the doctor set his nose, the nostrils swelling shut, and the way his nose still canted from the little bastard's sucker punch. He'd had raccoon eyes for days, but Max had gotten much worse when they caught up with him. The thought of what they'd done to Max brought him out of his reverie.

He'd read his personal copy of the case file on Max Day's murder a thousand times. There was nothing new, or at least nothing that would tank his chances for appointment as Chief. He'd meet with Mrs. Day. He'd be honest, forthright, and confident with just the right mix of compassion, sadness, and regret. He reminded himself to take it slow. Let her ask all her questions. Listen politely. Slow and steady wins the race every time.

Dick took a deep breath, released it slowly, and wiped his hand and iPhone on a handkerchief. He hit the green *call* button. It rang a long time.

"Hello," a woman's voice said.

"Hello, Mrs. Day. May I speak with you?" Dick asked.

"Who is this?"

"Deputy Chief of Police, Richard Dick," he said proudly, confident his title sounded impressive. "I want to—"

"You have some nerve," Mrs. Day scolded.

He bit back his retort and said, "Mrs. Day, I think it's time we talked. I'm willing to tell you everything that happened that night. Everything." He had no intention of telling her all of it. No one knew all of it except for a few trusted friends.

He was surprised when she said, "You'll have to come here. I don't drive much anymore. You come here and face me. Come to Max's home. You know where. I've seen you drive by from my window."

"That's agreeable," Dick said. "I'm five minutes away."

"Make it thirty." She hung up.

Sweat was dripping down the side of his face onto the collar of his uniform shirt. "Bitch!" he said into the dead line.

Chapter 3

Present day

"Can you believe she's already talking?" Liddell Blanchard said proudly. "She's smart, like her old man."

Jack Murphy responded. "That's called babbling. It's total nonsense. So, you're right, she does take after you, Bigfoot."

Janie Blanchard was eleven months old. She was born a little premature, but had caught up fast.

"Hey. I'm a proud father. You should be proud too—Uncle Jack."

Detective Jack Murphy was just shy of six feet tall and solidly built, with a shock of dark hair spiked in front. His gray eyes could turn dark when he was angry or threatened, and soft as a cloud when he was happy.

His partner, Liddell Blanchard, was a true Cajun transplant from the Iberville Parish sheriff department, where he'd worked river patrol until he'd met his wife Marcie and settled down in her hometown, Evansville. Jack called his partner Bigfoot because Liddell stood over six and a half feet tall and had the physique of a full-grown Yeti, with the temperament of a teddy bear unless he was angry.

Detective Sergeant Wolf opened the door to their office. A plaque on the door read MURDER SQUAD. Jack and Liddell still investigated other cases, but were primarily assigned to homicide cases.

"The Chief wants the two of you. Right now," Wolf said.

"Do you know what it concerns?" Jack asked.

Sergeant Wolf held the fingertips of one hand to his forehead and said, "Hmm. I'm getting nothing, Murphy. Now take your pet Cajun and get your asses up there. I'm not your damn secretary."

"Sarge is sure in a good mood today," Liddell said. Sergeant Wolf was a fair supervisor and made coffee when he emptied a carafe, but he had a dark side you didn't want to cross. "Maybe we're going to get an office big enough to smile in without hitting the walls."

"It's tiny, but still better than sharing cubicles," Jack reminded him.

"I guess."

"Maybe Double Dick's on a tear again," Jack said.

Double Dick was the nickname Jack had bestowed on Deputy Chief Richard Dick. It became popular because of Richard Dick's first two names and because of his propensity to punish a policeman more than once. He was like a velociraptor with rank.

"You're gonna get a spanking," came a detective's voice through the open door. Everyone laughed at that except Jack and Liddell.

"I've got dibs on their office if they get fired," a detective named Phil shouted.

Captain Franklin had created a new unit in the detectives' division. Jack and Liddell were now the murder squad. They had also been sworn in as federal special agents, attached to a new federal task force called USOC, or Unsolved Serial and Organized Crimes. It was, of course, called U Suck by the other detectives and police officers of the Evansville Police Department. Their new digs were the old file room. It was barely big enough for two desks, two chairs, and two men, but at least they could shut the door and block out some of the incessant clattering of keyboards, joking, farting, belching on command, and frequent cursing. It gave them some privacy when they were working on USOC projects.

A recent federal case involving a mass murder in Evansville had necessitated Jack and Liddell splitting forces to handle multiple scenes. Jack went to St. Louis, where there had been a similar case. From there it had taken him and a Missouri State Highway Patrol lieutenant named Jill Battles on to New Mexico. Jack had exceeded his authority and jurisdiction, according to his federal boss, FBI Assistant Deputy Chief Director Toomey, and he was promptly suspended before he was even sworn in. The feds were in a quandary what to do with him. He'd been assigned the case and had gone off-reservation when he took Lieutenant Battles—who was also suspended at the time—to New Mexico against procedures, orders, and legal authority. The reason he and Lieutenant Battles weren't in jail was they had successfully ended the murderous rampage of a killer responsible for over 600 deaths. Nothing says success like success.

"You guys should start a comedy club," Jack said as they left the office. "I hate meetings, Bigfoot. This is the kind of crap I was talking about when we were sworn in as feds. I don't have time to waste doing paperwork for bureaucrats. We've got a multiple-stabbing death to work right here."

"The stabber is in jail and he doesn't have a bond. We're just doing cleanup on the case for the prosecutor, pod'na. Think positive, like me. Maybe they have something good for us."

"Okay. I'm positive it's going to be bad news, Bigfoot. If this is another federal case like the last one, I'll resign." Jack said.

Liddell feigned a hurt face. "I know you didn't want to work for the feds, but I kind of like the challenge. Where's your sense of adventure? Your civic pride?"

"I left those in my other suit. Feds have too many rules and way the hell too many bosses," Jack said, but in truth he enjoyed the freedom of travel. He enjoyed being able to badge his way into other law enforcement agencies cases and the expanded jurisdictional authority.

USOC-Evansville was part of a larger regional task force that encompassed five states in the Midwest region. There were similar regional offices divided up like beats covering the whole of the country and other U.S. territories. The rule was that one region never poached on the jurisdiction of another region unless they were requested to assist.

Since Jack had expanded his own jurisdictional boundaries without the consent of Director Toomey, the FBI had rethought the regional procedure. Now, each region could continue an investigation in any other investigation with limitations. Jack promised to call the director of whatever region he needed to trespass in, and Toomey had given him dispensation to do so if he contacted him at the earliest possible time. Jack had promised Toomey. He'd try to keep it in mind.

"Even though you went about it ass-backwards, we caught the bad guy, saved the girl, found a home for a little boy, and became national heroes. Not bad for two local boys, if you ask me," Liddell said.

"Actually, many people died. Lieutenant Battles saved me. Not the other way around. And she's still on suspension. I can't believe they suspended her for an entire year," Jack said.

"She doesn't lie as good as you. And remember, you were actually assigned to the case. She was there for revenge."

Jack checked behind them as they headed toward the Chief's complex. "Sergeant Wolf isn't accompanying us. That can't be good, and don't make that into anything positive."

Liddell put the fingertips of both hands to his temples. "Positive thoughts, grasshopper. Positive thoughts. Positive…"

"Just shut up," Jack said. "I've got a bad feeling."

Judy Mangold, the Chief's secretary, buzzed Jack and Liddell into the complex's lobby. Some people thought she'd been there so long the building was erected around her. Her face was as expressionless as a poker player in a high-stakes game.

"Morning, Judy," Liddell said.

She didn't respond.

The door to the Chief's conference room was cracked and Jack heard Double Dick's angry voice vibrating the walls.

"You're in trouble, pod'na," Liddell said. "Twice."

"Why me? Why not you?"

"Because he doesn't like you twice as much as he doesn't like me."

"Shut up, Bigfoot."

The door opened so hard it slammed against the wall as Deputy Chief Dick came out in a rush. He glared at them with unmistakable hate and then he was gone.

Dick pushed his way through the exit and as the door snicked shut Jack heard the Chief's secretary say, "Good riddance."

Jack and Liddell entered the conference room where Chief of Police Marlin Pope and Captain Charles Franklin were sitting with a laptop open on the large table. Deputy Chief Dick's voice was coming from the laptop speakers. Chief Pope closed the lid, silencing it.

Marlin Pope was Jack's height, early sixties, skin the color of yellow coal, and the physique of a serious runner. He had risen through the ranks, the first black officer to be promoted to Captain, then Deputy Chief, and then Chief. He'd served as Chief of Police under two different city administrations and was on his third.

Captain Franklin, Jack's direct supervisor, was sporting the tan he'd brought back from his Miami vacation. He was slightly taller than Jack, late-forties, square-jawed, with perfectly groomed dark hair with streaks of silver at the temples. He resembled George Clooney, but without the millionaire cockiness.

A thin manila file folder lay open on the table next to the Captain. An old supplementary report was on top of four or five other sheets of paper.

Jack knew the supplement was an old one, because it was typed in all capital letters on a typewriter. No one did that anymore.

"Have a seat, gentlemen," Chief Pope said.

The Captain closed the file and he and the Chief sat quietly. Jack could hear the clacking sound of Judy Mangold's typing down the hall.

"If you're going to fire us, Chief, Jack can explain everything," Liddell said, pointing comically at Jack.

Captain Franklin responded, "You might wish you were fired."

Chief Pope said, "We're going to let you in on something. You are not to discuss anything you see or hear outside of the four of us. Understood?"

Liddell said, "Yes, Chief. What are we not discussing?"

Chief Pope said, "Mayor-elect Benet Cato will replace Thatcher Hensley on January first."

This was old news to the detectives. The mayoral race hadn't even been close. Benet Cato had no previous political experience, but Evansville's citizens were tired of the good ol' boy system of local politics. Jack thought it was time someone else's pockets were lined with public funds. Benet said the people's voice should be listened to. She promised greater transparency in local government. Heads would roll. Her speeches were held in public, in front of the Civic Center Complex. They were like a snake revival meeting and Benet had her own snake: Tilly Coyne. Coyne was a political activist, feminist, ex-journalist, who held several PhDs and reportedly spoke seven languages, depending on who she was lying to. Jack had never heard her speak, but her expression said more than words. Tilly was a sledgehammer and Cato planned to use her on the pebbles she deemed expendable.

Cato must have read the public's pulse correctly, because she had beat Hensley hands down. When she was sworn in, no one doubted there would be a tsunami of changes in local government and that included the police and fire departments. One of those changes would shake the police department to its core.

"I have it on good authority that I'm to be replaced by Richard Dick," Chief Pope said, confirming Jack's prediction.

Cato would be the first female mayor of Evansville, but this wasn't the first time Marlin Pope's position as Chief of Police was on the chopping block. Three years ago, Thatcher Hensley planned to replace Pope with Richard Dick, but he couldn't pull it off for several reasons—one being political suicide. In Hensley's estimation, to replace the first black policeman to ever attain the position of Chief of Police with Richard Dick, a blond-haired, blue-eyed Aryan Brotherhood poster child was unthinkable. And then Dick had gotten into hot water by stealing and hiding evidence from a murder scene in a high-profile case. Dick had skated on criminal charges somehow. Each new mayor had had the option of appointing a new Chief of Police, along with other department heads. Pope had lasted longer than most. Chief Pope was retained, but the mayor who tried to replace him would be gone soon. Politics was loads of laughs. But some city leaders wouldn't be laughing on January first.

Chief Pope opened the laptop on the table. "This audio is part of the reason you're here. I have an assignment for you. Listen and then I'll tell you what you need to know." He tapped the *rewind* button and the *play* button on the laptop.

The sound of knocking came through the little speakers. A door opened. Double Dick's unmistakable, condescending voice said:

Dick: "Mrs. Day?"

A woman's voice. Presumably Mrs. Day. "Why are you here, Richard? Why now?"
Dick: "You know who I am. What office I'm going to..."

Mrs. Day: "I know who you're hoping to be. You think you're going to be the Chief of Police."

Dick's voice took on an intimidating tone: "That's right. I *am* going to be Chief of Police. That's why I've come. I want to answer your questions. See if we can make this right. I know I haven't been forthcom—"

Mrs. Day: "You haven't spoken to me or to my family for thirty-seven years. You were there the night he was killed and you refused to tell us what happened. If your father wasn't who he was, you would be in prison."

Dick in a conciliatory tone: "Now, Mrs. Day. You know that's not true. I was never interviewed or charged with anything. I wasn't even a suspect.

None of my friends were. We all had alibis for that night, Mrs. Day. You know all of that."

Mrs. Day: "My husband was killed four years after my son's murder. The police investigation was a joke. A cover-up. Harry never heard a word of explanation from you or your friends during all that time. You refused to talk to us and heaven knows, we tried to meet with you and your father. And now here you are, trying to ease your guilty conscience."

Dick: "I'm here, Mrs. Day, to offer my condolences for the loss of your husband and your son, and because I want to say it was wrong of me not to have talked to you. I can't speak for the others, but I'll answer all your questions to the best of my knowledge. It was all so very long ago. I want you not to publicly oppose my appointment as Chief of Police. In exchange, I'll answer any of your questions. I swear."

Chief Pope stopped the audio and Captain Franklin asked, "You heard Deputy Chief Dick's voice on the recording?"

"Yes. I take it the Deputy Chief wasn't the one recording this," Jack said.

"No. The woman you heard on the recording is Mrs. Amelia Day. Her son, Maximillian Day, was murdered thirty-seven years ago today. He was seventeen and a senior at Rex Mundi High School. Mrs. Day's daughter, Reina, recorded the conversation between Deputy Chief Dick and her mother at Mrs. Day's home," Pope said.

Captain Franklin said, "According to Mrs. Day, she received a call from Deputy Chief Dick two days ago at around ten or eleven in the morning, asking if he could come by for a talk. She told him to come to her home at a later time that day. She called her daughter and told her about the call. Reina came to the house early and secretly recorded the conversation between her mother and Richard."

Chief Pope took over.

"They had a history, Max and Richard, that goes back to before the time Max was murdered in 1980," Pope explained.

"This is a cold case? Is there new evidence?" Jack asked.

"It is a cold case and there's no new evidence." Pope said. "The Days don't like or trust Richard, Richard's family, or the police department and city government. They feel the police failure to solve Max's murder was deliberate, a cover-up due to the fact that Richard was in a fight with Max the night he was killed, and Richard's father was a Captain over the investigations unit. Max's father, Harry, was killed in a robbery four years later in 1984. Harry's case was never solved.

"We obtained this copy of the recording from Mrs. Day and were just informing Richard when you came in. He admitted to the conversation, but didn't know it had been recorded and as you saw, didn't take it well."

That explained the temper tantrum Jack witnessed in the hall.

Jack said. "I take it this recording will somehow throw a wrench into the Deputy Chief's bid for Chief of Police?"

Chief Pope said, "There's quite a bit more on the recording, but you get the gist. Let me give you some background. Max Day was a seventeen-year-old senior at Rex Mundi in 1980. He and Richard were on the football team and there was bad blood between them."

Jack could imagine Dick being a dick to someone, but he couldn't imagine Dick in a football uniform unless it had a chest full of medals and rank insignia. Maybe that's what the bad blood was about. Maybe Max mussed Dick's medals.

Pope continued. "Richard was the captain and starting quarterback for the Rex Mundi Monarchs. As I said, Max and Richard had bad blood, but we'll get to that in a minute. Max was found shot to death inside his parked car near the back of Locust Hill Cemetery just before midnight on November twenty-sixth, 1980."

"Was Deputy Chief Dick a suspect?" Jack asked.

"For the sake of brevity, let's just all call him Richard. Not to his face, though," Chief Pope said. "Yes and no. Richard was a suspect according to the Day family, but not the investigators. The file"—Pope put his hand on the skimpy manila folder—"doesn't list any suspects. Nor does it mention a fight between Richard and Max, either before or the night of the murder. Mrs. Day says the investigators lied about there not being suspects. There were three suspects. I'll let her explain how she came to that conclusion when you talk to her."

"The Deputy Chief—I mean Richard—went to talk to Mrs. Day to ensure she wouldn't crap all over his chances with the new mayor," Liddell said.

"Yes. In any case, he poked a hornet's nest," Captain Franklin said. "That's where you come in." He added, "I wasn't on the police department when all of this happened and I don't remember hearing anything about either of these cases."

Chief Pope said, "I remember them vaguely from my motor patrol days. Richard's father was the Detective Captain in command of the investigations unit, so he was in charge of both investigations. There were rumors around the department that Max's murder would never be solved because the Captain's son was involved. Harry Day was killed in a robbery just before Richard joined the police department. That was four years later. I took it as station-house talk and didn't give it any credence."

"Holy shit, Batman!" Liddell said. "Sorry for the language."

Jack pushed forward: "Is Richard involved or connected to Harry Day's killing?"

Franklin said, "No. But Richard should never have approached the Days. Going to Mrs. Day now makes him appear complicit in Max Day's murder. Both mayors—outgoing and incoming—are demanding this one be resolved and Richard either be cleared of the murder or arrested. The Days have gone to the media with this."

The PD will be accused of a cover-up or fools for doing a poor investigation in the first place. In today's world, police were guilty even if proven innocent.

"So. You want us to investigate Deputy Chief Dick for a thirty-seven-year-old murder?"

Pope pushed the thin file folder across to Jack. "Read through this."

Jack flipped the file open. It was Maximillian Day's. Jack placed the open folder between himself and Liddell and they briefly scanned the pages. It took less than a minute. A police department offense report and a couple of short supplementary reports made up the entire file.

Pope said, "That is all we have on Max Day's murder investigation. I doubt there will be much evidence. We haven't even gotten that far yet."

Jack waited. There was obviously worse news coming.

Pope said, "They didn't specifically request a reinvestigation of Harry Day's case, but if we are to put the Days' complaint to rest we have to investigate both."

Jack had already decided that was the smart play.

"Mayor Hensley called me this morning, demanding to be briefed after we're done here. Benet Cato, the incoming mayor, has already listened to the taped conversation. She's aware of the Deputy Chief's predicament and wants this case solved before she takes office in four weeks. She wants total transparency as to your findings. I explained to her that we couldn't release details of an ongoing investigation, but she can be very persuasive."

"How in the hell did she get the recording before we did, Chief?" Jack asked.

Chief Pope said, "Mrs. Day's daughter. Reina Day, emailed the recording to Benet Cato."

Jack asked, "Does Deputy Chief Dick know Cato has the recording?"

"I honestly don't know," Chief Pope said. "I was explaining where we were and had just started the recording when he left. If this were a typical investigation with an officer as a suspect, police procedure says I should suspend the officer from duty until the officer is cleared. The recording of his conversation isn't real evidence. The Days obviously don't trust him and are claiming a cover-up by the police department in favor of Richard Dick. They are expecting us to continue to cover this up and you know that will be what the media pushes."

"This happened in 1980. That was thirty-seven years ago, Chief. Why didn't they raise a stink then?"

Captain Franklin answered, "According to Mrs. Day, they *did* raise a stink, but you can see by the very thin file that the case wasn't worked very hard, and if there were follow-up investigations none of the paperwork made it into the file. None of the complaints made by the Days made it into the file, either."

Jack asked, "Do we need to pull the file on Harry Day?"

"There is no case file, Jack," Captain Franklin answered.

While Jack was digesting this interesting tidbit, Chief Pope said, "I've talked with Mrs. Day. She said she and her husband requested meetings with Captain Dick, his son Richard, and the parents of two other boys that she claims were involved in the fight with Max close to the time of the murder. They all refused the meeting and Captain Dick wouldn't speak to them at all. If that's true, Mrs. Day's claims of a cover-up may hold water. She said she and her husband weren't allowed to see the case file and the detective who worked the case wouldn't talk to them."

Jack remembered Detective D. Olson was the name on Max Day's offense report. He didn't know Olson.

Jack said, "Is that even possible? I mean, wouldn't the news media have been all over this? I have a hard time believing the lead detective and the Captain wouldn't talk to the family of the victim."

"I don't have an answer for that. If there was wrongdoing by the police department, we have a duty to find the truth and that means a full investigation," Pope said.

Jack didn't like it. The whole thing stunk of political maneuvering. Why was Double Dick being considered for Chief to begin with? There were 385 other officers in the department, and a dozen or more sanitary maintenance people who could do a better job than that asshole. Also, who had the most to gain from sabotaging Dick? The Day family hated his guts, but Chief Pope would be out of his position. Jack knew Pope and couldn't believe Pope was ordering an investigation for political reasons. And he kept coming back to Reina and Mrs. Day. They hadn't done anything. It was Dick who approached them. He had whipped them into a frenzy with his haughty manner. If they kept Dick from becoming Chief, maybe that was the best justice they could hope for.

But there was one more consideration. Maybe Benet Cato thought the investigation would fail and if so, she wanted the failure to be on the previous administration, not hers. She could point out the reason these cases were never solved was because of the lack of transparency by the police department. Which would mean she was going to go public to show the voters that she was keeping her promise of transparency. The case smelled of corruption and she'd promised that heads would roll. Either way, four weeks was a short investigation window for a thirty-seven-year-old crime.

"Why us, Chief?" Jack asked.

"You can blame that partly on Benet Cato and partly on me," Captain Franklin said. "Benet Cato is clever. She apparently knows that you two and Richard are not on…the best of terms. She also knows that you have a reputation for doing the right thing. It's a win-win situation for her."

"We'll get on it, Chief," Jack said, picking up the slim case file and starting to get up.

Pope said, "We're not done yet. Come with me."

Chapter 4

The four men, Jack, Liddell, Franklin and Pope, stood outside the closed door to the Chief's office.

Pope said, "I don't want you working this case out of the detectives' office. Take it home. Take it somewhere private." He put his hand on the door handle. "Before we go in, you need to know that Claudine Setera is involved. She's here with Mrs. Day."

"Great!" Jack said. "The news media is going to saddle up and ride this to death."

"We'll handle the media," Franklin said. "You two do what you do best. Catch the murderer. Or murderers."

Jack understood the position this put the Chief in. More importantly, he knew what position he and Liddell were being put in. Murphy's Law said: *It's easier to get your tit in a wringer than to get it out.* Theoretically, Jack knew he could turn the case down, but he respected Chief Pope. Maybe he would find evidence that Dick was criminally involved. Murphy's Law also said: *Wish in one hand and shit in the other. See which one fills up first.*

Pope opened the door to his office and ushered them all inside.

Claudine and Mrs. Day were seated across from the Chief's desk on a leather love seat. Pope introduced Jack and Liddell to Mrs. Day and the men took seats.

Claudine spoke first, addressing Chief Pope. "We've been waiting over thirty minutes." It wasn't said angrily, but she was establishing the pecking order.

Jack ignored her and said, "What can we do for you, Mrs. Day?"

Mrs. Amelia Day was a small, attractive woman in her mid to late sixties, dyed red hair with some gray showing. She was well dressed and groomed, fingernails cut close, unpainted, and she wore no jewelry except the engagement-wedding ring on her left hand. A MedicAlert bracelet was on her right arm. Jack sized her up as stable, reasonable but no pushover, who didn't feel she had to dress to the nines to be taken seriously. And she had been smart enough to bring her attack dog—Claudine. She apparently didn't know Claudine would bite her as well.

On the other hand, Claudine Setera was dressed to meet the president or go on a date with an oil sheik. Cleavage was her top priority. Claudine was in her mid-twenties, dark hair worn long over her shoulders, dark eyes, immaculate olive skin. She was a Channel 6 news anchor and investigative reporter. She was as treacherous as she was beautiful. She had come up through the ranks, first working for a newspaper and then for Channel 6, where she moved up the ladder quickly. Jack had to admit Claudine was tenacious and usually got her story. He'd learned she was honest, fair even, but he didn't trust her. He saw her usual notebook was missing. Instead, she held a digital recorder. The red light was on.

Bitch.

Mrs. Day deferred to Claudine.

Claudine said, "Chief Pope was given a copy of a recently recorded conversation between Mrs. Day and Deputy Chief Richard Dick. Are you aware of this?"

"We're aware," Jack answered.

"And are you also aware that Mrs. Day's son, Max, was murdered in 1980?"

"Miss Setera," Jack began. "This isn't your interview. I can verify that the Chief assigned that case to us," Jack said and faced Mrs. Day. "We'll need to talk to you, Mrs. Day. Preferably alone, but you can have your daughter present, if you wish. She was the one who recorded the conversation, correct?"

Claudine's eyes flashed at the hint of being excluded.

Mrs. Day spoke for the first time.

"She did. Reina was supposed to meet us this morning at Channel Six, but Miss Setera was kind enough to come here with me until she gets here."

I'll bet she was.

"Would you like to wait for your daughter?" Jack asked.

"Reina's an ob-gyn," Mrs. Day said proudly. "She wanted to be here, but she must have been called to some emergency."

"Mrs. Day, if your daughter can add anything to the investigation, we should talk to her separately. We need to make sure we have your individual thoughts and memories."

Claudine was clearly unhappy with Jack's suggestion and was going to say something when Mrs. Day spoke again.

"Detective Murphy, my daughter and I have discussed the murder for the last thirty-seven years. I think it may be a little late to separate our recollections."

"Not necessarily." Jack leaned forward to emphasize his words. "My partner and I have had a few successes investigating homicides. We'll give this case our full attention and treat it as any other homicide investigation. Do you believe me?"

Mrs. Day had unconsciously made fists, but they now relaxed. "I knew your father, Jake Murphy. And Jake Brady. They were good policemen and good men. They built Two Jakes Restaurant, that place on the river?"

"That's right."

Jack's father was named Jake. He and Jake Brady had been partners on the police department their entire careers. They'd been hired at the same time and retired on the same day with the intention of building a floating restaurant on a barge docked on the banks of the Ohio River. They did so and named it Two Jakes Restaurant. Not satisfied, they dredged out an inland marina and a dock for the floating restaurant. When Jack's dad passed, he inherited half the business and a small, habitable river cabin two miles from the restaurant. Two Jakes Restaurant & Marina had become very successful.

Jack was a child when the murders had happened, but his dad and Jake Brady would have been patrolmen at the time. But his father had never mentioned the case to his knowledge. He made a mental note to talk to Jake Brady.

"I was sad to hear your father passed away. He used to talk about you a lot," Mrs. Day said.

"If I might ask, how did you know my father?"

"Harry was friends, or acquainted, with a lot of policemen. Harry was a Mason and so was your father. Your father was quite the dancer," she said with a wistful smile.

Jack didn't know how to take this. He forgot his father was a Mason. He remembered now there had been shindigs at the Hadi Shrine his parents had gone to. He didn't know much concerning that side of his father's life and that embarrassed him. But he remembered seeing his parents dancing in the kitchen. Jake would have never made it to *Dancing with the Stars*. Mrs. Day didn't have that part right.

"I hope he told you good things, Mrs. Day, but if it was bad, I have an excuse *and* a lawyer." Jack said this with a teasing smile. She cracked a tiny, short-lived smile.

"The world has moved on since the time of your loss," Jack said. "The police department has changed and I hope you can see that by how serious we're taking this."

Mrs. Day sat quiet for a moment, thinking. The moment of levity was over. She said, "My family requested many, many times to get the police to reopen my son's case. Harry pursued it and he was murdered. We've heard nothing from the police department. You can't know how frustrated I am with this place. My daughter is even more so."

Jack said nothing.

"If I trust you, you have to promise me right now, in front of this reporter," she said, meaning Claudine Setera, "you will include me in everything. You have to show me everything. I don't want to hear any of this 'ongoing investigation' stuff. I've had enough. My next step is to get an attorney."

Neither Chief Pope nor Captain Franklin responded to that last statement. Jack said,

"Will you talk to Detective Blanchard and myself, Mrs. Day?"

She surprised him with her answer. "Not here. Come by my house. My daughter will be there and will tape our conversation."

Again with the taping. Jack said, "That's perfect, Mrs. Day. That will give us time to do some digging and get some things together before we meet."

"One this afternoon. I'll be home. We can have tea and get comfortable in my kitchen," she said and gave them her telephone number and address. "Miss Setera, thank you for coming with me. I'll call you after I've had a chance to talk to these men."

"Chief Pope," Claudine said, "I have permission from Mrs. Day to use the audio recording. It will air this morning. I will mention that Jack and Liddell are on the case. Is there anything the police department would like to add? Is Deputy Chief Dick going to be put on administrative leave while this is under investigation? I would like to keep the public updated. Transparency is vital in a case like this."

Transparency? Jack was sure Claudine had been talking to mayor-elect Benet Cato. Transparency was the watchword of the day. This was just getting better and better.

"Claudine, I can't make a statement regarding the Deputy Chief's situation without knowing what my detectives discover," Pope said. "We have nothing to say yet—and no offense to you, Mrs. Day—but there are some things that shouldn't be made public in the interest of prosecuting a suspect when we catch them. That's in your best interest. Also, there may be legal questions in regards to taping someone's conversation without their knowledge and using it to slander them with the public."

"He has to do what he has to do, and so do I," Mrs. Day said.

Claudine wasn't satisfied, but she kept her peace. Jack figured she'd already cleared playing the recording on air with Channel 6's legal department. He also knew that Chief Pope was telling the truth about slandering Double Dick. The man's ego outweighed his common sense. Dick would most definitely sue the station and the Days.

As Mrs. Day and Claudine left the office, Chief Pope said, "Jack. Liddell."

Jack pulled the door shut and he and Liddell sat again.

Captain Franklin said, "I checked the cold case files in the detectives' office and in the record room. The file we gave you is on the Max Day case and it's all we have. I could find nothing on Harry Day's case from 1984. You'll need to do a more exhaustive search."

Chief Pope wrote on a piece of notepaper and handed it to Jack. "Here are some names. At least the ones I recall that might have worked on the case in some capacity. You can get a complete list of employees from personnel."

Jack read the names. Most of them were no longer with the department and some he'd never heard of. One of the names was Captain Thomas Dick.

Jack's father and Jake Brady's names were on the list. He took out a pen and scribbled *Mom* next to his father's name. He would call his mother and see if she remembered his dad ever talking about this murder. He might have told her something, but Jake was old-fashioned. He believed in keeping his family and his work separate.

Jack decided maybe he wouldn't call his mother quite yet. He'd need a scotch or three to make that call as she would talk /nag him into a coma. Her new focus was on being a grandmother. She would say things like, "You and your brother are too busy with your careers to give me grandkids, and God forbid either of you should come and visit your lonely mother. It's okay. I gave up my life to raise you."

Chapter 5

Reina Day was late leaving Deaconess Hospital. A common theme for a doctor. Her mother and Channel 6 anchor Claudine Setera were waiting for her at the television station. Her mother had given Claudine a copy of the recording by now. They finally had something to hold over the police department's heads to make them reinvestigate her brother and father's murders.

She dialed her mom's phone and it went straight to voice mail. *Well, Mom, if you don't answer your phone you deserve to wait.* She drove north on First Avenue and turned left onto Diamond Avenue. Locust Hill Cemetery wasn't far from Channel 6. She was already late, but a few more minutes wouldn't hurt.

On Diamond Avenue she noticed an SUV accelerating up behind her, its engine gunning as it pulled up close and swerved right and left as if it was going to pass her on one side or the other. It suddenly backed off. Just as suddenly, it sped up next to her, pacing her. She was already feeling a lot of emotion over the events of the last two days and now this jerk was video-game–driving beside her.

The SUV backed off and slowed. All she could see of the driver was a black hoodie. She thought maybe it was a kid who had mistaken her for someone else. A kid driving his parents' vehicle. She turned right on Kratzville Road at the light. The cemetery gates were just ahead at the top of the hill. She checked her rearview mirror and the car was gone.

She turned into the cemetery and followed the paved lane up a rise toward the mausoleum. Her brother and father's graves were in a small family plot near there. There were already headstones for herself and her mother, minus the end dates.

She felt an overwhelming need to visit Max and her father today, to tell them about Dick's visit and his possible appointment as Chief of Police. The man had no compassion. He was a joke. She needed to tell them that they weren't forgotten and the investigation might be reopened. She needed to say it out loud.

She parked the old Camaro SS in a gravel pull off at the side of the lane. She sat, thinking. Her mother had been through so much. Was it fair to bring all this up again and put her through another disappointment? The police hadn't done anything and weren't likely to, regardless of how they embarrassed Dick and the police department. Max was dead. Her father was dead. Nothing could change that. Max had been a fighter, but he never held a grudge. He didn't believe in revenge. But he did believe in the truth. Her big brother had taken up for her more times than she could count. He was always there for her. But that didn't mean he would want her to do this: Be part of the family obsession that bordered on mania.

Her father was the one who had obsessed over what he called "justice" for Max. Harry was a good man, but he had become obsessed. No one hurt Harry's family without consequences. When Max was killed and Harry saw the police were knuckle-dragging, it infuriated him. At Max's funeral, she'd told her father about the fight at Rex Mundi and he became convinced the police were doing nothing because the fight involved a cop's son. Reina was afraid he was going to do something stupid. Something violent if the police didn't find the killer. As it was, he'd gone to every television station, radio station, and newspaper in and around Evansville to plead for information relating to his son's murder. He'd offered a big reward.

The police warned Harry he was making a mistake by offering money. They said it would bring out every kook within a hundred-mile radius. That had turned out to be right. Their home answering machine was full of messages from people claiming to have evidence or to have seen something. Two psychics had called, stating they had been in contact with Max's spirit. It had been a waste of time and emotion. They had nothing.

Reina had watched her father spiral into a deeper depression each day, but he wouldn't give up. He hired private investigators and lost thousands of dollars for tidbits and lies while he was being strung along, kept hopeful. Harry stopped asking the police for help and started putting up posters on telephone poles and in store windows and bulletin boards, any place that would attract attention. He told her, "Reina, I know you think I'm crazy, but I've got to try. He would do it for me." And her father was right. Max would do anything for his dad and his family.

Harry's obsession ended four years after Max died. He was shot dead in a robbery at his store. Guns and money were taken, along with her father's life. The insurance barely covered the loss from the store and Harry wasn't a big believer in life insurance. Her mother had to sell the store. Her father's killer was never found. Like father, like son.

She got out of the car and a blast of cool air made her shiver. It was cold even for November. She walked down a row of gravestones and markers to two gray marble stones setting side by side with two empty plots beside them. One for her. One for her mother. There were fresh flowers near each headstone, so her mother had had the same idea this morning.

She took the digital recorder from her purse and pressed the *play* button. "Dad. Max. I want you to hear this."

The conversation coming from the tiny speaker seemed unnatural in this place where people spoke in whispers. When the talking ceased she pressed *stop* and put the device back in her purse. Playing it again stirred something in her, brought that night at Rex Mundi. She felt shame that she hadn't stopped Max from leaving. If he'd only stayed at school…

"What should I do, Dad? What would you do, Max?" she asked out loud. "Am I doing this to punish him or to get the truth, get your 'justice' for you. I could make sure he never becomes Chief of Police, but that won't bring you back. I hate him. I wish it was him and not you. Either of you."

She stood still, as if listening for the dead to speak, but she heard only the wind soughing through the trees and rustling the fallen leaves. Tears filled her eyes and cold determination replaced any uncertainty. She felt anger rising and clenched her fists at remembering the condescension in Dick's voice. "How dare he! How *dare* he talk to my mother that way. He's kept quiet for so long. So long…" she said.

She put the device in her purse, walked to her car and got in, closing the door. She wasn't conflicted now. Dick may not have murdered Max, but he was the reason the police never caught the killer. She swore she would ruin his life like he had ruined theirs.

Her eye caught movement in her side mirror, a brief glimpse of a man in a black jacket with a hoodie pulled around his face coming toward her. She heard an explosion and the Chevy's rear windshield shattered. Another blast and the front glass exploded, showering her. She ducked and threw her arms up over her head, but the explosions continued. She felt something hit her skull and tug at her hair. She was still reeling when her door was yanked open and a fist slammed into her temple, knocking her face-first into the dash. She was yanked toward the door by her hair and the fist slammed into her face and head again and again. Pain exploded behind her eyes. The noise, the pain, the gut-clenching fear, began to fade and she followed it into blessed darkness. The last thing she felt was her purse being yanked from her lap.

Chapter 6

Jack and Liddell had just left the Chief's office when Judy Mangold hailed them.

"Call for you from dispatch," the Chief's secretary said.

Jack took the phone, listened, and handed the phone back to Judy.

"We've got to go, Bigfoot," he said.

Five minutes later they were driving down an access road inside Locust Hill Cemetery. Crime scene tape sketched out a twenty-foot diameter around an older model red Camaro. The car sat in the back portion of the cemetery. Crime scene techs worked the inside of the tape, searching for evidence, photographing the scene from every angle, while other techs and uniformed police officers combed the surrounding cemetery grounds.

Jack parked behind a police car from which Officer Steinburg exited and came to the detectives. Steinburg was in his mid-sixties, with a full head of dark hair and the physique of a personal trainer. He had over forty years on the PD and would be forced into retirement when he reached sixty-five. Jack knew younger officers and brass that were in much worse physical and mental shape than Steinburg, but that was the way the system worked. Retirement might not end him like it did so many policemen, but police work was all he knew.

"I know you guys have your hands full, but when I called dispatch with the victim's name they said to get you out here."

"You haven't told anyone else?" Jack asked.

"No. Just crime scene and dispatch. I gave her Deaconess Hospital ID card to Corporal Morris."

"Is that the witness?" Jack asked, indicating Steinburg's police car. A man was sitting in the backseat, door open, his legs out and feet on the ground.

"You want him now or do you want to check out the scene first?"

"Have you talked to him?" Jack asked.

"He couldn't give me enough to put out a BOLO, but he saw part of what happened."

"Who was first arriving officer?"

"That'd be Sergeant Mattingly," Steinburg said. "The sarge turned the witness over to me and gave the ambulance an escort to Deaconess. He said you could catch up with him there."

"Do you know who Reina Day is?" Jack asked.

"I know *of* Reina Day. Who could forget a name like that? I've never met her, but a long time back her brother was killed right over there," Steinburg said, pointing toward the spot where Reina's car was parked. "I was a third-shift patrolman back then. Mattingly was the one found the body that night too. Ain't coincidence a bitch? Her getting attacked in the same place her brother was killed."

"Yeah," Jack said. *What are the chances Mattingly was first on scene at both murders?* He didn't believe in coincidence. But if Sergeant Mattingly was the one who found the brother's body, it followed that he might be familiar with this victim; it made a little sense that he would follow her to the hospital.

Steinburg admired the Camaro. "It's too bad what someone did to that car—a1975 candy-red Camaro. What a beauty."

Jack said to Steinburg, "Let's see this witness."

The witness was a big man, dark-skinned, taller than Liddell and a few pounds heavier. He was wearing a black hoodie jacket and black gloves, gray running pants. and kickers. The hood was pulled up tight.

"George Morgan," He shook each detective's hand. "Sorry. I don't take the hoodie or gloves off. Burns ain't pretty."

Jack recognized the name. "You were a Fire Department Captain?"

"*Was*," George answered.

Jack recalled George Morgan had responded to a house fire six or so years back. A meth head was cooking in a kitchen when his recipe went South and exploded. The resulting fire had engulfed the entire structure, but George had gone into the conflagration and rescued two children. The cooker had almost become the cooked, but the Great Turd God had protected him. He was blown through the kitchen door and landed in a baby pool.

George wasn't so lucky. He was choppered to Wishard Memorial Hospital in Indianapolis with second- and third-degree burns over much of his body. His act of heroism had ended his career and almost ended his life. The meth cooker had suffered singed hair and was released on bail. A week later the Great Turd God wasn't watching and this time the explosion killed the cooker. That's why they called it dope.

"I need to take a statement from you, George. Okay?" Jack took a recorder from his pocket.

"I know the routine," George said. "Talked to police a few times before."

Jack turned on the recorder and spoke the opening remarks that were required for a taped statement: name, address, age, telephone number, if the statement was given voluntarily, or if he had been coerced or made promises in exchange for what he said. The usual legalese.

"Tell us what you saw."

George clasped his big hands together. "I was visiting my mama's grave. That was eight-thirty or nine. I was right over there," he said, pointing to a knoll twenty yards north of shot-up car.

"I heard a couple of loud gunshots. *Bam! Bam! Bam!* That fast. I saw someone in black clothes, a black hoodie like this one, tall like me, thinner though, and he was moving in on that muscle car and shooting it up with a stainless-steel .50 caliber Desert Eagle. He was holding it in both hands, pushed out in front. Now that I think about it, he had gloves on. I'm pretty sure of that. I saw him shoot two, maybe three more times when he wasn't more than five feet from the driver's door.

"The shooting stopped and the guy yanked the door open and leaned inside. I didn't see who was in the car, but he was whaling away on someone. Pounding the hell out of them. I could see his arm coming up and slamming down inside."

Jack waited for him to continue.

"It all happened quick-like and I was caught off guard. I unfroze and yelled at him: 'Hey, you quit doing that! I'm calling the police.' He had to have heard me, but he didn't turn my direction. I saw him grab something and he took off running. Over that way." He pointed to the north.

They were standing on a slight rise and a couple hundred yards to the north could be seen the top of a flat roof building. Jack thought it might be the old work release building that was across Buena Vista Road.

"You didn't see a car besides the Camaro?" Jack asked.

"No. I guess he might have had a car somewhere else. I didn't see one on the grounds here."

"Where were you parked, George?"

"I walked from over there. I live on Hobart."

That was approximately three city blocks away. A short walk.

"So, your car wasn't here?" Jack asked.

"I left it at home." He dug his wallet out and showed Jack his driver's license. It showed an address on Hobart.

"I had to ask, George. What else do you remember?"

George motioned with his head in the direction he saw the suspect run. "There's no fence over there. Just a short rock wall. I didn't see where he went after that. There's that drop down to Buena Vista on the other side. It's pretty steep, but he was motivated."

Jack motioned for one of the crime scene techs. It was Joanie Ryan.

"Listen, Joanie. This guy saw the suspect run off over there and disappear down that drop to Buena Vista." Jack pointed the direction out. "You might be able to get some shoe impressions."

Joanie said, "Grounds still soft from that rain yesterday. I'll do it myself."

George told her, "I've been here since eight. There hasn't been anybody in the cemetery. At least not that I saw this morning. Except me and that poor woman and the bastard that beat her up."

Joanie went back to the scene.

"What did you do then, George?" Jack asked.

"I called the police and told them someone might have been shot and I ran over to see if I could help. I found that lady. She was knocked down on the floorboard. She was bloody as hell and wasn't moving. I thought she was shot dead, but I felt a pulse. I called dispatch again and told them to get an ambulance going. That's when the woman started coming to. I helped her set up and waited for the ambulance. Her head and face were all bloody and I was afraid to move her. Then Mattingly got here. What else you want to know?"

"You did good, George," Jack assured him. "You said *he*. Was it a man? Did you see a face?"

"Sorry, I didn't see the face, but it was a man for sure. Could have been twenty or fifty. White guy or a really light-skinned black guy. I know one thing for damn sure. The gun was a .50 caliber Desert Eagle. He was holding it, legs spread in a shooter's stance. And he was firing one shot after another into that car. It's a miracle that woman's alive."

"You're sure it was a Desert Eagle?" Jack figured George was more than twenty yards away.

"Detective Murphy, I did two tours in Vietnam. I know the difference between a little pissant pistol, a .45 and a .50 caliber. Dirty Harry gun. Muzzle blast would fry an egg. I don't know how many shots he fired exactly, but it was a lot. Sorry I can't help more."

"One of the crime scene detectives will want to talk to you, George. Can you sit in the car a little longer?" Jack asked.

"I'll wait. Hey, I know a couple guys from my old unit that carry one—I mean, that own a Desert Eagle. For target practice, you understand. Perfectly legal. They don't hunt deer or anything like that."

"What your friends do isn't my concern, George. Unless one of them shot up this car."

"They wouldn't do something like that. If you want, I'll talk to them and see if they know anyone else with a gun like that."

"That'd be a big help, George," Jack said and gave him a business card with his personal cell phone number written on the back.

Crime Scene Corporal Tim Morris came over holding out a gloved palm with several shiny steel casings. "These are .50 caliber pistol rounds, Jack."

"Told ya," George said.

Morris went back to work.

"Thanks for your help, George. We'll be in touch. Do you need a ride home?"

George said, "I'll walk. If you need me for anything, I gave Steinburg my number and address." He started to walk away and turned. "Detective Murphy."

"Yes."

"She's going to be okay?"

"She will be fine, George. We'll go see her in a bit."

"Would you let me know something. I mean, I know you're busy, but I can't help thinking if I'd just been a little quicker I might have caught that guy."

"You did good, George. Don't think that way. That's our job," Jack said, and George walked toward Kratzville Road.

"Let's go see the car," Jack said.

Jack and Liddell ducked under the crime-scene tape and stood by Corporal Morris. The car's doors and trunk were open. The front and backseat and floorboards were littered with glass. There wasn't much left of the back windshield and the front was a series of spider cracks. More of the glass fragments were spread across the hood.

Corporal Morris said, "We found five shell casings so far. He started shooting ten feet from the car, moving to the driver's side. One of the bullets is buried in the dashboard after it went through the trunk, the back-passenger seat, and the front passenger seat. If someone had been sitting there they would have gotten hit. We might be able to retrieve some slugs."

A crime scene tech called out, "Found another one, Corporal."

"Six," Morris corrected. "The victim took one hell of a beating. I'll send someone to the hospital to get pictures. Sergeant Mattingly followed the ambulance with the victim to the hospital. There's blood on the front seat and floorboard and dash. I don't know if she was hit by any of the shots, but the ambulance crew didn't seem to think she'd been shot."

"Is Sergeant Walker coming out?" Jack asked.

Sergeant Tony Walker was in charge of the crime scene unit. Jack and Walker were partnered when Jack first transferred to the detectives' office from motor patrol. They made a good team, almost reading each other's thoughts. Then Walker had gone and gotten promoted to sergeant and transferred to crime scene. Jack hated to break up the team, but it was a win-win situation. Walker brought his detective skills to crime scene.

"Walker took some vacation days, Jack. His wife put her foot down. He's worked every holiday for the last three years. She wants him home. Guess you're stuck with me."

"Works for me," Jack said and meant it. He'd worked many a crime scene with Morris and knew the man was thorough.

"Did you find a purse?" Jack asked.

"No purse. No wallet," Morris said. "Her hospital ID was clipped to her pocket. Not your typical robbery, is it?"

Jack agreed. He didn't think robbery for money was the motive.

"Holy cow! A .50 caliber?" Liddell said.

"Yeah. It's like using a bazooka on a fly," Morris agreed. "She's one lucky lady."

"We'll be at Deaconess," Jack said.

"I'll keep you updated."

Chapter 7

Jack and Liddell sat with Sergeant Mattingly in the emergency room lobby. He was a short man with a wide build. He resembled an old Volkswagen bus with a bad hairpiece and a temperament to match, but he was a good street cop with good instincts. He gave them a brief report on the cemetery incident and was anxious to go back to the scene. Jack had worked with him several times before and always thought him to be levelheaded in a crisis, but this one had shaken him. He seemed to take it personally and it came out in his brief verbal account of what they'd found at the scene. He told them the paramedics suspected a head injury, but she was conscious now and the prognosis was good. Mattingly told the ER receptionist to call him if there was any change, gave her his personal phone number, and left.

"Mattingly seems sure it wasn't a robbery," Liddell said.

"I agree. If the guy wanted to kill her, why not just walk up to the car and shoot her? George said the shooter took something and no one found Reina's purse and according to Mattingly, it wasn't brought in with her. I don't mean to sound gender biased, but have you ever heard of a woman not having a purse?"

Liddell shook his head. "It's like American Express. They don't leave home without it."

"Exactly," Jack said.

"This was personal, pod'na. If I was a betting man, I'd say this has something to do with Reina Day going to the news media about dear old Double Dick."

"Before we jump to conclusions, we should ask her if she had it with her. And we need to ask if she has an ex-husband or a boyfriend, or someone at work that she's pissed off. I agree this suggests it was personal, but that could mean domestic violence."

"Do you really believe the words coming out of your mouth, pod'na?"

"No."

Claudine Setera came in with a comforting arm around Mrs. Day.

"I thought you were barred from Deaconess?" Liddell said to Claudine. Several months ago, Claudine had been escorted by security from the emergency room after she and her cameraman snuck into a treatment room to interview a preteen male survivor of a mass murder. She frightened the boy so badly that he fled and had to be tracked down. But Claudine wasn't satisfied with that. She aired the attempted interview even though the boy hadn't spoken a word. The news media motto was, "If you don't know the truth, tell a sensational lie."

Claudine gave Liddell an oily smile. "The hospital called Mrs. Day. I'm here for support. You can't keep me out of the hospital, and you can't keep the truth from the public."

Jack ignored Claudine's bait. He said, "Mrs. Day, we haven't spoken to your daughter yet, but Sergeant Mattingly came in with her and said paramedics suspected a head injury, but she was conscious in the ER."

Mrs. Day's hand went to her mouth and the color drained out of her cheeks. "I have to see her."

Jack said, "I'll tell the nurse you're here."

Liddell said, "Let's find you a seat, Mrs. Day." He led her gently toward the row of chrome and red plastic chairs in the lobby.

Claudine latched on to Mrs. Day's arm like a barnacle to a hull and said reassuringly, "They should let us see her. We should know something soon."

Jack came back with the ER doctor in tow.

"I'm Dr. Hanson. Are you here for Reina Day, ma'am?" he asked Mrs. Day.

"I'm her mother."

Dr. Hanson glared at Claudine and asked Jack, "Is she with you?" Jack said nothing. To Claudine, the doctor said, "I thought you were barred from this hospital, Miss Setera. In case you don't remember, I am the doctor that had you thrown out."

Claudine said, "I'm here with Mrs. Day. You have no right to—"

"It's okay," Mrs. Day said. "She brought me. I didn't think I could drive. You can say what you need to say in front of all of us."

Dr. Hanson said, "Reina has a concussion and a pretty nasty cut across her scalp and facial bruising. The concussion doesn't appear to be severe, but she was confused when she came in. I've ordered a CT scan and depending on the results, I might keep her overnight for observation.

I understand from the paramedics who brought her in that someone shot at her. That might explain the cut across her scalp."

Mrs. Day's hand went to her mouth but she said nothing.

"She is coherent now and agreed to the CT scan, but I know Reina. She'll ask to be discharged as soon as we get the results. You know the saying that doctors make the worst patients. Maybe you can talk some sense into her, Mrs. Day. She really needs to stay overnight, at least."

"I need to see her," Mrs. Day said.

A nurse came out of the treatment area and Dr. Hanson said, "Excuse me a moment," and walked a short distance away to talk with the nurse.

He was gone a moment and came back. "The CT scan showed she has a mild to moderate concussion, but there is a little bleeding. I'm going to keep her overnight. Since she was unconscious, I'm ordering an MRI. She's being taken for that now and we're making a room ready. I'll have a nurse take you up to the waiting room."

Dr. Hanson said to Jack, "You and Mrs. Day can talk to her, but she needs to rest tonight. No excitement. No television or other excitement for the next twenty-four hours. No television interviews. No cameras. If you have no further question, I have patients."

Mrs. Day thanked him and Hanson motioned for Jack to follow him. They walked through the sliding doors of the ER treatment area. Dr. Hanson said. "I'm going to give the nurses and security here the order to keep that woman out of Reina's room. I can have them turn the phone off in there if you like." He was referring to Claudine. "She has a brain bleed and I have to take that seriously. That must have been one hell of a beating."

"You and I both know you can't stop Claudine, but thanks for trying."

A nurse came and they followed her to a third-floor visitors lounge.

Mrs. Day said, "I want to see her first. Alone."

"Of course," Claudine said, as if this was directed at her and not the detectives. "It shouldn't be long before she comes back, Amelia," she said to Mrs. Day.

Claudine was right. A few minutes later a nurse came and told Mrs. Day to follow her, leaving Jack, Liddell, and Claudine alone in the lounge. A small table sat in one corner with a coffee setup. There were two carafes, one with a quarter-inch of sludge in the bottom and in the other the coffee was so weak he could see through it.

He held the sludge carafe up and said, "I don't suppose you'd go to the nurses' station and get us some coffee, Claudine? Chop-chop."

"I'm impressed," she said. "That's the first sexist remark you've made. You didn't even call me *hon*."

"I'm inhibited by the female nurses," Jack said and took a seat.

Claudine sat by him and put a hand on his arm. "Poor you," she said with a pout. "We don't have to be enemies, Jack. This is a highly unusual situation. You'll need my help and I'll need yours. We're both after the same thing. The enemy of my enemy and so forth."

"I don't have enemies, Claudine."

"Yeah, right. What I meant was that we stand a better chance of solving this thing by working together. I'm willing to share everything I find with you."

"And the Golden Globe Award goes to Claudine Setera," Liddell quipped.

Claudine smiled at the jibe. "Okay. I admit I might need your help more than you need mine, but think of this: I have the trust of the family. They came to *me*. They don't trust the police department and that includes you two. I was the one who suggested Mrs. Day talk to Chief Pope. I can help. If I trust you, they'll be more likely to open up to you. It's as much about restoring the reputation of the police department as it is solving a cold case. Imagine the public impact we can make before Benet Cato takes office."

Jack could see she was almost salivating at the idea of being an embedded reporter, like Geraldo Rivera in Iraq, and he remembered how that turned out. It was a necessary evil in police work to keep the public ignorant until they needed to know something. No one liked you for it. He didn't enjoy it. But his job was to protect. That meant protecting his case, giving the jury the entire findings to ensure they could make an informed decision, and not try the case in Facebook court. When the case was completed, the public could have everything. He would be happy for the news media to dine off the case. It didn't make sense for the news to tell people what happened and color the jurors' memory, scare them, or worse, create a copycat situation.

Murphy's Law said: *There are two constants in life. One: You die. Two: Never trust the media.*

"I'll think about it," Jack said.

"That's all I ask," Claudine said and they both knew the other was lying.

Mrs. Day came back, sat down heavily beside Jack, and said, "I don't think I can take much more of this," she said. "Reina… I just… I can't lose my daughter too."

She broke down into tears and Jack put his arm around her. "We won't let anyone else hurt Reina, Mrs. Day."

Her face came up sharply. "You can't promise that. We've already lost so much. That asshole should never have called me. He should be in prison for what he did to my boy."

Jack said, "We don't know this is related to the other cases."

"I do. He found out somehow that I went to the news. He'll kill us all. I shouldn't have called you, Miss Setera. I've changed my mind. I'm not going to do this."

Jack wondered what Mrs. Day thought would be done. Didn't she understand that Dick would be talked to by the Chief? But Mrs. Day was right about one thing. The timing fit. Reina calls Benet Cato and then they make an appointment with Claudine. Reina doesn't show and they come to the Chief. Dick finds out and storms out of the Chief's office. Next thing you know, Reina gets pounded and her purse is possibly stolen. Maybe to get the recording.

Claudine Setera reacted just as Jack knew she would. "Mrs. Day," Claudine said, "Let's see Reina together first. If this is her decision also and you want me to drop this, I will. But I would like to hear it from her and at least see how she's doing. If you don't want to put any of this on the air I'll honor your wish."

Jack thought that what Claudine would really like to do was get some unguarded quotes from Reina. But it was really up to Mrs. Day and Reina at this point. Nothing was off the record as far as the media was concerned.

Mrs. Day asked Jack, "Did you find her purse?"

Chapter 8

Reina had asked her mom to send the detectives back. She wanted to talk to them alone. Mrs. Day accompanied them, leaving an unhappy Claudine alone in the visitors lounge. Jack was sure Claudine would be waiting for them when they came out.

Reina was propped up in bed with the covers pulled up to her chin. The television was tuned to Channel 6's weather report. The perky weather girl must have used grease to slide into the tight-fitting dress. She was announcing, "Partly cloudy with a chance of rain," with a brilliant white smile.

A bandage covered the left side and top of Reina's face and head. Her upper and lower lips were split. She was holding an ice pack to her face. An ugly red and dark purple welt peeked from under it. Her hair was long and thick and blond where it wasn't sticky with blood.

"Sit down, Mom. You're making me nervous," Reina said.

Reina lowered the ice pack. The white of her left eye was bloodshot. Scleral hemorrhage. Jack knew the medical term because he'd had a few himself over the years.

"Does it hurt?" Jack asked.

Reina put the ice pack back on her face. "I'm not laughing."

"I'm Detective Murphy and this is—"

"I know who both of you are. And the nurses told me all about *you*. Mom said she met with your Chief of Police this morning. Did he assign Max's murder to you?"

"He did. What did the nurses say?"

"They said you were a frequent flier," she said and winced. Her free hand went to her split lips.

"It's not that bad," Liddell said. "I mean, you'll hardly notice in a few days. A little makeup and—I guess I'd better shut up now."

Jack said, "Your mother said you wanted to talk to us."

"Did you find my purse?" Reina asked.

"No," Jack said. "A witness thought he saw the person that attacked you take something."

Reina closed her good eye. "I was afraid of that. The recording I was going to play during my interview at Channel Six was in my purse." She used her arms to adjust her position on the mattress, but it was painful to move.

Mrs. Day said, "I'll get the nurse to bring you something."

"No, Mom. I've taken Tylenol and that's all I can have." To Jack she said, "Detective Murphy, the man who did this and stole my purse is connected with Max's death. I'm sure of it. I don't know how he could know I was going to Channel Six, or how he knew to take my purse, but it wasn't a robbery. Have you ever heard of someone getting robbed and beat up in a cemetery?"

Actually, Jack had heard of that exact thing, but it wouldn't help her to hear that.

"Do you know anyone who would want to harm you?" Jack asked.

She was wearing an expensive wedding ring. "No. I don't, and I'm divorced. I wear the ring to keep from being bothered, and it's the only thing of value I got out of the marriage. I'm on good terms with the ex. No fights. No children. No financial disputes. No reason to harm me. Whoever did this wasn't trying to kill me."

"Miss Day, I'm just doing my job. Checking everything. I have to ask these questions. Was there anything else of value in the purse?"

She came back smartly with, "I see. Do you think I took prescription drugs from the hospital and was in the cemetery to sell them? Is that what you mean?"

"That's not what I'm asking," Jack said.

"He didn't say that," Liddell added.

"I'm sorry for being so rude. The answer is the usual stuff was in my purse. Driver's license, credit cards, three dollars cash, some change, hair ties, cell phone. The only thing of value would have been the digital recorder, but you don't believe that was what he was after, do you?"

Jack and Liddell were quiet. Mrs. Day stood by the bed and patted Reina's arm.

"Sorry. I'm a little pissed and I hurt," Reina said.

"Understandable," Jack said. "What I can tell you is that we have every available policeman searching for the suspect. If you can give me a description, it will help us."

"What did the witness say?" she asked.

"I need to hear what you remember."

She took a breath and calmed herself. "I was on Diamond Avenue going west. A dark blue or black SUV was tailgating me. I'm not sure what year or make; they are all the same, except for the ones that are designed like little toasters. It was still right on my tail when I turned onto Kratzville. He crossed into the other lane and zoomed up next to me. I slowed down to let him go around, but he paced me. I couldn't see his face. I got near the entrance and he took off."

"You said *he*," Jack said.

"It seemed like a man. He was wearing a black hoodie jacket with the hood pulled up hiding his face."

"Did he seem familiar to you?"

"I didn't see a face. I thought it was some kid. I'm sure that it was the same man who attacked me."

"Okay," Jack said. "Why were you at the cemetery?"

"I was on my way to Channel Six to meet my mother…" Her voice trembled. She took Mrs. Day's hand and squeezed it. "I'm all right, Mom," she assured her mother.

"Can't you talk to her later?" Mrs. Day said.

"Not later. Now. I want to do this now, Mom. I'm okay. Really," Reina said.

Liddell pulled a tissue from the container by the bed and handed it to her.

"Thank you," she said and dabbed under her eyes.

"Why were you at the cemetery?" Jack asked.

"We were going to do an interview with Claudine Setera. That reporter at Channel Six news. My mom wanted to go to the police, but I didn't think it would do any good. I decided to visit my brother and father's graves before going to the television station. I parked and went to the graves. I guess Mom told you the conversation she had with Richard Dick?"

"She did," Jack answered.

"I recorded it. I made a couple of copies on thumb drives. I emailed one to Benet Cato."

Mrs. Day added, "I gave Claudine one and she made a copy."

Reina said, "The recorder was in my purse. I was sitting there, getting myself together. I saw someone coming toward my car. It was the black hoodie guy. The one that was following me in the SUV."

"You're sure it was a man?"

"Yes. He was white. The hoodie was pulled down so I could see just the mouth and the bottom of the jaw, but it was a man and he was white."

"Could you tell his size?"

"He was tall. As tall as you are. He was wearing that jacket and I only saw him for a second. Then the back windshield exploded. I ducked. The blasts were loud, like a shotgun and he kept shooting one right after the other. He grabbed me and he hit me and kept hitting me. I must have blacked out, but the last thing I remember was someone yanking on my purse. I woke up in the ambulance and then here."

"Did you see a weapon?" Jack asked.

"No. But it sounded like a shotgun. I know what they sound like because my dad owned a gun shop."

Mrs. Day's voice was thick with emotion. "Harry never let the kids go inside the gun shop and we didn't keep guns around the house."

"Dad let me and Max shoot a shotgun once," Reina said.

Mrs. Day was shocked. "He never did."

"Yeah, he did, Mom," Reina said. "And Max had his own shotgun, but Dad made him keep it at the store under lock and key. Dad let him shoot targets sometimes. I know, because Max used to bring the targets home and show me. He was pretty good."

"I didn't know," Mrs. Day said.

Jack imagined Mrs. Day didn't know a lot of things about her seventeen-year-old son.

Reina squeezed her mother's hand. "I miss them too, Mom." To Jack she said, "You said you'd tell me about the witness."

Jack said, "Before I do, I need you to tell me one more time about the SUV that followed you to the cemetery."

"It was him. He was wearing a black hoodie, a jacket or a pullover sweatshirt. I didn't see him that well. The guy in the car was wearing the same hoodie. It would be too much of a coincidence they were different men, don't you think?"

"Did you see anyone else at the cemetery when you drove in? Anyone out by a grave? Any other vehicles?"

"There was another man in the cemetery. A retired firefighter. He heard shots, but he was pretty far away. He saw the guy hitting you and he thought the guy stole something before he ran away. He gave a similar description you did, but he didn't see any vehicle." He didn't tell her that George was wearing a black hoodie jacket. For now, George was just a witness. Jack didn't suspect him, but he'd have to be checked out. Everyone was a suspect until they weren't. That's what they taught you in Detective 101.

"You're not going to find him, are you?" Mrs. Day said. When neither Jack nor Liddell answered right away, she said, "I knew we shouldn't have gone to the police. Harry was right."

Jack said, "We haven't had a chance to read the case files yet. I'll talk to the Chief and ask him to assign your case to us, but it would really be better to have other detectives work it. If it's not related to our cases it will slow us down." To Mrs. Day he said, "Mrs. Day, are we still on for one o'clock? We can reschedule, considering what's happened."

"Hell's bells," Mrs. Day said. "One o'clock at my house. Reina needs to rest and she can't do that with me standing around crying. I've got my husband's notes and such."

"We'll be there at one," Jack said. "Miss Day, you get some rest so we can talk again. I'm sure we'll be back to talk to you. Maybe later this afternoon, if the doctor says it's okay."

"Give me your card," Reina said and Jack did.

"If you think of something, call the number on the back. That's my personal cell phone. But try to rest."

"I'm resting. You're not supposed to sleep with a head injury. That's why I can't have any strong painkillers. But it will help if I can be quiet for a little while. You'll come back, won't you?"

Jack assured her they would and he and Liddell left Reina's room. Claudine was gone and a police officer was sitting on a bench where he could watch the elevator and the door to Reina's room. His name tag read D. DOOLAN. Jack never knew what the D stood for because everyone just called him Droolin' Doolan. He hoped the man's first name wasn't really Droolin'.

Doolan stood and said, "Hey, Jack. Liddell. Sergeant Mattingly said I was to guard someone at Deaconess. Security gave me the room number and said you were up here. Who am I guarding and from what?"

"The woman in that room." Jack pointed at Reina's door. "She was beat up pretty good and we think it might be a domestic violence kind of thing."

Doolan wasn't convinced.

"Okay. I'm lying," Jack said. "Her name is Reina Day. Someone just shot her car up and beat the hell out of her and stole her purse, so it may have been a robbery. She's being kept overnight, so I don't know if Sergeant Mattingly wants twenty-four-hour postings or not. We don't have much of a suspect description."

Doolan grinned. "Thanks. I bet Steinburg ten bucks that you would lie."

"Do you have a description?" Jack asked.

Doolan said, somewhat sarcastically, "White male, black jacket and hoodie. About your height. No one like that is getting near her room. It'll be pretty damn hard to hide a Desert Eagle under hospital scrubs, don't you think?"

Jack was a little ticked at his attitude, but grateful for an armed guard. "No one goes in except nurses, doctors, or her mother. There's an older woman in there with her. Her mother."

"Okay. I got it," Doolan said. "Is she involved with the Double Dick shit that's going on?"

"I'm not going to tell you and you don't want to know."

"You guys never talk about anything fun. I guess you can't say nothing because it's Double Dick's ass flapping in the wind. Figures." Doolan asked Liddell, "How's little Janie?"

"She's saying some words already," Liddell said proudly. "Smart, like her old man."

"I might point out you work with this guy," Doolan said, meaning Jack.

"Bite me, Doolan," Jack said.

Jack and Liddell got on the elevator and when the doors shut Jack said, "He's right."

"About Janie being smart like me?" Liddell asked.

"No, smart-ass. Doolan's right. If it didn't involve Double Dick we wouldn't be messed up in this."

"Do you think an armed guard is really necessary, pod'na? Sergeant is overreacting a little? If the guy didn't kill her at the cemetery, he sure as hell isn't coming here."

Jack said, "Mattingly's just playing it safe. If he didn't tell Doolan to babysit, the Captain would have, just for appearance's sake."

"Do you think Mrs. Day is right that the police department deliberately or negligently flubbed the original investigation?" Liddell asked.

"I find that hard to believe."

"Double Dick is involved, pod'na."

"Good point." Dick had totally screwed up a stakeout that Jack was running and that had resulted with Jack almost being killed. Dick had caused such chaos that Jack had to chase an armed bad guy down a narrow alleyway in pouring-down rain. He still had nightmares. The blade coming down, gouging along the side of his face, through his cheek and jaw, down his neck and across his chest. Liddell had called him Franken-Jack for months because of the red, jagged scar. But the bad guy was dead, so it evened out.

Murphy's Law said: *Where there's a Dick, there's a major screwup.*

Jack and Liddell left the hospital and headed for their office. Mattingly would have officers scouring the neighborhoods around Locust Hill Cemetery for witnesses. Captain Franklin would have already assigned a detective to take witness statements and everything would be funneled to them without telling the officers or detectives squat about Max or Harry Day's murders from way back when.

"We're going to piss a lot of people off, keeping all of this under wraps," Jack said.

"When don't you piss a lot of people off?"

"Another good point, Bigfoot. You're on fire today."

"One o'clock is right around the corner and I'm a little peckish," Liddell said.

"It's not even nine o'clock."

"Tell that to my stomach." As if on cue, Liddell's stomach grumbled.

"You win. You pick the place. You drive."

"Hallelujah! Hey, let me tell you a joke I heard from Johnny Hailman," Liddell said. Johnny Hailman was a K-9 officer known for his horrible jokes.

"If you tell me, I'll have to kill you," Jack said.

* * * *

Claudine Setera had gone to get coffee and was just coming from the nurses' break room when she saw a uniformed police officer get off the elevator. She ducked back and watched Jack and Liddell come out of Reina's room down the hall and go talk to the policeman. She knew Murphy had conspired somehow to keep her from talking to Reina and she was having none of it. She went back in the break room and kept the door cracked, but she couldn't hear what they were saying.

Jack and Liddell got on the elevator and she watched the policeman drag a chair down the hall and take a seat outside Reina's door. She'd have to be creative.

Claudine straightened her skirt and unbuttoned two of the buttons on her top to maximize the cleavage output to 150 watts. She poured another coffee and carried them both down the hall toward the policeman.

Chapter 9

Warrick County was dotted with stripper pits created by open coal-mining operations. He knew the back-county roads like the back of his hand. He slowed the SUV, preparing for the cut in the brush that led back to the abandoned stripper pit. He and his buddies had partied in the pits in high school. Girls, beer, swimming, pot, more beer, maybe something that made them feel better than all those. He found the cut and turned down a grass and weed-covered path. He drove over some manageable tree limbs downed by a storm. This section of Indiana was known as Tornado Alley for a reason.

The pit was exactly where he remembered and full of mud-colored water with a sheen of oil floating around the banks. The kids called these man-made mini-lakes swimming holes; the adults called them "drowning pits." Each year a half-dozen people—even some old enough to know better—drowned.

This path he'd come by was the only path back to the road, but hikers had created their own trails over the years. He'd have to hurry. There was always the chance of meeting a nosy deputy on his way out. They used to check these stripper pits from time to time and the path wasn't wide enough for two vehicles.

He drove right up to the water and backed the SUV around, hearing the grit crunching under his tires. He parked and went through the purse. Lipstick, chewing gum, facial tissues, nail file, condoms, elastic bands, a leather wallet with credit cards and an Indiana driver's license, loose change, a small ring of keys, and a digital recorder. He opened the door and pitched the condoms out on the ground. "You won't be needing these for a while. Not with the face I gave you."

The recorder was slim, lightweight, perfect for clandestine recordings. He wondered what use a doctor would have for it. The display on the recorder showed one recording. He pushed the *play* button and listened to the conversation all the way through. The entire conversation was less than four minutes. He played it again, listening more closely this time for incriminating statements. There was nothing. Absolutely nothing.

He had done nothing but stir the hornet's nest. With Murphy and Blanchard investigating Max's death he would have to mind his steps, but Murphy wouldn't have any more than the original investigation and that had gone nowhere. All of the evidence, what little had been collected back then, was disposed of long ago. There were no witnesses. This recording proved nothing. He was in the clear. He'd lived through worse and to be honest, he'd enjoyed the intrigue. He was a man of action.

He stuffed the purse's contents back inside and got out of his SUV. He started to pitch it into the water and thought better of it. For all the police knew it had been taken in a robbery. He could use it to arrange a suspect, if needed.

Chapter 10

Mrs. Day's manner was reserved when Jack and Liddell arrived promptly at 1:00. She invited them in, but hardly said two words while showing them into the kitchen, where she brewed a pot of coffee. She thawed as she watched Liddell decimate the platter of homemade pastries he'd sniffed out on the kitchen table. She said to Liddell, "You have a healthy appetite, Detective. Just like my Max. He ate like three teenagers and must have burned it all off."

"I'm eating for two," Liddell said. "We just had a baby. My wife and me, I mean."

Mrs. Day made a sound that may have been a humorous chortle or a disgusted grunt.

The coffee finished brewing and she brought a tray with a carafe of coffee and three mugs to the table. She poured each of them a cup. Liddell asked for cream and sugar and she put these on the table.

Jack waited for her to have a seat and then laid the case file he'd brought on the kitchen table. He opened it and slid it toward her.

No one spoke as she took the documents out and read them one by one in entirety. When she finished, she put everything back in the folder.

"You're telling me this is all you have?" Mrs. Day asked Jack.

"Mrs. Day, we're just beginning. You have no reason to believe this, but we will work this like it's a new case. We've been taken off our other assignments to concentrate solely on this."

She put her coffee down and crossed her arms over her chest, never taking her eyes from Jack's.

Jack said, "I know you suspect a cover-up or, at the very least, that we were incompetent. Let me ask you a question: Do you want me to tell you the truth, or do you want me to lie to you?"

Without hesitation she said, "I want the truth."

"That's what we're after," Jack said. "I'll give you the good, the bad, and the ugly facts as we see them right now. Bad first: Your son's case is thirty-seven years old, your husband's case is thirty-four years old. What I just showed you is the entire file on your son's case. The file on your husband's case is missing. Therefore, we may or may not have any physical evidence or witnesses."

She didn't seem surprised.

"The ugly part: Due to the age of the cases, most, if not all of the detectives, patrolmen, or support personnel at the police department are old enough to have retired or are deceased. The retired ones aren't known to stick around Evansville, so we'll have to track them down. But we will."

Again, she wasn't surprised. "And the good?" she asked.

"The good. You have Jack Murphy and Liddell Blanchard working the investigations. We're very good at what we do, Mrs. Day. We're having a list compiled of everyone employed by the police department during those years. And another list of every officer on duty the days your son and husband were murdered. We've also hired a forensic computer analyst. The Chief has taken us off our other duties to concentrate exclusively on this. We have Chief Pope's word that we will have every resource. I know that doesn't sound like much, but believe me, we have solved cases with much less." He didn't think she needed to know this was the oldest case either of them had ever worked.

She came to a decision.

"Okay. I'll trust you, but I have to tell you hearing from that ridiculous man opened deep wounds. I'll curse him with my last breath. He wasn't a good boy back then and he's a most callous and arrogant man now."

Jack bit his tongue. He didn't know Dick as a teenager, but she was right about him being a dick now.

She said, "I wish my daughter was here to help with this." She left the kitchen without another word. Then she came back with a fistful of Kleenex and a Bankers Box, which she set on the table. She removed the lid and Jack saw several large mailing envelopes and two leather-bound bereavement books inside. The books were covered with white faux leather. IN LOVING MEMORY was inscribed in gold lettering on the outside.

"This is everything Harry collected."

"Mrs. Day, I won't make excuses for the Deputy Chief or for the past. He is who he is." *A prick.* "Things were done very differently back then. DNA wasn't used by the courts until 1986. I can't promise you we will find evidence, so I can't say we'll be able to run DNA tests. I can't promise you we will find the person or persons responsible. What I *can* promise you—what *we* can promise you—is we will do everything possible to get to the truth."

She said, "I suppose neither of you are old enough to remember any of this. I see you're married, Detective Blanchard. Do you have children?"

"Yes, ma'am," Liddell said and fumbled in his pocket for his cell phone. He pulled up the photos and scooted his chair closer to Mrs. Day.

"That's Janie. She's eleven months old this week. She has her mama's beauty, but she's a talker like her daddy." He flipped through a couple of photos and stopped. "That's Marcie, my wife. We met in Louisiana where I used to work. We hit it off right away. Married eight years now."

"Do you love your wife and daughter?"

"Of course."

"And you would do anything to see that they're safe. If someone hurt them, would you do anything to find that person?"

"We get your point, Mrs. Day," Jack said. "We both have families."

Satisfied, she removed the white leather-bound bereavement books. She handed one to Jack and the other to Liddell, saying, "Dick nor any of his family attended Max's funeral. Not once did he come to see us or call us. Not once. I suppose you know about the fight Max was in at Rex Mundi the night he was killed?"

"Tell me." This was the first he'd heard of this.

"Dick and two of his friends got into it with Max at football practice. Thirty-seven years ago, tomorrow. They were the last ones to see my boy alive. But we never heard a word out of any of them. The decent thing to do would be to talk to us."

Jack agreed and scanned the several pages of visitors' names in Max's album. One name stuck out: Ted Mattingly. Dick wasn't in attendance unless he failed to sign the book. Olson wasn't there, either.

"There was one policeman who came to Max's funeral. He was helpful at first, but then we didn't see him again for a long time."

"You said he was helpful at first. What do you mean?" Jack asked.

She said, "Mattingly was the policeman who found my son that night. He came to the funeral and talked to Harry and Reina. Harry's face was red and I could tell he was getting angry. Not with the policeman. I asked Harry later what was said. Harry said the detectives were a bunch of incompetents. He wouldn't discuss it. Reina had told us there was a fight at school and she said she told the policeman about the fight. He said he would turn the information over to the detective working the case. Harry and I had talked to the detective. He was worthless, just like Harry said.

"Harry was killed on the Fourth of July, 1984. I remember the detective supposedly working on Max's murder came to the house the day after Harry was killed."

Jack asked, "Was that how you found out your husband was hurt? The next morning?"

"No. That policeman, Mattingly. He came by my house late the night Harry was killed. I was getting worried Harry was so late, and when there was a knock on the door I thought it was Harry." Her expression went blank. "It was Mattingly, telling me Harry wasn't coming home. He made sure Reina was home with me before he left. He said the coroner's office would call and..."

"So, the detective didn't come and talk to you that night, Mrs. Day?" Jack asked.

"He came the next morning and talked to me and Reina," she said.

"What did he tell you about your husband's death?" Jack asked.

"He told me Harry was killed during a robbery. He knew Harry was asking a lot of people questions about Max's murder and he asked a lot of questions about what Harry had found out about Max's murder, but he hardly asked about Harry's friends or enemies and stuff like that.

"He asked me if Harry kept business records at home. I had a bad feeling about this man. I told him Harry kept all his business records locked in the safe at the store. And Harry kept a notebook for himself. He kept track of his daily sales and a tally of how much money he'd left in the register and what was in the safe." She stared off into space for a moment and said, "He always kept that notebook with him in case he got robbed. The detective said they never found it."

"Did your husband leave much money in the cash register?" Jack asked.

"Nothing but a few rolls of coins and loose change."

Jack said, "The detective may have wanted a list of what was stolen, Mrs. Day. Those are routine questions."

"He *wanted* in the safe," she said. "He said he'd found the safe in the back room. He offered to go with me to unlock the safe so he could go through the books. I said I'd get our accountant to do that and I'd let him know if anything was missing. We didn't have an accountant. Harry always did his own books and taxes and stuff. But I didn't trust this guy. Not after Max and all that.

"I remember asking him how it could be a robbery when he didn't know if anything was taken. He said it had to be a robbery because the cash register was empty. He told me there were other recent robberies downtown recently, but I never saw anything in the news about other robberies. Especially about shootings during a robbery. Harry would have told me if there was and I watched the papers for a month or so. That detective was lying."

"Did you ever let the detective go through the safe?"

"Hell no! Excuse my language. It was a day or two before I could bring myself to go to the shop to find his books. When I got there the safe was locked, but everything that should have been inside it was gone. The detective had told me the safe was locked. I called the detectives' office and he called me back the next day. He said maybe Harry hadn't locked the safe that night and the robber cleaned it out. He couldn't explain why the door was shut and locked. I asked him if they found a notebook and he said he hadn't seen one, but he'd check with crime scene. I told him Harry always had the notebook in his pocket. He said if Harry had it on him it would be at the coroner's office. I told him the coroner had returned the property already. He said Harry must not have had it or it may have gotten lost when the coroner came and got Harry."

"Could that have happened?" Jack asked. "Did it ever turn up?"

"I wasn't in a good place, Detective Murphy. I had to take his word for whatever he told me, didn't I? In the end it didn't matter what I thought. The notebook was never found. Reina helped me search the house, the garage, the business, everywhere we could think of. Nothing. I had to go back through our old tax records and contact the businesses Harry dealt with for some receipts, but I never came close to getting all of it. I remember it was a nightmare trying to deal with the insurance companies and then pay our taxes. Those are some heartless people."

"Do you remember the detective's name?" Jack asked.

"Detective Olson," she said. "His name is on some paperwork in those envelopes."

Jack took several mailing envelopes from the Bankers Box. The one on top was dated November 26, 1980. He opened this one and took a sheaf of papers out. On top of the stack was an offense report made out and signed "Det. D. Olson." It was a duplicate of the offense report they were given by the Chief of Police earlier. The other documents were basically the same as the ones Jack already had, except for a crime scene report and several newspaper clippings recounting the murder of a Rex Mundi High School senior by an unknown assailant. There were very few details, but Olson was quoted as saying the victim had been shot inside his car and it was under investigation.

The crime scene report at the cemetery stated they had taken photos of the body, the car, but no mention of a broken taillight lens as Mattingly had told them. The photos weren't in Mrs. Day's papers, and Jack didn't have any with his copy of the file. The crime scene report in Mrs. Day's papers didn't specify any evidence was collected and the report wasn't signed, which was unusual. There wasn't a name for the reporting crime scene officer.

Jack opened another envelope dated in 1984—Harry Day's murder. The offense report was marked robbery/homicide. There were two brief supplementary reports, both authored by Dan Olson, and one report from crime scene. The crime scene report was brief and like the others, was unsigned and didn't give the names of the crime scene techs filing the report. There were more newspaper clippings, these of Harry's death, but this time there were Xerox copies of Polaroid photographs. The photos were of a closed safe and a cash register lying open on the floor. No evidence number was written on the Xerox copies. Either this was a totally messed-up investigation, or someone had doctored the paperwork.

"Do you who made Xerox copies of these Polaroid photos?" Jack asked, showing her the copies.

"Your Officer Mattingly said he found those in the police files."

"I thought you said you hadn't talked to Sergeant Mattingly," Jack said.

"I forgot about those pictures. Mattingly came to the house a week after Harry was killed and asked me a bunch of questions about Harry. I had already talked to a detective and found the safe was empty. Mattingly brought what's in that envelope, all except for the pictures. He asked if I'd found anything missing from the store and I told him about the safe being emptied. He was surprised. He seemed to remember being told the safe was locked. He came back a few days later and brought those. I told him that's what I saw when I was there to find Harry's business books. He told me to hang on to all of the stuff he'd given Harry and he'd keep digging."

"Did you talk to Detective Olson again?" Jack asked.

"Detective Olson came out here a week or two later, but he didn't tell me anything except they were following some leads. I called him several times over the next weeks and he told me he was still investigating. He didn't sound hopeful. He asked if I could remember if any weapons were missing and I told him I would have no way of knowing. I asked him about Harry's notebook. He told me he hadn't found anything like that. He told me to keep an eye out for it and he'd do the same. That was the extent of my contact with him."

"Did you call anyone else at the police department?" Jack asked. He knew from the Chief that she said she and Harry had made repeated requests to meet with Captain Dick and/or the Chief and had been rebuffed.

"When Max was killed Harry was like a hunting dog. He called the detectives' office and spoke to Captain Dick—that's Richard Dick's father—and the man wouldn't discuss the case with Harry. He suggested we leave police work to the police."

"Did you?"

"Definitely not. Harry talked to every policeman that came in the store after that and believe me, there were plenty of cops who came in. Of course, they all said how sorry they were, but nothing ever came of it. They were afraid to go against Captain Dick, if you ask me. Mattingly and Harry became friends because he was the single person willing to help us. Mattingly..." She stopped and asked, "This isn't going to get Mattingly in trouble, is it? I don't want him to be punished for helping us."

"He did nothing wrong, Mrs. Day. He's a good police officer and I'm sure he was doing his job," Jack said.

"Okay. Well, Mattingly got some information on the fight at Rex Mundi. He confirmed that Dick and his two friends were in a fight with Max and had gone after Max when he left the school that night. There was a girl involved. I think her name was Ginger Purdie. Mattingly said she told him that she didn't see the fight, but Reina said that when Max was leaving Ginger had come up to him and asked if he was hurt. So, she must have seen the fight. I mean, she was part of the reason they were fighting."

"Richard Dick and Max were fighting over Ginger Purdie?" Jack asked.

"Max and Dick had some history going back to when Max was on the football team at Central High School. Max played against Dick, who was with Rex Mundi. Dick was the Rex Mundi quarterback and Max was a Central tackle. Max bragged that he'd taken the Rex Mundi quarterback down a few times. When Max transferred to Rex Mundi in his senior year they were on the same team, but there was a lot of animosity between them. Anyway, Ginger was supposedly Dick's girlfriend and Max was taking her away. To be honest, I don't think my son even liked her."

My kind of guy. "Did they ever fight before that night?" Jack asked.

"Not that I heard of," she answered. "But I didn't approve of Max fighting. That's why we had him transferred to Rex Mundi in the first place. We thought he would get more supervision there at a Catholic School. We didn't know that he and Dick had a score to settle or we would have never put him in that position."

"It's not your fault, Mrs. Day. Even if you had known Max and Richard Dick didn't get along they would have met somewhere else and fought," Jack said, but she wasn't convinced. She'd been beating herself up over this for a long time.

"It was Dick and his friends that killed Max," she said. "Some other people told Mattingly they knew about the fight, but they wouldn't come forward."

Jack knew that even if someone *had* come forward they couldn't prove anything. Secondary witnesses and even eyewitnesses were wrong 50 percent of the time. These were teenagers showing off. Dick had an ego as big as outdoors now, so he probably did back then too. But he had always pegged Dick as a bully, a coward, and a blowhard. He couldn't imagine Dick going toe to toe with anyone who would defend themselves.

"Mrs. Day, I have to ask. Did Max or Harry have any other enemies that might have wanted to hurt them? Anyone who threatened either of them?"

"Harry never had an enemy in the world," she said. "But Max loved conflict. He wasn't a bad boy, but he never let a slight pass. He was easy to anger and quick to react. Dick and his friends were always getting under Max's skin."

"Explain."

"We let Max go to Central when he started high school, but we put Reina in Rex Mundi. After we transferred him to Rex Mundi, he found out one of Dick's friends was heckling Reina. You know. Teasing, touching, that kind of stuff. We didn't know about it until Harry and I were called to school to pick Max up one day. He'd been in a fight with Carl Needham. Reina said Needham was Dick's best friend. Well, Max said Needham had been asking Reina out and wouldn't take no for an answer. She embarrassed him in public and he started a rumor that Reina was… pregnant. Reina didn't tell us this was going on because she knew Harry had a temper and so did Max."

"What happened?" Jack asked.

"Well, Max found the boy and that's why we were called to come pick Max up. The rumors stopped."

"Was Needham one of the boys with Dick the night of the fight with your son?"

"Yes. Reina told me it was Dick, Carl, and Dennis."

"Do you know their full names?"

"Richard Dick, Carl Needham, and Dennis James."

Jack thought if it was Carl and Dick who had pursued Max that night there was a good possibility that another fight would have occurred. Max had publicly humiliated both of them.

"Anyone else you can think of, Mrs. Day?"

"Max liked to fight. He'd never run no matter what the odds. But I'll tell you something else. Max's car was really banged up when we got it back. There were dents and scrapes and part of the front bumper was pulled off. Harry said it had a lot of damage."

"Did Max have a wreck before that night?" Jack asked.

"No," she answered. "And Max loved that car. He would hand-wash and wax it a couple of times a week. If there was a scratch in the paint he would have had a fit."

The crime scene report listed a broken taillight lens, but it didn't say what type of car it was on. There was nothing about what happened to the victim's car after crime scene released it.

"What kind of car did Max have?" Jack asked.

"Reina has the car now. A 1975 red Camaro Super Sport. Harry had it repaired and gave it to Reina. She's still driving it."

Jack felt a chill run up his spine. Max had been killed in that car and Reina was almost killed in the same car at the same place in the cemetery. What were the chances?

"The car has been towed to our crime scene garage, Mrs. Day. I'll ask them to release it as soon as possible," Jack said.

"I don't care about the car. As long as Reina is safe. Thank you for having a policeman watch out for her."

"Are you going back to the hospital tonight?" Jack asked.

"Yes."

"Call me before you do and I can have someone take you."

"That's not necessary, but thank you."

"That's all the questions I have for now, Mrs. Day, but I'm sure I'll have more later. Do you have any questions for us?"

"You'll get him, won't you?" she asked. "Richard Dick shouldn't get away with this again."

Jack and Liddell took the Bankers Box of material with a promise to make copies and return it.

Chapter 11

Deputy Chief Dick hung up his desk phone. The news wasn't good. In fact, it was horrible. If the recording got out he would be humiliated. He had to prepare for that. Victory goes to the prepared mind, or something like that. Today would be a test of his internal fortitude.

He should have known Chief Pope would give the investigation to Murphy and Blanchard. If there was a detective who hated him more, Chief Pope would surely have assigned that detective the case.

Dick wasn't impressed with Murphy like some people seemed to be. Murphy was lucky. That was all. Dick brought Murphy up on disciplinary charges several times in the past. It should have resulted in his firing. Murphy was no doubt ecstatic at the prospect of bringing him down.

He stood in front of the full-length mirror on the wall beside the office door, straightened his tie, brushed at his shoulders, and picked a speck of lint from his sleeve. His dress shoes were immaculately shined, pants creased to a knife edge, badge and ribbons carefully shined and placed. He went back to his desk and picked the gold three-star collar-dogs that designated his rank as Deputy Chief. He took a polishing cloth from the middle drawer of his desk, wiped the smudge of his fingerprints from the gold, and worked the pins back into his collar. Perfect.

He debated whether to take his tricked-out police cap or try to appear more casual. He decided on casual. He didn't want to seem anxious or desperate. He stood erect, head held straight, and examined himself one last time. He was ready.

Deputy Chief Richard Dick left his office and spoke to Lieutenant Brandsasse as he passed by. Brandsasse was still working as Dick's receptionist for an extended punishment period. Dick had it on good authority that Brandsasse had been disrespectful of him. Had berated him to civilians, no less. Brandsasse was a lieutenant and should have more loyalty. More discipline. It was the sign of a good leader-to-be to have the respect of one's subordinates. He'd teach the man or eventually break him.

Dick said, "Lieutenant, I'll be in a meeting. If anyone needs me you can text my cell. If it's not important, take a message." With that, Dick turned and walked out of the office. Lieutenant Brandsasse gave his boss a disrespectful one-finger salute as he disappeared through the door.

He took the stairs to the main floor and went through the back entrance, taking the long way around by the court building to get to his car. The minor detour before his meeting was necessary. He'd forgotten his notes and his breath mints. He passed two uniform officers walking to their cars. They didn't greet him. He made a mental note of their names. He retrieved the items from his car and went back to the civic center.

Dick walked down the hall, enjoying the solid clicks his heels made on the tile floor. He ignored the receptionist. He could never remember her name. It began with an L. Lucrecia. Leticia. Lamika. It didn't matter. She'd been there less than a year and she wasn't in his circle.

He stopped in front of the elevators and punched the *up* button. The elevator was on the third floor. The damn things were insufferably slow. He'd have to mention that to Thatcher. But then, Thatcher wouldn't be mayor much longer, and he was sure Thatcher had other things on his mind right now besides slow elevators.

The doors whooshed open. Dick stepped on and punched the button for the third floor. A hand stopped the doors from shutting. A young woman, twentysomething, with dark, unkempt hair, no makeup, blue jeans, cowboy boots, and a stained sweater over an equally ugly shirt stepped inside. She didn't attempt to talk to him or notice he was there. Maybe she was one of the cleaning people. He didn't know all the maintenance people. They weren't in his circle. He punched the third-floor button again and she punched it after him.

Mayor Thatcher had summoned him for a meeting. He had a good idea what the meeting was concerning, but what was done was done. He'd endure whatever the man said, go back to his office, and make plans to repel the new assault he saw coming. He never imagined that doing a good thing—talking to the family of Max Day before he took over the reins of the EPD—would be taken so out of context. He should have known that no good deed goes unpunished.

The elevator door opened and the young lady brushed past him into the hallway without a "sorry" or an "excuse me" or even a "watch it." He couldn't help but watch as she moved down the hallway at a quickstep march. The city comptrollor, Bob something, was just leaving the mayor's office and held the door for the woman, but passed by Dick without acknowledging him. Rudeness must be catching.

Dick opened the mayor's office door. He was mildly curious what business the badly dressed young woman could possibly have with Thatcher, but she was nowhere to be seen.

"He was expecting you five minutes ago," the mayor's secretary said without addressing him by name or rank. "Go in. You don't have to knock."

Dick felt his stomach tighten. The secretary was always uppity, but something was off. Something bad was happening and he hadn't a clue. He rapped his knuckles on the door, regardless of what the secretary said, and was greeted with a "come" by Thatcher Hensley. That voice sounded tired.

Dick entered the spacious office to see that many of the awards and photos had already been taken down from the walls and were now in boxes stacked on chairs and the floor beside the desk. He wished he had the nerve to say, "Going somewhere, Thatch?" But he didn't know what was going on. Therefore, caution was the watchword.

The young woman from the elevator was with the mayor. She set a box of Hensley's personal belongings on the floor and pulled the chair to the side of the mayor's desk. Hensley's rolling chair was turned facing her and he'd scooted back off the chair mat.

"Have a seat, Richard," the mayor said.

Dick sat on an empty chair across from the mayor. The woman's eyes never left Hensley as she said, "We've got a problem, Thatcher. What are you going to do?"

Dick could tell Hensley was relieved that another person, a man, was in the room. He'd never seen Thatcher cowed by anyone, much less some little spit of a girl.

"Richard, do you know Tilly?" Hensley asked.

"Tilly Coyne," the young lady said, but didn't move to shake hands, didn't take her eyes off Hensley.

Hensley cleared his throat and said, "She's—"

"I'm Benet Cato's campaign manager," Tilly interrupted. She asked Hensley, "I'm going to ask again: What are you going to do with this problem?"

Mayor Hensley said, "Richard, we need to discuss the elephant in the room, so to speak."

"Elephant?" Tilly said and stood. "This is not an elephant, Thatcher. It's a goddamn bull in a china shop. It's a Hiroshima. I'll ask for the last time: What are you going to do?"

Hensley backed his chair off the mat and took a long, deep breath. "I was just made aware of this 'problem' an hour ago, Miss Coyne. A better question is: How does Benet plan to handle it? It's really not my problem. If she was so interested, why didn't she come herself?"

The minute those words left Thatcher's mouth Dick knew it was a mistake and he grinned inwardly. It was about time someone took the arrogant asshole on.

Tilly said, "She lets me handle pissant problems if the people in charge don't have the balls to keep their employees in line."

Dick glared at her. She was undoubtedly talking about him. How dare she!

Thatcher finally found his voice. "And how would you deal with this problem, Tilly? Perhaps you'll give me the benefit of your non-experience in handling these types of things."

Dick, who had sat quietly during this exchange, had had enough. "Stop it! Would someone please tell me what you're talking about. I might have something to say about it."

Tilly fixed Dick with a stare that made his scrotum shrink. "You."

Dick managed to say, "What does that mean?" He knew what it meant.

"You are the problem, Deputy Chief Dick," Tilly said derisively, coming to her feet. "We are discussing what should be done with you. And before you say that you are under a merit system and therefore can't be fired except with just cause. Before you say anything, I want you to remember whose name appears on your paycheck. I want you to remember what happens after the first of the year. I want you to remember that Benet ran her campaign on a clean-sweep slogan. You are an embarrassment."

Dick folded his hands in his lap and struggled to keep the emotion out of his voice. "I'm assuming you've had a complaint by a Mrs. Day."

Tilly sat down. "Duh. You think?"

"It was just a conversation," Dick said to the mayor.

"A conversation that was recorded," Tilly said.

Hensley focused his attention on the top of his desk and she tore into Dick.

"A conversation that was emailed to mayor-elect Benet. She heard the entire 'conversation'. She, to say the least, is concerned that someone of your supposed intelligence, and someone in charge of day-to-day operations of a three-hundred-eighty-five-person police force, would have a conversation with the family of a boy who was murdered thirty-seven years ago. A murder that you have been connected to by rumor. You, of all people, should know the family wouldn't welcome your comments, nor your presence."

Thatcher was staring at Dick now. "Just what the hell were you thinking, Richard?"

Dick saw the handwriting on the wall. Hensley had just found his way out. Cato wouldn't appoint him Chief. He would be castigated, ridiculed in public, and the blame for an investigation that he had no responsibility for—he was eighteen when it happened—would be hung around his neck like a burning tire. He was being sacrificed in the name of politics.

"I thought I could reason with her," Dick offered.

"You thought?" Hensley said with a sneer.

Tilly said, "I think we're done here, Thatcher. I'll report back to Benet that you don't have a clue what is going to be done. According to you, it's not your problem. I'll handle it."

Tilly got up and left the office. The door snicked shut behind her and Hensley rolled to his desk and put his clasped hands on the top. "I can't protect you this time, Richard. Maybe this will all go away. Just tell me one thing. No. No, don't tell me anything. I don't want to know. I'm told Jack Murphy is working this one and I'm sure he'll catch the bastard. He always does. I hope you appreciate a man of his caliber."

Dick was dismissed and as he passed the secretary's desk he could swear he heard her snort. Well, her days were numbered too. Clean sweeps included nosy, good-for-nothing clerical help. He'd gloat as she cleaned her desk out. He'd have her escorted from the building. Perp-walked out the door.

Chapter 12

Liddell pulled up to the drive-through window at the First Avenue branch of Donut Bank.

"How can you possibly be hungry again, Bigfoot?" Jack asked.

A young girl came to the window and asked, "Can I help you, sir?"

Liddell said, "I'd like to make a withdrawal," and the girl giggled. He asked Jack, "Do you want something, pod'na?"

"No. I just worry you'll go into a sugar coma and wreck the car."

Liddell gave her his order and asked for coffees.

"So, you're not worried about me, you're really worried about the car? That hurts," Liddell said.

His order came, two boxes of mixed pastries and two large coffees. He handed one of the coffees to Jack and set the boxes on the seat between them.

"I thought I'd bring a little something to the meeting with the Chief and Captain," Liddell said.

"Right," Jack said. "We need to keep this meeting short. I want to move everything to the war room. You can take them there."

They had dubbed a back room at Two Jakes Restaurant as the war room. It was a place where they had worked before. A place where they could run their investigations in privacy and anonymity. Plus, Liddell was in food heaven and that meant less downtime feeding the Yeti.

"Is Jake cooking today?" Liddell asked. Jake was a part-time cook—he called himself a chef—at Two Jakes Restaurant. Jake had hired a man named Vinnie to act as bartender. Jack had never known Vinnie's last name and hadn't worried over it, since Jake trusted the man. Jack knew Vinnie had a colored past, but he had proven himself a willing ally time and time again when Jack was in a scrape.

"I think Vinnie is standing in. Jake sounded like he was coming down with something when I talked to him yesterday," Jack said. "What do you think of Mrs. Day's take on all of this?" Jack asked, trying to get the focus back on the case and away from food.

"First off, I don't like the fact that Max and Harry Day were both shot to death. And I don't like that most of Max's and all of Harry's files are missing from headquarters. And the way the scenes were handled. If there is a complete file on either of these cases, maybe Detective Olson took them home and just never brought them back. Then there's the little fact that Sergeant Mattingly is tied to all of this. I mean, I like Mattingly, but this is suspicious, don't you think?"

Jack agreed. "The whole thing stinks, Bigfoot, but we can't get ahead of ourselves. We'll find Harry's robbery/murder file when we get downtown. Then we go to property and see what evidence they have for us." He hoped the files were just misplaced. If Olson had taken them home, which was a good possibility, he might still have them. Olson hadn't done much and what he'd done was done badly. "When I was young, my father told me, 'Jack, real life is different from what people think. Keep your eyes open and your mouth shut and you won't catch flies.'"

"Wise man, your father," Liddell said. "Wiseass, his son."

"Bite me, Bigfoot. Can you drive a little faster?"

Liddell responded by pulling to the curb and stopping. "If you want to drive, it's okay by me, pod'na. Maybe you can take some of that aggression out on the other drivers."

"Sorry, Bigfoot," Jack said. "I guess this case—these cases—are getting under my skin. You don't drive like a sissy. I apologize."

"Does this mean you're going to get off my butt for my safe driving habits?" Liddell asked.

"Don't get carried away," Jack said and grinned. "You still drive like an old woman. So, put your big foot down on the gas and let's get this party started."

"I love you too," Liddell said, put his left signal on, and pulled back onto First Avenue.

The truth behind Jack's temper was their getting assigned to this case. He'd planned a romantic evening at home. Him, Katie, no dog, no phones, wine, scotch. Maybe some more scotch and wine. He'd had a hot tub installed at their house. The water would be the perfect temperature and the tub was the perfect place for drinking.

The special evening was for Katie. She hadn't been feeling well. Yesterday morning when he woke up he found her in the upstairs bathroom.

She said she didn't want to wake him, but he could tell she'd been crying. He knew better than to be an insensitive lout and ask her what was wrong. She either wouldn't answer or he wouldn't like the answer and then he'd try to fix whatever was wrong and would make it worse—"just like a man," as women were fond of saying.

He thought about having flowers delivered. She loved flowers. But should he have them delivered, or should he bring them? He'd put together a picnic basket with candles, a tablecloth, her favorite cheese, chips, dip, her favorite wine, his favorite twelve-year-old Glenmorangie scotch and glasses. Screw the flowers. If the rest of that didn't get him laid, nothing would.

It was going to be a surprise. Instead, the Captain and Chief had surprised him with this damn case. Political cases never ended well. Or on time.

As if to prove his point, 3:30 traffic on First Avenue going south became a rolling parking lot with workers heading home toward the Twin Bridges and on into Henderson, Kentucky. It was always bumper-to-bumper down First Avenue. Liddell had taken a shortcut through side streets that the crowd of driving dead must have discovered. Now they were sitting, stuck in traffic on St. Mary's Drive, behind Berry Plastics.

"Oh, like you could do any better," Liddell said.

"I didn't say anything."

"Yeah, but you were thinking it."

"Was not."

"I can tell by that little tic in the corner of your eye."

"Bite me, Bigfoot."

They turned off Martin Luther King Boulevard and onto Sycamore Street, then a sharp right into the parking area behind the Chief's complex. Double Dick's reserved parking spot was taken. Jack said, "Pull in there." He was pointing to the police garage doors. A large sign on the roll-up door declared NO PARKING and under that said that violators would be towed.

Jack took the FBI placard from the glove box and placed it on the dash. "Now it's our spot, Agent Blanchard. No one messes with the FBI."

They went to the side door. Jack pushed the intercom button, the lock clicked, and they entered.

Judy Mangold, the Chief's secretary, sat at her desk, said "He's waiting," and hooked a thumb toward Chief Pope's office. Jack knocked on the Chief's door and heard, "Come."

Jack and Liddell entered. Chief Pope and Captain Franklin were listening to the audio recording of the ill-advised conversation again. The recording stopped and the Chief motioned for them to take chairs.

Jack said, "Maybe we should go to the conference room." They did.

Jack arranged the documents on the conference table. "We're going to need some direction here, Chief," Jack said. "We need to get into central records and find any material they have relating to Max's case. Also, the robbery-murder case of Harry Day."

"I can get whatever you need, Jack," Captain Franklin offered.

"I appreciate the offer, Captain, but I would like to recruit someone from records to work on my team," Jack said.

"You want the record-room sergeant?" Chief Pope asked. "He's pretty new at the job and wasn't around when all of this took place."

Jack said, "I want someone who will dig until they find—"

"Any piece of dirt or gossip they can," Pope finished the thought. "Penny Pepper?"

"Yeah."

Central records was staffed by a gaggle of civilians, mostly women, and gossip was measured in half-lives. The rumor mill was headquartered in central records and their supreme commander was an early-sixties-year-old blond dynamo named Penny Pepper. She knew everything there was to know about everything and everyone. Penny was the ninja master, the Red Power Ranger, and the Xena: Warrior Princess of all police-related rumors.

"Penny," Chief Pope said. "You're serious?"

"If anyone knows any background, it will be Penny. I can make her my supersecret agent."

Chief Pope picked up the phone and punched a button. "Judy, is Pepper working today? She is. Tell her you need to see her. Tell her you have something juicy if she doesn't say anything. Then show her in here. Yes. I'm aware."

He hung up and said, "Judy said Pepper will sell us down the river. She's right. Do you really need her, Jack?"

Jack didn't have time to answer before there was a knock on the door and Penny Pepper was shown in by Judy.

Pepper said, "Whatever it is, I didn't do it." She said it jokingly, but her expression said she was guilty of something.

"Penny," Captain Franklin said. "We need your help with something extremely sensitive."

Penny's face began to glow as if she had won the powerball lotto and was bursting at the seams to tell someone. "I'm your girl," she said. "I can keep a secret."

There was an old saying: *Two can keep a secret if one of them is dead.* He'd have to kill her. He asked Penny, "What have you heard?"

"I haven't heard a thing, Detective Murphy."

He noticed she had called him by his title and not Jack like she usually did. His mother would do the same thing when she was mad at him. She would call him Mr. Murphy. As in, "Mr. Murphy, you take your hands off that boy's throat this instant." Penny would call him Detective Murphy when she had been snooping into his affairs.

"Penny, what have you heard?" Chief Pope asked.

"Okay. I've heard that Jack and Liddell are investigating the old murder case of Max Day. And I heard that Deputy Chief Dick went to Mrs. Day to tell her to keep her mouth shut because he was going to become Chief."

"Is that all?" Jack asked.

"Well, I know that Captain Franklin took the Day case file from records," she said, confirming what Jack had suspected. Their discreet investigation had already been blown to hell.

"So..." Jack prompted her.

"I know he didn't find much. I could tell by how much space the file had taken up in the cabinet drawer. The date of the file he took was around the time Max Day was murdered. Then he got in another cabinet that would contain records dated around the time Harry Day was murdered. He didn't find Harry's file. I couldn't find it, either. You'll need the missing files and so I started doing some investigating on my own," she said proudly. "That is what you want, isn't it, Jack?"

"I think you chose well," Chief Pope said to Jack. To Penny he said, "Penny, I'm going to ask you to do something that is not in your job description, but..."

"I'll be happy to, Chief Pope," Penny said. "As long as I don't get fired by the incoming mayor, that is, or let go by Double—erm, I mean Deputy Chief Dick. I don't think he cares for me. If he finds out I'm helping you build a case against him he won't be happy. Not at all."

Pope frowned. "We're not building a case against anyone, Penny. This is a discreet investigation. A peek, if you will. I can promise that *I* won't fire you. Unless you compromise Jack's investigation, of course. That means no talking to anyone except for the people in this room. No one can know what you're doing or what you provide to Jack. If you don't want to be involved, I'll understand."

"No. I'll do it. Whatever it is. Just ask."

Chief Pope said, "It sounds like you have a handle on what I want. I remind you—"

Penny put her fingers to her lips and mimicked turning a key. "My lips are sealed. I have to keep quiet about this," she finished for him. "I'll be glad to help with anything that keeps you here, Chief Pope. I like things just the way they are."

She was dismissed and Jack watched down the hall to be sure she left the offices. Chief Pope said, "I hope this doesn't bite us in the ass."

Jack wanted to say, "Chief, we've already been chomped," but he said, "Let me show you what we have and tell you what we suspect. You'll see why we need to take the chance with Pepper."

Jack took them through Harry's collection of papers, the remembrance books, the copies of police reports, and a little notebook log Harry had kept of all the dates, times, and who he spoke with at the police station. Mrs. Day hadn't remembered the notebook was in the bottom of the box. Captain Thomas Dick's name was mentioned several times. There were also a dozen notations of people he'd spoken to that he considered possible witnesses, but he didn't say why he thought so.

Jack said, "The file we have right now doesn't have any corresponding reports to show any of these people were ever interviewed."

Chief Pope was going through Harry's notebook and he put it down. Captain Franklin closed the remembrance book. Jack put the documents back in the mailing envelope.

Chief Pope said, "I can certainly see why they thought the police were covering something up."

"Mrs. Day wants us to copy this and give it back," Jack said.

Chief Pope leaned out of the conference room. "Judy," he called. She came and Jack handed her the box.

"I'll make a copy," she said.

"The family seemed to just give up after Harry Day was killed," Jack said.

Pope said, "I was a motor patrol officer when Max and Harry were killed. I seem to remember that Detective Olson worked Harry's case."

"He was the investigator on Max's case too," Jack said. "Hopefully, Penny will find something. We'll check the cold case cabinets in the detectives' office. We need to check the property room. If we don't find anything, we'll visit Olson."

There was another knock at the door. Judy stuck her head in and handed Jack a piece of notepaper. "Penny said you'd need this," she said and closed the door.

"What is it?" Liddell asked.

"Dan Olson's home address," Jack said.

"She's a mind reader," Liddell whispered.

Jack asked, "What can you tell us about Harry Day's murder, Chief?"

"I remember he owned a gun shop downtown. It's still there. Earl's Gun Emporium. At least, that's the name now," Chief Pope said.

"Mrs. Day said they sold it after Mr. Day was killed," Liddell said.

"It's been a long time back, but I remember Harry was shot and killed during a holdup. Dan Olson worked the case. I remember, because there were some rumors going around that he helped himself to a couple of guns while he was in the shop alone. Of course, detectives weren't very popular among the lowly street cops back then and rumors were in abundance," Pope said.

"The documents Mrs. Day gave us have copies of two different offense reports made out when Max was killed," Jack said. "One of them was handwritten and signed by Officer T. Mattingly. The other was typed and signed by Detective Olson. The reports give different facts. For instance, Mattingly's report indicates signs of a scuffle outside of Max's car."

"And Olson's report?" Pope asked.

"Olson's report concludes there was no suspect and doesn't mention any type of scuffle. There's not much more than basic info on Max or the car he was found dead in. Olson's supplementary report was minimal at best. There's no mention of interviews, evidence, nothing but Max being found in his car, dead from a gunshot wound to the head. His report sounds like Max was sitting in the car and someone just walked up and popped him. No tire tracks, no scuffle, nothing to indicate a fight or whether there was one person or twenty there when it happened."

"Don't forget Mattingly was a new patrolman, Jack," Chief Pope said. "Maybe he turned in the report and Detective Olson decided it wasn't correct and made out his own."

"That would be more plausible if Mattingly's offense report was in the file you gave us, Chief. Mrs. Day had both offense reports. She said Mattingly was in touch with her husband and giving him information as to Max's murder. She didn't seem to notice the reports were different."

"I don't know what to tell you," Pope said.

"The common denominator in all of these, if you include Reina Day, is Sergeant Mattingly. He was the one who found Max's body. He also found Harry's body. He was involved with investigating Harry Day's killing, and he was the first officer on scene at Reina's attack," Liddell pointed out.

Jack said, "The remembrance book from Max's funeral shows that Sergeant Mattingly attended the service. Mrs. Day said he was the only policeman who came to the service to her knowledge. He talked to Harry and Reina at the service and she said Harry was angry afterward, claiming the police were incompetent. She said Mattingly began getting together with her husband and discussing Max's case. She said he supplied Mr. Day with some of the documents she gave us today. He never came to their house, but she knew they were talking because Mr. Day would tell her things they said to each other. When weeks had passed and there was nothing new from the investigation, Mattingly went to Rex Mundi and talked to several students about a fight that occurred between Max and Deputy Chief Dick and two of his friends. The fight is not mentioned in Olson's paperwork." He told them that Reina Day, according to her mother, said Double Dick and two of his friends were involved in the fight and it was over a girl named Ginger Purdie. Dick and Max were vying for Ginger's affection. "She said Mattingly suddenly backed off. She thought he'd been warned not to talk to them anymore. From what she told us, I think the idea of a cover-up began with Mattingly."

He told them about Olson's contact after Harry's death and the suspicious questions he asked, then the missing ledger. He told them Mrs. Day couldn't determine if any guns were missing because of the missing ledger, and that the money was locked up in the safe. And how Olson had offered to open the safe and check the contents. She declined.

"This doesn't prove anything, Jack," Captain Franklin said, because he was expected to play devil's advocate. "Could be coincidence. We need something solid to clear these cases."

Jack didn't believe in coincidence. Everything happened for a reason. Everything was connected. He just couldn't see the links. Yet.

"What do you know about Olson, Chief?" Jack asked.

"Olson was a detective when I came on. He's been retired for a while," Chief Pope said. "Did you know him, Charles?"

Captain Franklin said, "Vaguely. He retired right after I came on the department. I knew who he was."

Chief Pope mused, "He wasn't a real good detective, but he was connected. Politically. And more."

"What do you mean by 'more', Chief?"

"He was part of the Masons, Jack. The Masonic Lodge here in town. Everyone in the detectives' office was a Mason. A lot of the upper ranks were too. Your father also belonged," Chief Pope said. "Jake Brady. But they didn't make a big deal out of it. Your dad and Jake were street cops to the core. I'm glad to see the business those two started has done so well. A lot of guys here were jealous of their success."

Jack didn't know what to say. He was seeing his dad from a totally new perspective. He knew his dad never wanted to be anything but a street cop, but he had no idea about the influence that being a Mason had with the PD in the past. It made him respect his dad even more. Jake Murphy wasn't an ass-kisser or game player.

"I'm well aware of your war room at your restaurant, Jack," Chief Pope said.

The war room was supposed to be a secret. Liddell, the Captain, Sergeant Walker, Angelina Garcia, and a select few knew they had used the back room at Two Jakes to run off-the-record investigations.

"I told him, Jack," Captain Franklin admitted. "It's the perfect place for you and Liddell to work in private."

There was a knock at the door. Judy Mangold stuck her head in again and said, "Penny's back." Judy sat the Bankers Box inside the door and handed Jack the material she'd copied. She showed Penny in.

Penny handed Jack several sheets, still warm from the printer.

"I found some reports that were misfiled. I made you copies. Do you want me to file the originals where they belong?"

"Let me have them for now." He skimmed over the papers. "This is an evidence report from Harry's death made out by Sergeant Mattingly," Jack said and handed it to Liddell.

Liddell handed the paper to Captain Franklin. The Captain took Harry's offense report from the box and compared it with the evidence report. "The time on the evidence report is a couple of hours after the murder was discovered. Mattingly must have gone back to the scene. Odd."

"Odd that Mattingly went back to the scene?" Liddell asked.

Captain Franklin said, "No. Odd that crime scene wouldn't have found this evidence."

Pope said to Penny, "Good work, Penny. Does anyone else know about these reports or what you're working on?"

She said proudly, "I know how to keep a secret."

Jack had to choke back a laugh. Penny's idea of a secret was sharing it with a dozen people.

Jack said, "There was another shooting this morning, Penny. Crime scene may still be working on it, but any paperwork that comes in on a Reina Day—from anyone—I want you to make a copy for me and one for Captain Franklin. Don't put them in my mailbox. Give them to Captain Franklin directly."

"I'll check all the cabinets again to see if anything else has fallen through the cracks."

After Penny was out of earshot, Jack said, "The handwritten evidence report Mrs. Day gave us from Max's case was also signed by Mattingly. It showed things you'd expect to find if there was a fight or scuffle at Max's scene, but there was no evidence number. Now we have an evidence number from Harry's scene, courtesy of Sergeant Mattingly, and the report was conveniently misfiled."

"Without a witness who saw another fight at the cemetery, that doesn't mean much, Jack. And we still don't have Harry's case file to see if Mattingly's evidence was collected by him or crime scene, or even put in evidence," Captain Franklin said.

"But Sergeant Mattingly's evidence report clearly shows he collected shards and pieces of broken beer bottles around where Max's car was that night. He also found a tire iron near the car with blood on it. It should have been sent to the state lab for testing," Jack said. "We didn't have DNA tests in 1980, but if we still have the tire iron we can run it through the process."

Chief Pope said, "Captain Franklin, please call Sergeant Mattingly to your office. Jack and Liddell should be there. Anything else, gentlemen?"

Jack said, "Yeah, Chief. Two things. We'll need a list of police and civilian personnel from 1980, and I don't want to ask Deputy Chief Dick for it." Deputy Chief Dick was currently in charge of the personnel unit, where all those type records would be stored.

"What's the second thing?" Chief Pope asked.

"We'll need unlimited access to the property room and any records that pertain to evidence in Max or Harry's cases," Jack said.

The Chief said, "I don't think we have to worry about keeping this investigation quiet anymore. Claudine Setera will see to that. But I still want you to work from your war room. I can't take a chance that anything else goes missing. Do you want me to call the property room sergeant?"

"No," Jack said. "But I need Angelina Garcia."

"That's three things, Jack. But I'll approve it," Chief Pope said. "Can she get the personnel records for you?"

"I still want them from personnel. Maybe it will be good that the Deputy Chief sees we're pursuing this. He'll be less likely to interfere if he sees we're asking for the records, Chief."

"Okay."

"I'll call Sergeant Mattingly in," Captain Franklin said. "I'll let you know when he's here."

Jack and Liddell left. When they were in the lobby, Liddell asked, "Property room?"

"Yeah. Then we talk to Sergeant Mattingly," Jack said. "I'm going to call Angelina."

"She'll be thrilled to be working for us again. Especially the part where she's getting paid."

"She always gets paid, Bigfoot," Jack said defensively.

"Not for the hundred little things you asked her for on our other cases."

"Oh, and I guess you never ask her for favors."

"Point taken," Liddell said.

* * * *

Deputy Chief Richard Dick was angrier than he'd ever been. So much so that he left work early, telling Lieutenant Brandsasse he wouldn't be back and that Brandsasse could just lock the office up. Then he countermanded that order. Brandsasse was to stay until 8:00 this evening and monitor his calls, take notes, and pass on only the emergency calls or those from Chief Pope. Dick knew Brandsasse worked an off-duty job that he was required to be at right after he got off work at three. This would make him at least five hours late to his other job. Too bad.

Deputy Chief Dick left the building still smoldering. His personal driver, Captain Dewey Duncan, was on vacation and Dick had been lowered to driving the Cadillac Escalade he'd commandeered from the narcotics unit seizure pool. He missed the convenience of having a driver and someone to bear his anger. With everything going on he didn't need the headache of finding a temporary replacement for Captain Duncan.

He backed out of his reserved parking spot and headed to Highway 62 and took the ramp going east at twice the speed limit. Red Brush shooting range was in Warrick County, north of the Alcoa aluminum plant. He'd been a member of Red Brush for a very long time and spent several days a month sharpening his shooting skills with handguns, shotguns, and rifles. He'd once shot a Thompson .50 caliber machine gun similar to the one reputedly carried by the infamous killer Machine Gun Kelly who had, ironically, never shot his machine gun at anything other than tin cans. Rumors and reputations and lies. It was disgusting that his appointment as Chief was being held up by the spreading of rumors and lies. He knew the lower ranks of the police department called him Double Dick behind his back. He knew who had started that too. When this witch hunt was over they would show him respect or they would suffer the consequences.

His thoughts were a red blur and had occupied his mind until he arrived at Red Brush. The range itself was a couple of benches, a canopy, and a small Quonset hut where the targets were locked away. The shooting distances were set for seven, fifteen, twenty-five, and fifty yards for the handguns and shotguns. The rifle range was separate.

He unlocked the hut and took two silhouette targets and a staple gun to the seven-yard target posts, stapled them up, and walked back to the canopy shelter. The targets he'd chosen were designed for law enforcement, depicting a man with a gun in his hand. He imagined the target as Tilly Coyne and felt his anger boil up like acid in his throat.

He was angry at the mayor. He was angry at Tilly Coyne. He was angry at the Chief of Police, who didn't have the sense to step aside and let a better man take over. But he was mostly angry with Maximillian Day. Mad Max indeed. This was all his fault. And Murphy. He couldn't forget Murphy.

He went back to his car and lifted the hand-carved wooden box from under the front seat. He opened the box and took the Desert Eagle .50 caliber semiautomatic from the velvet-lined box and worked the slide a few times. The Desert Eagle was a true work of art.

"Do ya feel lucky, Tilly?" he said in a menacing voice. "Well, I do. You're going to make my day."

Chapter 13

The police property room was located in the basement of the Civic Center in a steel room with fifteen-foot ceilings with a heavy chain-link barrier covering the entrance. Inside there was evidence from criminal cases, found property, and weapons seized from an assortment of crimes and from suicidal people. The gun safe was a spacious 1940s Keystone brand simply called Fat Boy because it held forty-eight long guns, plus twenty-five to thirty handguns. The door to the safe stood open, the inside bulging with long guns, pistols, and more propped against the outside of the safe. More were stacked on two long folding tables. Several large boxes and another folding table barely held the remainder of the handguns seized over the years. When Marlin Pope had become Chief of Police, the long-held practice of auctioning weapons ceased. Now, if weapons couldn't be returned to their owners they were destroyed.

Row upon row of heavy metal shelves filled the room from floor to ceiling, bursting with box upon box of evidence. Two seventeen-foot stepladders leaned against the shelves. It was a hoarder's dream.

Recently promoted Sergeant Alistair Simms stood blocking the doorway of the property room and made a sweeping motion with her arm. "What can I do for you, detectives?"

Simms had made sergeant exactly five years after joining the force, which was the minimum number required to become a sergeant. At twenty-six, she was the youngest sergeant on the Evansville Police Department. She was dressed snappily in her police uniform, her gold badge, gold name tag, and gold collar dogs were highly polished, as were her Corfam dress shoes. She was cute, in a *Terminator* sort of way. Even her welcome was serious and exuded competence and leadership. Jack couldn't help but think she was destined to become a female version of Double Dick.

He handed her a scrap of paper with the report numbers for Max and Harry's cases and the evidence number for Harry's case written on it. He didn't want to give her the reports themselves. He had the only copies now and wanted to keep it that way.

Sergeant Simms read Jack's note and asked, "Where's the report?"

"You don't need that," Jack said. This wasn't his first time in the property room."

"I make copies of the offense reports and evidence supps when I'm requested to retrieve property, Detective Murphy. I have a separate file cabinet with the paper copies cross-referenced to evidence. I also enter all of this in the computer recording the time, date, and who makes the request."

"Is that a new policy?" Jack asked.

"It's *my* policy. This place was a mess when I took over."

She was right about it being a mess. The last time he was down here you could barely walk between the shelves. If you found what you needed it was customary to yell "Eureka!" You never wanted to hear "*Timberrrr!*"

"I'm not allowed to give you the reports, Sergeant Simms. You need to call Captain Franklin. I can give you his number," Jack said.

"He's not my direct supervisor, Detective Murphy. I work for Deputy Chief Dick."

Jack had forgotten that fact. *Well, hell!*

"The Chief of Police, then." Jack brought the Chief's number up on his cell phone and handed the phone to Sergeant Simms, the property room Nazi.

She took the phone, spoke to Chief Pope briefly, said "Yes, sir," handed the phone back to Jack, and motioned them to come inside.

"These are *old* case numbers," Simms said.

"Thirty-seven years and thirty-four years, to be exact," Liddell said.

"The oldest is the Max Day murder, right? I don't know what the other number is for," Simms said. Seeing the expressions on the detectives' faces, she said, "Hey, I work in a dark corner of the basement, but I'm not a mushroom. I heard you were investigating Deputy Chief Dick concerning the murder of Max Day. He was a teenager, I hear. You must have really pissed someone off to get this case. Your asses are hanging out in the wind—excuse the language."

Jack said, "We don't know that he *did* anything yet, Sergeant. Rumors are dangerous."

Simms blushed at the recrimination. "I never said he did anything. Did I say that? I said that's what I heard."

"And I wasn't directing that remark to you, Sergeant," Jack came back. She'd evidently grown a big head with her promotion. If she made lieutenant he might have to ask for a lawyer before talking to her.

"Right," Simms said before sitting down at her Army surplus desk. She opened one of the index file drawers and her fingers crawled through the cards. She stopped and pulled out another drawer and then another. Finally, she found the catalogue card.

"That's the right offense number," she said, showing the card to Jack and Liddell. Typed on the card was the set of numbers Jack had written down for Max Day's case. The items of evidence recorded on the card were blackened out and indecipherable. At the bottom of the card someone had scribbled in *property destroyed.*

"Try the other case number," Jack said and added, "Please, Sergeant."

Simms dug through the cabinet again in several places before giving up. "Are you sure there was evidence? I'm not finding a card."

"Can you search by evidence number?" Jack asked.

"I haven't had time to cross-reference all the old files yet. Let me see." Simms went to a similar file cabinet with a Dymo label reading EVIDENCE NUMBERS stuck to the front top. She searched several drawers where the number should have been and found nothing. "It's not here. Hang on."

She closed the file drawers with a bang. "These *are* both murders, aren't they?"

"Right."

"Well, the damn cards should be in the drawers no matter how old the cases are. Now you can see why I'm working my ass off down here. What a damn mess. I'll go through all of this to see if it was misfiled, but it may take some time. This really pisses me off."

Jack asked, "Is there a system to the shelves? Are the boxes arranged by the offense date? Maybe there's a bag or box with a date from those years. We can help you."

She said, "You've got to be kidding. This type of sloppy work drives me batshit crazy. It's police department policy that no one but the property room commander is allowed to retrieve evidence. I'll give it my best shot. That's all I can promise."

Jack and Liddell left the property room and could hear Simms swearing loudly behind them.

"Now she's not just a regular sergeant, she's a commander," Liddell said.

"I've got news for her," Jack said. "She's not in command as far as I can tell. I hope she's had her tetanus booster."

* * * *

Jack and Liddell swung by their office to check their messages when Detective Sergeant Wolf cornered them. Sergeant Wolf was shorter than Jack, heavily built, but solid like a tree trunk. He'd put in a lot of years assigned to motor patrol and made a decent detective sergeant.

"I've reassigned your other cases," Wolf said. "The Chief said you would be on a special assignment. That sucks for you and the rest of us."

"I told you we were special, pod'na," Liddell said to Jack.

"Not my idea, Sarge," Jack said.

"Jesus, you two. If you're not working for the feds you're off on some flight of fancy case. This thing is old as Methuselah. Dick will get even for whatever slight he imagines you're responsible for. What makes anyone think you can solve it now?"

"Because we're the A-team," Liddell said with a straight face. "My code name is Condor. Jack is Sparrow."

Wolf gave them a grudging grin. "Your code names are mud one and mud two. Get this done and get back here. The guys are bitching about picking up your slack and I gotta listen to it. I don't like listening to bitching. You hearing me?" Wolf said.

"*Jawohl mein kommandant*!" Liddell said, clicking his heels together and giving a Nazi salute.

Wolf walked away, shaking his head.

"Don't piss him off, Bigfoot," Jack said. "We might need him for a reference when we get fired."

"There's the negative Jack we all know and love," Liddell said.

"We need to call the ladies," Jack said, and they crept into their office, shutting the door behind them. They could still hear a couple of detectives call out "USUCK!"

Liddell called Marcie and told her he would be very late getting home and blamed it on Jack. Jack called Katie and told her to stay out of the garage. As soon as he said it he knew it was a mistake. That would be her first stop when they hung up and she'd find his surprise. Damn it!

Jack hung up and called Two Jakes. "Jake, I'm going to need the meeting room," he said when Jake Brady answered.

"I heard," Jake said. "I've got it ready for you. You'll need computers and that other stuff, but I put extra chairs, a coffee maker, cups, and a couple of folding tables in there. Sounds to me like you've got a tiger by the tail, son."

Jack didn't ask how Jake knew what they were doing. The grapevine was mighty. "I don't know when I'll be there. You might want to warn Vinnie that we'll be coming and going. Angelina too."

Vinnie had living quarters in what was once the pantry—a big pantry—in the back of Two Jakes. Vinnie kept the stock current, cleaned, served, and bartended during the day. And Jack suspected he smoked weed most of the night.

Two Jakes was, at the very least, a two-man operation. When Jack's father died, Brady couldn't cook and tend bar by himself. Jake Brady hired Vinnie, a small, wiry man with a tan so deep his skin was like leather. His face was creased sharply with lines that belied his true age, whatever that was. Thick blond hair was pulled back in a nub of a greasy ponytail. Year-round he dressed in short-sleeved tie-dyed shirts; blue jean cutoffs, and deck shoes. For all Jack knew, Vinnie could very well be one of the original flower children of the 1960s. But, unlike any of the flower children, Vinnie was extremely clean and polite and didn't smoke dope in front of him. The drink-slinger had a questionable background, but a rare talent for mixing drinks and keeping customers happy.

The last call Jack made was to Angelina Garcia. She began her career as the IT person for the Evansville Police Department and proven herself invaluable in digging up—read that *hacking*—information using computers and her connections in the cyber world. She had first come to Jack's attention several years back when he was chasing a serial killer who was staging his murders as nursery rhymes. At that time, she was a data analyst with the vice unit, but after working with Jack and Liddell she was transferred to work in the violent crimes unit.

She met the sheriff of Dubois County, Mark Crowley, during an investigation; they married and she eventually semi-retired from the EPD. She was now a consultant for the Evansville Police Department and several other agencies.

Jack told her he was setting the war room up again and before he could explain further, she said, "I'll bring my stuff."

"You can work from home if you want, Angelina," Jack said.

"Mark's out sick for a few days. It's no problem."

Jack thought for a moment and said, "You can stay at my cabin. Hot tub, beer, privacy."

"I get enough privacy here, Jack. I'll stay at the casino hotel. Lots of people, pool, spa, exercise room, slots, restaurants. When do you want me to start?"

"There's no big hurry, Angelina, as long as you get set up in the next couple of hours."

"Can I go to the bathroom first?"

"Well, I didn't mean…"

"I'm just kidding, Jack. Let me get my stuff together and I'll head that way. Is Jake there?"

"Yeah," Jack said and the phone vibrated in his hand. "Got to go, Angelina. I'll see you at the war room in a bit."

He disconnected and answered the incoming call.

"Sergeant Mattingly is in my office."

"We'll be right there, Captain."

Chapter 14

The fluorescent environment of the Civic Center basement was replaced by the sunset when Jack made it to the Chief's complex. He could see the sun was already setting. It was early evening and the days were getting shorter. His confidence he would be able to solve this case was waning as well. They had so far gotten no further than the original poorly done investigation. Evidence was missing, reports were missing or replaced with fakes, there was one partial witness—George Morgan—and he didn't have much of a description of the guy. But George knew his guns and was able to tell them the attacker used a semiautomatic handgun. A specific handgun. A .50 caliber Desert Eagle. His information was partly confirmed by the .50 caliber shell casings found at the cemetery this morning.

As far as the older murders, they had one witness, the person who found the bodies: Sergeant Mattingly. They still had to interview Double Dick and his friends from Rex Mundi, but that would have to wait until they got background on all of them. At least he knew Dick's background. He was a dick. That was all he needed to know.

Jack felt the black cloud follow in his footsteps as he and Liddell made their way to the Captain's office. Judy Mangold had already gone home for the day. Captain Franklin buzzed them inside. The Chief's complex was dark.

"Sergeant Mattingly is in my office, but I have something to tell you. It may not mean anything, but I thought you should know. I just got off the phone with Lieutenant Brandsasse. He has the 1980 and 1984 personnel lists for you. He said he'll be in the office for a few hours if you want to come and get them."

Jack thought he knew why, but he asked, "What's he doing here so late?"

"Lieutenant Brandsasse said Richard had him pull the 1980 and 1984 personnel records right after he returned from the meeting this morning."

"We hadn't asked for the records yet," Jack reminded him.

"We hadn't. Actually, we weren't going to involve Richard in that task. He must have known we were going to request them is all I can figure."

Jack could think of another reason. Double Dick wanted to see if there was something in the files that needed to disappear. That meant Angelina would have to also get the city personnel records and compare them to the EPD personnel records to see what was missing. Richard wasn't going to make this easy on them.

"Lieutenant Brandsasse said Richard took the records to his office."

Bingo.

Franklin continued. "Lieutenant Brandsasse said Richard locked himself in his office and made several phone calls. Richard then left and told the lieutenant to take messages unless it was an emergency or Chief Pope wanted something. Richard told him to stay until eight."

"Did the lieutenant say what time he got the call from the mayor's assistant?" Liddell asked.

"I didn't ask. When you pick up the files you can ask him."

"It's not like him to leave early," Jack said. "I hate to say this, but from the way things are shaking out, we may need to keep an eye on him. We were just in the property room talking with Sergeant Simms and she couldn't locate any of the evidence. She found a property card from Max's murder and the items entered were redacted and someone wrote *property destroyed* on it with no explanation."

Franklin's shoulders fell. "We don't have squat, Jack. Excuse my language. We can't do anything without appearing that we're trying to sabotage Richard in favor of Chief Pope."

"Angelina is setting up the war room, Captain," Jack said. "I can get her to run some history and financials on Richard and every name mentioned in what we do have. She can check phone records and the like. Or don't you want to know any of this?"

The Captain said, "I don't want to get the Chief involved in any further details unless we need his authority. What's said in Vegas…"

"Understood, Captain."

Jack also understood the thoughts that must have been running through Double Dick's mind. Even Sergeant Simms had heard Dick was a suspect in the old murders, and she made it sound like the rumors were true. Dick had his sources, so he had heard all of this. He may have been covering his ass while he was locked in his office making phone calls, or he might have been checking to see what his attorney might need. There would have to be an attorney involved sooner or later.

"Let's see what Sergeant Mattingly has to say," the Captain said and they went to his office.

Mattingly sat in a hardback chair in the corner of Captain Franklin's office, holding a thick accordion binder on his lap. He didn't show any curiosity or nervousness. If anything, Jack had the impression Sergeant Mattingly was relieved to be able to unload the secrets he'd been harboring for more than three decades.

Sergeant Ted Mattingly was a rookie patrolman just off his probationary period at the time Max Day was murdered. He was the one who found the body. Mattingly was mid-fifties now; tall, sturdily built, thick, jet-black hair, and carried himself like a man who had seen and done it all. Nine hash marks were sewn on his left sleeve, indicating his thirty-eight years of service. He joined the police department five years earlier than Richard Dick.

Jack and Liddell entered the office behind Captain Franklin and said, "I guess you have some questions for me."

They sat and Jack said, "You know what we need."

"Give me the *Reader's Digest* version," Jack said.

Sergeant Mattingly took a cleansing breath and began. "I know how this appears. I'm the one who found Max and Harry's bodies and then I'm first on scene at the cemetery with Reina this morning. Let me start by saying I'm glad the Chief gave these cases to you two."

"Yeah," Jack said. "We're just thrilled too. So. My first question, Sergeant Mattingly, is why you didn't notify the Captain here that you had special knowledge of several murders, not to mention the possible connection to what happened to Reina Day this morning?"

Mattingly said sheepishly, "I was going to. But I've been living with this information, these suspicions, for my entire career."

Jack gave him a skeptical look.

"Jack, there is no *Reader's Digest* version. Sorry. I'll tell you what I know and what I've done, but it may take a while."

"Should I call Katie and tell her to put the scotch away?" Jack asked to lighten the mood and Mattingly chuckled. It was obviously hard for Mattingly to share what he'd been holding back for over thirty years and he needed to know he wasn't in trouble. Yet.

"I'll answer your question first and then I'll go back to the beginning," Mattingly said.

"Take your time," Jack said.

"Why didn't I come forward earlier? Well, I had tried to make something out of the murder of Max Day and later on Harry Day and was, more or less, ordered to cease and desist inquiring into those cases by the then–Detective Captain Thomas Dick, who is the father of Richard Dick."

Jack was thinking cover-up.

"Captain Dick was a smart detective. He directed the investigations and when he found out—from Detective Olson, I guess—that I was digging into the murders on my own time he promised to not only ruin me, he would put me in jail for tampering with evidence, obstruction of justice, falsifying court documents; you name it. I was on the sergeants list by the time he and Olson caught on to me. He told me it would be a shame if instead of making sergeant I went to prison. You know what they do to cops in prison."

"Did you do anything wrong?" Jack asked.

"Hell no! But I'm sure they could have manufactured evidence, witnesses. Even the stink would be a career ender."

Jack said, "You opted for door number one."

Mattingly was embarrassed. "I thought I was helping the family by nosing around, but I realized I was only giving them false hope. I figured I couldn't do any good for anyone if my career ended. Call me an asshole."

"Asshole," Jack said with a grin.

"Screw you, Jack," Mattingly said and then, "Sorry for the language, men. You too, Jack."

"Good one," Liddell said.

Mattingly's grin faded. "In 1980 I was third shift, motor patrol north. The beats weren't as small as they are now. Mine was all of the north from Diamond Avenue, east of Highway Forty-one and west from St. Joe Avenue. I was married back then and working two off-duty jobs to keep my wife happy. I had one kid and one on the way. I was always tired. I tried to catch a few winks whenever I could, so I would drive to the backside of Locust Hill Cemetery, turn the police radio up, and instead of taking my meal I'd get some shut-eye. The wife left me anyway. Ran off with the milkman. Seriously. The guy delivered milk and dairy products to the grocery store where she shopped."

He gripped the binder tighter, concentrating on its cover, and said, "Sorry. Okay. On the night Max Day was killed I had just left Dunkin' Donuts on First Avenue, where I was having coffee with two other units, Turpin and Preske. They're both deceased now. Anyway, I got a dispatch to Locust Hill Cemetery. It was just a 'suspicious circumstance' run. I figured it was a couple of teenagers doing the nasty. A lot of kids went there to make out or pull pranks. Still do.

"Everyone knew about the cemetery. I had the idea I was being set up because I was the new guy. Someone was always pulling pranks back then. Anyway, I pulled into the cemetery and saw a car parked back by the mausoleum with its lights off. Then I noticed the driver's window and windshield was covered with something dark.

"I put my spotlight on the car, punched up my bright lights, and flipped on the light bar. The car was facing away from me. All I could see was a shape in the driver's side. Nothing moved. I called it in and went to check the driver. When I saw he was dead I called for backup. Turpin and Preske were still at Dunkin' Donuts, a few minutes away, but Olson got there before them. Detective Dan Olson was working third shift that night by himself. No other detectives.

"I was pretty new. I'd seen dead bodies when I was in training. Natural deaths, a few stabbings and shootings. Nothing like this. This boy, Max Day, was slumped against the driver's side window and part of his head was missing. There was blood and stuff stuck to the ceiling.

"Turpin and Preske got there right after Olson pulled in. I remember thinking Olson must have been real close because I had barely got there myself. This was about one in the morning. The kid hadn't been dead long.

"Preske came up to see what I had, but Turpin stayed back. Olson ran Preske out of the scene and took over. Then he bent over and picked something up off the ground by the car. Olson declared the weapon used was a handgun. He held up a shell casing for me to see and then put it in his pocket. He told Preske and Turpin they could take off. He told me to make out an incident report and not an offense report. I asked him if he was sure he didn't want an offense report and he got real mad and told me to go ahead and do an offense report if I wanted. I told him I needed some ID on the victim and he told me to leave that part blank, he'd fill it in later.

"I made out the offense report and started a supplementary report while Olson called for crime scene and the coroner. I thought it was strange that Olson would be doing all of this himself. He didn't call for another detective or call his supervisors, which was department policy. He'd dismissed Preske and Turpin. He didn't ask me to help crime scene do their search. But I was new. You never questioned the detectives."

"Go on," Jack said.

"Crime scene got there and Olson said something to them. They took a few pictures and a wrecker showed up. The coroner came and took the body, the wrecker took the car, and Olson told me to leave. The whole thing took thirty or forty minutes."

"That's all you can remember?" Jack asked.

"I remember it very well. I was new, but I wasn't dumb. I thought Olson was cutting way too many corners. I made out two identical offense report forms and a supplement form. The supplement was handwritten and I wasn't done, so I didn't give him that one and I kept one of the offense reports. On the one I gave Olson I put the crime down as a murder. I included the car description and plate number and a description of the scene. He told me that the report should have said suicide, but he would fix it later. He said that was it for me and I should leave, but he stayed."

"You said he didn't call for another detective or supervisor," Jack said. "Was that uncommon?"

"There may have been other detectives scheduled to work that night, but back then detectives working third shift were home in bed, meeting some woman, drunk, or all three. Olson was a skirt-chaser, a drunk, and low on the seniority totem pole. I don't know if other detectives were on duty that night but, in any case, Olson got there real fast. I wondered if this was his first homicide because he was guarding the scene, keeping everyone out—and I mean *everyone*.

"I knew detectives didn't even talk to other detectives about their active cases, and definitely motor patrol was kept in the dark. They locked the files up in their desks or took the case file and evidence home. They didn't turn in an offense report on an active investigation until it was necessary or they were ordered to."

Jack didn't tell Mattingly that he'd been ordered by the Chief to do exactly that.

"Olson told you to leave. What did you do then?"

"I left and waited about twenty minutes until Olson was gone, then I went back and searched the area. I saw scuff marks in the grit where the front of the car had been. Crime scene, Olson, and the wrecker had messed up most of it, but I could still make out where the fight was. Something on the ground glinted in my headlights and I found pieces of broken beer bottles. Maybe three or four bottles in all. A tire iron was off to the side of the road maybe twenty feet away, near one of the headstones. The tire iron had blood on the lug end. I collected the bottles and the tire iron, but I didn't have a camera to take pictures of where I found them. I thought about calling Olson or crime scene back out, but he got pretty mad about being questioned the first time. I figured I'd put it in evidence myself and turn a supplement in to crime scene. Let them notify Olson. You know?"

"I made out an evidence supplement, the details of what I'd collected and where I found it. When I got downtown I made a copy of my evidence report. That time of night I had to leave the evidence and supplement in records because the property sergeant was a first-shift job.

"I checked the records room the next day. The evidence was gone—I thought it had been picked up by the property sergeant. I asked to see the reports and I saw Olson had changed my offense report from homicide to death investigation/suicide. His signature was on it instead of mine. I couldn't believe he would call it a possible suicide when a weapon wasn't found. He didn't know about the tire iron and I doubt Max clubbed himself to death. My evidence report was gone from records.

"I made a copy of Olson's offense report and compared it to my offense report. He didn't mention the description of the victim's car. He didn't mention the broken beer bottles or the bloody tire iron. He didn't mention any type of struggle or fight. Just a dead kid sitting in his car."

Jack said, "You definitely turned in the broken glass and tire tool as evidence?"

"Yeah," Mattingly said. "I made a copy of the evidence report when I turned it in. I didn't have a camera, but I saw Olson taking some Polaroids and crime scene was photographing the body and car."

"What did you think happened?" Jack asked.

"I've thought about this almost every day. I believe there was a fight outside the car. I remembered seeing one of the taillight lenses broken. Pieces of it were on the ground. The car was banged up pretty good; dents in the trunk lid and roof. I didn't think that was from a wreck because of the broken pieces of tail lens on the ground. Something had to have happened right where the car set. I need to tell the rest of my story."

"Go ahead," Jack said.

"Okay. I talked to some of Max's family a few days after he was killed and they didn't remember seeing any damage to his car. It was a nice car and his dad said he took good care of it. I haven't talked to any of the family for a long time and until this morning I guess I forgot Harry had the car restored and gave it to Reina. When I heard the run called in I was real close. I can tell you, seeing that car, the bullet holes, it brought back some memories."

"Do you have any idea why Olson didn't do more?" Captain Franklin asked.

"Don't get me wrong. Olson was an okay detective, but not great. He made sergeant shortly after Max's murder. At the time I thought that was because he was a Mason. Most of the detectives were Masons back then. A lot of the brass were too. Sorry, Captain. No offense."

"None taken, Sergeant," Captain Franklin said.

"And later?" Jack asked.

"Later I was convinced Olson had made rank because he knew something about someone."

Jack let that go for the time being. "What made you keep investigating this?"

"It was my first murder. So, yeah, I did some snooping around in the files and the more I snooped, the more I didn't like the direction the case was taking. My reports were gone and the property sergeant wouldn't tell me if the evidence I'd turned in was still there or if it had been sent to the state police lab. I was being shut out."

Jack waited for Mattingly to continue. From what Mattingly had hinted about Olson, there could be other reasons for the reports to be missing. On the other hand, Jack knew of detectives that kept a case locked in their desk to keep everyone out. Olson might not have wanted to put the files where anyone could read them. For that matter, he could still have them.

"Did you ever find out what happened with the broken bottles or the tire tool?" Jack asked.

Sergeant Mattingly answered, "No such luck." He added, "I went to Max's funeral service and talked to Harry. I'd bought a gun from him once so I knew who he was. We got to talking about the murder and he called Reina over. She told me about a fight between Max and Richard Dick at Rex Mundi the night Max was killed. I remembered seeing a Rex Mundi varsity jacket on the body in the car. Reina said Max left in his car and shortly after another car left going the same direction as Max. She recognized the driver as Richard Dick. She said the fight was between Max, Richard Dick, Carl Needham, and Dennis James. All of them were on the football team."

Amelia Day had told them about the fight and had given them the same names, but Jack kept this to himself for now.

"We talked some more and Harry didn't like what I told him. I left. A few days later I went to Rex Mundi and talked to the football coach—he's deceased now too, by the way—and the coach told me Max and the other boys were on the varsity football team. He said Max had missed practice. He didn't see him at all that night and heard the next day that he was dead. He couldn't believe Max would commit suicide. He claimed he didn't know about the fight during practice, but he wasn't surprised.

"When I was leaving the school, a teacher caught me and said she heard talk that Max had been in a fistfight at the practice. She told me it was because Max had his eye on a cheerleader, Ginger Purdie, who was Richard Dick's girlfriend. She said there was bad blood between Max and Richard. I asked her who she'd heard this from and she wouldn't tell me. I couldn't exactly question all the students. I wasn't even supposed to be there at the school. I was doing this on my own time, since I worked third shift. It's all in here," he said, indicating the binder on his lap.

"We'll get to that," Jack said. "Tell me what Reina said about the fight."

"She said she saw Max down near the bleachers by the locker room area. He was watching the cheerleading practice. Richard came up behind and hit Max in the head with a football helmet hard enough to knock him down. Two of Richard's friends were there. Carl Needham and Dennis James. She said they were all standing around him like the fight wasn't over. Richard said, and I quote, 'I'll make you sorry, Max. Next time I'll put you in the ground and not on it.' Reina said that Max went to his car and had left his car keys in the locker room, so she gave him the extra set she carried for him. Richard and the others were coming toward Max and Max got in his car and left. A minute later Richard took off in his car and she thought he was going after Max.

"I found Ginger Purdie and talked to her. She didn't admit to seeing the fight or knowing anything about it. I didn't believe her. Reina had told me that Ginger came up to Max after the fight and was fawning over him, asking if he was okay. Max made some cute remark and left. Reina said she must have seen the fight, but Ginger was Dick's girl. I didn't think she would tell the truth back then."

"Do you know where Ginger is now?"

Mattingly said, "She moved to France after college. She married her French teacher and was going to teach English. Her parents told me she is a free spirit and they could hardly keep up with her. You might be able to find her, but I didn't get much more out of her than what I've told you. Dick hated Max, they were fighting over her, and she didn't see or hear anything. I've got the address and phone number for the parents from my contact back then."

"Do you know who saw Max last?" Jack asked.

"That would be his sister, Reina. I didn't get an opportunity to talk to her until Max's funeral service. I didn't want Olson knowing I was talking to people, since he was the investigating detective on the case. I hoped he wouldn't talk to Reina and find out she'd talked to me."

Jack said, "Good work for a rookie."

"When I heard the names of the boys involved in the fight, I had a better idea why Detective Olson did what he did. Richard Dick's father was Detective Captain Thomas Dick, retired now. I don't think Captain Dick wanted to have his son involved in a murder inquiry."

"You seem to have something more to say," Captain Franklin said.

Mattingly was uncomfortable, so Franklin added, "Anything you say in here will stay between the four of us."

Mattingly said, "I didn't mean to infer anything by what I said. If it was my kid, I'd want to keep him out of trouble too."

"What else did you find out?" Jack asked.

"When I talked to Rex Mundi's football coach, he said Richard was a standout quarterback. The coach thought he might even be recruited by one of the big universities with a full-ride scholarship, but he didn't think that would ever happen because Richard's father was grooming him for the police department." He paused to let that sink in.

He continued. "The other two boys were only involved in the fight at Rex Mundi as hecklers, as far as I could gather. One boy, Needham, is the son of a wealthy family; mother and father were doctors—surgeons—involved in local politics, charities, that sort of thing."

"And the other boy? Dennis James?" Jack asked.

"Yeah, Dennis. I remember him from back then as a little punk. I've heard his name over the years since. Nothing good. But nothing more than thefts, fights, drugs, that kind of stuff. I haven't any idea what happened to Carl Needham and Richard Dick is—you know—a Deputy Chief now."

"What did you do next?"

Mattingly was quiet, gathering his thoughts, then said, "Harry owned a gun shop downtown. Most of the cops knew him. He was a nice guy and he gave sweet deals to policemen. Guns, ammo, hunting equipment. He'd sell it at cost. Dirty Harry. That's what we called him. You'd hear guys say, 'I went down to Dirty Harry's and got a new shotgun for X dollars.' Stuff like that. That's how I knew him." He sat quietly again.

Captain Franklin said, "We talked to Mrs. Day. She gave Jack and Liddell the documents you gave Harry."

Sergeant Mattingly steepled his fingers and put them under his chin. "I know I wasn't supposed to do that. I did it because no one here was answering Harry's questions. And there were things missing from the records and crime scene hadn't done squat. I checked with the property room sergeant and he said he couldn't tell me anything about the evidence I had entered. I pressed him and he said he couldn't find the things I put in evidence. He said maybe it had been checked out before it got to him. Maybe by Detective Olson.

"Harry kept saying his son's murder had been covered up. He knew about the fight at Rex Mundi and he was convinced Captain Dick was burying the investigation. Harry thought Richard Dick had killed his son."

"Did you think that too?" Jack asked. "That Max was killed by Richard Dick?"

"I didn't. I mean, it just didn't seem possible to me that three boys had committed a brutal murder and kept it quiet. Kids brag. But then you have to remember who his father was. Richard Dick could have easily gotten his hands on one of his father's guns. Max's dad owned a gun shop. Maybe Max brought the gun to the fight. One of them got it away from him and shot him.

"Over the years I've ruled that notion out because of the mess in that car. No. The killing happened inside the car with Max in the driver's seat. There had to be someone else in the car. I mean, the gun didn't walk away on its own, did it? Someone took it."

"Did you tell Harry any of that?" Jack asked.

"Harry wanted to blame someone. He would never consider the possibility that his son was shot with one of his own guns. I asked Harry once if he'd had any .50 caliber guns missing and he got really pissed at me. We didn't have someone arrested, so he blamed it on the Dicks."

"When did you give all those files to Harry?" Jack asked.

"Harry kept digging around. He would ask me to check the files from time to time for him. I did for a while. A couple of months before Harry was gunned down in his store, he talked me into checking on the progress of the investigation again. I made some inquiries and found out the state police lab had never received anything from Max's case. They had no record of a .50 caliber shell casing—the one Olson found that night—being presented for ballistics. I checked with central records and the case file was still missing.

"I got the Rex Mundi yearbook out, called the office at the school. The three boys had graduated but I talked the secretary into giving me addresses and phone numbers for the families. I called Carl Needham's house and talked to his mother. She said Carl was in law school and they didn't know how to reach him. She wouldn't tell me what school and said I was to leave her son alone. I called Dennis James's home. His father didn't know and didn't care where he was. He said to try the county jail. I did. He was a frequent flier. Drunk, disorderly, small-time drugs. He wasn't in jail. I called Captain Dick's, hoping to catch Richard. Captain Dick answered the phone. Dick Sr. wanted to know what I was doing. He reminded me I was a patrolman and not a detective. He said he'd bring his son in if detectives needed to talk to him. I'd heard that Richard Dick was due to be sworn in as an officer in the next few days and I told Captain Dick so. He suggested I tell my concerns to Detective Olson and he hung up on me.

"I was about a month away from making sergeant, although I didn't know that at the time of that call. I met with Olson. I was already in pretty deep, but like I said, I thought I had a responsibility to follow up. Harry was a good guy and I just wanted to show him that someone cared. Well, Detective Olson shut me down before I got the first word out of my mouth."

"How so?" Jack asked.

"It came up that if someone was as sharp as I was—*and* a team player—that person would be put in for sergeant. He made it sound like if I wasn't a team player I was the enemy of the police department. I reminded him that you needed five years of service to make sergeant's rank. He said, 'not necessarily.' I'm ashamed to say it, but I dropped my investigation. My career was on the line. I had a family to think of. Max was dead and I couldn't bring him back. At least that's the way I justified it."

"You made sergeant early," Jack said.

"Yeah. About a month after I quit snooping, I was put in for promotion to sergeant. I went in front of the merit board along with two other patrolmen who each had over ten years on. I had less than five years on, but I got the promotion. Richard Dick was sworn in the next week."

"But you kept working the case after you made sergeant, right?" Jack asked.

"Captain Dick was still around. Olson was still around. The Chief back then might as well have lived in Florida because he was never around. Always on vacation. Anyway, Harry made request after request to have the case reinvestigated and they placated him by saying Olson was talking to some unnamed witness or a possible suspect. They never told him how any of that turned out and he thought—even I thought—they were lying about Olson talking to anyone. No one to my knowledge ever took statements from the three boys involved in the fight that night. I knew all that, but I kept out of it."

"And then Harry was murdered," Jack said and Mattingly's face reddened.

"And then Harry was murdered," he said.

Chapter 15

Claudine Setera sat at a table in the far back corner of Duffy's Tavern. The lighting in the bar was deliberately dim so the men at the bar could pick up the even dimmer women sitting at the tables, laughing hysterically at the men's bad and raunchy jokes.

One of the men at least twenty years her senior had come to her table with two mugs of beer. She told him she was meeting her husband, a policeman, and the drunk had moved on, saying, "Your loss, bitch." She thought she would have to go home and take a bath to get the odor of stale beer, piss, and cigar smoke out of her hair. The back door opened. letting sunlight in. The man coming through the door of the bar wasn't her husband, but he did draw everyone's attention, especially one of the drunk women.

"Ms. Setera," Deputy Chief Richard Dick said. He pulled a seat near her and sat stiff-backed, lacing his hands on the tabletop. He had changed into street clothes, which for Double Dick was a handmade Italian suit with a name and shoes with a price tag to match. His dad had taught him not to waste money on substandard clothing. The price of Dick's clothes closet could feed a small nation.

"Deputy Chief," she said. "I wasn't sure you'd come."

"Well, we have some important issues to discuss."

"Like?"

Dick leaned toward her. "We can deal with this investigation to each other's benefit."

Claudine gave her Cheshire cat smile. "Detective Murphy and I were discussing much the same point earlier," she lied.

Dick sat up straight again and his palms lay flat on the table. He cleared his throat. "I'm innocent of any perceived wrongdoing, Ms. Setera. When this is over you won't want to have been on the wrong side. I think you'll want to work with me instead of against me."

"I may," she said. "Work with you, that is."

Dick's posture relaxed slightly.

"I mean, I may if you can convince me of the benefit to my station. I'm sitting on a national news story here. Why would I give that up?"

"Because I'm being unjustly targeted by the current Chief of Police and the thugs he's assigned to investigate me."

"Do you mean Jack Murphy and Liddell Blanchard?"

Dick gave a disgusted grunt as an answer.

"Are they investigating you specifically for a thirty-seven-year-old unsolved murder? Are you saying you're a suspect in Max Day's murder? Or are you saying you're a suspect in Reina Day's assault? Or both?"

"Pah!" he said. "I'm not saying anything of the sort. If I'm a suspect in *anything* it's a lie and a travesty of justice. It's a deliberate attempt to besmirch my spotless reputation and attempt to stop the inevitable."

"And the inevitable is?"

"I will be Chief of Police." Dick held his head high.

"Just to be clear: Are you asking me *not* to interview Detective Murphy and Blanchard?"

"On the contrary, Claudine. I may call you Claudine, may I not?"

"Yes, you may, if I can call you Richard."

"Claudine, I encourage you to do your job. If that includes interviewing Murphy or his sidekick, then by all means, do so. But I want you to keep me informed, so to speak."

"So to speak," she said.

"Yes," Dick said. "It will benefit us both, but mostly you."

"Me?"

"You will know who the real killer is. That is, if Murphy can find them. If he can solve this case. And frankly, I don't think he's up to the task. He's an arrogant blowhard and not a very good detective in my opinion and—" Dick stopped mid-sentence. "This is all off the record, by the way."

"Of course, Richard."

"I think we will be close friends after I'm Chief. Let me tell you something off the record."

"You're off the record," Claudine said.

"I'm thinking of creating my own press corps. Every agency with power over people's lives has a responsibility to keep their charges—the citizens—informed. We can best do that if we work together. The media and the police. Imagine how that would benefit the citizens of Evansville?"

"And you."

Dick straightened his tie and smoothed the front of his shirt. "Yes. Me. But I'm thinking of the city. Cato's campaign ran on transparency of government. I assure you she will support my decision to bring the media onboard."

Claudine smiled genuinely. She knew Dick was right about the mayor-elect working more closely with the news media. And Dick was hoping to garner a little limelight for himself with a little ass-kissing all around.

"I'll have to clear this with the Channel Six legal department, Richard, but as for me, I'm onboard with your plan."

"Would you care for something?" Dick asked and wiped his hands on a napkin.

"Thank you, Richard, but no thank you. I have to meet with my boss and between us, I wouldn't drink a canned soda in this place."

He smiled, they stood, shook hands, and she left by the back door.

He sat long enough to allow her to get out of the parking lot. He hoped she'd say no to a drink or, God forbid, a meal. He wanted to get out of this disgusting, filthy place. He'd picked it because it had been suggested by one of his minions, Larry Jensen, as a quiet meeting spot. After the debacle with Benet Cato's pit bull, Tilly Coyne, he didn't want anyone reporting his meeting with Claudine. There were ears everywhere at the police department. Jensen was right about it being quiet, but he felt he'd have to send the suit to the dry cleaner's and disinfect himself.

One of the ladies playing cards at a table turned toward him, smiled, and waggled a hand. Her teeth were missing and a bright red wig sat askew on top of her drunken head.

"Good lord," he muttered and left.

Chapter 16

"Independence Day, 1984, Harry was killed—gunned down in his store." Sergeant Mattingly took a small plastic evidence bag from his shirt pocket and handed it to Jack. Inside was a spent shell casing. The bag was marked with a black Sharpie. The date: July 4, 1984. Time: 7:34 p.m. The case number was the same one for the homicide/robbery of Harry Day. There was no evidence number written on the bag. It was sealed with red tape marked with the initials T.M.

"I've kept this at home in my desk since that night. It doesn't have an evidence number because I never put it in evidence. The supplement, my report of the incident, is there in the file I just gave you and I never turned that in to records, either. I'll explain in a minute.

"I was a new sergeant when I found Harry murdered. First policeman on the scene. Again. Harry was shot in the back of the head. Point-blank. I think that was the bullet that killed him."

Jack manipulated the object in the bag. "That's a .50 caliber casing."

"Yeah. It's the same type of bullet used on Reina's car today," Mattingly said. "And the same caliber of bullet Olson found at Max's murder scene."

They all sat thinking about that.

"Why did you keep this?" Jack asked, shaking the bag.

"Let me start at the beginning."

Captain Franklin said, "Go ahead, sergeant."

Mattingly collected his thoughts and said, "I was working second shift as a motor patrol sergeant when Harry was killed. I already told you about my promotion."

Jack said nothing.

"I'd quit giving Harry any information, but I still stopped by his store now and then like a lot of other cops. I think Harry understood the position he was putting me in and he didn't pressure me. Harry closed up shop at six o'clock. I'd swing by after he closed and check the building for him.

"That night, July fourth, all the other shops downtown had closed for the holiday or closed early. Harry stayed open until six like he always did. The city's fireworks display on the river wasn't scheduled until nine that night. I had to help with crowd control, traffic, that stuff, so I didn't get by his shop until after seven."

Evansville had a monstrous firework display every Fourth of July. Jack avoided the half a mile of riverfront where it was wall-to-wall crowds of men, women, and screaming kids. He wondered why kids screamed so much and over anything. He was never a screamer. He was always making some other kid scream.

"Okay," Jack said.

"I drove by Harry's shop at seven-thirty and saw the lights were still on. Harry never left that many lights on unless he was open. I sat there watching and when I didn't see him I got out of the car. The door was unlocked, so I went in. He had this little buzzer in the back room that would go off if the front door was opened. I could hear the buzzer go off, but he didn't say anything. I called out to him. Still no answer. I started to go toward the back to see if he was back there and I found him lying in a side aisle up near the front door. He was on his stomach, arms stretched out above his head, and most of his face was gone. There was a smear of blood from the center aisle leading to where his head lay. Someone had shot him and dragged him out of sight of the front door.

"I got on my WT and called for backup and started clearing the business on my way to the back. Harry had storage back there, a little work area, and a one-person gun range. He worked on guns and would test-fire them back there. I heard a noise coming from the back.

"I got on the radio again and told dispatch to send backup code three. I yelled 'Police! Come out with your hands up.' I was ten feet from the door leading to the back. I damned near shit myself when Olson walked out of that door with a gun in one hand and his badge in the other."

"What the hell?" Liddell said.

"Exactly. I told him to put the gun down and he laughed and called me a rookie. He said he came by to check the store, saw the lights on, came in, and found Harry dead. He said he'd just got there and was checking the store when he heard me come in. He said the back door was standing wide open and the suspect must have fled."

"Did you check the back room?" Jack asked.

"He told me to leave it with him. Said he'd get crime scene and the coroner and I should go back to my duties."

"Did you?" Jack asked.

"Hell no. Olson holstered his gun and got on his radio and called dispatch for crime scene and a coroner. He told dispatch to continue the backup, but tell them to go code one—everything was under control. He must have heard me call for backup."

"What did you do?"

"I called for more cars and had them set up a perimeter. Olson didn't have the authority to cancel cars or give them a disregard. I didn't have any suspect information, description, vehicle, direction of travel, but I told the cars we had a shooting at Harry's and told them to stop anyone suspicious in the area. Olson just stood there the whole time. He was a little shook up, but I thought it was because I still hadn't holstered my weapon.

"Olson said if I was staying I should go outside and start an offense report. He said to make it a robbery/homicide. The cash register was on the floor. Boxes of ammo were strewn around like someone had swept them off the shelves. But if someone was robbing Harry, they would have had him open the register or the safe. They wouldn't shoot him and take a chance on not getting any money and then just throw things around.

"I told Olson I didn't think it was a robbery. Nothing appeared to be taken except maybe a few dollars. I know people have been killed for less, but Harry was one tough hombre. He would have put up a fight. He had a carry permit and he wore a nine-millimeter Beretta on his belt. When I found him, the gun was still in its holster. I'd expect to find his body back by the register and not near the front doors, shot in the back, like he'd tried to run. Harry didn't run.

"Olson laughed at me. He said some of the guns had been stolen. He pointed out several empty spaces in the gun cases and racks. To me, I couldn't tell. I told him the cases weren't broken into. Harry never left them unlocked. Why not smash the glass and take what you want? It was too clean. Nothing was broken. Just some boxes of shells knocked on the floor by the register. It seemed to me as an afterthought. He said I should go be a cop and leave detective work to the professionals."

Jack asked, "You think the robbery was staged?"

Mattingly said, "I think Harry was murdered, plain and simple."

Jack was beginning to think the same thing, but then he wasn't there at the scene.

"How did Olson know the guns were missing?" Jack asked.

"Exactly my thinking," Mattingly said. "He claimed he'd gotten there just before me and was clearing the store for suspects. I didn't see signs of a burglary when I came in. I was worried about Harry. Then I found him dead. Olson would have too. So how come he hadn't called in the murder? I couldn't see anything was missing until he suggested it. I still don't know for sure anything was stolen. And he'd been in the back room. He said the back door was standing open. Why wouldn't he have started a manhunt? Set up a perimeter?"

Jack agreed that Olson's story to Mattingly about how this occurred was suspicious. For one thing, everything Olson did flew in the face of police procedure and common sense. You didn't go into a building, find a murder victim, and then clear the building without calling for backup. And if Mattingly's account was accurate, Olson didn't want Mattingly to go in the back room of the store. Why? Mattingly had an answer.

"I always thought Olson stole some guns. Harry would have had keys to the locked cases and keys to the doors—front and back. The back door had an audible alarm unless you opened it with a key. I didn't hear an alarm."

"Did you find the keys?" Jack asked.

"Somebody must have taken them," Mattingly said, stressing the word *somebody*.

"Where did this shell casing come from?" Jack asked and held up the plastic evidence bag.

"Crime scene was taking their time getting there. Olson just stood around with his thumb up his ass watching what I was doing. I found that casing up under the edge of a shotgun rack. When I spotted it, I told Olson and he came over, got down on his knees and picked the casing up with his bare hands."

"Seriously?" Liddell said.

"Yeah. I offered him an evidence bag, but he just tossed the casing in the trash. He said it wasn't relevant. He said this was a gun shop and there were likely shell casings all over the place."

"Was there?" Jack asked.

"Harry was a meticulous man. He kept his place spotless. He'd never leave something like that on the floor for a customer to step on or slip on. Anyway, when officers arrived I posted them at the front and back doors and told them I'd make out the offense report. Crime scene got there and while Olson was talking to them I got the shell casing out of the trash and gave it to one of them. I was going back outside and I saw Olson take it from the crime scene tech and throw it back in the trash. I retrieved it and now you have it."

"Did Olson know you collected it again?" Jack asked.

"Yeah. He just smirked at me like it didn't matter."

"Were other shell casings found?" Jack asked. "Or a weapon?"

"Just one shell casing and that was odd. After crime scene did their thing and the coroner's office took Harry's body, Olson asked me for the report. Again, I'd made out two of them, one for me and one for him. Then he asked me to do another sweep inside."

Jack raised an eyebrow.

"Yeah. That's what I thought. Crime scene had already gone through it, but he insisted. I did a walk-through and lo and behold, a .357 magnum shell casing was on the floor. It wasn't there earlier and it was in plain sight. He made a big fuss over me finding it and reminded me that he'd said there would be shell casings everywhere. He bagged that one himself. He said he was going to chew some crime scene ass."

"Did it get into evidence?" Jack asked.

"No. I checked a couple of weeks later. I found Olson in the detectives' office and asked him why he didn't enter it into evidence. He told me he'd personally taken it to the state police lab."

"Was it there?" Liddell asked.

"I called them. They'd never logged it in. Back in that time, detectives all carried 9 millimeter Smith and Wesson semiautos. Olson had come from the back room where Harry had that little gun range. The casing could have come from there. I think Olson planted it and made sure I found it."

"Why didn't you turn this casing over to crime scene at some point?" Jack asked, meaning the .50 caliber.

"Stuff has a way of disappearing when it involves the Days' murders. Or when Olson is involved and Olson and Captain Dick were around for several years after Harry's murder."

"And you've been keeping the binder and shell casing all this time? Why didn't you bring it to me?" Captain Franklin asked.

"Olson worked for Captain Dick. Dick was still in charge of the detectives' office when Harry was killed. I had just made sergeant after being threatened to leave Max's investigation alone. I didn't get involved officially this time, but I kept track of the case."

"When those two retired, why not come forward then?"

"I was ashamed to be honest."

Jack was getting a sick feeling in the pit of his stomach. He said to Mattingly, "Then when Reina was shot at…"

"I panicked," Mattingly said. "I thought I was responsible for not doing more. If I'd kept after the cases maybe Harry wouldn't be dead. Maybe Reina wouldn't have been attacked."

"You should have come forward," Captain Franklin said. "But Reina put herself in danger. That wasn't your fault. I approved the guard you put on her room just in case someone might take a second shot."

Mattingly's face turned a little red. "I guess I took the initiative. Sorry for jumping the chain of command, Captain."

Captain Franklin asked, "Do we have anything solid to connect the murders and Reina's attack?"

Jack said, "I don't think we've proven the murders are involved with what happened to Reina, Captain. The .50 caliber weapon and a lot of conjecture. No offense, but we haven't ruled out old boyfriends, ex-husbands, or maybe some disgruntled pregnant patient or a coworker."

"That's why I'm assigning Reina's case to another team, Jack," Franklin said. "And before you start complaining, I want to remind you that you already have two cold cases going."

Jack wasn't sure he could take on a third case, but he needed to act upset just for future reference. Murphy's Law said: *Never pass up an opportunity to make your boss feel like a heel.*

"I can see your point," Jack reluctantly agreed. "But… I want to be kept informed. And if this turns out to even smell like it's related, I take the case over. Agreed?"

Captain Franklin said, "I'm not agreeing to anything."

"I'll take that as a yes," Jack said.

Mattingly handed Jack the binder. "My notes are in here with everything I had on those cases. Reina's shooting will be in records before the end of the day. I don't think anything will go missing this time. If you need anything from me, I'm available any time. Here's my phone number." He handed Jack a piece of notepaper with his home number on it and left the office.

Jack heard the door up front shut and said, "Captain, will you tell the Chief what's going on? I think I'll run by Two Jakes and see what's needed and then we need to take a break."

Captain Franklin said, "Yeah. You two need to get some rest. I have a feeling tomorrow is going to be one hell of a day. I'll put a rush on the shell casings with the state police lab."

"Claudine Setera was at the hospital," Jack told the Captain.

"She's called here. The Chief is talking to her, but not telling her anything she doesn't already know. She wants to have a meeting with you two and us."

Jack was silent on the subject. He took out his cell phone and called Corporal Morris at the number that had been given him. Morris was in the shower, but his wife said she'd have him call Jack shortly. He hung up.

"I'm going to have Morris put the .50 caliber casings under lock and key. I don't think anything will happen now, but then it's hard to believe that someone would try to kill Reina Day," Jack said.

"Good idea," Captain Franklin said. "And you need to make sure the little paperwork we do have is safe. Especially what Sergeant Mattingly just gave us. We don't need all of this getting out before we're ready."

"I'll put razor wire and Bouncing Bettys around the war room," Jack said. They all laughed and Jack and Liddell left the Captain's office.

"Do you want me to go to Two Jakes with you?" Liddell asked.

"Why don't you go home? Kiss the baby for me. Tell Marcie I'm sorry. I'll be a few minutes and then I'm heading home myself," Jack said.

"You're lucky to have someone understanding like Katie. We both are. This work doesn't lend itself to good relationships. I'm going to keep my family close."

"Yeah. I had a perfect evening planned. Just me and Katie, a bottle of wine, a bottle of scotch, a hot tub, and relaxing. Maybe I can still get home and do that," Jack said.

"It's not that late, pod'na," Liddell said. "Just go home. Two Jakes can wait. It's not going anywhere and this case has been stalled for a long time."

"We'll talk to Olson tomorrow," Jack said. "You'll have to type up your notes at home for now, Bigfoot. Jake said he got us a printer and stuff, but you know how tech savvy he is."

"Yeah. I'll email a copy to you tonight."

Liddell got in his car and Jack went back to the detectives' office. He called Morris at home again and this time he answered. He told Morris what he wanted and asked him to meet at Two Jakes at six in the morning. To his credit, Morris agreed without asking questions. Jack then called Two Jakes. Vinnie answered.

"Vinnie, is Angelina there?" Jack said.

"Been and gone," Vinnie answered. "Said she would be back early in the morning."

"Thanks, Vinnie," Jack said. "Tell Jake we'll have four or five guests tomorrow, so…"

"I know. Lots of bacon and eggs and pancakes. Enough to feed a Bigfoot," Vinnie said and laughed.

"I'm headed home, Vinnie. We'll need a better lock on the war room."

"I'll take care of it."

Jack hung up and walked to his Crown Vic.

Chapter 17

Jack left for home. He hoped Katie hadn't found the surprise picnic in the garage fridge. That made him think of something she had said the other day. There was a new teacher, Craig something or other, at Harwood where she worked. She said she thought he had a crush on her. She said this guy had brought her a lunch and had offered to walk her to her car. He had even broken up a fight in Katie's classroom. Big deal. It was two twelve-year-old girls. That didn't make him a he-man. He would have to meet this putz. Maybe show him a good place to hide a body.

He pushed Craig and a shallow grave out of his mind and thought about an evening with Katie under the stars. Wine. Hot tub. Scotch. The big head fogged up and the little head was taking over. But then another thought intruded. This one overpowered even the little head. He had been given a chance to pay Double Dick back in spades. Give him a taste of his own medicine. But he didn't work that way. Did he? Okay, maybe he did, but he would try to get to the truth. That's what a police investigation was all about. The truth. On television and in the media the cop was always portrayed as a villain who would lie or plant evidence to put an innocent person in jail or in the ground. That was a lie. He would try his damnedest to prove Dick didn't commit any of these crimes. He would keep politics out of this. If he couldn't prove Dick was innocent, Jack would frog-march him up and down Main Street. If he wasn't guilty…well…

He was passing Deaconess when his thoughts turned again to the latest victim of this fiasco. He should check on Reina. That would mean he'd have to forgo the sex and scotch, in any order, for another thirty minutes, but then he'd go home. It was the right thing to do.

He pulled into the emergency room drive and parked behind an ambulance. It was late. It was a detective's car. But just in case he stuck his OFFICIAL FBI BUSINESS placard on the dash. His job with the federal task force had some benefits. Now if could get the feds to give him a take-home car, free gas and maintenance, he'd be set. He went through the double doors, waved at the off-duty policeman working the desk, and went to the employee elevator.

Coming off the elevator, he met Mrs. Day, who was just leaving.

"Is Reina asleep?" he asked.

"They won't let her sleep, poor girl. Some nurse or other comes in every hour, taking her blood pressure, checking her pupils, asking stupid questions. Reina practically threw me out I was fussing with them so much."

"I was going to stop by and check on her. Maybe I should just go. I'll walk you out."

Mrs. Day pushed the *call* button for the elevator. "Nonsense. She'll be glad to see you. She hates having a policeman outside her door. They call security to relieve them even to go to the bathroom. Is she really in that kind of danger? Should I stay here with her?"

Jack said, "We have her under our protection, Mrs. Day. You need some rest too. This must be exhausting for you. I promise you she will be well taken care of."

"Have you made any progress, Detective Murphy?" she asked. Her eyes were red-rimmed. She probably hadn't slept well since Double Dick came a'calling. That was the problem with cold cases. To investigate them properly a detective had to dig up the past. A past that had been made peace with, or at least had brought resignation that it would never be solved.

"We're getting a clearer picture of what happened. We've already talked to several officers who remember the case and we're going to reexamine the evidence and statements. We've also been assigned your husband's case on the off chance it's involved. I'm not saying it is, but we have to consider it to cover all the bases."

The answer seemed to satisfy her a little. The elevator doors opened and when they started to close she stopped them.

"Thank you for helping my daughter, Detective Murphy. I can't—" Her voice broke and her eyes teared up.

Jack held the elevator door and let her get under control. She'd had one too many big shocks in the last few days. "I'll make sure she's okay," Jack said reassuringly. "But I suspect she can hold her own."

That brought a smile and she said, "She's a fighter, that one. She's got a lot of her father in her. Just like Max."

"Mrs. Day, I meant to ask you something and then I'll let you get home."

"Anything," she said guardedly.

"Do you have any of your husband's work documents? Bills of sale? Who has a federal firearm license? Anything from his gun shop?" Jack asked.

"The cops called it Dirty Harry's Gun Shop. Did you know that?"

"We heard that somewhere," Jack said.

"Most of his customers were cops—excuse me, policemen. They were always buying or trading or wanting him to sell something for them. He was proud to help them. My Harry was always a cop at heart. He'd been in the Army and was discharged because he had a bad ticker. If he didn't have that he would have been a cop, like you and your father." She seemed far away for just a moment and then said, "Yes. He kept detailed records. When he died Reina was in medical school in Nashville. Vanderbilt University.

"Reina wasn't going to run the shop. Harry always meant to keep it in the family. But he was gone and I hated guns. Still do. I sold the place to Earl Dickson. He was Harry's competitor. He paid a good price for it and he promised to hang on to Harry's records. That was such a long time ago that I doubt he still has them."

Jack had seen Earl's Gun Emporium downtown, but he'd never been inside.

"Are you sure it's okay to visit?"

"She's asked about you today," Mrs. Day said.

"I'll just stick my head in the door. Where did you park?"

Mrs. Day said, "In the emergency patient parking lot. I'll be fine. Thank you again, Detective Murphy," she said. "The family is grateful. I'm sure Harry would be pleased." The elevator closed and she was gone.

Jack went around the corner and spoke briefly with Office Doolan, who was standing guard. Or sitting guard. Doolan was pulling a double shift for time-and-a-half pay.

Jack was about to knock and Doolan said, "Double Dick was up here checking on her. He didn't go in because her mother was in there with her. He seemed scared and told me not to tell anyone he was here."

I'll bet he did. "Did he say what he wanted?" Jack asked.

"He didn't say much. He acted like I was an ant to be stepped on, but it might dirty the bottom of his shoe. Is it true that he might be the new Chief?"

Jack shrugged. He wasn't to talk to anyone if it wasn't absolutely necessary.

The officer said, "I sure as hell hope not. He hates me."

Mrs. Day hadn't said anything about Dick contacting her again, so why would he risk coming to see Reina in the hospital? But then, why did Double Dick do anything? It pleased him. Or it was to his benefit. Double Dick didn't have time for anything or anyone but himself.

"Welcome to the club," Jack said, knocked on the door, and entered the room.

Reina was sitting in a comfortable chair beside the hospital bed. She had a blanket pulled up around her shoulders and it draped down her lap to the floor.

"How's my favorite gunslinger?" Jack asked and this drew a smile.

"You're so full of it," she said. "My mother just left if you're here to see her."

"I'm here to check on you, Miss Day," Jack said.

"Oh God! That makes me feel older than my mother. Call me Reina. Or Dr. Day."

Jack pulled his familiar line. "Okay. You can call me Supreme Commander. My phone always does."

"What do you want, Supreme Commander?" Reina asked with a straight face.

"Seriously. I just came by to check on you."

"Well, you checked just in time. I'm going to check myself out. As you can see, I'm fine and I have things to do. I have a patient early in the morning and I've got to get clothes and a real shower and food. And I feel like I'm in jail. I don't like having a policeman stand outside my door." She started to get to her feet and a dizzy spell dropped her back in the chair.

"Maybe you can leave in the morning, Reina," Jack said. "Doctors are always the worst patients. I'll pull the guard off your door if you want." He didn't intend to release the guard. He'd just have him move down the hall a little.

"The poor man may want to do something else tonight. Maybe a doughnut shop is open," she said jokingly. "I'm sorry. I didn't mean that."

"You saw my partner, Reina," Jack said. "Three hundred pounds of pure doughnut muscle."

The smile was back and a twinkle in her eye he hadn't seen before, but it faded as another wave of dizziness hit her. She was pale and Jack called the nurses' station for her.

"Before she gets here, I want you to leave. A lady doesn't like to get sick in front of a man."

Jack got it. He stayed in the doorway until the nurse arrived.

Doolan was mimicking sticking his finger down his throat and making gagging noises.

"You realize everything in this hospital is being video-recorded," Jack said, but it didn't faze Doolan.

Jack got on the elevator and remembered he hadn't asked Reina if she'd had any current run-ins with patients or a patient's family. He'd done what a detective should never do and assumed her shooting and the theft of her purse was tied to his investigations. He felt she'd be safe enough tonight with police protection ten feet away. He'd stop at the hospital first thing in the morning and ask her more questions. Katie, his hot tub, and scotch were waiting impatiently.

* * * *

Jack didn't notice the black SUV parked in the Superior Court parking lot when he left police headquarters. The SUV pulled slowly onto Sycamore and followed at a distance.

The SUV driver watched the Crown Vic pull into the Deaconess Hospital ER and park behind an ambulance. The SUV pulled into the ER visitors' lot and parked facing the ER entrance. He watched Detective Murphy get out and go into the ER. He could see through the automatic doors. Murphy said something to the policeman who was working extra duty in ER. Murphy pointed out of the doors, most likely telling the officer where he'd parked so his car wouldn't be towed. Murphy was an arrogant ass. He watched him head down the hallway toward the main elevators.

He took a hand-carved wooden box from under the passenger seat, held it on his lap, and unlatched it. Inside was the .50 caliber Desert Eagle semiautomatic, snugged into its blue velvet– lined cushion.

He pulled on a pair of tight-fitting leather gloves before touching the weapon. The weapon was produced in stainless steel, but the oils from his skin would degrade the finish. He kept part of his attention on the ER entrance as the other part of him admired the weapon that he'd been given by his father many years ago. His father had admonished him with "guns are not toys" and "never point a gun at anything you don't intend to kill." He never had.

He was lost in thought and had missed seeing Mrs. Day come out of the ER and she was now walking toward the SUV. He felt a small, tingling sensation at the thought that she might be coming to confront him. He took the Desert Eagle from the case, put the case on the passenger seat, and jacked a round into the chamber. If she approached him he would finish this here.

She turned left into a row of vehicles and got into a Toyota Prius. He'd seen it in her driveway when he'd gone by earlier. Nearby there was a loud blast. His finger had tightened on the Desert Eagle's trigger. He watched her slump against the steering wheel. Her body shuddered and her arms hung down. *Did she shoot herself? Had someone else?* It wasn't possible. Then he saw her shudder and recognized it for what it was. She was crying. The blast must have been a car backfiring somewhere else on the lot.

Mrs. Day was sobbing. She raised up and slammed her fists on the steering wheel. She was hysterical. Good! She'd put him through hell all these years. She couldn't accept the fact that her snot-nosed little prick of a son was dead. She and her crazy husband had continued to stir the pot until they had to be dealt with. She should have quit while she was ahead, but now... now it was too late.

He waited patiently until, at last, she sat up, put the car in gear, and drove out of the lot. He did likewise.

She headed toward the west side down Columbia Street and north on St. Joseph Avenue. He followed, not too close. She was heading home. He knew where she lived. No need to spook her.

She turned onto Meyer Road heading west again. They were out in the country. Houses were thinning and interspersed with wooded fields. He considered running her off into a ditch, doing it here, but there were still too many houses close to the road. He knew the area well. It would have been so much better if she had stopped at the cemetery like Reina had done earlier. He could have done her there. The symbolism, the lesson, wouldn't be lost on Reina. But this woman was like an old horse that had been out of the barn too long. It knew one direction. Home. Alone. Always alone. He would be doing her a favor.

She turned onto Kleitz Road and he dropped further back. He decided to let her get in her house. To think she was safe. Her taillights winked in the distance and disappeared as she turned into her driveway. He proceeded past the house at a normal speed and watched her making her way from the unattached garage, down the cracked walk, up two concrete steps to her porch, and then go inside.

He slowed and turned around and saw light come on in the front room. He drove to the house, pulled onto the edge of the driveway, put his headlights on the high beam, and angled the car facing the front door about twenty feet distant.

The front door opened and Mrs. Day stood framed in the doorway, squinting, one arm held up to block the bright light. He watched her. She was curious, scared, but more curious. More stupid than scared. He left the engine running and stepped out of the SUV with the Desert Eagle held down by his leg.

"Mrs. Day," he said loud enough to be heard.

Her head cocked. She couldn't see him. He was just a shape. But she was listening, trying to discern the voice. He stepped closer. "Mrs. Day," he said again, a little louder.

She stooped a little, her hand held up to block the light. He saw realization dawn as he stepped forward. She dropped her arm, her shoulders slumped, and she said, "You."

He stepped forward so she could see his face more clearly. "Yes. It's me, Mrs. Day," he said, raised the gun, and blew the top of her head off.

The impact knocked her backwards through the open door. He walked up on the porch, kicked her foot inside the door, and pulled it shut. He got back in the SUV, wiped the slide and receiver down with a soft cloth to get the burned gunpowder off. He admired the gun, the weight, the perfect balance, before he put it back in the box and shut the lid. He backed out of the driveway and turned west.

He wasn't worried about the noise. People were always shooting guns out here in the country. The only thing on his mind now was the enormous muzzle flash the Desert Eagle made. Flames shot out of the muzzle two or three feet. A fireball. Blinding. Spots still danced across his field of vision. It was the cleanest kill yet.

Chapter 18

Jack parked inside his garage and retrieved the picnic from the fridge and set it on a little table on the back patio. He was proud of the small additions he'd made to the house since moving back in with Katie. This was his house when he was growing up, and he'd purchased it from his mother after his father passed away and she'd moved to a Florida retirement community. He'd brought his new wife to live here and they had made it their home. Everything was perfect. Perfect wife, perfect life. Perfect pregnancy. And then they lost the baby; a little girl, full-term, stillborn, no explanation.

Jack had never gotten over the sight of Katie, blood running down her legs, pale to the point of death, rushing her to the hospital, and then he fell into the mental void where waiting, patience, fear, and anger met and fought for his attention. He was mad at Katie, mad at himself, mad at the doctors for not seeing this coming, mad at Him. How could He have allowed this to happen? What had he, or Katie, or Caitlyn, the baby they were trying for—what had any of them done to deserve this? He got sick to death of people telling him, "It's God's plan. She's in a better place now." Talk like that made him want to knee someone in the nuts. She wasn't in a better place. She should have been at home. With them. That was the better place. He was Catholic and wanted badly to believe in heaven, but he'd lived most of his adult life in hell or sending assholes there. He needed to chill. Have a scotch. But the past wasn't done with him.

After Caitlyn was buried, Jack had thrown himself into his job. He'd begun neglecting the things he'd talked about doing when they'd moved into the house. The yard turned to weeds. The fence needed whitewashing. The garage needed roofing. He was neglecting his friends. Neglecting

Katie. He found himself becoming impotent, and not just sexually. He felt unable to breathe sometimes and was on meds to control his anxiety, but that only shifted the problem to drinking.

Katie had withdrawn. He was losing her too. He had finally put them out of their misery and they divorced. He gave her the house and he'd moved into the river cabin he'd inherited from his father. He buried himself in his job and drinking became a requirement. He'd tried to pull himself out of the pit he was digging, but the more he tried, the deeper he dug. Through it all Katie hadn't abandoned him. Not completely, anyway. He'd fought his way back to her and would never leave her again.

He remembered that while they were apart, he had dated around, had come close to getting engaged, but it didn't work out. Katie had dated a couple of guys and it bothered him even though he was seeing someone else. It didn't really get to him until she announced her engagement. Then he had a come apart.

He looked across the spacious backyard. Katie's engagement party had taken place right there. A smooth-talking Chief Deputy Prosecutor had come along and swept her off her feet. Eric Manson, tall, dark and a dickhead. Eric had deserted Katie without a word and fled Evansville when he came under indictment for his part in a sex scheme run by his boss, not to mention he was complicit in the death of the then-prosecutor. But the prosecutor's office had survived both of their absences. Cut the head off one snake and five more grew in its place.

Since Jack had come home he'd done the improvements Katie wanted. He replaced the fence, planted a flower bed, updated the garage to hold both of their vehicles, put an alarm system in the house. He'd done that for her, and for him, he bought Katie a gun and taught her to shoot. He'd done all that, but he hadn't touched the room that would have been their daughter's. He couldn't bring himself to open the door to that room. He missed little Caitlyn. Mourned her. He couldn't face what he'd become because of it. What that cost them as a family.

But tonight—tonight was about being back. Back in Katie's life. Back in society. Back in the knowledge of true love. Katie had pulled him out of his funk, but he could still feel the edge of something bad waiting in the wings. He was afraid he'd screw this up like he'd screwed up before. He loved her completely, but he didn't know if he was ready for a baby; trying again, risking it all again.

He had a special surprise for her tonight. He'd been carrying something in his glove box for ten months, never finding the right moment. Tonight, he wouldn't wait for the right moment. He'd make one. There was a full moon tonight. Liddell had told him the *Farmer's Almanac* called it a *frost moon* or a *mourning moon.* It was a full moon, so he didn't really care what it was called. He was finished mourning.

He lifted the hot tub cover. The water temperature was perfect. He laid out the picnic items on the table. A tray of cheeses and chocolate-covered strawberries, a bottle of her favorite wine. He wasn't a wine drinker. He put out two glasses: One for wine, the other a tumbler for scotch. He decided to enjoy the romantic evening. Let the job fade. If it didn't, he'd stuff its ass in a metal cage. Nothing was going to interfere with this evening.

He put his key in the kitchen door and found it unlocked. He'd cautioned Katie dozens of times to lock the doors. It annoyed him, but he wasn't mad. She was a sunshine person and dark thoughts didn't hang over her head like they did over him. She was the light to his dark. They balanced each other. Besides, he had a dog. A mean dog. A big poodle-looking thing with a bad disposition named Cinderella. He hadn't picked out the name. He'd inherited her from a homicide victim. He didn't blame the dog for the disposition with a name like that. Problem was, Cinderella didn't know the difference between friend or foe. She hated him. Loved Katie. Hated him.

He stuck his head inside and said in a fake Cuban accent, "Oh Lucy. I'm home." No answer. No dog. *Damn dog. Do what you're supposed to and bark.*

He heard a whimper and saw Cinderella lying on the floor under the kitchen table. She didn't bare her teeth at him, as was her usual first reaction to seeing him. "What's the matter, pooch?"

Cinderella's snout lifted from the floor a few inches and lay back down.

The kitchen light was off, but there was a light on in the stairway. Cinderella whimpered again and a chill ran up his spine. The whimper wasn't coming from Cinderella. Even before the hair stood on the back of his neck, his .45 was in his hand. His senses picked up everything, analyzed his surroundings, heard everything down to the ticking of the grandfather clock in the hallway, and the humming of the refrigerator.

His gun led the way, finger keeping a slight pressure on the trigger as he swept the downstairs and moved to the stairway. He thought he heard movement and then a woman's scream and a pain-filled moan.

Jack rushed up the stairs without feeling his feet touch the risers. The scream had come from the nursery. Jack pushed the nursery door open with his foot. Katie sat cross-legged on the floor by the pink bookcase they had bought way back when and were going to use for the baby's toys. On her lap was a pink-padded leather-bound book that reminded him of the remembrance books Mrs. Day had shown him. This book was open to the pages that would have been the baby-to-be's first photos.

There was one of Jack holding a tiny football in one hand and a doll in the other when they first found out she was pregnant. There were photos of Katie at different stages of pregnancy, a photo of Jack putting the pink cabinet and the crib together, and a shot of them making ugly monster faces in the camera. He'd insisted on that selfie after a night of drinking and making love.

Katie turned her face toward him and his heart broke. He sat down beside her, put an arm around her shoulders, and pulled her close. They sat that way for a long time before she shut the book.

"I'm sorry, Jack. I didn't want you to see me like this," she said and pulled away. Jack wrapped his arms around her and held her against him. He firmly, but gently, took the book from her, set it across both of their laps and opened it again. She met his eyes, crying and smiling at the same time.

"I was just tidying up in here and…"

"Shhh," he said, squeezing her tighter. "It's a frost moon tonight," Jack said and pointed up. "What say we melt it?"

"Let's," Katie said and he kissed her in a way that would make the French blush.

He reached in the pocket of his sport coat and held up a diamond ring, sans box. "Katie Murphy, I love you more than I can ever say. Will you—"

"Jack…" she said, and the panic in her voice set his teeth on edge.

"What is it, honey?"

She pushed him away at arm's length. "I have to tell you something. You may not want to do this when you find out."

Jack was stunned. He'd waited so long for the right moment and obviously this wasn't it. He felt stupid and embarrassed. She was scared and that made him scared.

"Wait," she said and left the room. She came back carrying a digital thermometer and held it out for him to see with a curious expression on her face.

Jack read *New Choice* and realized it wasn't a thermometer. Two red lines in a small display window. According to the instrument that meant…

"I'm pregnant, Jack. I've been having morning sickness for a few days."

He felt the blood leave his face. "So, you—" He couldn't get the words out. "I—"

"You don't have to do anything," Katie said. "It's my fault. I know how you feel about having a baby. I know you're not ready."

"I'm—"

"You don't have to explain. I don't expect…"

He came to his feet. "Katie, I—"

"I know you're not ready. I know that. I took precautions, but it happened."

"Will you stop finishing my sentences? I'm happy. Are you sure? I mean, of course you are. I'm going to be a daddy? God, that's fantastic!"

"Take a breath, Jack. Yes. You're going to be a daddy." She touched his face and her voice softened. "If that's what you want."

"If that's…Of course that's what I want. I'm going to be a daddy!" He hugged her and kissed her and twirled her. "Sorry. I didn't mean to do that. Maybe you should sit down. Do you need something from downstairs? I'll get it. You just sit and I'll get—"

"Jack. I'm pregnant, not an invalid."

"But you were crying, Katie. Are you okay? What can I do?"

"Just hold me and listen."

He held her and kissed the top of her head. "Okay. Talk and I'll be quiet."

She said, "I've been feeling a little ill in the morning, but I wasn't running a fever. I bought a pregnancy test kit. It was positive. I went to the doctor a few days ago and it was confirmed. I'm a little over four months. I'm sorry for waiting. I didn't know how to tell you. I'm pregnant. I'm going to have a baby. Then I started cleaning the nursery and found the baby book and then it hit me." She buried her face in his chest, sobbing. He could barely understand the next words. "I'm –going—to—lose—you—again."

"Katie," Jack said, holding her face in his hands and kissing her everywhere. "You never lost me. You'll never lose me, honey. I've always loved you. Always. I want to have this baby with you. I want to marry you. Maybe not in that order, but you know what I mean."

Katie snatched the ring out of his hand and slid it onto her finger. "I thought you'd never ask, you stubborn man. What took you so—"

She didn't get to finish.

Chapter 19

Jack was up early and walked past the picnic he'd planned for Katie. The hot tub was still partially uncovered and some of the napkins had blown around the yard. He was starving. He snagged a little wedge of the cheese that was Katie's favorite, popped it in his mouth, and spit it right out. *How could anyone eat this crap?*

As he got in his Crown Vic, his back and knees popped loudly. He and Katie had spent the night on the floor, in the nursery, the picnic totally forgotten. Some things were just meant to be. Katie was pregnant. He was okay with this. Better than okay. It would be fine this time. He would spend more time at home with her. She would worry less and that had to help. Right? And when little Jack was born he could teach him to play baseball and win fights. "Always go for the nose or the nuts."

He'd also teach him why he shouldn't follow in his old man's footsteps like he and his father and grandfather had done. The Murphy curse would be broken. No law enforcement for little Jack. He was going to be a jet pilot. Strike that. He was going to be a scientist, like Jack's brother, Kevin. Kevin had the perfect life. Kevin was smart, travelled the world, made a great living. Kevin was alone. Had been alone since a close call with a woman in Florida five years ago. Kevin was married to his job. Maybe it was a Murphy curse to live their work. He'd make sure Katie had a bigger hand in little Jack's world. Maybe he'd grow up more like her. He could be a teacher.

He pulled out of the garage. The horizon was a milky-blue and red streak. The sun wouldn't be up for a bit. It felt much colder than the forty-seven degrees the garage thermometer showed. Then he remembered the thermometer didn't work. Another thing on the to-procrastinate-list.

There was no traffic as he made his way to Riverside Drive and drove past the Blue Star Casino to Waterworks Road. He pulled into the parking lot of Two Jakes. Liddell was already there. Jack pulled up next to Liddell and they rolled their windows down. No other cars were in the lot except for Vinnie's old Indian motorcycle.

"Remind me to get you a set of keys, Bigfoot. Strike that. I don't have the budget to feed you," Jack said, rolled his window up, and got out.

Liddell leaned across and pushed the passenger door open. "Better ride with me, pod'na. I've got bad news and even worse directions."

"What happened?" Jack asked and changed vehicles. He feared the worst, of course. Reina had been shot. The guard on her room had been shot.

"It's Mrs. Day," Liddell said. "She was murdered last night. Shot. I just got a call from the sheriff's department."

Even with directions Liddell would have gotten lost if Jack hadn't corrected him twice. They pulled to the narrow shoulder on Kleitz Road behind a Vanderburgh County sheriff's two-tone brown Dodge Charger. A sheriff's crime scene van was parked across the street. Yellow and black caution tape was strung and two white-clad crime scene detectives stood on the front steps of the house talking to a sheriff's sergeant who Jack recognized.

The sergeant waved them in and Jack and Liddell slipped under the tape and approached the steps. As they did, Jack noticed an orange marker flag in the grass just beside the driveway.

Sergeant Elkins had the distinction of being the last deputy sheriff to make the rank of sergeant under the patronage system. He openly bragged about paying a past sheriff a thousand dollars for sergeant stripes. He paid another five hundred for a guarantee to stay on the street as a motor patrol sergeant and not work some chickenshit job like admin, or doing evictions, or serving subpoenas. He liked working the street, knew his people, had his favorite hangouts, coffee, knew where available bathrooms were, and knew places to hole up and sleep if he was so inclined.

He was solidly built for a man in his early sixties. He had a full head of curly hair that he claimed was salt-and-pepper, but was mostly gray. His hands were calloused and the size of wooden mallets. An ever-present cigar was clamped between the teeth of a face that exuded annoyance.

"This shoulda been yours," Elkins said.

"Good morning," Jack said. "They haven't gotten rid of you yet?"

Elkins took the cigar out of his mouth. "I decided not to leave until I get better insurance. Vanderburgh County isn't as generous as the police department. I retire, I have to pay twenty dollars a month. You guys get it free. I'm going to file an ADA lawsuit if they try to make me go."

"That's the civic spirit I like to see in a dedicated law enforcement professional," Jack said sarcastically.

"You want to know what I got or you want to turn around? I wouldn't blame you if you did," Elkins asked, the niceties over.

"We came to party," Liddell said and Elkins gave what would have been a chuckle for most people.

Elkins said, "The coroner took her and left already. The deputy coroner gave a ballpark TOD—time of death—from six to ten yesterday evening. Neighbor drove past about ten o'clock last night and noticed her lights were on. Same neighbor drove past around midnight because she had to go get some milk. At midnight? Oh well. Anyway, she saw the lights were still on. Then this morning about four she drove past on her way to work. She owns a bakery in town. She makes doughnuts, Liddell. And she's single."

"I'm happily married and I can always buy doughnuts," Liddell answered.

"I'll give you her information anyway," Elkins said. "She and the victim, Mrs. Amelia Day, have been friends and neighbors forever and she stopped to see if Mrs. Day was okay. The front door was unlocked. She opened the door and—surprise! The top of Mrs. Day's head was splattered on the couch and back wall of the living room. You're welcome to go in, but I can save you the time and I don't have to add you to the crime scene log."

Good idea. Jack waited for him to continue.

"Like I said, the body is already at the morgue by now. We're closing her up. She was standing in the doorway. Shot once in the head. Killer drug her inside and pulled the door shut. There's drag marks but, so far, no prints of any kind. No suspects. No weapon. We did find one thing in the yard."

Liddell said, "A .50 caliber shell casing."

"Yup," Elkins said. "Right over there by the side of the driveway."

There was an orange flag stuck in the ground as a marker.

"The killer must have shot from there. Not far, but still a good shot to hit her in the face like that."

"Was anything taken?" Jack asked.

"I don't know. I've been trying to find some family to come and check the house. Her only family is in Deaconess Hospital. I heard Dick's conversation with her on the news last night. He's so stupid he should run for Congress."

"Did you know Mrs. Day?" Jack asked. He suspected that Elkins knew something about everyone in the county. It was his superpower.

"Her boy, Max, was killed when I was still a lowly deputy sheriff. Shot in the head in his car in a cemetery, if I recall correctly?" Elkins asked.

"Right," Jack said.

"The dad, Harry, owned that gun shop downtown," Elkins said. "Nice guy. Good family man. He was shot during a robbery. Shot in the head. Reina was shot at in the same cemetery where Max was murdered. That was on the news last night too. You got to pay better attention, Jack. Claudine Setera didn't say anything nice about the police department last night. Is there any chance Double Dick will take the throne?"

Jack said, "Come out to the car. I'll tell you what we know." The three men moved out of earshot of the crime scene detectives.

"We've been ordered not to discuss the cases with anyone, but since you're not anyone I can tell you. And we might need your help. We're investigating the murder of Mrs. Day's son, Max. Thirty-seven years ago the boy was murdered in Locust Hill Cemetery like you said. Most of his head blown off. We have reason to believe the weapon used was a .50 caliber. There were apparently no suspects, but since we've reopened the case we're making some headway." Jack didn't really believe they were making headway, but sometimes seeding the clouds, so to speak, yielded results.

"I heard it was a .50 caliber that shot up Reina's car," Elkins said. "Listen, Jack. Maybe you shouldn't tell me. Last time I got involved with a case of yours I covered for you and caught some heat."

Elkins had let Jack go into a burned structure to recover evidence without reporting it anywhere. It could have gotten Elkins in serious career trouble, but luckily the home's owner was killed and Jack had caught the culprit. "We're investigating Harry Day's murder as well."

"I heard you was a fed now, so you can take this one off my hands. Seems you hit the trifecta, Jack," Elkins said.

"You wish," Jack said and continued his accounting. "According to the Days, Deputy Chief Dick was, or is, a suspect in Max's death. We have information that Dick and two friends were in a physical fight with Max at Rex Mundi the night he died and may have pursued him in Dick's car. Dick's dad was a Captain in the detectives' office and the feeling is that he whitewashed Dick's role so Dick could get on the police department."

Elkins asked, "Is old Double Dick a suspect in Harry's murder too?"

"Not yet," Jack answered. "But he's a contender for appointment by the incoming mayor, Benet Cato, to be our new Chief of Police, so now we've got that interference. Plus, it may go to the motive for several of these killings."

Elkins said with a straight face, "Life sucks and then you die, Jack."

"I'm ever-hopeful we will prevail," Liddell said. "Good always triumphs over evil."

"Not always," Elkins said. "Imagine Chief of Police Double Dick. I think you got that backward, Liddell."

Jack continued. "Double Dick approached Mrs. Day two days ago and wanted to meet. Mrs. Day said Dick had never contacted her before. They already thought Dick was involved in Max's death and wanted to get some leverage to make the police do a better investigation. Dick came to the house and Reina secretly recorded the conversation. Reina sent a copy of the audio to Benet Cato and they gave a copy to Claudine Setera."

"No shit?" Elkins said with a smile. "Good for her."

"Evidently it wasn't such a good move," Jack pointed out. "Reina's in the hospital and now Mrs. Day is dead."

"Someone is cleaning house. You think it's Double Dick?" Elkins asked.

"There were others involved in the fight with Max. We have a couple of people we need to check on," Jack said.

"I can get you two deputized," Elkins suggested.

"Bite me," Jack said.

"Me too," Liddell said.

"We might go to the morgue," Jack said. "If you don't mind."

"Whatever floats your boat," Elkins said. "Should I not put that in my report?"

"We were never here," Jack said and they got back in their car.

"Morgue?" Liddell asked.

"I'll call them first," Jack said and called the coroner's office.

"All our rooms are taken," Lilly Caskins answered.

"Lilly, you're in awfully early," Jack said.

"What. You think I'm so old I need my beauty sleep?"

"I apologize for whatever you think I might have said improper, Miss Caskins," Jack said. "I just wanted to know if you've scheduled the postmortem on Amelia Day."

"What do you think? You got the boy wonder, Elkins, with you. Ask him. He seems to know everything."

Jack muted the call and said, "Holy cow, boy wonder, she got up on the wrong side of the bed this morning."

"I heard that, dummy," Lilly said.

Jack checked the display screen. He'd hit the wrong button.

"Will you call us when Dr. John is coming in for the autopsy? Please," Jack said.

"This one's from the county so it's not your case, but I'll think about it," she said and the connection was broken.

"War room?" Liddell asked.

Jack laid his head against the headrest and closed his eyes. "Sounds good."

"Didn't you get any sleep?" Liddell asked him.

"Mind your own business and watch the road," Jack said testily.

"You didn't? You finally popped the question last night, didn't you, pod'na?" Jack said nothing.

"That's why you're so tired this morning. What did she say? Yes, I hope. Me and Marcie been betting when you'd finally come to your senses. You showed me that ring ten months ago or more."

Jack still said nothing and mimicked a loud snore.

"Come on. Let me live vicariously through you."

"That's a mighty big word for a little mind," Jack answered.

"Well, me and Marcie still have a very active sex life," Liddell said. "Last night we—"

"Will you quit! I don't want to hear about your mating habits, Bigfoot. Yes. I, as you so delicately put it, popped the question. And Katie said yes. Why wouldn't she? She's getting a stud like me. That's it. Now, let's get back to work."

"Huh," Liddell said, and was quiet until they turned onto Waterworks Road.

"Think you can walk when we get there or should we stop and get crutches?" Liddell asked with a huge grin.

"Smell that," Jack said, changing the subject. "Smells like Vinnie's cooking breakfast."

Liddell stepped on the gas. "I think better on a full stomach."

"So that's where your brain went? You ate it," Jack said.

Chapter 20

Liddell pulled in behind Two Jakes and parked next to Jack's Crown Vic. Angelina's light green Toyota RAV4 with smoked windows was there along with the black and showroom-shiny Ford 500 belonging to Captain Franklin.

Jack and Liddell entered through the delivery door and could hear voices coming from the front dining area: Captain Franklin, Angelina Garcia, and Vinnie.

"Eggs and bacon, please," Liddell said as they stepped into the dining area of the restaurant. "Good morning, everyone."

Vinnie split off from the conversation and headed for the kitchen.

Angelina Garcia was a petite Latina of twenty-four. Her long, dark hair had been bobbed into a beautiful frame for her smiling face. She had taken up running after getting married to Mark Crowley. Not jogging. Running. Jack had asked her why she decided to do that when there were perfectly good cars. He had likened it to jumping out of a perfectly good plane. Her response had been "Exactly."

Angelina had helped them with a recent case where a killer was targeting illegal immigrants. The death toll was over three hundred. She had started her career with the Evansville police as a part-time computer technician and ended up starting her own company and working part-time for ICE, Immigration and Customs Enforcement.

Captain Franklin was sitting at the table. "Jack. Liddell," he said with no emotion, giving Jack that "uh-oh" feeling.

"What's happenin,' Cap'n?" Liddell said and took a seat.

Captain Franklin said, "I hope you're still in a good mood when I tell you what happened overnight."

Jack's stomach fell a few inches. He feared the worst, that the killer had eliminated Reina's guard along with Reina herself. But he had the wrong Day.

"Mrs. Day was gunned down last night or early this morning," Captain Franklin said. "She was found inside the doorway of her house. One shot to the head. Large-caliber. Another .50 . She was found this morning about five o'clock. Sergeant Elkins of the sheriff's department called me about twenty minutes ago. I knew you'd all be here early and I wanted to keep this among us as long as possible."

Jack didn't have to tell Captain Franklin there was little chance of that. It would undoubtedly lead the news this morning. But he did say, "We've already been out there, Captain."

"Why didn't you call me?" Captain Franklin asked.

"Sergeant Elkins is working that case and he called us. They collected a single .50 caliber shell casing at the scene. County's crime scene is still there. They haven't found the slug yet, but Elkins said there were tire marks on the grass by the driveway. He thinks the killer pulled up, Mrs. Day came to the door, and he shot her one time in the head. They might find the bullet if it's still in the house."

"Given the circumstances, do you want to bring Sergeant Elkins into these investigations?" Captain Franklin asked.

"Can you have Chief Pope talk to the sheriff?" Jack asked. "I know Elkins won't talk to the media."

"I've already called the Chief and he's waiting for me to call back to tell him I notified you two. I'll let you get to work," Captain Franklin said.

"Elkins said Channel Six played the conversation on-air last night," Jack said.

"You didn't hear it?" Liddell asked.

"I was tied up last night and didn't get to sleep until late," Jack said.

"He was tied up," Liddell repeated. "Literally."

"Why don't you stay for breakfast, Captain?" Jack asked.

"Thanks," the said, "but I'm sure you've got things to talk about that you don't want the brass to hear. Besides, I have to call the Chief and then I have meetings. Are you going to make the death notification to Reina?"

Jack hadn't asked Elkins that question. He'd assumed since the death was in the county that Elkins would make it. "I'll call Elkins," Jack said. Jack didn't want to give Reina more bad news, but it might be better coming from him.

The Captain left.

Liddell said, "Angelina, why don't we go see what you've got? We can eat in the war room, can't we?"

"Go ahead," Jack said. "I'll call Elkins and see what he wants to do about the notification."

Angelina and Liddell went to the kitchen and Jack called Sergeant Elkins.

Chapter 21

Sergeant Elkins met Jack at Deaconess Hospital to break the news to Reina Day. Elkins was talkative until they reached the door of her room. A policeman was down the hallway in a chair by the door.

"You think he's bored?" Elkins asked and chuckled.

"With nothing to do but drink coffee and urinate all day. Yeah," Jack said.

"You can do the talking," Elkins said. "I've done my share of these. I'd rather eat a turd than do another one."

Jack said, "You were eating one of those this morning."

"I was eating one of what?"

"That black thing you had stuck in your mouth," Jack said.

"Are you calling my cigar a turd?"

"Hey, if it smells like a turd and looks like a turd…"

As they approached the room the officer came to his feet.

Elkins stuck out a hand. "Elkins. Glad to meet you."

Jack said, "He's a detective sergeant with the sheriff's office. He's with me."

"Sergeant Elkins," the officer said and shook hands.

"Has anyone been in there while you were on duty?" Jack asked.

"Yes, sir, Detective Murphy. I've been here since eleven last night. The nurse was in there a bunch last night. Holy cow. I don't know how anyone gets any rest in the hospital."

Elkins asked, "She woke you up, did she?"

"Yes, sir, Sergeant. I mean, no, sir."

"Have you talked to the lady in that room?" Elkins asked.

"Just to say hello and introduce myself," the officer said. "She was nauseated some. I think they're worried about the concussion. She's feisty.

She wanted to check herself out a couple of times and we had to call a doctor. It's been quiet for a while."

Jack read the officer's name tag. "Officer T. Bone," Jack said. He felt for him. Policemen were like mean kids when it came to name-calling. T. Bone was just asking for it.

"It's Thomas Bone, sir. Shortened from Bonet. We came here from France originally and the T got left off the end of our name. No one bothered to change it back. Like Shakespeare said, 'What's in a name?'"

Apparently a T-Bone, Jack thought. Even the Ellis Island cops were mean kids too.

Elkins surprised Jack. *"Thou art thyself though, not a Montague. What's Montague? It is nor hand, nor foot, nor arm, nor face..."*

Officer Bone smiled. "That's exactly right, Sergeant Elkins. I'm glad someone finally gets it. Do you know Shakespeare?"

"Not personally," Elkins said and the T. Bone laughed.

"The nurse was in about half hour ago, so I think Reina—Miss Day I mean—is awake. Her TV was going all night, but I don't hear it now." Officer Bone knocked lightly, opened the door a crack, and said, "You have company."

Jack could hear the sound of soft sobbing. He and Elkins entered to find Reina sitting on the side of the bed with an emesis basin—a kidney-shaped dish—in her lap. She was pale and shaking. Elkins pushed the *call* button for the nurse and Jack held the basin for Reina.

"The nurse is on the way. Do you—?" Jack said before a large nurse elbowed him aside.

"She was like this when we—" Elkins managed to say before the nurse pointed toward the door. They left.

Outside in the hall, Jack said, "Yesterday she seemed to be getting better."

Officer Bone spoke up. "Well, she might've been reacting to the news this morning. Like I said, the TV was on in her room and it's on every channel. I saw it on the TV in the nurses' station over there." He pointed down the hall to a television facing out into the hallway.

"What's on every channel?" Jack asked.

"About her mama getting killed last night," Officer Bone said. "Isn't that why you're here?"

"Yeah," Elkins said.

Jack had found out an hour ago. How in the hell did Claudine get this? Maybe she was monitoring their radio. Maybe she had another source. Who?

"Did you give this to the media?" Jack asked Elkins.

"Them's fightin' words," Elkins said and T. Bone laughed again.

"Yeah," Officer Bone said. "If I'd known, I would have unplugged her TV. You working on her mama's murder, Sergeant Elkins?"

Elkins's complexion turned pale. "Excuse me," he said and walked down the hall to a restroom.

"You did nothing wrong, Officer Bone," Jack said to the concerned officer. "Morning sickness."

"Yes, sir. I mean…huh?"

"He's got a very weak stomach. He gets sick every morning. He's prone to emotional outbursts."

"I feel bad, sir. Is there something I can do?"

"Nah," Jack said. "He'll be fine as soon as he pukes."

"I meant, is there anything I can do for that woman in there?"

"Yeah. Don't become a snitch for the news media."

"Got it," Bone said. "I wouldn't, sir."

It was several minutes before Elkins came back. He wasn't pale anymore, but his shoulders slumped. The wind was no longer in his sails. He'd been at this all morning. Making a death notification was hard enough. The news media would usually wait to name a victim until the family was notified. Claudine was the exception.

The nurse came out and despite her earlier wrecking-ball image she seemed reserved and Jack could see she'd been crying too.

"I'm sorry, fellas," she said. "That poor woman has been through hell. I gave her something the doctor ordered to calm her down, but she's fighting it. You can go in, but she may conk out on you."

Elkins shrugged. "You go in. She doesn't need us both in there and I think she's more familiar with you."

T. Bone said to Elkins, "Can I get you a ginger ale, Sergeant Elkins?"

Jack went in. "I'm sorry, Reina. I came to tell you." He sat on the foot of her bed and she latched onto him, squeezing him like her life depended on it. He could feel her shake with sorrow.

He put his arms around her and rocked her gently. "I'm here. You're going to be okay. We're going to finish this." He could feel the impotence of his words. Finishing this thirty-years-plus stagnant case wouldn't be easy and it wouldn't bring back her mother, father, or brother. Justice was blind and dumb and deaf and just plain senseless at times. All that was left was revenge. The shit-meter's needle had reached that point. He had reached the end of being nice.

Reina sat back and said, "Do you promise? Promise me." Her words came out frail and lost, but there was an underlying strength in her that refused to be beaten. "Promise me!"

"I promise, Reina," Jack said. "I promise. Now you have to promise me something."

She watched his face, her expression slipping between hope and impending disappointment.

"Promise me you won't give up. Believe in me. Okay?"

Chapter 22

Jack brought Sergeant Elkins in and left him talking to Reina. There were questions to be asked. It was the way it was. Jack felt her sorrow. It was a hard thing to answer questions after the loss of a loved one. And it was a hard thing to be the one asking those questions when someone had lost their entire family.

Jack drove to Two Jakes and made a mental list of things he needed to do. The list was a mile long. He gave up on it and drove on autopilot, thoughts of last night invading his ability to sort and categorize and prioritize the things that needed done. He was going to be a father again. He was going to be a husband. Again. He was still going to be a cop. He would still be on call twenty-four hours a day—weekends, holidays, birthdays, anniversaries, and any other inopportune time someone acted out like a violent animal and he was needed to bring them to ground.

Katie had married him once, knowing what their life would be like. She had not been okay with it, but she'd done the best she could to give him the freedom to do what needed to be done. She knew he was fighting for the right reasons. Helping people even when it cost him. She knew he could never walk away from a case. It was who he was. He was losing his soul, bit by bit. It was being eaten away by the evil he fought again and again.

He was who he was. That was the problem, wasn't it? He couldn't—or wouldn't—change. What he thought was the right thing was so much a part of him that it was like breathing. He hoped he could still do the job and keep his marriage. He owed that to Katie. To little Jack. It was going to be a boy.

He had this deep feeling that everything would be all right this time. He'd grown up. He'd faced most of his demons. Killed a few of them.

When he found out Katie was pregnant last night he thought his heart would explode, but in a good way. This morning there were thoughts of repurposing the nursery from a sometimes guest room back into baby Jack's room. The garage was big enough for a workshop. He'd build the furniture and new shelves for toys. He wasn't a great carpenter, but he could learn. He'd take the time.

Baby Jack. He couldn't call the little fella that, but he wondered how Katie would feel about Jake. Name him after his grandfather. If it was a girl they could call her Jackie. He'd talk to Katie about it tonight.

He parked behind Two Jakes and was energized now. When he walked inside he could smell freshly cooked bacon and homemade biscuits. Jake Brady hailed him from the kitchen. "You'd better get in there before your partner eats the tables and chairs."

"What? Again?" Jack said and Brady chuckled.

Angelina was sitting behind a bank of computer screens, a BLT sandwich in one hand, typing with the other. Corporal Tim Morris had arrived and was arm wrestling Liddell for the last piece of bacon and Angelina was laughing at their antics. A woman had just been murdered, but Jack didn't see this behavior as callous. This case was a political hot potato to begin with and it had just taken a deadly bent. That made it all the more important for the team to be able to blow off steam. The possible endgame of the cases could mean an end to any one, or all of their careers.

"All right, you can have the last damn piece," Morris said, and rubbed at his arm where Liddell had given him a noogie.

Jack interrupted them. "We still have a guard on Reina Day. She'll be in the hospital a little while. That's good for us because we can keep a better eye on her."

Liddell said, "We've got to get ahead of this, pod'na."

"Here's the plan," Jack said. "We take the gloves off. Politics or no politics. If we have to arrest the damn governor, we do it. We can apologize later if we're wrong. Right now, I just want to shake the bushes, start fires, bring the fight back to the bastard that's doing this. I believe attacking Reina was a warning and when we didn't drop the investigation, he or she decided to up the ante. You'd better believe the pressure will come down hard now. I don't care how the news media got Mrs. Day's story. I want their next story to be that we strung this guy up from a streetlight."

Liddell raised his hand. "Are we going to talk to Double Dick now?"

"Damn right," Jack said. "Angelina, can you give me a list of people we'll need to talk to? Addresses, phone numbers, employment, and the like?"

"Way ahead of you, boss man." She handed him a sheaf of papers. "Current address, personal info, telephones, employment, and vehicle they drive, including registered license plates. I'm still running criminal and tax histories, phone records."

"If I wasn't married, I'd kiss you," Jack said.

"If you kissed me, Mark would kick your ass," she said and everyone chuckled. "You seem extra-happy this morning. What's up?"

Jack was absently flipping through the papers.

Angelina nudged him and said, "Hey. You seem extra-happy."

Jack put the papers down. "What? I'm just happy. And this is good work, Angelina. Just what we needed."

"You're never happy," Angelina said. "Where's Jack? Who the hell are you, mister?"

Liddell said, "Leave him alone. He got lucky last night."

Jack turned his back to them. "I'm trying to read this damn stuff and make some connections."

"There's the Jack we all know and love," Liddell said. "Welcome back, pod'na."

Jack turned around. "You want to know why I'm happy? I'll tell you."

Angelina said, "Let's hear it."

Jack put the papers on the table and picked up a mug of coffee. He took his time and sipped at his coffee.

"Jesus, Jack! Say something," Angelina said.

"I asked Katie to marry me last night."

Liddell wrapped Jack in a ferocious hug, spilling coffee everywhere. "My man."

Angelina turned it into a group hug and kissed Jack on the cheek. "I assume she said yes. I'm happy for you two."

Jack struggled to extricate himself and when he could breathe, he said, "I'm going to be a daddy too. We're—she's—pregnant."

"Damn, you work fast," Angelina said admiringly. "You did all that last night?"

Jack allowed them to squeeze him to death again and when they stopped, he said, "Okay, let's get back to work. I want to go home sometime and see my soon-to-be and very-expectant wife."

"I'm gonna be his best man," Liddell informed Angelina.

"Okay, let's get to work. You're on, Angelina. Tell us what's in this stack of papers that you didn't let me concentrate on," Jack said.

"Well, my news isn't as good as yours, but I think it's a step forward. I numbered the cases. Max, Harry, Mrs. Day—I put Reina in a separate category. I created a master list of every name mentioned in the reports. These names are broken down by the cases they were involved in and I've got their personal information. Some of the names came up in three or more cases, so I put these on top. The last pages are the victims and their personal information."

Jack was flipping through the pages while she talked. They weren't assigned the case, but he was glad she had included the murder of Mrs. Day. There were a couple of dozen names that came up more than once. He was surprised there wasn't more, since they now had three murder investigations and a shooting.

Ted Mattingly's name was on three of the cases, Max, Harry, and Reina. He was also someone the family trusted. He would have access to all of them, but what would his motive have been to hurt them?

"Angelina, can you dig a little deeper into Ted Mattingly's past? I want financial, lawsuits, anything you can find that may have connected him in some way to Max or Harry," Jack said.

"You want me to search for drugs? Gunrunning? That kind of stuff?" she asked.

"See if he has had a big infusion of cash at any time."

"Okay."

"Have you got the sheriff's department reports on Amelia Day's murder?" Jack asked her.

She handed him a small stack of papers. "This is what I have on her so far. Elkins hasn't filed the offense report yet and there's not much except a report entered by one of their crime scene guys. You might want to take a gander at that."

Jack found the report. "They recovered the slug that killed Mrs. Day," he said. "It was buried in the living room wall."

Corporal Morris said, "I'll call them and see if they can get a rush on the comparison with what you gave me this morning."

"They have a .50 caliber shell casing too," Jack said.

"Got it."

"And can you tell them and the state lab that the results are not to be released to anyone but you, me, or Sergeant Elkins?

"And if you can find any paperwork on Max's or Harry's case, that would be something."

"I better get downtown and get on this," Morris said and left.

Jack flipped through the scant file on Mrs. Amelia Day and noticed his own name on that list.

"I'm on here?" he asked Angelina.

"You were the last person to see her alive," Angelina answered. "Sergeant Elkins will put that fact in his supplementary report and on the offense report, so I thought you should be on the list."

She was right, of course. The last person to see the victim alive, the one to find the body, and the relatives or significant others, were always the first suspects. He waited for her to continue.

"This Olson guy is a weird duck," she said. "He retired as a sergeant but has a substantial bank account. Over 200 K. I checked and didn't find a 401K plan and I know he didn't get much from his retirement pay. He owns his house. Owns his car, albeit it's fifteen years old. He's divorced. Four times. He paid support of nine-hundred dollars for twenty years until about ten years ago. I checked his exes out and they don't stand out in any way, except they were stupid to marry this greaseball."

"Have you met him?" Jack asked.

"No. I put his picture in your papers there. He's a greaseball."

Jack flipped to Olson's photo. He was a greaseball.

"Mattingly is divorced and has one child. I say *child*, but she's twenty now and in school at Purdue. Psych major. She's doing pretty good too. Hey, maybe she can talk to the Yeti and find out why he wants to be your bridesmaid."

"Ha-ha," Liddell said, and Jack made a twirling motion with his finger for her to continue.

"I've got a lot on Mattingly in your file, but I will need to do some more digging. But I just started my check on Mrs. Day and, financially speaking, she's had a hard time. She didn't get squat from the sale of her husband's gun shop. It barely paid for Reina's medical school training. She was on Social Security and was living on that and a small life insurance policy from Harry. There's a second mortgage on the house, but it wasn't much. I couldn't trace what happened to that money. Nothing from Max, as you'd expect. I don't think parents had life insurance on their kids back in your day."

Jack said, "My parents had life insurance on me."

"Well, pardon me."

"Did the gun shop have insurance?" Liddell asked.

"Good question," Jack said.

"Yeah, but Harry let it lapse and they didn't pay out," Angelina said.

Jack filled Angelina in on the conversation they had with Sergeant Mattingly yesterday to bring her up to date.

"So, Sergeant Mattingly was bribed to drop the investigation," she said.

"Technically he wasn't assigned to the investigations. It was more a threat than a bribe. He was assigned to the area where Max was killed, so it follows that he would be first to arrive there. He was assigned to check on traffic and crowd control down at the river on the night Harry was killed. We can't check that because there are no dispatch records that go back that far. According to Officer Steinburg, when Reina was attacked Mattingly showed up after he'd heard her name called in to dispatch. Understandable, also. But what doesn't jibe is that motor patrol sergeants, like detective sergeants, tend to stay available at headquarters most of the time. They were dispatched on runs when they were requested or a sergeant was needed. Mattingly seems to do patrol as well as administrative duties."

Liddell said, "We've known Mattingly a while, pod'na. You can't really suspect him, can you?"

"I suspect everyone until they aren't a suspect," Jack answered.

Jake Brady had attached a large whiteboard to a wall in the war room and a couple of blue markers were on a table nearby. Jack picked up a marker and printed on the board:

VICTIMS
1-MAX 2-HARRY 3-REINA 4-AMELIA

SUSPECTS:
MATTINGLY (1-2-3)
R. DICK (1)
CARL NEEDHAM (1)
DENNIS JAMES (1)

LEAD INVESTIGATORS:
DET. DAN OLSON (1-2)
MURPHY AND BLANCHARD (3-4)

OTHERS:
CAPT. THOMAS DICK (1-2)

PROPERTY ROOM SERGEANT
??

Jack turned to Angelina and asked, "Do you have the name of the property room sergeant during the first two cases?"

"Deceased," she said. "I ran the name but there wasn't anything that stood out."

"What's missing?" Jack asked the group.

Angelina said, "Obviously, the names of the crime scene techs involved. And the crime scene logs, so you know who was at each scene. But you asked Morris for all that. If there's something there, he may find it. I can't tell from the personnel records you gave me. Keep in mind that computers weren't used for the first two cases. Someone will have to go through records manually."

Jack told her, "Sergeant Mattingly said he found parts of broken beer bottles and a bloody tire iron at the cemetery where Max's car would have been. We checked with the property room and the evidence from that index card had been blacked and the property marked *destroyed*."

"You don't destroy evidence in a murder case, do you?" Angelina asked.

"Not supposed to," Liddell said. "But a lot of things are missing from these cases. I doubt Olson did much work."

"Greaseball," Angelina said as if that explained that.

"These are the next people we need to talk to," Jack said. He drew a red circle around Carl Needham, Dennis James, and Double Dick's names.

"Dennis James is going to be the tough one," Angelina pointed out. "I found a lot of information, but I couldn't find *him*. He has a record for criminal recklessness with a handgun. I pulled the affidavit of probable cause on that one and it's in the file. It was a Smith and Wesson .357. But there's something else more interesting in there."

Jack sat down and spread the sheets of paper on the table in front of him. Angelina had been very thorough. He wouldn't have expected anything less. Dennis James's data trail started with his Indiana driver's license. The address on the license was in the North Park area. The license was suspended and had expired a year ago. He had a police record. Drunk driving, battery, public intoxication, public indecency, possession of marijuana, and then about eight years ago Dennis decided to step it up in his criminal career: Possession and distribution of heroin, possession of cocaine. He'd somehow managed to get into a rehab program for the drug charges. He'd walked away from a rehab program and committed a home invasion robbery and that's where the criminal reckless charge came from. He was sentenced to four years and did two. He was released and promptly rearrested and convicted of felon in possession of a handgun. A .50 caliber semiautomatic Desert Eagle.

"Do we know where that gun is now?" Jack asked and Angelina shrugged. Jack remembered the condition of the property room and doubted the gun would be found even if it hadn't been destroyed.

"He just moved to the top of the list. We need to run him down before he talks to Needham or Dick," Jack said.

"You think these three boys are behind all of this?" Liddell asked.

"We have to start somewhere. We need to find Dennis James. Let's concentrate on Max's murder for now. I think that will lead us to the other killings, including the attack on Reina Day. Either these boys are involved or they're not. We need to know."

"James is my choice," Liddell said. "He has the background. He likes .50 caliber handguns. He's a troublemaker with a drug problem. And he's disappeared."

Angelina got busy on the computer and said, "I'm with Liddell on this one. I just found that James closed his Old National Bank account on Main Street two days ago. Twenty thousand was deposited in the account the morning he closed it. He doesn't have credit cards, employment records, and I can't find a vehicle registered to him. His cell phone number was on his bank account, but it's been discontinued. As of two days ago he went dark again."

"I'll call a friend at the bank," Jack said. "We can get security camera footage of him when he closed the account."

"Where does a guy like that get twenty thousand dollars?" Angelina asked.

"Good question. Let's find out." Jack picked up the phone to call his banker friend before he realized it was six in the morning.

"Drugs," Liddell said. "James made a big score."

"I don't think his buyer would deposit the money into his account. I may be wrong. Angelina, can you call narcotics to see what they have on him? Everyone knows what we're doing, but you can tell them it's for a background check for one of your clients. I don't want to release any more of this than I have to."

She jotted a note.

"Okay, on to Needham. Tell me what you can about him," Jack said to Angelina.

"What I have is in the folder," Angelina said. "He's in Columbus. He's a bigwig now. An Ohio state senator and a lawyer."

"Of course he is," Jack said.

"He went to law school in Ohio. Worked for a big firm and later ran for office. Got elected. He has a private practice, but I don't see where it made much money last year. I pulled his financials and the guy is loaded.

I mean, really loaded. No wife. No kids. Parents were killed in a house fire here in Evansville seventeen years ago. I'm checking to see if he inherited. He owns a horse farm just outside Columbus. No property here in town that I can find."

"What's his zodiac sign?" Liddell asked with a smile.

Angelina ignored him. "His current address is in the file. He has an office in the state office building in Columbus. The address is in the file. The address for his law practice is his home." She struck a few more keys. "*And* he has a federal firearms license, Ohio unlimited concealed carry permit, NRA member. He's a big voice in the recent movement to train and arm teachers."

"Any guns registered to Needham?"

"A Smith and Wesson .38 caliber revolver."

Jack was incredulous. "The guy can legally buy and own a fully automatic arsenal and he registers a peashooter revolver."

Angelina said, "It doesn't mean he doesn't own an arsenal. He's just careful about what he registers."

"We'll do Needham before we get to Double Dick, but we need to focus on Dennis James," Jack said.

"The autopsy on Mrs. Day will be this morning, pod'na. Maybe we should go to that and while we're there we can see if they have any records on Max or Harry's autopsies."

"Okay. Let's go," Jack said.

Angelina said she was going to run home and check on Mark, who was in bed with the flu. She reminded them she had a husband and a life.

That reminded Jack of how his life had changed overnight. He was engaged and he was going to be a father. *Maybe Kate or Katie if the baby is a girl. Or Maureen, after Katie's mother.* If the kid was like him that would lead to fistfights. He'd have to teach him to fight dirty.

Chapter 23

Dennis James was living the dream. He'd closed his old account at the bank as he'd been advised and took the money out in cash. Twenty thousand large was a lot of cash to carry around, especially in some of the places he went. He'd gone to the bus station and stored half the money in a locker. Then on to the casino, where he promptly lost a little over five thousand at the craps tables. One of the cocktail waitresses—Suzy, her name was Suzy—had kept bringing him drinks and she let him feel her up a little. He knew it was a ploy to get his money, but he didn't care. Suzy was cute. Then he'd won a thousand and decided to quit. Four grand down the toilet. He'd never do that again. It was a shame. He could have bought Suzy and a room for the night with that much.

He took a cab from the casino to the Red Roof Inn in Warrick County and had given the cabdriver a big tip. He was feeling generous. There was more money where that came from.

He checked into the Red Roof under the assumed name he was told to use, went to his room, and waited for the call. He waited an hour. The time crawled by. He was sweating like a pig and he felt achy all over.

He had the dough he needed, so when the call didn't come, he took another cab to a biker bar on the outskirts of Chandler and scored some China white. Plus, he bought one—no, two—bottles of Tennessee whiskey. He went back to his room and snorted a couple of lines while he waited for his call. He was promised he would get what he needed. So where was it?

He'd finished the China white, then followed it with a Jack Daniel's chaser. He didn't like being kept waiting. It was disrespectful. A friend shouldn't treat another friend like they were nothing. He didn't have rich folks. He didn't get to go to the finer schools. If he had money like his friend, he sure as hell wouldn't be wasting his life as a civil servant. Going to that fancy school had made him a putz. Dennis had learned from his daddy that a man had to watch out for himself, first *and* last. He would never be a servant for nobody.

"Civil servant," he said derisively and wiped his mouth with the back of his sleeve. That started him thinking. Maybe he didn't get the call because he was being set up. The cops would come barging in any minute now. He'd go back to prison. Maybe a whole SWAT team was outside his door right now!

He struggled to his feet and staggered to the peephole and saw nothing. He cracked the door, stuck his head out, peered up and down the hallway. No one was there. But that didn't mean they weren't coming for him. He didn't think his buddy would do that, but then again, he might. Dennis regretted making those threats to expose everything, but he'd explained that he was desperate. More desperate than he'd ever been in his life.

Before he'd done the China, he was feeling feverish and flu-like symptoms. The onset of withdrawal. He needed more. Something stronger. Damn if it didn't seem like each time he needed more. He had money now, but he knew it wouldn't get him through the month.

Since that "thing" had happened in high school, his buddy had kept him supplied with a teensy bit of cash and a place to crash. Then he'd gone to some parties and soon the drugs called to him like in one of them vampire movies. Drawing him in. The money wasn't enough and he couldn't seem to hold a job. It wasn't his fault his life sucked and he'd gone down this road. He'd started stealing, selling cheap or pawning to get the money for what he really needed. When that wasn't enough he started breaking into houses and businesses. He'd gotten caught by a homeowner once and they beat the hell out of him. He got a gun to protect himself after that. Then the cops caught him in a dope house with a gun that he'd stolen from the guy that had beat him up. He didn't remember beating the guy so badly he went to the hospital, but being told that he did kind of cheered him up.

His dad was worthless but he still remembered what the old man had told him. "You take care of yourself. First, last, and always. No one else will. You remember that, you little faggot. You remember it was me told you that. You don't and you'll make a fine punk in the joint."

He needed money. He knew stuff. He was owed big-time. He started calling his buddy. His buddy had given him a hundred bucks here, a hundred bucks there, and had even bailed him out when he got himself throwed in jail, but now he needed a lot more. He'd called his buddy and asked for the whole ball of wax. A hundred grand. Cash.

It was suggested to him that he was as guilty as anyone and if he went to the police he would be as likely to get the needle as anyone. He didn't care. He just knew what he needed right now. It was a different kind of needle. Something to keep the monsters at bay.

He didn't get the whole one hundred, but Mr. High-and-Mighty agreed to give him 20 G's up front with a promise to get that much every month and all he had to do was keep his mouth shut. Easy-peasy pie. It was more money than he expected. But, hey, he thought, his buddy had the money. That made him giggle. "Buddy had the money," he'd said out loud and giggled again. He was getting drunk on top of high. But the alcohol would just postpone the sweats.

He'd left the Red Roof Inn that night and took a cab back to the casino. He had over ten grand and he was feeling stupid for staying in a dump like the Red Roof Inn. He checked into the Le Merigot across the street from the Blue Star Casino at midnight. He paid for one night with cash and tipped the clerk a hundred. He went to the casino and won five hundred smackeroos in the first spin of the roulette wheel. He switched to the craps table and lost a grand, but he wasn't worried. He'd hit the damn lottery. He'd latched onto the main artery of a cash cow. The world was his oyster, and in fact, he could afford to eat in these expensive joints and enjoy oysters on the half shell and all the whiskey he could drink.

The next thing he knew he was being escorted from the restaurant and from the casino by security. He groped a waitress, but he'd offered her two hundred bucks and he could swear she said okay.

They were taking him back to the hotel and he saw the sun was up. He pushed the uniformed security guards away and staggered back to his room. His key card didn't work on the lock. He double-checked to see if he had the right room. The key card didn't have a number on it. He held onto the wall and worked his way down the hall, trying the card in every lock.

"Peckerheads gave me the wrong damn key!" he yelled and heard doors opening. People were coming out in the hallway. "What are you looking at?" One man went back in the room and locked the door. Dennis read the door numbers. He was on the wrong floor. "Sorry," he said loudly. "S'not my floor. Sorry."

He took the elevator up one floor and found his room. The card worked. He slumped down inside the room against the door and sat, trying to focus. That was what his life was like. One day he was picking a cigarette butt out of a glob of mashed potatoes he'd gotten from the trash behind a greasy spoon restaurant and the next day he was here at Le Merigot effin' hotel. Life was full of surprises.

He got up and turned his pockets out. He still had five hundred dollars and some chips. He wanted to go back to the casino, but he had to check out at noon. He said, "Rent the room for another night. Check. It's my lucky room. Check. I gotta get more Jack Daniel's. Check. And I gotta go get the rest of my cash. Check and double-check." But he thought maybe he'd go to the bus station and get the rest of his money later. He didn't think he could walk that far right now. And the casino was just across the street. But he didn't have any money for that.

He stepped outside his door and noticed a man in a black suit, white shirt, black tie, and sunglasses at the end of the hall. The guy wasn't wearing a uniform, but he was security. The guy was watching him but didn't say anything. Did the casino call security on him? Or maybe it was that prick who had been staring at him down below. *He* called security. The little sissy. What did he think he was going to do? Kill him? The nosy little bastard had nothing to worry about. The only thing he was going to kill was another bottle of Jack Daniel's and maybe a craps table.

He brushed past the security man on his way to the elevators and got on. The man got on with him. He got off at the lobby level and went to the desk clerk with the security man following. Dennis glared defiantly at the security man, dug deep in his jeans pocket, and plopped the five hundred dollars on the counter.

"I want the same room for two more nights," Dennis said to the prissy clerk, and said to the hovering security guy, "Tell him my money's as good as anyone else's."

The security guy gave the clerk the okay. When Dennis had registered earlier he'd given the night desk clerk an extra fifty bucks and didn't have to show identification. He gave this clerk a twenty and said, "That's for your trouble, my good man." Dennis turned to the security guard and said, "You ain't getting nothing, you prick."

"Have a lucky day," the security man said and walked away.

Dennis shot him the bird and strode back to the elevator, then turned around. He yelled back at the clerk, "You got some assholes around here, you know that." He went back to his room. He needed a drink.

As he walked in the room, a phone rang. He picked up the receiver of the room phone and yelled, "What now!"

The line was dead but the phone kept ringing. He felt something buzzing in his front pocket and remembered the cell phone he'd been given when he checked into the Red Roof Inn. They were finally calling. Great timing.

"Hello," he answered more moderately.

"You were supposed to stay out of Evansville, Dennis," the voice said. "You aren't where you're supposed to be."

"Well, hello Mr. Big Bucks," Dennis said, more than half drunk. "You're the one that wants me out of the way. I was doing just fine before you told me to go to that dump."

Silence.

"You there? Hey. Hey, I was just giving you a hard time. I didn't mean nothing by it," Dennis James said. He took a swig of the Jack Daniel's and flipped the cap across the room. He was still pissed, but it wasn't at his friend. That security guard had better watch himself, though. The line was silent still and he said, "Hello. Hey, I didn't mean nothing." He found the top and screwed it back on the fifth of Jack Daniel's, thinking maybe he'd better slow it down. He might have been an idiot, but he wasn't stupid enough to mess up a golden opportunity like this. He was getting the money because he knew about that night. The night Max died. He'd be quiet even if he didn't get the money. Plus, he didn't want to get his tit caught in a wringer for keeping quiet for so long. One of them had killed Max, but they were all guilty.

"I'm still here," the man said.

"Good. I'm sorry. Okay? I'm sorry for my smart mouth. I'm kind of drunk right now and I get that way. You know how I am," Dennis said.

"I remember."

"Well, listen. Here's the thing. I need more money," James said. "I've gotta get some things. You know? Maybe I could go to Caesars casino in Kentucky? That'd be better, wouldn't it?"

Silence again.

"Okay, I'll stay here," James said. "But I need more money. I gotta eat. And I need some clothes and stuff."

There was an unmistakable snort on the phone. "Dennis, you will always need things. Always need money. Don't lie to me. You've been using again. What is it this time? Not crack. You sound too rational."

"I ain't using. I ain't. I swear. I'm just drunk. That's all. I swear to God."

"Listen closely, Dennis. I left another twenty thousand for you at the place where you were supposed to stay. It's in the safe, in an envelope, with the name you're using. Take a cab from the casino back there in the morning. Tell the clerk you have a package in their safe under the name you're using now. Remember our agreement, Dennis. Don't move again unless I tell you. Understand?"

Dennis shuddered at the tone of voice. "I kept quiet all these years and I didn't do nothing. You guys started this. I don't want to get involved at all. I don't want the money anymore. Just leave me out of it. Okay?"

"It's too late for that, Dennis. You are part and parcel of everything that's happened. You know what happened and you know what he's capable of. You don't mess with someone like that. I'm only taking care of you so that he won't. Understand? There is no out for any of us. If you don't do as I say, I won't be able to protect you anymore. Do we have an understanding?"

"Uh, I guess," Dennis said.

"You have to be invisible a while longer and then you'll be a rich man. You can move wherever you want and start fresh. I want to do that for my old high school friend. Will you let me?"

Dennis thought about how they had been friends. He would have done anything for any of them back then. All he being asked to do was stay underground and keep his mouth shut. He'd been more or less doing that since high school, hadn't he?

Dennis said, "I mean, yeah. Got it."

"Excellent, Dennis."

Chapter 24

Jack and Liddell had no clear idea how to track Dennis James. On paper he was like a nomad, never staying in one place. They checked homeless shelters and soup kitchens for a couple of hours, but no luck. Jack called his friend at the bank again and got the name of the teller who was involved.

He hung up and said to Liddell, "I guess we'll go talk to this young lady. Dennis James had an account with Old National for twelve years and suddenly he withdraws everything and closes the account yesterday. The bank is on Main Street by the McDonald's. My friend says the teller is working right now. She doesn't have a driver's license, so maybe she lives nearby."

Liddell drove while Jack sifted through the file Angelina had given them. She'd added police personnel files obtained by Captain Franklin for Double Dick, Sergeant Mattingly, retired Detective Olson, and Captain Dick. There was also a ream of single sheets for each policeman who was working in 1980 to 1984.

Jack said, "Half of these people are deceased and most of the other half are retired. Most of the current addresses are in Florida and some in Mexico."

"Don't bitch, pod'na. We might get to go to Florida."

"With our luck, they'll send us to Mexico and we won't get back in the U.S." Jack closed the folder. "We can call the ones we can find. If we don't find Dennis James today, we'll retrace our steps. I don't want to talk to Needham or either of the Dicks until we have more of the story. Needham and Double Dick can cause the most problems. You agree?"

"Do you really think Double Dick will be appointed Chief?" Liddell asked.

"I thought you were a glass half-full person, Bigfoot. If you're worried, I guess the sky really is falling."

"I'm not worried, exactly," Liddell said. "I just wonder what it will be like working for Gestapo Central."

"Well, I'm not giving up on the new mayor having some common sense. If need be, we'll go to work full-time for the feds."

Liddell slowed suddenly. "Who are you and what have you done with my pod'na?"

"Bite me, Bigfoot. Just drive."

Liddell pulled into the curb next to Old National's entrance. There were no customers this time of morning, but a uniformed policeman was seated behind the counter. His name was Jim Kelly and he was a third-shift detective when he wasn't moonlighting as a bank guard.

Jack bumped knuckles with him. "I'm surprised you still have a uniform," Jack said. He was kidding, of course. Department policy was that even detectives must have a complete usable uniform in case of a mass call-up for things like riots, mass unrest, disaster duty, etc.

Kelly was muscle-bound to the point of ridiculousness and as tall as Bigfoot. He gave them a bodybuilder pose accompanied by a toothy smile.

"You still waiting for Hollywood to call?" Jack asked.

Kelly gave him a toothy grin. "Nah. I'm going to bodyguard Lady Gaga. I think she's got a thing for me."

He was also a Lady Gaga fanatic. He went to her shows several times a year and came back with some type or other of memorabilia. One time he brought home a multicolored wig and kept it on his desk until he got tired of being whistled at by the other detectives.

"I think what she has for you is a restraining order," Jack said. The two tellers behind the counter giggled.

"He's just playin' around," Kelly said to the two young women and showed Jack and Liddell into the manager's office.

A balding man sat behind the desk typing away on a keyboard. The nameplate on the desk said WALTER HIGGINBOTTOMS. This was the manager, but not who Jack had talked to on the phone. Another man was sitting in a chair in the corner. He was tall and thin with a full head of blond hair. This was Gerry Gorman, a retired policeman who was on his second career as Security Chief for Old National Bank Corporate.

"Hi, Gerry," Jack said to the Security Chief. "I guess this is the safest bank in Evansville with you and Kelly on duty."

Gerry Gorman shook Jack and Liddell's hands and said to the man on the computer, "I'll take care of them, Wally." Wally got up and left the office.

"If you're here to arrest Wally, I need to see your badges, guns, warrants, and orders from the president."

"Bite me, Gerry," Jack said and introduced Liddell.

"So. You're crazy enough to ride with Jack?" Gorman said.

Liddell said, "I have a degree in psychology and keep sedatives on hand."

"Sedatives for you or for him?" Gorman said.

Jack didn't think it was funny.

"Have a seat," Gorman said and they all took seats. "What can I do for you, Jack?"

"Like I said on the phone, we need to talk to one of your employees. Janet Cummings. Concerning the account of Dennis James."

Gorman went to the door and spoke briefly with the head teller. A minute later a striking brunette came into the office. She was young, early twenties, armed with a pair of thirty-eights worn high on her chest. She smiled and crossed her arms. Jack knew from years of interviewing experience that stance was body language for *My eyes are up here, gentlemen.*

Gorman said, "These men are detectives and have a few questions for you about an account you closed. Dennis James."

"Yes," she said. "He closed the account a couple of days ago."

Jack asked, "Regular customer?"

She hesitated.

"You can answer their questions, Janet," Gorman said.

She said, "He was a regular customer. I should say he was regular for the last two years. He had an account here for twelve years, but he doesn't now. I think I said that already. Sorry."

"It's okay to be nervous," Jack said. "Just take your time. We're all friends here."

She took a breath and gripped her hands tightly in her lap. "Well. Yes, he was a regular for as long as I can remember. There was a monthly deposit from an Indianapolis bank of one thousand dollars a month for the two years I've been here. I know he had the account longer, because when he closed it I saw regular deposits and withdrawals going back twelve years."

She hesitated again and Jack wanted to tell her to quit stalling and just answer the damn question. He said, "Mr. Gorman said you can answer all of our questions. I promise not to get you in trouble. Continue, please."

Gorman gave her the okay and she said, "Denny would come in and withdraw small amounts. Usually twenty dollars. Sometimes he did this two or three times a day."

"Did you know Denny well?"

"I meant Mr. James. Sorry. It's just that when you have a regular customer you get to know what they like to be called."

Jack hid his impatience and asked, "What did you think about him? What impression did you get from him?"

"I felt sorry for him. He seemed lonely. To be honest, I think he just came in to talk to me. It was kind of creepy at first, but he never asked me out or made inappropriate remarks. Hey, he's not in trouble or a psycho or something, is he? Oh my God!"

"You have nothing to worry about, Miss Cummings," Jack said. "When he closed his account, did you find that unusual?"

"That's what this is about."

"What do you think this is about?" Jack asked.

She gave a knowing smile. "That transfer of twenty grand—I mean, twenty thousand dollars that was put in his account the same morning he came in and closed the account. This one wasn't from Indianapolis. It came in from someplace really far away."

"From out of the country?" Jack asked.

"No. I mean it was from Minnesota. Mr. James never had more than a thousand dollars in that account, and it dwindled fast. You'd be surprised how fast money disappears when you keep spending ten here, twenty there. He was always cleaned out before a new deposit was made."

"He came in and closed his account..." Jack prompted.

"He came in and said he was closing his account and wanted it in hundred-dollar bills." She hesitated a third time, but Gorman sat stone-faced. Jack thought Gorman was going into a coma. He was starting to feel groggy himself. Maybe he'd take a nap and when he woke up she'd say something.

She finally spoke. "We don't keep that kind of money in the drawers. I had to get Wally—he's the bank manager—to get the money out of the safe. We both—I mean me and Mr. Higginbottoms—counted the money in front of Denny—that's Mr. James—but he seemed to be in a hurry and didn't want us to count it. It's bank policy that we count any money as we give it to the customer."

"Okay," Jack said.

"Then after we counted it out he changed his mind and wanted fifties and twenties. Wally went back to the safe and got it. *Mr. James* put the money in his pockets. I know you don't think he could put that much in his pockets, but a bundle of ten-thousand dollars in twenties and fifties is about an inch thick." She demonstrated with her thumb and forefinger.

"And then..." Jack said.

"And then he pulled two fifty-dollar bills out of his pocket and slid it over the counter to me. Then he winked at me and said something like, 'You've been nice to me. You won't see me again.'"

Jack waited.

"I told him we weren't allowed to take money from customers. I didn't take the money," she said to Jack. "Honest."

"You did the right thing," Jack assured her, although he didn't believe her.

Gorman explained, "Every now and then a customer will try to give a tip to a favorite teller. Bank policy prohibits this." To Cummings, he said, "Was Wally there when this happened?"

"No, sir."

"Did you report this to Wally?" Gorman asked.

Her expression said she hadn't. He was losing patience with her.

"Did Denny give a reason for closing the account?" Jack asked.

"No. He just said he was going away for a while. I told him he didn't have to close the account if he was going to come back, but he said he didn't think he'd be back."

"Do you know where he lives?" Jack asked.

"I think he's homeless. He used an address on the far northside to open the account, but I had a note from the main office to ask him for his current address when he came in again. I asked him for a new address, but he said he didn't really have a permanent address."

"Did he show you a driver's license when he made withdrawals?" Gorman asked.

"I knew who he was, Mr. Gorman. He was in here all the time. I didn't ask for one. I'm not in trouble, am I? I really need this job."

"You're not in trouble," Jack assured her, but Gorman's demeanor said something else.

"There was that deposit each month, but it didn't seem like a lot." She put a hand to her mouth and said, "Is he a drug dealer?"

"That's exactly what we're thinking," Jack lied. "He's a suspect in a couple of murders, so if you see him again, you tell Wally to call me. Okay?" Jack thanked her and she was dismissed.

Gorman took an envelope from his suit pocket and handed it to Jack. "This are the best shots I could get from the bank film. I got you some close-ups of his face."

Jack opened the envelope and pulled out a dozen still shots of a man at the bank counter wearing the clothes Janet Cummings had described. Jack recognized Janet Cummings in the pictures. She appeared to be a lot more than customer-friendly.

"I can track his account withdrawals and see if we have video of those if you need them."

"That would be great," Jack said. "I can't tell you what we're investigating, but I can promise you the bank is not involved. We're just trying to run this guy down."

Gorman said, "Follow the money. I'll see what I can get for you and I may have to mind Miss Cummings's transactions a little closer. Why don't I believe that gal?"

"What do you mean?" Jack asked.

"I know she's not involved with those cold cases you're working, but she's hiding something. I didn't always work in a bank, you know."

"What cold cases?" Jack asked. "I never told you what we were working on, Gerry."

"Maximillian Day. Harry Day. And now I hear Mrs. Day has been killed. Her daughter injured and in the hospital. Jeez, Jack. You've gotten yourself into a hornet's nest," Gorman said sympathetically.

"Where did you hear all of this, Gerry?"

"Don't you ever listen to the news? It's been all over Channel Six."

Chapter 25

Jack called Angelina. She was still at home getting Mark taken care of, but would be back at the war room within the hour. Jack had put her on speakerphone and she told them about the recent Channel Six news special. She said Claudine had released everything she could possibly know and some things that were mere rumors at this point. Claudine had played just enough of the taped conversation between Dick and Mrs. Day that her audience would conclude Double Dick was an arrogant, unfeeling ass. Angelina quoted Claudine, "The public has questions about the systematic slaughter of the Day family. If the police have answers, Chief of Police Marlin Pope isn't sharing them with this reporter. Deputy Chief Richard Dick couldn't be reached for comment."

Dick truly was an ass and he was arrogant... but a killer? Claudine had suggested there was a cover-up by the police and had hinted at the guilt of Double Dick in the murder of Max Day. The one thing she missed was deriding Jack and Liddell personally.

Angelina said, "Jack, Claudine mentioned you and the Yeti. She said you were assigned to all these cases and had gotten nowhere. What a bitch."

Jack got off the phone with Angelina. Claudine had stirred the pot. He was sure Double Dick would strike back. He was surprised the man hadn't already approached them in his bullying, authoritative manner, making demands. He was arrogant and thought he could manipulate Mrs. Day, but he'd found out different. He was stupid enough to try and visit Reina Day in the hospital. His ego was so big there was no telling what he might do.

He called Sergeant Elkins and learned the autopsy on Mrs. Day had already begun.

"Let's go to the morgue," Jack said.

At the coroner's office they were met by a very large young man named Ivan Ivansky. Ivan was a behemoth in his early twenties, with dark, tanned skin and blond hair worn in a spiked crew cut. He topped Liddell's six-foot-six by at least two inches, maybe more, and had at least forty pounds of muscle on Liddell. His shoulders were broad and the sleeves of his lab coat stretched taut. Jack and Liddell had first met him over the winter when he had started interning for Little Casket. Jack's first impression was of a young Dwayne Johnson, "The Rock," a Samoan-Canadian WWE wrestler-turned-actor.

Ivan started as an unpaid intern with the coroner's office, but was recently hired as a full-time deputy coroner. That made him Lilly's assistant.

"Detectives," Ivan said, and shook both men's hands.

Jack worked his fingers and rubbed his hand after he'd gotten it back from Ivan's death grip. "I might need that hand later," Jack said. "You been crushing coconuts again?"

Ivan grinned. "They're in the back. The doc and everyone. Sergeant Elkins is here."

From behind them came the voice of Lilly Caskins, the Chief Deputy Coroner. "Igor, we got business to do. Go get the stuff you were sent after. Chop-chop." Ivan hurried down the hall.

Lilly said, "Igor's not house-trained yet. For the life of me, I don't know how we can afford a new assistant. I'd like to replace him with a box of new surgical gloves that we can't afford." With that, she turned and stomped toward the room where the autopsies were carried out.

From as far back as Jack could remember, Lilly Caskins had been nicknamed Little Casket by the rank-and file-policemen. It was a nickname that suited her well, because she was evil-looking and diminutive, with large, dark eyes staring out of extra-thick lenses and horn-rimmed frames that had gone out of style during the days of Al Capone. Jack respected her work for the most part, but she had an annoying habit of being blunt at death scenes. Jack wasn't surprised Little Casket called her new assistant Igor. She had a nasty temperament and was equally rude regarding the living and the dead. But in this case his size and appearance must have prompted the name.

Ivan came back with a large box of supplies and followed Jack and Liddell to the autopsy room. On the way Jack asked him, "How do you like your new job?"

"It's been interesting, Detective Murphy."

"Lilly hasn't fired you yet, so you must be doing a good job," Liddell offered and this got a smile from the gentle giant.

Ivan said in a low voice, "She's not so bad, Detective Blanchard. I like her."

From the other side of the autopsy room door Little Casket said, "This isn't a popularity contest. Come in or leave. Your choice."

Liddell said, "She's got spooky good hearing, pod'na."

Jack agreed, quietly. He just wanted to get what they needed and get out. Being around Lilly was like being under Nazi occupation—voluntarily.

They entered the autopsy room and the post on Mrs. Amelia Day was already underway. Dr. John Carmodi, Sergeant Elkins, and a female Jack didn't know were gathered around the stainless-steel table. They turned their attention to the new arrivals.

Elkins said, "We're just about done here, Jack."

"Just in time then," Jack said. He didn't particularly care for autopsies. The smell, the violation of a person's body and privacy, the reminder that life was limited. Police liked to feel invulnerable. Death was a constant reminder that just wasn't the case.

Liddell offered a hand to the new girl. "I'm Blanchard, he's Murphy."

She held up her gloved hands and said, "Sorry. I don't want to touch anything. I'm Beatrice. Bea. Crime scene."

Jack assumed Beatrice was one of the new hires under the county's program to put more sworn deputies on the road. The city had started a trend when they hired three civilian crime scene employees trained in forensic science as well as criminal justice. It was a trade-off. Three civilians making less money and three higher-paid trained police officers put back on the streets. Of course, this had been resisted by the rank-and-file police officers, but it turned out that with proper training and hands-on experience the three civilians had proven to be invaluable.

The one kink in the system was the turnover in crime scene with the civilians. Once they were trained and had some experience to list on a résumé, they were snatched up by other progressive police agencies all over the country. Which proved one of Murphy's Laws. *No good deed will go unpunished.* Or *There is always a dark cloud at the end of the rainbow.*

Elkins said, "Bea's a good girl. Excuse me, I mean crime scene investigator. She'll send you a copy of everything we get from the scene. Won't you, Bea? Of course she will."

Bea was no longer interested in Jack or Liddell's presence, and didn't even acknowledge Sergeant Elkins's misogynist remark. She snapped a few more pictures and said, "I'll take care of it, Detective Murphy."

"Call me Jack."

"If you insist," she said without taking her focus from the body.

Elkins said, "Don't mind Bea, Jack. She had a tough day. Didn't you, hon?"

Bea deliberately ignored him, but Jack saw her jaw tighten.

Elkins continued, "We pulled a young girl's body from the river down in the river bottoms. It must have gotten snagged on submerged root. She was missing for nineteen days from across the river in Henderson. Fish ate most of the face." To Bea he said, "First floater is always the worst. You'll get used to it after a while."

"She was fifteen," Bea said. "My sister is fifteen. Her skull was caved in. I'll never understand how someone could do this. Or why."

Jack had no answer. He'd seen hundreds of murder victims, mangled and burned bodies, hacked up, hung, shot, tortured. It had numbed him to Bea's reaction. He had compartmentalized the shock and horror of such atrocities. Locked it away in a hidden bunker deep in his heart and brain to draw on its power when he needed a reason to keep fighting this evil. He worried that the hidden depths of death would outdo his ability to use the feeling for good or to seek justice. He feared that one day he would become the monster. He would become the thing he hated most.

The body on the autopsy table was Mrs. Amelia Day, but no longer Mrs. Amelia Day. Now she was a hollowed-out vestige of the woman who sought justice for her son and her husband and was killed for believing she would find it. He wondered how many more would have to die before this was over. He could only think of one that had to die.

Jack got close to Elkins's ear and whispered, "You need to go easy with Bea."

Elkins responded. "Jack, she got sick at the scene. I'm trying to toughen her up. If she wants to do this kind of work she can't be running off to cry. I'm doing her a favor. Ain't that right, Bea?"

Bea said nothing.

"Not everyone is as callous as us," Jack reminded him. "Remember when you were new and still normal?"

"Guys like us were never normal."

Dr. John said, "I hate to break up this little disagreement about *normal*, but I should have the report finished by this evening. Elkins said a .50 caliber is suspected and I concur. One entry, front of the head; one exit wound, back of the head. No other medical conditions present. Cause of death is massive damage to the brain. Manner of death, gunshot wound to the head. Her death was instantaneous. No stippling around the entry. Not a contact wound."

Elkins said, "No weapon found."

Bea said, "The shot was fired from twenty to twenty-five feet from the victim. We found the shell casing beside the driveway about twenty-five feet from where the victim was standing in the doorway of her home."

Dr. John pulled a sheet over the body.

Jack asked Sergeant Elkins, "Anything else we need to know?"

"Yeah," Elkins said and took a small plastic envelope from his pocket. It contained a mangled lead and brass bullet. "Bea found this lodged in a wall in the living room. She says it's good enough for a ballistics match if we find the gun."

Liddell said, "Way to go, Bea."

Jack said, "Morris is going to contact you about comparing the ballistic evidence we have. Do you have anything else?"

Elkins said, "Yeah. Little Casket can't keep her eyes or her hands off me. I'm feeling used."

Jack gave an involuntary flinch at Lilly being called Little Casket out loud. But he remembered she and Elkins had some kind of history. Jack didn't want to know.

Lilly responded, "In the old days, Deputy Dawg here could be had for a wink and a bottle of Night Train." Her face twisted into something that might be a grin on anyone else.

"Let's go, Bigfoot," Jack said. "Too much information."

Lilly called after them, "I'll try to find the autopsy records on your other cases."

Jack didn't even have to ask how she knew at this point. "Thanks."

Jack and Liddell hurried outside, got in the car, and Liddell drove. "Where to now?" he asked.

"Now we go see retired Detective Sergeant Dan Olson," Jack said. "We can't find Dennis James. People that are part of our investigation seem to be getting killed. We know where Reina is and she's safe. I would love to take Double Dick into custody, but I don't think that would fly. And he is quickly becoming a suspect."

Chapter 26

Retired Detective Sergeant Dan Olson lived on North Fulton Avenue across from Cedar Hall Elementary School in a badly weathered shotgun house. Most of the neighboring houses had been torn down to make way for the much-needed road project and sewer drainage construction. But Olson's house, with its green clapboard siding and sixty-plus-year-old shingle roof must have sat farther back from the road and was untouched.

This neighborhood had been part of the original area known as Boxtown, where the government had thrown up houses for the returning World War II veterans. The houses were called shotgun-style because you could fire a shotgun through the front door and out the back without touching a wall. The rooms generally consisted of a front room, bedroom, bathroom, kitchen, and back door. The design was simple, cheap, and good enough for mortgages that were affordable to the returning troops so they couldn't say Uncle Sam never gave them anything.

The only out-of-the-ordinary aspect of Olson's property was the six-foot tall newer chain link fencing with two padlocks on the front gate. All that were missing were coils of razor wire, angry dogs, and a guard tower.

"This guy's around seventy-five years old. Right?" Liddell asked. The curtains were drawn in every window. The property didn't give off the vibes of an occupied structure. A ramshackle shed sat in the backyard inside the fence and it too had a heavy padlock on the door. Jack imagined there was a brick paved alley on the other side of that fence. A lot of the old vets had gotten work laying brick streets and alleys when they came home from the war. A lot of the bricks got misplaced and found their way to the alleyways behind the workers' houses.

Liddell parked on the street's narrow shoulder in front of the house. Jack took out the list of names, addresses, and phone numbers Angelina had supplied them with this morning and found the phone number for Dan Olson. He called and saw the front window curtain shift. There was no answer.

The front door opened. The man who stepped outside in jeans, house slippers, and striped bathrobe was all of five-foot-two inches tall and wide in the hips. He was in his seventies, but had dark hair that was parted on the side and held in place by some kind of product—maybe Brylcreem that was advertised back in the day as "a little dab'll do ya." He'd used the entire tube. To continue the description, Olson was wearing a face that didn't welcome visitors. The face went with the fence.

Jack held his credentials out of the window. Olson pointed a remote control at them. Jack heard the lock on the gate click and the gate opened a few inches.

"Let's go."

They got out, Liddell locking the doors on the Crown Vic, and they went through the gate, pulling it shut behind them. The paranoia was catching. The yard was gravel with blades of grass poking through here and there.

"I guess he doesn't have to cut grass," Liddell said.

They walked across the gravel and stood at the bottom of two concrete steps leading to the door. Without taking his focus from them, Olson pointed the remote at the lock again and Jack heard it lock. He stepped back, allowing them to enter. To Jack's surprise, Olson left the door wide open.

"Anyone that would break in on three cops has a death wish." Olson didn't grin. He was holding a gun down to his side.

"Thanks for the armed reception," Jack said and Olson gave a snort.

"I heard you was a smart-ass, Murphy," Olson said. "Yeah, I know who you two are. Your mugs are plastered on the news enough you could start your own PI business and make a killing." He motioned outside and said, "You try living around here. It's like *Night of the Thieving Dead.* Drugs, prostitutes, gangbangers, burglars. The little kids are the worst. I was in Nam, you know. If I had me a Huey I still couldn't keep these sewer rats from overrunning my position."

He said this last and chuckled, leaving Jack to wonder if that was a joke or if the thought of gunning down the community was a favorite fantasy.

"I'm sorry," Jack said.

Boxtown was a depressed community. He didn't blame Olson for being cautious. Most cops were trained to live in code yellow. But Olson was a little over-the-top.

"I was wondering when you'd get to me." Olson said. "Have a seat."

The living room consisted of a sofa and an overstuffed La-Z-Boy recliner. The recliner had a cup and remote holder built into one arm. A holster for a semiautomatic had been screwed and glued to the inside of the other arm. All that was missing was the beer and snacks and some targets. He was equally ready for game time or bloodshed.

Jack and Liddell sat side by side on the sofa and Olson plopped down in his overstuffed, weaponized throne and slid the Smith & Wesson .45 semiautomatic into the holster beside him.

Olson was no beginner at dealing with police. He waited for Jack or Liddell to start speaking first so he could establish the pecking order and decide what to tell them.

"How long have you been retired, Sergeant Olson?" Jack asked.

"Nearing twenty years," Olson answered.

"Before either of us came on the department," Jack said. "Is retirement what it's cracked up to be?"

"Hmpff." Olson adjusted his ass in the chair and his hand laid across the butt of the gun.

"Did you turn the .50 caliber shell casing from Max Day's murder scene into evidence?" Jack asked.

This had the desired effect. Olson sat forward in the recliner. Jack could see the man was shrewd as a fox, but he had gone from paranoid to intelligent, maybe dangerous. Jack found himself watching for Olson's hand to pull the handgun.

Olson relaxed, smiled tightly, sat back, and said, "What evidence? Who you talking about?"

Shrewd. But Jack wasn't out of ammunition, no pun intended. Not yet.

"You were lead investigator on two murders: Max Day in 1980 and Harry Day in 1984," Jack said.

Olson's eyes were guarded, never breaking with Jack's. He said, "Yeah. I remember."

Jack switched gears again. "You were a detective sergeant for quite a long time, Sergeant Olson. I remember my dad talking about you. He was always telling stories about you and some of the runs you were on together." Jack said this with a deliberate—and he hoped sincere—smile.

Olson's shoulders visibly relaxed. Jack continued. "My dad was Jake Murphy. He and Jake Brady went into business together when they retired."

Olson said, "I remember them. Opened that floating restaurant, didn't they? We all thought they was crazy, but it turned out to be a smart move, didn't it? Most of the guys that worked during those days are dead or gone to nursing homes…or worse, and with nothing to show for it. Take me, for example. I didn't end up with anything except this house."

Jack had gotten him started talking, so he'd let him talk.

Olson said, "I've been to your place a few times. Two Jakes, right? Nice. Real nice. Your dad did right by you. I bet it's a moneymaker."

"It does okay," Jack said.

"I hear you got a cabin cruiser and a dock at that old river cabin he owned. I used to fish down there sometimes. Your dad didn't care. He let a lot of us fish on the bank, but he wouldn't let us stay in that cabin. Said he was keeping the rats out. Hey, what kind of boat you got?"

Jack said, "It's a Chris-Craft. I call her *The Misfit*."

Olson laughed and pushed back against the seat. "That sounds like a cop's boat. You're a riot."

"He's a funny man," Liddell said, speaking for the first time.

Olson focused on Liddell. "You're the one they call the Cajun. How tall are you?"

Liddell stood and easily touched the ceiling without reaching.

"I bet you don't have anyone screw with you," Olson said.

"Only once," Liddell answered. It was the correct response and Olson laughed again.

"Okay. I think we like each other enough for me to talk to you now. That's what you were doing. Am I right?"

"Right," Jack said.

"Damn right. What now? You want me to just talk and you ask questions when I'm done, or are you going to ask all the questions? I'm not a detective anymore and everything's gone to shit these days. I heard all you guys take sensitivity classes. Hmpff."

"My dad taught me to let a *witness* talk or not talk. *Suspects* were allowed to talk or else," Jack said and now Olson laughed wholeheartedly.

"Yeah. Old Jake would have put it just that way. What a cop. He would have been a good detective too, but he was too smart, your dad. He stayed a street cop and let the rest of us dummies get stuck in the quicksand of rank and politics. I hated every minute of it. I can't tell you the number of times I wished I'd stayed in uniform."

"My dad always said you were a good sergeant. A good detective," Jack lied. His dad never talked about Olson. Maybe because he didn't make it a habit of airing other people's screwups.

"Oh yeah? I never knew he was a fan," Olson said.

Jack had to remember not to lay it on too thick with this one. Whoops!

"Okay. Sorry about giving you a hard time. I've seen the news and let me tell you something, there's not much that bimbo said that was true. If you're here to lay the blame on me for not clearing those murders, you can leave and don't let the door hit you in the ass."

"We're not pointing fingers," Jack said. *Yet.* "We just want to know what you remember about the investigations."

"Okay, I'll start with the oldest murder. Max Day. Thirty-five or so years it's been." Olson leaned back in the chair and put his hands behind his head.

"I was a pretty new detective. I made sergeant after that one. Anyway, I got the call. They sent me to Locust Hill Cemetery. I was on third shift because I didn't have any seniority and I wasn't connected. Back then, those were the criteria for making rank and getting assigned to good shifts, you know. Hell, I barely made detective, but that's another story."

His eyes returned to the spot on the ceiling where images of the past were playing.

"I got there and Mattingly and two older cops got there ahead of me. Mattingly said it was a shooting death. I told the other two guys to take off." He explained, "Back then it wasn't unusual for cops to take souvenirs away from big crime scenes. You know. Nothing big. Nothing important. Just little things. I don't know what they took. Maybe Mattingly found a shell casing. He never gave it to me. I don't know nothing about that. Okay?"

Jack said, "Got it." Olson wasn't wrong about souvenirs being taken by police, but he'd contradicted the story Mattingly told.

"So, I kept Mattingly there to keep watch while I checked the scene. I called crime scene. I knew a suicide when I saw one. This kid's head was nearly destroyed and I didn't see any evidence of a fight or struggle or anything. There wasn't any evidence, like I already said. It happened in a damn cemetery, at night, so no witnesses."

"Did you ever find a weapon?" Jack asked.

Olson's eyes became slits. "It's been so long I don't remember. But if it was a suicide, the gun would be there or someone had already taken it. There were three uniforms there when I got there."

"Okay," Jack said, but not understanding a bit of Olson's reasoning and wondering if he was getting senile or deliberately not remembering clearly. Olson hadn't mentioned the broken bottles and tire iron Mattingly found. He already said there was no sign of a fight or struggle—or anything. Why would he put it that way?

"I remember it was colder than a witch's titty," Olson was saying and he shivered, supposedly remembering everything. "It had rained cats and dogs earlier, but it wasn't raining when I got there. If someone said there was a fight, the tracks or footprints or any such must have washed away in the downpour."

Jack wasn't buying it. Olson was lying.

"I took a couple of Polaroids. I don't recall what crime scene took, but I know they didn't collect any evidence. The car got towed and went over really good by our guys later. They didn't find anything but pieces of the kid's brains scattered around inside. If you want to know the truth, I think he was out there buying drugs and it went sideways on him. He was sitting in the driver's seat and someone blew his head off from outside the car. All the brain matter was on the ceiling and passenger window. No one in the neighborhood heard or saw anything. And...there was no shell casing. If Mattingly told you that, he's making it up."

Mattingly had actually put in his report that the blood was on the windshield and the driver's window. The shot couldn't have come from outside the car.

"Why would Mattingly do that?" Jack asked.

Olson didn't miss a beat. "He wanted to be important. That was the way to make rank or get into the detectives' office. You did a good job, solved a murder, found a big piece of evidence when no one else could. Stuff like that. That's what got you promoted. You understand? And now, I guess Mattingly heard you got hold of this old case and he wants in on it."

Jack had had the same thought. He didn't believe it; his gut told him that wasn't the case, but he couldn't discount it, either. Of course, Olson had contradicted himself so many times he was obviously making it up as he went.

Olson crossed his arms, which was textbook body language for "I'm going to lie my ass off. When are you getting out of here?"

"Was my dad involved in Max Day's investigation?" Jack asked, throwing another nonthreatening question into the conversation.

Olson said, "No. No. Not Max Day's. Jake was there during the other one. Max's dad. Harry. Right? I'd say, ask your old man, but he's gone. Sorry to hear that. He was a good street cop."

"Thank you," Jack said. "Let's continue with Max's murder."

"Sure. Like I said, there wasn't no evidence of a fight, or evidence of a weapon that was used to kill the poor kid. I heard later this kid was a certified prick. Always starting fights, skipping class. Tough guy. He got kicked out of Central High School and his parents sent him to Rex Mundi. Everyone knew both those schools were full of druggies, even if Rex Mundi was supposed to be so religious. I mean, what the hell has happened to our kids? Shooting each other to get some attention because they don't feel loved. I don't even want to get into that. For all I know it was one of them Romeo and Juliet–type suicide pacts. Maybe Max wanted some cutie-pie and if he couldn't have her, no one would. She shot him and lost her nerve. That would account for no gun being found."

"Are you saying a girl killed Max?" Jack asked.

"I'm just throwing out ideas. That's what detecting is. Am I right? Anyway, in my day, if a girl jilted you, you just went to the next one. And if I had a problem with another kid I'd punch him in the nose and that was that. We'd be best buddies next day. Now some little pansy gets his Capri pants in a twist and they bring a gun to school. I mean, what the hell? But I don't want to go there."

Then he went there again. "We didn't have all this getting-a-lawyer hassle because some numbnuts was wearing fag clothes. He'd get his lickings and shut up after that. Someone was messing with you, it was settled right there in the classroom. The only reason I can see that Max was shot was because he was dealing drugs. Forget what I said about a girl. It was over drugs. Drug dealers was the only ones carrying guns around."

Olson was exhibiting a classic pattern Jack had noticed in liars. Make the victim the bad one. Blame them for creating the incident. Getting off the topic and keeping it there. Stall for time and confuse the investigator.

"Nothing ever came to light?" Jack asked. "No one came forward with evidence or saw something or heard talk?"

"There's always people coming in claiming to know things. You know that. There was this one psychic nut that read it in the cards that Max was killed by a cop and that was why we didn't find any evidence. Can you believe it? Horseshit! Am I right? You know it. And Sergeant Mattingly was going around asking leading questions. People who weren't even witnesses. Stirring up the crazies. A lot of people would say anything they thought would get them some attention. You know?"

"I heard there were rumors going around after Max's murder that the police didn't do enough to find the killer," Jack said. "I'm not saying you didn't do your best. But that's what I've heard."

Olson's jaws clamped shut. He forced them to relax before saying, "You listen to me, Murphy. You know those crazies I was just talking about? That's the Day family. All of 'em. Loony tunes, the whole inbred bunch. I worked my ass off on that boy's case and the old man's too. There was nothing there. I was a good detective. Anyone says there was some sort of cover up because of Captain Dick is a liar. And an asshole with a grudge. Back in my day we took care of each other. The thin blue line. But we didn't cover up a murder."

Jack hadn't mentioned a cover-up. Of course, Olson said he'd watched the news and Claudine had stressed the cover-up angle.

"Captain Dick was Chief of Detectives at the time, wasn't he?" Jack asked.

"Yeah. What's that got to do with the price of potatoes? Someone is making a shit sandwich. Am I right?"

"Did Captain Dick direct your investigations?" Jack asked.

"Of course, he did. He was my commander. Listen up, Murphy, there was a lot of guys on the department that were related. Father and son, brothers, uncles, spouses. I think I'm done here. I ain't answering no more of your questions if you're on a witch hunt. I know you and Richard don't get along. And I know he's a royal pain in everyone's ass. But he's still a cop and I don't spread rumors about cops."

"I'm sorry if I offended you. I'm not 'after' Deputy Chief Dick, or his family. I don't even know his family, but I've heard good things about the Captain. My job is to find the truth. To find Max and Harry's killer," Jack said. "This is all background information. You've asked other people these same questions a thousand times." He wanted to say: "You screwed up two murder investigations because you're a dick." Instead, he asked Olson a question he already knew the answer to. "Do you recall what caliber of weapon killed Max or Harry Day?"

Olson sat silent. Jack sat silent. Liddell was a ghost. Finally, Olson sat back in his recliner and said, "Max was shot with something big-bore. His head was exploded like someone blew up a watermelon. We never did know. Like I said, we never found the weapon. And there was never a shell casing. Mattingly must be yanking your dong."

Not what Mattingly said.

"What about Harry?" Jack asked.

"Harry was shot with a .357 magnum. We found a bunch of different spent casings on the floor. Surprise, surprise. He was shot in a gun shop where there was a little shooting range in the back. Anyone could have dropped the casings. We didn't have any of that fancy equipment like on *CSI*. The coroner said it was most likely a .357, and we found some of those on the floor."

Again, not what Mattingly had told them. Jack remained silent.

"Mattingly made sergeant just before Harry was killed. He thought that gave him extra rights to wander around in a crime scene. I was a sergeant too and detectives were in charge at a crime scene. He wasn't too happy when I threw his ass out. He wasn't crime scene. He wasn't a detective. I didn't need him and I told him to get his ass out, but he kept snooping

around like he was Columbo or something. He always thought he was
smarter than the detectives."

"Did Mattingly find anything when he was snooping?" Jack asked.

"He had a spent bullet that he *said* he found on the floor. He insisted
it was from the gun that killed the guy. I don't remember what caliber it
was. I just put it in an evidence bag with the rest of the shell casings we
found. The floor was littered with them. This was a gun shop. Am I right?"

Jack agreed it was a gun shop.

"Well, Mattingly was still climbing the ladder. He was testing for
lieutenant, if I remember right. Yeah. He was wanting to be a lieutenant.
More weight to throw around. I didn't believe a word that came out of
his mouth then and if I was you, I wouldn't believe him now. Once a liar,
always a liar. Am I right? You know I am."

Jack asked, "Do you think Sergeant Mattingly had it in for you
and Captain Dick?"

"I didn't say that. Did I? Personally, I wouldn't piss on the man if he
was on fire. But hey, what's that they say? Live and let live. Am I right?
You know I am."

"I believe you," Jack lied. "I don't trust him, either. I couldn't tell you
that right up front. Am I right?" he asked, using one of Olson's expressions.

Olson responded with a chuckle, "You know you are. You know what?
You're an asshole, Murphy, but you're a pretty fun guy. We could have
been friends in the wayback."

Jack forced a smile and thought, "Not on your life, you worthless, lazy,
lying piece of filth."

"Okay, let's kick this up a notch," Jack said. "You were a good detective.
You've still got detective blood in you. I can see it. You've got this place
locked down like a fortress. Nothing gets by you, does it?"

"Quit yanking my dick and ask your question."

Jack asked, "The robbery and murder of Harry Day? What did you
think that was about? Your honest gut feeling."

Olson's eyes took on a cautious glint. "You have to remember that was—
what? Thirty, forty years ago? You was still shitting your diapers. Didn't
your old man tell you about it? He was there. I remember him being there."

"All my dad taught me was how to drink scotch and win fights," Jack
said and Olson grinned. While he was on a roll, Jack said, "Dad would
always say, 'Drink up, Jack. There're sober kids in China.'"

Olson thought this was hilarious. When he stopped laughing he said,
"Yeah. He was a drinker, your old man was. And not the cheap stuff, either.
You might say him and Jake Brady were scotch-a-seurs. You know. Like

connoisseurs. Anyway, I remember when we'd all be at Jericho's Tavern telling stories; your old man would get a bottle of Blue Label and sniff the cap before he'd let the bartender pour it. What a card. He was a good cop. Everybody liked him. He wasn't a pain in the ass like you." Olson laughed like he'd told a big joke.

We're buddies now.

Jack said, "So no one back then, at least none of the real cops, thought Captain Dick was covering Max's murder up?"

"That's right."

"When my dad passed, I found Bankers Boxes full of notebooks, tapes, pictures from the job, all kinds of stuff. I put a lot of it in storage. I'll have to drag it out and see if he had notes on those cases. Maybe he kept something. Did you keep any of your notes or tapes or pictures—that kind of thing?"

Olson's expression slipped, but he recovered quickly. "Yeah. You should see if Jake kept any. When I was done with the job, I was done. But your dad—he might have kept some stuff…"

His words trailed off and he began rubbing his thumb across the curled finger on his right hand, his eyes fixed on the wall. He stopped rubbing and said, "I knew some guys that kept stuff. It was more political back then. You know? Some guys kept things for insurance so they could stay on a certain shift, or keep the same partner, or just to keep their job. You know?"

"I can understand that," Jack said. "Did you keep anything… for insurance?"

Olson adjusted his position and cleared his throat. "I wasn't talking about me, was I? But hey, if you find anything embarrassing about me in your dad's stuff, don't spread it around. I used to drink him and Brady under the bar. You may not think it to see me now, but I was a ladies' man back then. Broads like the badge and gun, danger and passion, bad-boy stuff. Am I right? You know I am. And I had aplenty of passion. I could tell you stories." He chuckled.

Jack waited.

Olson said, "I do remember something, though. May be nothing. I didn't think it was suspicious back then, but hey, you got my noggin working."

"What's that?" Jack asked.

"Mattingly was first on the scene at both of the murders. Max *and* Harry. *And* he spent a lot of time at Harry's house while Harry was at work. That was after Max was killed. I know that to be true, because I seen his car out there sometimes. What if he was doing more than comforting the grieving mother? Am I right?"

"You think?" Jack said.

"You know I am. You know how cops are. Any hole in a storm and all that. I heard stories. The man would do a snake if he could hold it still. He'd do a knothole. Maybe he was putting it to the missus and Harry found out? Harry was a gun nut. Who knows what a guy like that might do," Olson said, rubbing his thumb against his forefinger again. "Harry goes off on Mattingly in the gun shop and the shit hits the fan."

"Amelia Day?" Jack asked. "You think Mattingly had something going on with her?"

"He was a real pussy hound, is all I can tell you. Hell, if he'd plant evidence at a murder scene and then make up a story, maybe he wasn't just trying to get the glory. Maybe he's the one that killed Harry? Am I right? You know I am."

"You just said Mattingly was the first officer on scene at Harry's and at Max's murder. Earlier you said you were first at Harry's," Jack said.

"Yeah. I did say that. Maybe I got it wrong. It's been a lifetime ago." Olson pushed himself up straighter in the recliner. "I remember now. I was there at the gun shop after Mattingly. I remember I was close by. Maybe I'd just left headquarters. Anyway, Harry's gun shop was right downtown. Mattingly was working west sector, not south, so he shouldn't have been anywheres near the downtown area. Him and Harry was supposed to be friends, so I didn't think anything about him being there back then, but now you got me thinking I was wrong."

Olson took a deep breath and let it out all at one time. "Anyway, I got there pretty quick and Mattingly told me Harry was on the floor. Gunshot in the head. We thought it might be a robbery because the cash register was emptied, the drawer was still out, and there was change all over the floor behind the counter. We searched, fingerprinted everything, talked to anyone and everyone. I ran all my snitches, but I came up empty."

"So, Mattingly was there when you got there and the register was on the floor. Right?"

"Yeah. Mattingly called it in and I arrived before the troops. Did he tell you I was there when he got there? Why, that lying sack of shit!"

"Did Mattingly search inside the shop with you?" Jack asked.

Olson changed the subject. "I don't want to speak ill of the dead, but…"

Jack waited for him to continue.

"I bought a couple of guns from Harry. He sold them cheap to cops. Cop discount. But I never saw the place doing much other business. I couldn't see how he kept his door open. Unless he was buying hot and selling cheap. Know what I'm getting at? Am I right? You know I am."

"You're saying Harry was buying stolen weapons and selling them?" Jack asked.

Olson's response was a shrug.

"So—what—you think someone killed him over the guns? Someone he was buying from?" Jack asked.

"You know how word passes around the criminal element. Somebody may be thinking, 'Hey, this guy's got stuff I want and I ain't got no money,' and so…" Olson made a gun out of his finger and thumb. "*Pop*. Now I got something too."

"So now you don't think Mattingly was the one who killed Harry?" Jack said.

"Hey. I don't know who killed the guy. I'm just telling you possibilities, is all. Maybe him and Mattingly were dealing in guns. One of them got greedy. There were lots of guns. We didn't know how much was missing because Harry was a terrible bookkeeper. Accidentally on purpose, if you ask me."

"I hadn't thought of that," Jack said. "You've still got a good mind for this stuff," he said. "Help me out here. Do you think Max's and Harry's murders were connected?"

Without hesitation, Olson said, "The only connection I see is Mattingly. He was always there first."

Jack didn't bother to point out that Olson had just said he was at Harry's murder scene first. He let Olson run out the rope.

"When Harry was killed, it was pretty late at night. The shop should have been closed, but Mattingly would have had access because they was friends or partners. And—Harry's old lady and that daughter, Rainy or Rita or something, was making noises about Max's murder being done by a cop. Maybe Mattingly wanted to scare them all into shutting up, and when that didn't get her attention—*pow*, Mama's dead. You see where I'm coming from here? Am I right? Damn straight, I'm right."

Jack had to admit it. Olson had a point. Only it was the top of his head. The man wasn't even a good liar.

"Her name is Reina," Jack said.

"Yeah. Reina. She grew up to be a doctor. But I guess you knew that with her getting shot up and all. Hey, not meaning to change the subject, but that Channel Six babe is some kind of hot, ain't she? I know I ain't much now, but I was a mover back in the day. I could tell you stories. What I wouldn't give to be five years younger."

Try forty years.

"We can swap stories next time," Jack said.

"Yeah," Olson said with a nervous chuckle. "Sure. You don't have time for an old fart's stories of conquest. I get it. I'll just say this: That family has had nothing but bad luck. You'd better keep a guard on that girl, Rita."

"Reina," Jack said again.

"Yeah. Rainy Day. She's got some name, don't she. Reminds me of that Mick Jagger song, 'Ruby Tuesday'—you know that one?"

Jack nodded.

"Well, someone don't seem to like the Day family. Know what I mean? Maybe you should check on the whereabouts of a certain sergeant when these tragedies seem to happen?"

Jack said, "One more question, Sergeant Olson, and then we'll leave you alone. Did you attend the autopsies on both of the victims? Max and Harry Day?"

Olson sat quiet for a moment.

"I went to Max Day's. Still have bad dreams about that one. I even went to the funeral service. You know. See who shows up and that. Nothing, except I saw Mattingly there. What the hell was he doing there? I didn't have to go to Harry's autopsy. It was obvious he'd been shot in the head. That was the cause of death. Me being there wouldn't have made a difference. We never caught the guy that did it, so it wasn't important."

Jack wondered why Olson was lying about going to Max's funeral service. He hadn't signed the remembrance book and Mattingly had said Olson wasn't there. But somehow Olson knew Mattingly was at the service. Had he been watching Mattingly?

"So, did you take pictures at Max's service?" Jack asked.

Olson made a dismissive gesture with his hand. "Taking pictures of everyone at a funeral hoping to see some creep hanging out watching. Bah. That only works on television. Am I right? You know it."

Olson was right about that. Criminals rarely, if ever, returned to the crime scene to gloat over their handiwork, but it made for good TV.

"One more question," Jack said. "Did you ever talk to the boys that were involved in the fight with Max Day at the high school the night he was killed?"

Olson's face turned red and he shook a finger at Jack. "I see where this is going and like I said a couple of times now, there wasn't any evidence of a fight at the cemetery. I'm not saying there weren't rumors that Max was in a fight at the high school, but a lot of people hated that boy. Anyone could have done it. Don't you go stirring up the pot. Captain Dick's had enough of that shit thrown at his family."

What about the Day family, asshole? "Thanks for your time, Sergeant Olson. And hey, if you find any notes or anything on either case, you'll call me? Am I right?" Jack handed him a business card.

"You know you are," Olson said, but he didn't chuckle this time. He got up to show them out.

"Just one other question, Detective," Jack said.

"I ain't a detective anymore, so you can cut the crap, Murphy."

"Okay. Earlier you said you took some pictures of the scene at the cemetery."

Olson blinked and then stared Jack in the eyes. "Did I say that?"

"Yeah, you did. What happened to those?" Jack asked.

"Hell if I know." Olson showed them out, hit the button on the remote, and unlocked the gate.

Jack heard the lock click behind them. When they got in the car, he saw Olson watching them from the doorway.

"Do you think he's scared, Bigfoot?" Jack asked.

"I'll bet dollars to doughnuts he's still got the pictures," Liddell said.

"That's a risky bet for you, Bigfoot. But yeah. He's done something with the pictures and whatever other evidence he has or had. The best thing he ever did for the police department was retire."

When they drove away, Olson picked up the phone and punched in a number. It rang once and was answered.

"It's me," Olson said and listened. Then, "Yeah, they were just here."

Chapter 27

Le Merigot was a respectable hotel. The spacious lobby with its glass front giving onto a magnificent view of the Blue Star Casino riverboat said so. It smelled of money and money was respect. The hotel operations manager was a close relation of one of the owners. That meant the manager's relative was loaded. That made the boss respectable by blood and he let his desk clerks know it. He expected them not to tarnish his or the hotel's reputation; thereby his respectability. Many a desk clerk had found themselves out of a job and unable to work at another hotel if they forgot.

That's why Bob Werner, a nineteen-year-old, one semester short of an associate degree in hotel management, decided not to push his luck by questioning the self-important prick who had strolled into the lobby and asked for someone by name, but didn't know a room number. When he told the guy no one of that name was registered, the guy demanded to see the hard copy of the register. The guy must have been in management if he knew the hotel kept a paper ledger of the guests, as well as having one on computer. Bob hesitated briefly before handing over the register. If this guy was in management, he knew the boss and if the boss got pissed off, he could kiss his already tenuous job good-bye.

The man's face was slightly familiar and he had an important air about him. Arrogant, cocksure, preppy.

"If you give me a description of the person…" Bob began, but the man seemed to find what he was searching for and shoved the ledger across the counter without a word of thanks.

Bob watched the man go to the elevators and punch the *call* button and get on. When the elevator doors closed he said, "What a prick. One day you'll all be working for the Bobster. Oh yeah. And then we'll see who's what 'n shit." He then promptly forgot the man and went back to the business textbook he had hidden under the counter.

* * * *

When he went to see Dennis James at the Red Roof Inn, the room was empty. He'd given Denny a cell phone and apparently Denny had taken it with him. That was good. He could track the phone.

This was getting tedious. He hadn't expected Denny to give him this much trouble. If Dennis James hadn't been so pathetically predictable he might have even admired the junkie's attempt to avoid being found, but he didn't understand why he had changed hotels. All he could think of was that the drugs and drink were finally taking their toll. The man was losing it. The end stages of the addiction. Paranoia and hallucination. The paranoia had saved his life. For a time. But that time was over.

He exited the elevator on the third floor, turned left, and then another left. His spit-shined shoes whispered on the thick burgundy carpeting. He had dressed in the black suit, white shirt, and black tie he'd seen hotel security wear. He'd changed his appearance, enough even his own mother wouldn't recognize him. She hadn't been around for a very long time.

He stopped at the door to room 3120. The DO NOT DISTURB placard was hanging from the door handle. He could hear the television playing.

He reached inside his overcoat and took out a 9mm-Beretta fitted with a heavy silencer. He knocked on the door three times, then again, louder, and watched the peephole for movement. Nothing. He stepped to the side of the door and reaching across his body, fired three shots into the door's locking mechanism. He fired two more where he knew the safety latch would be if it was engaged. The armor-piercing rounds punched through the metal door like it was made of paper. He pushed the door open and stepped inside. The bathroom door was closed and he could smell dampness.

An empty whiskey bottle was on the floor, and another one was on the still made-up queen beds. The other bed was all rumpled sheets and covers. He walked to the windows, checking the floor beside each bed. Denny wasn't passed out there. He went to the closed bathroom door and called out, "Denny. Come out. It's me." Nothing. He stood back and fired six times through the cheap bathroom door, starting at chest-high and staggering the shots, moving downward. He turned the handle and opened the door. The room was empty.

He went back to the bedroom and found the cell phone he'd given Denny next to one of the pillows. It was laying on a folded piece of hotel notepad. He spread the paper open and read, in large, cursive letters:

The next time you see me
will be on the news.
I'll call you.

He crumpled the note and went back to the bathroom. There was still water residue in the sink and a damp hand towel. He tossed the note in the toilet and flushed. He'd just missed him. Dennis James was full-blown paranoid or he was smarter than he'd given him credit for, but Denny had made a fatal mistake. He didn't think Denny would go to the police. Or the news media. He was an accomplice, after all. And with Denny's reputation and the absence of any evidence, who would believe a junkie? He was as good as dead.

He took the stairs down and exited through a side door. Denny didn't have a car and he knew Denny couldn't rent one, so that left cabs or maybe city buses. He'd left the cell phone behind because he was afraid he could be tracked. He was right about that.

Dennis James wouldn't go very far, but he couldn't risk the man getting picked up by the police. He was a drunk, he liked to fight, he was a burglar and thief, he would commit some type of crime when he ran out of the money he'd been given. With the investigation open again, he couldn't afford for Denny to be found and interviewed by Murphy and Blanchard. It would ruin everything. He was angry with himself for not taking care of the Denny issue years ago. He'd had several opportunities to orchestrate a fatal accident, maybe an overdose. Instead of killing the man, he'd helped him out all these years and this was how he was being repaid for his kindness. He'd heard it said a thousand times in his career: "No good deed goes unpunished." Well, no bad deed would go unpunished, either. Denny was dead. He just didn't know it yet.

Chapter 28

Back in the car they sat quietly, each in their own thoughts. Janet Cummings told them nothing that would help. They still were unable to locate Dennis James, and if the teller was right, he had no home, no friends, no work of any kind, and worst of all, he might have left Evansville. Angelina's information seemed to back that view up. And now Claudine had compounded things by airing Double Dick's taped conversation and adding her own spin on the other incidents. If Dennis James was smart and saw the news, he'd be on a bus and far away from Evansville.

Talking to Dan Olson hadn't gotten them very far, except to strengthen the rumor of a cover-up. Dan Olson was a pathological liar, or worse, he was complicit. He and Mattingly had butted heads over these cases and it was a toss-up as to who was being truthful. Jack's money was still on Mattingly.

Jack felt a vibration in his jacket pocket, pulled out his phone, saw the caller ID, and put it on speaker.

"Jack, where are you?" Captain Franklin asked.

"We're near downtown, Captain."

"You need to come to the Chief's office right away."

"Okay."

"I called Sergeant Walker in. He has the ballistics back. Claudine has started a tsunami of public opinion. We've set up a special telephone line to take calls from the public expressing their outrage, asking about rewards, etc. But that's not why I called."

Jack waited. He hated that Tony had given up his vacation just to get mired in this political marsh. But police officers and doctors were always on call. If they didn't answer the call, bad stuff happened.

Captain Franklin said, "Mayor-elect Benet Cato wants to talk with the investigators of the Max Day case. We haven't told her that you're also investigating Harry Day's murder or that of his wife, but she's not stupid."

"Captain, she's not the mayor yet. *And* she's not a cop. I hope the Chief told her to piss up a tree?" There was a pause and he added, "sir."

"That's the other thing. Mayor Hensley will be here also. He's the one who called Chief Pope and insisted on the briefing along with Benet Cato. Chief Pope will be there, as will I."

All the king's horses and all the king's men...

"That's swell, Captain. Will Claudine be there? Can I bring a date?"

"Don't be childish, Jack. You know what's at stake here. Behave yourself, and that's an order."

"I do know what's at stake, sir. Can't you do anything?"

Captain Franklin said, "If I could, we wouldn't be talking, Jack. Just come in. Behave."

The call was disconnected. Jack said, "Are we going to tell them everything or should we lie to our boss?"

"You'll do what you want, pod'na. You always do."

"Damn right." Jack allowed himself a few choice curse words and added, "*Behave*, my ass."

"You're cute when you're mad," Liddell said and batted his eyelashes.

"Maybe Double Dick will be there and we can question him in front of his current boss and future boss."

Chapter 29

They were pulling into the rear of police headquarters when Liddell's phone rang. It was Little Casket.

"You might want to get over here ASAP. I've got something good for you." She hung up.

"That was—"

Jack said, "I heard. I wonder what she's got for us. Well. She'll have to wait. We've got bigger sharks to deal with at the moment."

They entered headquarters and the Chief's secretary, Judy Mangold, buzzed them inside and pointed at the Chief's conference room.

Jack and Liddell entered the conference room. Chief Pope, Captain Franklin, and Mayor Thatcher Hensley were seated around the large table and a chair was in a corner away from the door and the other men. It was occupied by the slouched figure of a young woman in her mid-twenties, dark, short hair combed across her forehead into uneven bangs. Her clothing was more appropriate for hiking than meeting with the most powerful men in Evansville. She appeared more at ease than anyone in the room.

"These are Detectives Murphy and Blanchard," Chief Pope said. "And—"

"I know who they are," the young woman interrupted and remained slouched in the chair.

Chief Pope continued as if she hadn't interrupted him. "…this is Tilly Coyne. Mayor elect Benet Cato's campaign manager. She will be the new mayoral assistant."

Good behavior. Don't get mad. Correction: Don't get madder. "I understood Mrs. Cato would be joining us?"

Tilly's eyes narrowed, daring anyone to challenge her. "Do you see her?"

Jack bit his tongue. She reminded him of someone. Then it came to him: Tilly could be Little Casket's love child. He said, "I was hoping to meet her."

"Oh, I'm sure you'll be in a meeting with her after the first of the year. Have you cleaned up this mess yet?"

Thatcher Hensley cleared his throat. "Detectives, I hope you have some good news for us."

Jack said, "Mr. Mayor. Jilly… I'm sorry—I didn't catch your last name."

Tilly said with a slight smirk, "Get on with it."

I really dislike this bitch.

"Mr. Mayor, we were given this case yesterday. It's gone unsolved for thirty-seven years. It most likely won't be solved immediately, since most of the witnesses and evidence are in the wind. We're in the process of running down some leads." Jack wasn't sure how much the Chief wanted either the mayor or Cato's assistant to know about the missing files and physical evidence.

Chief Pope said, "My detectives are working diligently on this, Mayor Hensley. We have hopes of—"

Tilly interrupted the Chief of Police. "Hope in one hand and shit in the other, Chief, and see which pleases the voters more."

Thatcher must have found his balls and said, "Miss Coyne. Your disrespectful remarks are not helpful, nor wanted. If you can't behave in a professional manner, you'll leave. You're in my office as a courtesy to Miss Cato. Personally, I think Benet herself should have come."

"As far as any of you are concerned, *I am Benet.*"

"I refuse to deal with you any further," Mayor Hensley said. "And you can tell her that."

Jack could see a vein pulsing on the mayor's neck. This was the first time Jack ever felt like hugging a politician. "Mr. Mayor," Jack said. "I think Tilly here needs to hear the truth about what we're doing. Undoubtedly the news media will be feeding off the investigation, and since Miss Cato campaigned on a transparency platform, she needs to see for herself why total transparency isn't always the best option."

Hensley seemed grateful for Jack to take Tilly's heated glare off of him.

"Yadda yadda," Tilly said. "Listen closely. I'm here because I get results. I know people. I know what works and what will sink a government. You think I'm a hired gun, but I'm a nuclear response. You're a screw. Don't screw with the screwdriver."

Jack ignored her. She might come in handy if he needed resources or permissions and someone had to light a fire under Hensley's ass. He asked, "Is Sergeant Walker going to join us, Chief Pope?"

Tilly again. "I saw him and told him not to bother. You can talk to him later. I don't need to hear a bunch of forensic jargon. I want results. I don't care what you've done unless you've caught the asshole that's messing Cato's plans up. Do I make myself clear?"

Jack took his cell phone from his pocket and said, "Just to make myself clear, I've been recording this conversation since entering the room. In the interest of transparency I can make this recording available to Claudine Setera and I'm sure she'll have an orgasm." He watched Tilly Coyne and saw a bit of perspiration on her top lip. "Or I can keep it for the memoirs I always wanted to write. I don't like being bullied. I don't like self-important pricks. I don't like a lot of things. But to be crystal clear, Miss Coyne: I don't like you. When you get some power to back up your mouth, you can fire me. Until then, keep your mouth shut and your ears open or get the hell out. And you can tell Benet Cato what I said."

Tilly's mouth drew into a straight line, her jaws clenched and she gritted her teeth. He had to give her credit for having balls. She'd sat through all of this and still thought she was the alpha male.

Jack decided to finish her off. *In for a penny, in for a pound.* "Have you heard of Murphy's Law, Miss Coyne?" He didn't wait for her to answer. "Murphy's Law says don't screw with Jack Murphy. You should take that to heart. Now, if you're done marking your territory, I'd like to answer these men's questions. I have an investigation to get back to. You're dismissed."

The Chief's lips twitched in a quick smile.

Tilly's face was a mask of rage. She started to speak, but Jack interrupted, stood and pointed at the door. "I'm sorry if that wasn't clear enough. I said *get out!*"

Tilly rose from the chair and walked to the door. She opened it and said evenly, "I've got things to do. Call me if you make any progress." She left without another word or a glance back.

Jack watched Judy Mangold buzz her through the doors and flip her the bird as she left.

Jack gave Judy the thumbs-up and returned to his seat, awaiting his punishment.

"I apologize for my detective, Mr. Mayor," Chief Pope said.

"Not at all," Hensley said. "Magnificently put, Detective Murphy, even if it bounced right off her. That woman has a hide like a rhino. Please continue with the briefing. Chief Pope, please ask your sergeant... uh..."

"Sergeant Walker," Jack offered.

Hensley said, "Have Sergeant Walker called back to the meeting if he's not too busy."

Jack saw Walker come in the door and say hello to Judy Mangold. Jack motioned for him to join the meeting and said to him, "I thought you were ordered not to come to the meeting?"

"She's not the boss of me," Walker said with a grin. He was, of course, referring to Tilly.

Walker was introduced to the mayor and when they were all settled around the table, Jack said, "Do you want the short or long version?"

"Jack, you might want to wait until I give you my report," Sergeant Walker said.

He was given the floor.

Walker said, "I have the ballistic comparisons from the bullets and casings from Reina Day's scene, Mrs. Day's murder, and the one Sergeant Mattingly found at Harry Day's murder scene. I was told there was a spent casing found by retired Detective Dan Olson at Max Day's murder scene, but that is not available."

Jack noticed Walker had skirted the issue of Olson's mishandling of evidence.

Chief Pope interjected, "Mr. Mayor, Jack and Liddell are working Max and Harry Day's murder cases. They are assisting the county sheriff in the murder of Mrs. Day. And we are keeping them in the loop on the assault on Reina Day."

The mayor shook his head sadly. "How can one family be so unlucky?"

Jack said, "Not unlucky, Mr. Mayor. Targeted." He let that sink in for a moment before saying, "These cases all appear to be connected, by victim if not by a suspect."

The mayor seemed to be lost in his thoughts and said nothing.

Walker continued: "The shell casings are all .50 caliber. Hornady .50 caliber Action Express, three hundred grain brass jacketed hollow points. Sergeant Mattingly found one of the .50 caliber casings at Harry Day's murder scene. Six of these were found at the cemetery where Reina Day's car was shot up. County CSU found one of these at Amelia Day's house and they found the projectile.

"Ballistics show they weren't all fired by the same gun. There are two .50 caliber handguns involved. The six from Reina's assault match the casing from her mother's murder. The one from Harry Day's murder doesn't match any of the others."

Mayor Hensley asked, "So the same person who killed Mrs. Day also tried to kill her daughter, Reina? And a different person killed Mr. Day? Is that what you're saying?"

"Not necessarily, sir," Walker answered. "The same gun was involved in Reina and Mrs. Day's cases. Another gun of the same caliber was used in Harry Day's case. Whether they were both owned or fired by the same person of different persons will be hard to prove. We were unable to get any latent fingerprints from the shell casings, sir."

The mayor said, "So the same gun that shot at the daughter, later killed the mother. Is that right?"

"Yes, sir," Walker said. "The gun that killed Harry Day may be connected to the one that we suspect killed his son, but we don't have a shell casing from the boy's case. Either one wasn't found, which is a possibility, or it has been disposed of because of the age of the case. That's the oldest case, sir."

"Disposed of?" the mayor asked.

Chief Pope jumped in. "In cases as old as Max Day's, sometimes evidence is misfiled or was disposed of. We tightened up our handling of evidence a long time ago, but this was almost before even my time."

"I would think you never disposed of anything involving a murder case," Mayor Hensley said.

Walker changed the subject. "My news is that we found a slug—a projectile—in the dash of Reina Day's car. It was sufficient to match to a weapon if we find one."

If the mayor saw the condition of the property room he would understand why there needed to be more money in the police budget. There was too little room and too big of a job for one person to maintaining evidence properly. It would all come to a head one day when an attorney filed for dismissal of charges, citing the conditions in which evidence was stored and maintained. Sergeant Simms was working diligently to straighten out five decades of crap, but it was like emptying a lake with a spoon.

Jack said, "A witness at the cemetery said the gun being used was a Desert Eagle .50 caliber semiauto."

Walker said, "That's a strong possibility, but there are other semiautos that fire the .50 caliber. Not that many, but a few. Unless we find *the* gun it will be hard for me to make a definitive match."

Mayor Hensley interrupted. "I don't understand something. Do you mean to tell me you're involving us in a Vanderburgh County investigation? Mrs. Day's murder happened in the county. We don't have jurisdiction, unless I'm mistaken."

Jack said, "Mr. Mayor, we will be working alongside the county police. They have jurisdiction, but in a case like this we need to share information and resources. We do this all the time."

"And you say all these cases are related, yet you don't think they were done with the same weapon. Is there one killer or two? Or three or four, for that matter. Next thing you'll be telling me is we have a serial killer that's killing again after three decades. The public will be terrified. I can't have that. They'll think me negligent. The news media is already saying the police department covered up the boy's murder. If they can't trust their law enforcers, they won't trust their mayor."

Thatcher Hensley rose from his chair unsteadily and color had bloomed in his cheeks. "Well, gentlemen, I'll leave you to it. I have much to do. My mind was occupied and I didn't hear much of what was said after Miss Coyne's interruptions. I trust that you will get to the bottom of this, Chief Pope. I think your men are doing great work. Keep me informed." And with that, he left the room. Jack got up and shut the door.

"He doesn't have a clue what he's gotten into, does he?" Jack asked.

"He's a good man, basically, but I think he's ready to take his bows in public and go home," Pope said. "This is getting a little deep for someone who has a month left in office. He's a proud man. He doesn't want this to stain his reputation."

It always came down to saving face for a career politician. The fact that three people from the same family were ruthlessly murdered meant nothing. Jack expected no less, but it still pissed him off.

Screw his reputation, Jack thought, but said, "I understand, Chief." But he didn't understand. Every one of them in the room had more to lose than Hensley. Hensley could walk away. They couldn't.

Jack continued his briefing. Some things the Chief and Captain had already heard from Mattingly, but they hadn't heard Olson's story and denial that there was a fight at Rex Mundi or signs of a fight at the cemetery the night of Max's murder. Jack told them about the Xerox copies of two Polaroid photos that Mattingly had given Mrs. Day after Harry was murdered. The original Polaroids, like the case file, were missing. Jack told them about Olson's suspicion that Mattingly was having an affair with Mrs. Day, or that he was dealing in stolen guns with Harry, or that they were running drugs. They all agreed that the stories were so different and yet so similar that someone was lying.

"This all started with the death of Max Day," Jack said. "When Harry wasn't happy with the police investigation and basically started his own investigation, I believe that's what led to his being killed. Then it's quiet from 1984 to now, until Richard Dick is recorded by Reina Day, and they go to Claudine. The killer must have been concerned the investigation would be reopened."

"That seems logical," Captain Franklin said, "but how did the killer know the Days were going to see Claudine? The only ones they told about the recording were Benet Cato and Claudine. Claudine was the one who brought it to us."

"Richard must have told someone about going to see Mrs. Day," Jack said. "Whoever that was knew it was a stupid move and that set the ball in motion. Or Dick realized he'd screwed up going to Mrs. Day. The person who tried to kill or scare Reina Day must have suspected she had some piece of evidence. Her purse was stolen. The recorder was taken."

Jack asked the Chief and Captain, "When you asked him to come to your office, did you have the feeling he already knew what it was about?"

Chief Pope said, "He may have suspected I knew he'd gone to see Mrs. Day, but he was genuinely surprised and angry when we started playing the recording for him. Is that your impression, Charles?"

Captain Franklin said, "He was embarrassed. But that doesn't mean he wasn't aware of the recording. It's hard to say."

"You both knew Captain Dick, right?" Jack asked.

"Are we back to the cover-up, or is there a motive for murder?" Chief Pope asked.

"Both," Jack answered truthfully. "What can you tell me about him?"

Chief Pope chuckled, but there was no humor in it. "He was a…stern man. He was a Captain when I came on the department. Maybe motor patrol, but I seem to remember him being in investigations. No one seemed to like him. Some stayed clear just because he was hard to please, but most feared him. He was quick to lay blame if he ran into a problem with an investigation. Motor patrol was his favorite target."

Jack thought, "Like father, like son."

Jack asked, "When his son came on the department, how did he treat him?" Jack wasn't sure why he'd asked that question, but no information was ever wasted when you had no information.

"I never really thought about it," Chief Pope answered thoughtfully. "But you could tell that Richard worshipped the ground his father walked on. Thomas Dick was the man who Richard came to be. Personally, I prefer Richard to Thomas. There was something hard and cruel in that man."

Jack asked the question. "Do you think Thomas Dick is capable of murder?"

Pope said, "Jack, you've been a detective long enough to know that anyone is capable of killing, given the right set of circumstances. The nicest, most religious person joins the military and kills the enemy. The reason for the killing needs to be justified. Does that fit Thomas? I don't really know. Did Thomas kill Harry? I can't tell you. But he could very easily have been behind covering up his son's implication of involvement in the death of Max Day."

Jack digested this and asked, "What can you tell us about Dan Olson?"

Pope didn't have to think. He said, "Olson was dishonest. Everyone knew that. He retired long ago, but I think he was under internal affairs investigation when he left. He was a detective, then made sergeant and stayed in investigations instead of going to motor patrol. If he showed up on one of your runs you never expected the case to go well. I don't want to speak ill of someone who's not here to defend themselves, but I would say all this to his face. Do you think he killed Harry to cover up something he did wrong on Max's investigation?"

"It's possible, Chief," Jack said. "But he isn't the one that shot up Reina's car. According to our witness that guy ran like a gazelle. Olson needs a nursing home."

"And that leaves Thomas Dick out as well," Captain Franklin added.

"Good point," Jack said.

"That leaves us with Dick, Needham, and James," Liddell said. "They're the only ones that would fit the description from Reina's case."

Jack didn't say anything, but he wasn't going to rule anyone out yet. It was possible there was more than one person involved in these attacks. Working together, or working separately, but accomplishing the same thing. To stop an investigation into the earliest murder. Max Day.

Jack said, "Mattingly and Olson should be able to tell one story, but they're giving conflicting accounts and pointing fingers at each other. One thing they both agree on is that these killings are meant to put an end to the Days' meddling."

"Who do you believe?" Captain Franklin asked.

"They both made some good points, Captain," Jack said. "My gut goes with Mattingly and tells me Olson is a liar. But if you've followed a case for over thirty years, maybe some of his thoughts have been skewed by what he thinks he remembers. Olson seemed more concerned with keeping Captain Dick out of the investigation than he did about being accused of helping with a cover-up himself."

Sergeant Walker said, "Well, I've got some good news for you. Sergeant Simms found some of the evidence in the Max Day case. A paper bag with some broken beer bottles. She also found a tire iron with blood on it. She said they'd fallen behind one of the shelves."

"It's a miracle Simms found anything," Chief Pope said. "I was a detective when someone got the bright idea to purge the oldest evidence from the property room to have more space. The city didn't have a budget to expand the area. A lot of things from closed cases got pitched, sold at auction, or burned, as well as old unsolved cases."

"That's the kind of forward thinking I've come to expect from those days of policing, Chief," Jack said, then, "Did I just say that out loud? I'm sorry."

"So, where are we, Jack?" Chief Pope asked.

"We know that the ballistic evidence connects Max, Harry, Reina, and Mrs. Day's cases. We suspect there was a cover-up. We suspect retired Sergeant Olson was involved in the cover-up. Sergeant Mattingly is the single known person to come up in all the cases. He found two of the bodies and found Reina. It's still a little of a stretch for a coincidence."

"I agree, Jack," Captain Franklin said.

"Should we be suspecting Mattingly? Maybe take him off duty until this is over?" Chief Pope asked.

Captain Franklin answered that. "I don't think that's a good idea. We know where he is right now. If we temporarily relieve him we'll have to assign surveillance. Let's wait and see what Jack comes up with."

Liddell said, "What about the Deputy Chief? He's the pièce de résistance in this."

He got his answer when Chief Pope said, "If there's nothing else, gentlemen, let's all get back to work."

Jack said, "Chief, just one thing. I heard Claudine Setera might be here. What's her status, or can I push her off a bridge? Metaphorically speaking."

Chapter 30

Jack and Liddell drove to the Vanderburgh County coroner's office to meet with Little Casket. When they were buzzed inside they were met by a gentleman holding a calabash meerschaum pipe and wearing a wool shawl-neck sweater at least two sizes too big. He was tall and shaped like a bowling pin: narrow shoulders, thick hips and legs. The sweater's pocket bulged with a leather tobacco pouch and was tar-stained.

Little Casket came down the hallway carrying a tray with four coffees on it. She said, "This is Dr. Eric Schirmer, the coroner-surgeon who, before he retired, performed the autopsies on Max and Harry Day."

"I'm Detective Jack Murphy and this is—"

"I'm well aware who you both are," Dr. Schirmer said. "Detective Murphy. Detective Blanchard," he said, shaking hands with each of them. "You two remind me of my past. Cops and coroners were well acquainted. Quite a few detectives were required to assist me with the autopsies. A few of them passed out when you asked them to do something as simple as remove the top of the skull."

Jack had felt nauseous himself during the first post he had attended. It was done in the garage of a funeral home on a body that had been laying in the heat for two weeks. They had to scoop it onto a body bag because it came apart when they tried to pick it up.

"Let's get comfortable, shall we?" Little Casket said.

Jack and Liddell were caught off guard by her courteous behavior.

"Yes. Let's," Liddell said.

Little Casket glared at him and shoved the tray into his hands. "Make yourself useful, Hoss."

Dr. Schirmer chuckled at that until it turned into a coughing spasm. Little Casket took him by the arm. "Let's get you to the conference room, Dr. Schirmer."

Schirmer shook her loose. "Unhand me, woman. I need to speak to these men. In the autopsy room, if you don't mind. Get my case, will you? There's a good girl."

Little Casket hurried off and came back with an aged brown leather case. They went to the autopsy room. Dr. Schirmer stopped in the doorway and said, "Imagine what we could have done with a place like this, Lil?"

He instructed her to put his bag down on one of the stainless-steel autopsy tables and opened the flap. He took out several X-ray films and said, "Where's the damn—Oh, there it is." He took the X-rays to the light box mounted on the wall and began putting X-rays under the clips.

Jack whispered to Little Casket, "Does he have the autopsy reports?"

Schirmer said, "I'm ninety years old and can't get around like a twenty-year-old, but I sure as hell haven't lost my hearing. Have I, Lil?"

Lil?

Schirmer said, "I have those reports and more. What you make of it is up to you. We had to rely on detectives for a second pair of hands. No money for a pathologist assistant back then. Budgets and favors were something we had to get with blackmail. Just me and Lil. Isn't that right, Lil?"

Little Casket smiled.

Schirmer said, "She wasn't so quiet when she worked for me. What's important is what I have for these detectives." He flipped a switch that turned the light on.

"These are X-rays of Maximillian Day. I had copies made and given to me. I understand from Lilly that her copies are no longer in her files."

"The whole damn file is missing," Little Casket complained. "Excuse my language, Doctor."

"I performed the autopsy myself. One of your detectives was present for part of it—Detective Olson, I believe his name was—but he wasn't interested in anything but getting my report."

"Do you have a copy of the autopsy report?" Jack asked.

"I keep a copy of all my reports. The originals went in the coroner's files."

Jack examined the two X-rays, a skull in profile and frontal. "What am I seeing, Dr. Schirmer?"

"I was told by Detective Olson that this boy was shot with a large-caliber weapon." He pointed to the profile view of the skull. The left side of the skull near the ear and the skullcap were not there. Instead there was a jagged, cratered edge. "See here," he said and put his finger beside a shadow on what would be the right side of the victim's head.

"I see a pencil-sized shadow," Jack said. "What is it?"

"That's the point of entry. You can't see it clearly on the X-ray, but this wound wasn't caused by a lead projectile. My notes explain. I'm sorry I don't have any 35mm pictures. You'll have to take my report and my word for it."

"What was the cause the death, Dr. Schirmer?" Jack asked.

"Compressed air," Schirmer said and watched Jack's expression. He tapped his finger on the pencil-shaped shadow on the right side of the X-ray. "That's the entry point." He pointed to the left side of the skull, where a funnel-sized crater was missing. "That's where the blast exited."

Jack said nothing.

"I can see you don't believe me. Detective Olson didn't believe me, either."

Jack said, "It's not disbelief, exactly, but most of Max's brain is missing, along with the left side of his skull. A rifle bullet or a contact gunshot might do that. But compressed air?"

Schirmer said, "The victim was reportedly found in the driver's seat of his car. Brains and tissue were all over the ceiling and driver's-side window. The windows were up. Isn't that right?"

In the skimpy case file Jack had there was no mention of the windows being up or down. Olson had told them the blood and brains were on the windshield and all over the passenger side of the car. He thought Max had been shot from outside the car, and then waffled on that.

"Did Olson tell you the condition of the car, or did he show you photos?"

"Olson said the driver's window was up. That would indicate the shot had to come from someone on the passenger side of the car, correct?"

"Olson led us to believe the shooter was standing outside the car," Jack said.

"Then the window would have been damaged. According to Olson, the window was intact. The injury was close contact, so the killer must have been inside the car. Maybe in the passenger seat, maybe in the backseat. I can't tell you that. But he had to be close to cause that kind of wound."

"Okay, let's say the killer was in the passenger side of the car. Inside. What kind of compressed air weapon does this kind of damage?"

"A diver's weapon. A shark dart or something like it."

"Did you say a shark stick?" Jack said incredulously. He'd seen them being used in movies to kill aggressive sharks, but the idea of someone getting in the passenger side with a spear-sized weapon was really out there.

"I assure you I don't have dementia, Detective Murphy. This boy was not killed with a lead projectile. It was a projectile of compressed air. CO_2, to be exact. I'll explain. The skin around the entry point appeared to have been flash frozen. The skull was distorted, the scalp was torn open, much of the brains were expelled through the tear, and the rest were turned to mush. But the inside of the skull was ice cold at the time of the autopsy."

Dr. Schirmer opened his bag again and took out a textbook and an old magazine. The cover of the magazine read *SCUBA*. The textbook was a very old medical manual from World War II depicting injuries. A page was marked.

"With a gunshot, a lead projectile, fired into the side of the head, you would see stippling around the wound. The gas behind the bullet enters the skull and fills the cavity, causing the skull to literally explode. It happens in microseconds. With CO2, the wound fills with frozen air—not so fast as from a gunshot—and the skull bulges and opens like you're seeing here. I can promise you, this is not a wound caused by a lead projectile."

Dr. Schirmer opened the book to a black-and-white photo of a man's body lying on a steel autopsy table. The body was disemboweled from the pubic area to the solar plexus. Schirmer turned the page to a close-up of the torn skin and put his finger on the photo.

"Do you see that? That little mark there, and there." Schirmer was pointing to the edge of the skin. Jack could see an abrasion. Small. Round. Like a puncture mark. Similar to the wound on Max's X-ray.

"In this photograph, you can see where the shark dart entered the stomach just below the sternum. This was an accidental death, not a murder, but my point is this weapon is designed to inject air suddenly into the shark, and in effect, blow it up." An inset picture showed a round handle, about three-quarter inch in diameter, with a three- or four-inch spike protruding from the end. The spike was round like a tenpenny nail, only larger, and a piece of orange plastic was clipped on it where it entered the handle. Another inset picture showed the handle in pieces with a CO2 cartridge screwed into the handle at the spike end.

Schirmer said, "Imagine what this would do to a person's head."

Jack imagined the exact damage they had seen on Max's X-ray.

"The tip of the dart is extremely sharp, like a needle, to allow it to penetrate a shark's thick hide. It could easily penetrate a human skull, especially on the side where the bone is not so thick."

He pointed to the inset picture again. "The dart is hollow. Like a big hypodermic needle, if you will. The compressed air is released when the CO2 cartridge is ruptured and pushed through the dart. It's like an explosion of air and not gas created by igniting gunpowder. Its purpose is to kill sharks or predators, not to deter them. The air creates a cavity that expands until it causes what you see here. This poor man was accidentally stuck with the dart and the expanding gas literally eviscerated him."

Jack didn't know what to say. This put a new spin on the case.

"I know you're skeptical, Detective Murphy. I've had personal experience with sharks. I wasn't always a doctor. I was a Navy Seabee and I've used these, or a variation of them. I'm sure with the world at your fingertips, given the current technology, you can find many other examples of these types of deaths."

Jack turned a couple of pages. In another picture the shark dart was attached to a pole. He wondered if it could be detached.

"Can this be used like a knife?" Jack asked.

Schirmer opened the magazine to an advertisement for a Farallon shark dart. "The company doesn't make this for divers any longer, but they are still available for military use. As you can see, the handle and dart are screwed onto a longer spear, but the CO_2 cartridge can be used with just the handle. Like a big ice pick."

"Were these available in 1980 when Max was killed?"

"The first I heard of them was in the late 1960s. Sharks aren't as big of a problem for divers as television makes out. They're like our Lil here. You don't want to piss them off or you'll get bit."

Little Casket grinned and thumped Schirmer on the arm.

"I have to sit for a minute," Schirmer said.

They retreated to Little Casket's office. She made another pot of coffee. They relaxed and drank coffee while Jack and Liddell absorbed what the old surgeon had said.

Dr. Schirmer finished his coffee and said, "Let's get to it." He got up and they all followed him back to the autopsy room. He was limping now and Little Casket was visibly resisting taking his arm.

When they got back to the light box and X-rays, Jack pulled one of the desk chairs over for Dr. Schirmer. "Sit," he told the doctor and Schirmer didn't protest.

"You have more for us," Jack said.

"Lil, take all of those down except the profile one," Schirmer said to Little Casket. "Now get my bag."

She did as he asked and he took another set of X-ray films from the bag. Little Casket clipped them to the light board. One was an X-ray of a chest, the other a left shoulder.

"These are Max's?" Jack asked.

"They are. I want to show you what that boy endured before someone killed him," he said.

"There"—he pointed to a rib on the X-ray. "See that break? See the jagged edges? That's from a direct blow from a blunt object."

"A tire tool?" Liddell asked.

Schirmer said, "Could be. Yes. Whatever it was, it was swung very hard. And by a left-handed person. The blow to his ribs damaged his lung. That's not what killed him, but it would have, given time."

He moved onto the X-ray of the shoulder. "Here we have a fractured left clavicle and damaged acromioclavicular joint. That's where the clavicle joins the shoulder. See where the joint is separated here? You can't see the other injuries on the X-rays, but my report indicates a bruise on his right ulna near the wrist. Nothing was broken, but it appeared he fended off a blow. He also had abrasions on his face and the knuckles of both hands. He was definitely fighting when he took this beating."

"Did Olson tell you a tire iron was found at the scene?" Jack asked.

"If I had been told, it would be in my report. It's not."

"Got it," Jack said.

"We have some new information that suggests Max was in a fight the night he was killed. That's between us," Jack said.

"Who am I going to tell?" Schirmer said, dismissing the notion with a wave of his hand. "Detective Olson attended the post and I showed him the X-rays just like I'm showing you. He said he didn't see anything unusual on the X-rays. He insisted it was a gunshot. He seemed in a hurry for the autopsy report and suggested very strongly that I stick with the obvious and say the boy was shot in the side of the head. I didn't agree and I said I wouldn't put my name on a finding like he was suggesting."

"You say he suggested very strongly. Do you mean he threatened you, Dr. Schirmer?" Jack asked.

"No one would dare threaten the doc," Little Casket said.

"I told him to go to hell," Dr. Schirmer said. "I couldn't prove the weapon was a CO2 shark dart, so I gave a finding that the instrument of death was unknown. Where my report went after that is anybody's guess, but I kept a copy just in case I was called to court. I never was."

Jack asked, "If you had questions, why not a coroner's inquest?"

"Detective Murphy, there hasn't been a coroner's inquest in Indiana since the late 1800s. Plus, I didn't think it would change anything. The police were still investigating and I didn't want to interfere. No suspect was ever found."

Jack knew what the political climate in Evansville was back in the days of Max's murder. A coroner was an elected position and he wouldn't want to rock the boat too much. "You're sure it was Detective Olson you spoke to?" Jack asked.

"Dan Olson. The man had no imagination, and imagination is a necessity for a good detective, don't you think?"

Lilly jumped in again. "Olson was a moron. He couldn't think his way out of a paper bag. The dumbass!"

"Language, Lilly," Dr. Schirmer reprimanded.

"Sorry, Doctor," she said, chastened.

"A shark dart," Jack said again.

"Yes. I've got my report for you and supporting documents. I would like a complete copy back, if you don't mind."

Little Casket took the file and hurried off to make the copies.

Jack imagined the handheld shark dart. The killer in the passenger seat. Max was already hurt. His lung collapsing. The killer stabbed him and blew his head off.

Schirmer said, "I suggest you should talk to someone in the Navy. Or Special Forces. Maybe at a dive school. Someone familiar with the tools of the trade."

Jack didn't doubt Schirmer believed the weapon was a shark dart. If it was a CO_2 weapon the injury could have appeared to have been from a large-caliber handgun.

"You performed the post on Harry Day, Max's father."

"I did. The cause of death was a contact gunshot wound to the back of the head. I knew Harry. Hell, everyone did. He was generous with people in law enforcement, and I guess that included the likes of me."

"You don't happen to have a copy of Harry Day's autopsy report do you, Doctor?"

"I knew you'd ask." He retrieved another X-ray film from his case and put it on the light board next to the X-ray of Max Day.

"You see?" Dr. Schirmer asked.

Jack saw. There was a perfectly round hole in the back of Harry's skull. The front of the skull and most of the sinus cavity were obliterated.

Schirmer added, "This was a large-caliber handgun. See the stippling around the entry."

Stippling was when burned and unburned cordite, or gunpowder, gathered at the site of entry and adhered to the tissue, which formed a black circle or pattern. The stippling showed up on the X-ray as a shadow.

"I'd say the barrel was an inch or two from his head. Detective Olson came in with the body and stayed a short time. He didn't like to watch. He called the murder a 'robbery gone bad'. I remember him using those words several times. Even after all these years. It was like he had practiced saying them."

"Did he take an autopsy report?" Jack asked.

"Yeah and then Sergeant Mattingly came in about a week later. He was suspicious that Harry's murder was more than just a robbery. He said the family was auditing the store inventory but nothing seemed to be missing. In fact, he asked questions about the boy's murder."

"Did you tell Sergeant Mattingly what you told us about Max Day?" Jack asked.

"Yes. He asked for a copy of my autopsy report, but I told him he'd have to get it from Sergeant Olson. Sergeant Olson told me not to give it to anyone and he had mentioned Mattingly specifically. I don't know if he thought Mattingly was a suspect, or if he just didn't like the man. Personally, I didn't know Mattingly well. I didn't tell him I had copies. Why? Is that important?"

"Maybe," Jack answered.

Dr. Schirmer shrugged and said, "Well, I guess I've answered all your questions. The Max Day death has troubled me greatly. And now the mother being murdered. It will be interesting to see if she was killed with the same weapon that killed Harry. Two murders in the family might be a coincidence, but three...never."

Jack didn't believe in coincidence. The revelation that Max didn't die from a gunshot threw a wrench in the works, but he was sure these murders were committed by the same person or persons.

Dr. Schirmer said, "I'm happy to see these murders being investigated again. But for now, I'm an old man and an old man needs his rest. I'll let you get back to work. I have some catching up to do with my little rose."

Jack eyebrows tented.

Schirmer smiled warmly at Little Casket. "Little Rose was her nom de guerre when I was the coroner. Did she tell you that? No. I'm sure she wouldn't."

Liddell couldn't hold it back. "But I can see why you would call her that. She's our little rose too. Always smiling and always so cheerful. So much fun to work with."

Lilly was careful to not let Schirmer see the death-star glare she focused on Liddell.

Chapter 31

Dennis James was a devout Catholic. He'd forgotten that about Dennis. They'd all gone to Rex Mundi Catholic high school where Religion 101 and 102 were required classes. He himself had stopped going to any church many years ago. He didn't see the point. Religion didn't advance anyone. Success was more important than spiritual needs. He did unto others as they thought they could do unto him. He was better at it.

He made a few calls and found that Dennis went to the 8:00 mass at St. Anthony's every Saturday. Still. Tomorrow was Saturday. He would likely find Dennis there. It was time for Dennis to stop worshipping and meet his maker. The daughter, Reina, had seriously pissed him off, but in the grand scheme of things she didn't matter. She knew nothing but the rumors and lies she had heard all these years. If she stayed out of his way, he might let her live. Might.

Chapter 32

Jack would have liked for Sergeant Walker to be present while they talked to Dr. Schirmer, but he hadn't expected to meet Schirmer. Liddell was able to get some good pictures of the X-rays and Schirmer promised to make them available if they were needed. The old surgeon didn't want to let them go and understandably so. Jack called Walker and they agreed to meet at the war room.

Walker arrived before they did and was in the war room talking to Angelina when they arrived.

"Angelina has some interesting information for you," Walker said.

"I need to tell you about this first," Jack said. "Sorry, Angelina."

Jack put the autopsy reports on the table and related what they were told by Dr. Schirmer. Liddell let Angelina download the pictures from his phone. She made prints and taped these to the whiteboard.

Walker examined the X-rays of Max's head. "A shark stick?"

"He called it a shark dart," Jack said. "How many murders have you heard of committed with something like that?"

"I've never even heard of a death like that. This goes beyond my training and believe me, I'd remember. But you've got to admit we've seen some pretty inventive weapons and weird killings," Walker said.

Jack said, "Neither Olson or Mattingly found the weapon at Max's or Harry's scene, but both thought the deaths were caused by a large-caliber handgun. Mattingly said Olson found a .50 caliber bullet casing at Max's scene, but Olson denied finding it. At Harry's scene, Mattingly found a .50 that didn't match the shell casings from Reina or Mrs. Day's scenes. Olson accused Mattingly of trying to grandstand or advance himself by claiming to find evidence."

Walker said, "I've worked with Mattingly on many cases, both as a detective and as crime scene. I've never had that impression. If anything, he takes the blame for his guys screwing up sometimes."

Angelina said, "When you know someone it's hard to see a bad side of them. Forget you know Mattingly and decide on what you do know, who you believe. What does the evidence tell you?"

"I think Olson is the one that's lying to us," Jack said. "He practically derailed the investigation from the get-go. Dr. Schirmer said Olson wasn't interested in the autopsy results and just wanted Schirmer to say it was a gunshot wound that killed Max. Schirmer showed us Harry's X-rays and it was obvious he'd been shot, but I agree with the doc about Max's being a different type of weapon."

Walker agreed. Angelina asked Liddell, "What do you think?"

"What he said," Liddell said.

Jack said, "Okay, Angelina. You're on. What did you find?"

She put her hand on top of a stack of printouts. "These are phone records for everyone you've given me. You don't have to go through them. I just wanted you to see that I really do work." She took the top sheet and said, "I'll give you the *Reader's Digest* version. First, I couldn't get phone records from thirty years ago. I had to start somewhere, so I started with Mrs. Day's phone records for the day she said Dick called her. She received a call from Dick's personal cell phone at eleven that morning. The call lasted one minute and ten seconds.

"Dick made four calls that day to phone numbers in Columbus, Ohio. The first call was made a few minutes after the call to Mrs. Day. Then around noon and the other around three p.m. The number he called is the switchboard at the Senate Building in Columbus, Ohio."

"Carl Needham?" Jack asked.

"Must be," Liddell said.

Angelina continued. "The fourth phone call was made at seven that evening to a cell phone with a Columbus area code. That cell belongs to Carl Needham. Senator Carl Needham. The call to Needham's cell phone lasted twenty-three minutes and seventeen seconds."

Liddell quipped, "That's a pretty long conversation, or a lot of Muzak."

"I can't tell you all four calls were to Needham, but I read online that thirty-one of thirty-three Ohio state senators have offices in that building. Needham is one of them.

"We can safely assume Dick and Needham were in touch the same day Dick went to see Mrs. Day. It would make sense to talk to the others involved in the fight with Max. But we still don't have a fix on Dennis James."

Angelina admitted, "If Dick or Needham called Dennis, I didn't find it."

"Do me a favor," Jack said. "Add Janet Cummings to your list. She's in her early twenties and works at Old National Bank. I'll call and get her info for you."

While he was saying this Angelina was punching keys. She said, "Don't have to. I've got her pulled up." She hit a few more keys and said, "Personnel records. Phone numbers. The number she's given the bank doesn't match any on the list I've run."

"She's tied to Dennis James somehow," Jack said. "Maybe. I don't know for sure, but why don't you see if you can make a connection?"

Angelina jotted a note.

"Angelina, how hard will it be to see if any of Mattingly's calls went to Ohio or to Dick's phone—Richard Dick or his dad Thomas?"

"You telling me how to do my job?" she asked.

"Just thinking out loud."

"Okay then," she said. "I already checked. Mattingly didn't call Ohio or either of the Dicks. And he didn't call Reina Day or Mrs. Amelia Day. I checked calls going back a couple of months and there was nothing to any of the people you gave me. He made a lot of calls from his cell and home phones, but I didn't check the recipients out. Do you want me to do that?"

"No need for that yet," Jack said. Mattingly was divorced, had two daughters and a son. His family would account for the majority of the calls. He didn't expect to find anything there.

She continued the report. "There were several calls from Mrs. Day's cell phone to a medical answering service the morning Reina was attacked. Two calls to Reina's cell phone and two to the answering service."

"Reina's cell phone wasn't with her property at the hospital," Jack said. "Can you keep an eye on it and see if someone tries to use it?"

"I tried to locate it," Angelina said. "It's been disabled. The last location was the cemetery."

"Figures," Jack said. He privately thought that he was dealing with a smart killer. Of course, the ability to locate a phone was common knowledge to every eleven-year-old kid in the country. But to have just shot a car up, rob and beat the owner in public, run from the scene, *and still* have the presence of mind to disable the phone—that took a special mentality.

Reina Day called Mrs. Day's phone several times, but the calls lasted only seconds. Reina's cell phone had placed a couple of calls to Channel 6 the same day as Dick's visit. After that there were several calls to and from Claudine Setera's personal cell phone.

"Reina called Channel Six a few hours after Dick's visit to Mrs. Day. There are so many calls from Claudine to various locations I'll have to work on that more. Unless you want me to concentrate on finding Dennis James?"

"Find Dennis James," Jack said.

"Okay, boss," she said and threw him a little salute.

"And see if Dick or Needham made any large withdrawals or transfers of money from their accounts recently," Jack added. "Specifically deposits to or any transfers or withdrawals using Old National Bank."

"I was getting to that," Angelina said. "Both of them have a flurry of financial activity. A week before the deposit in Dennis James's account, Dick transferred twenty-five thousand from his quite substantial savings to an investment company in Minnesota. Monarch Investments. The same week Carl Needham transferred thirty thousand of his personal savings into his private business account and from there it went to Monarch Investments in Minnesota. Financial companies have to register with the state where they are located in order to do business. Articles of incorporation need to be filed naming the officers, etc. Double Dick and Carl Needham are listed as CEO and CFO respectively. There is a silent partner listed: Dennis James. Dennis has no say-so or duties, he just collects part of the earnings."

"You're telling me Dick and Needham have an investment company in Minnesota?" Jack asked.

"It's not actually in Minnesota. That's where the business is licensed, but the infusion of funds is coming from Ohio and Indiana, like I said. Twenty thousand dollars was disbursed two days ago to Dennis James's bank account. I'm a genius," Angelina said.

Walker jokingly said, "Angelina, I thought you'd have this all solved by now. Who killed JFK?"

Angelina locked eyes with Walker. "Should I remind you I can ruin your credit rating?"

Tony looked away first. Smart man.

"Have you found anything else on Double Dick?" Jack asked. "Besides the Minnesota connection."

"He's divorced. His ex-wife is remarried to an Alaskan state trooper. His son died at the age of three. He lives a pretty frugal existence," she said. "He has a hefty savings and is making a good return on his 401K investments. For a dick, he's got a lot of money."

Jack didn't smile at her play on words. In fact, he felt an inch tall. He had shoveled insults on Double Dick for—well, since he'd known him. He'd never once imagined the man might have cause to be such a ruthless bastard. He thought, *There but for the grace of God go I.* When Jack became divorced he'd been able to throw himself into his job. Double Dick had thrown his authority and abuse at the people working for him. Dick was truly a sad case, but Jack still wouldn't piss on him if he was on fire.

"Now, his father, Thomas Harrison Dick, is a different matter," Angelina said and put a hand over her mouth, not quite covering a smirk. "I still can't say his name with a straight face. You know. Tom, Dick, and Harry. Never mind."

"The family must have a humorous way of coming up with names," Liddell said.

"A Dick by any other name..." Walker added.

"Don't encourage them, Tony," Jack said.

"Maybe we should start calling her Littlefoot," Walker suggested. "They make a good pair of cutups."

Angelina expressed her opinion by punching several laptop keys. "Your credit rating is fifty. You have three federal warrants outstanding for your arrest. And if you don't stop, I'll put the Child Sex Crime Unit onto you."

"Jesus, Angelina! You didn't?" Walker said, making his way over to see what she was doing on the computer.

"Nah. I just sent a message to my husband telling him I was going to kill you, so come bail me out."

"Message received," Walker said.

"Also..." Angelina drew the word out. "There were three calls to Captain Dick's home, two from Needham's cell, and a third from the Ohio Senate Building. All this morning. The calls were short and may have gone to an answering machine. I couldn't find any corresponding calls from Captain Dick's phone to anyone we've identified."

She paused to let Jack chew on that.

"And right after you left Olson's house this morning, he called a cell phone number that's not registered."

Jack asked, "A pay-as-you-go phone?" Angelina agreed.

"Can you find out where the burner was when the call was received?" Jack asked.

"Working on it, but burners are nearly impossible to trace."

"But not impossible?" Jack asked.

"I've got friends with NSA that might be able to, but I hesitate to use them unless this is national security. Even I can only go so far."

It wasn't a matter of national security, but it was a serious concern for the Evansville Police Department. If Double Dick became king he'd rule with an iron fist and a whip.

Angelina mistook Jack's silence as his consideration of going ahead with the search. "So, do I contact NSA?"

"No," Jack said. "At least, not yet." He smiled to let her know he was joking.

Jake Brady came from the kitchen and motioned for Jack. "Phone call."

Jack excused himself and answered the portable phone on the counter of the bar. He listened briefly, disconnected, and went back to the war room and said, "Reina checked herself out of the hospital and ran the security detail off."

* * * *

Liddell sped down Riverside Drive to a neighborhood Jack was intimately familiar with. While Jack and Katie were divorced he started dating the Chief Parole Officer in Evansville, Susan Summers. Susan owned an historic home on Sunset Drive that she had converted into a bed-and-breakfast. The B and B was a hit with visitors who wanted the true Evansville experience while in town for various events and it was close enough to walk to the Blue Star Casino riverboat or the new Ford Center stadium. Reina Day owned another of the historic homes, this one a three-story with an elevator at the west end of the park, eleven houses west of Susan's B and B.

As Liddell turned down Sunset Drive he saw a police car sitting on the wrong side of the street facing west. He slowed and pulled up beside the car. The officer rolled the window down.

"You here to talk to the queen?" the officer asked them.

"Why are you here?" Jack asked. "The woman you're protecting lives at the end of the block."

"Orders," the officer said. "She's refused protection. You here to relieve me?"

"We've come to visit the lady of the house," Liddell said and drove on. He parked in the driveway of the huge house at the dead end of the street. Sunset Drive was about two uninterrupted city blocks with houses on the north side of the street facing south. Each of the houses were built in the late 1800s or early 1900s by the wealthy and each had once been blessed with a picturesque view of the Ohio River. Progress had taken care of that blessing. So instead of watching the riverboat traffic move along Riverside Drive, the property owners opted to create a tree-lined private park. Now the park was open to the public and kids ran and screamed and slid down slides and threw up by the merry-go-rounds. Progress.

Liddell let out a whistle. "According to Angelina, she owns this outright. No mortgage. No husband. No children. I'd need a map with *you are here* on it to find my way to the bathroom."

"Let's go see why she's being so difficult," Jack said.

They went to the front door and rang the bell. The door was yanked open by a man with an angry expression and wearing only a Speedo. Speedos had gone out of style a millennium ago, but this guy was wearing a florescent yellow one with a bulging happy face on it that emphasized his scowl, among other things.

"She doesn't want to see you," the man said.

"I understand," Jack said. "But this is police business." Jack showed his badge and when that didn't get the desired cooperation, he pulled his jacket back, revealing his .45 Glock. "May we come inside?" Jack said and brushed past the man.

"Hey, you can't do that. I'm a law student."

"Do you know Murphy's Law?" Jack asked.

The man just stared at him.

Jack said, "Murphy's Law says: 'Don't screw with the man with a gun.'"

The man was about to protest when Jack heard a voice coming from the next room.

"It's okay, Aldo. I know them. You can go back to the tanning bed." Reina Day stepped into the large foyer and said, "And for God's sake, put some clothes on."

"You'll catch your death," Liddell said and mouthed to Jack, "Aldo."

"I was just getting dressed and I saw these two coming to the door, Reina. Sorry." He hurried away.

Reina said, "Aldo means well. He heard what happened and he's trying to protect me. He has a little crush."

"He appears… excited," Jack said and she tried not to smile.

"If you're here to give me a safety speech you can save your breath," she said.

"I've got plenty of breath, Reina," Jack said. "To be honest, I'm a little pissed at you."

Red began to creep up her neck, but before she could say anything Jack said, "I promised your mother that I would protect you and find the truth."

She shot back, "And see how well that turned out."

"You're going to make me regret getting involved, Reina. We're on your side. That doesn't make us very popular with the politicians. This is the type of case that ends careers even if they're solved. So instead of being a problem, why don't you use some of that brain and work with us?"

She was quiet for so long Jack thought she was working up a head of steam. Instead she said in a quiet voice, "Aldo is a black belt in Tae Kwon Do. I don't need extra protection. I'll be fine here. And I have patients. I'm going to work in forty-five minutes to prepare for a surgery and I don't need a policeman following me around making my patients nervous."

"I appreciate your work ethic," Jack said. "I take my work serious too. I'll make you a deal."

She crossed her arms.

"I want to keep an officer inside here. At least when you're home. And one to follow you to work. They will be invisible, I promise. I can even have the inside cop wear a Speedo to blend in."

She smiled and said, "I'm supposed to trust you now. After everything that happened. I think I'll turn down your deal and make you one."

Jack waited.

"You spend your time finding the bastard that killed my mother. I'm a surgeon. It takes my entire focus to perform safely. You're trying to work several things at one time and from experience, I know you'll miss something important. I don't want you or your department to worry about the media fallout. I can't help what they will do, but I will promise not to talk to the news again if you promise to stay out of my way."

"Okay. Deal," Jack lied. She couldn't stop them from posting a security guard to watch the park across the street, or one driving on city streets to Deaconess Hospital.

"I mean it. I've called the mayor and I *will* sue the city for violation of my civil right to privacy. If a car follows me, I will file harassment charges and that will add to my lawsuit. I can get a protective order if necessary. Please leave my house and do your job. The best thing you can do for me is to find the bastard that's killing my family."

She opened the front door and showed them out.

Once outside, Liddell said, "That went well."

Jack got on the phone. "Captain. She's refusing any and all protection?" He listened. "We came when we heard she was home from the hospital. Are you saying we can't go near her again?" He listened and ended the call. He turned to Liddell and said, "Before we got here, she'd threatened the Chief that she would get a restraining order. We can't even talk to her now."

"That doesn't make any sense," Liddell said as they got back in their car.

"Unless she doesn't want us to know what she's doing," Jack said. "Maybe she thinks she and Mr. Speedo can take this guy on by themselves."

Liddell said, "He was scary. I'll have nightmares tonight."

They made a U-turn and drove past the park. The sky was clear, the temperature had risen. In the park, two boys were being pummeled by a good-sized girl and trying to cover their faces to dodge the punches. She was screaming something that sounded like "I told you—"

"That's us, Bigfoot. Reina just kicked our asses," Jack said.

"Should we break the fight up?"

"Nah," Jack said. "She's just slapping them. To the victor go the spoils."

"It's a different world we live in, pod'na."

Jack called Sergeant Elkins and there was no progress on Mrs. Day's murder. Elkins wanted to meet them and Jack told him to bring his file to Two Jakes early tomorrow morning.

He called Angelina. She was still sifting through telephone records, IRS records, financials, gun registrations, and police records. The list of people with some involvement in all four cases had grown to over forty law enforcement, legal, and civilian persons. Jack didn't envy her the task.

"Angelina, find a stopping point and go home to Mark," Jack said. "Tomorrow is Thanksgiving. I'll see you after. Sorry, that's Sunday. Come in Monday."

"I can come in tomorrow, Jack. Mark will understand. He can make a Hungry-Man turkey dinner. I don't cook anyway. All he ever wants are steaks, hamburgers, or meat loaf. What is it with you guys?"

"You'll be here by yourself if you come in tomorrow," Jack said, although he planned to meet with Elkins. "Go to Buy Low and buy a Thanksgiving dinner. Mashed potatoes, dressing, cranberry stuff. He'll think you cooked all day."

"I'll have to do the airplane thingy with the fork to put that stuff in his mouth," she said and laughed.

"Get some rest. I'll need you sharp on Monday. We're going to find Dennis James and squeeze him for all he's worth." He ended the call.

"Does this mean I get to stay home Thanksgiving Day?" Liddell asked.

"Yes. You can eat a whole herd of turkeys, Bigfoot. I'm just going to meet Elkins for an hour to discuss what we can do."

"Did you know that a group of domesticated turkeys is called a *rafter*?" Liddell asked, surprising Jack with his useless knowledge.

"Then go eat a rafter," Jack said. "Hell, eat the whole roof."

Liddell chuckled. "What are you and your new fiancé going to be doing? I mean, after you meet with the sergeant?"

"What do you think? How about you?"

"I think I'm going to be explaining to Marcie why I'm going to get fired by the new mayor."

Jack agreed. They had a lot of circumstantial evidence, conflicting statements, missing evidence, and political pressure up the wazoo. They weren't exactly swimming in leads and if they interviewed Dick or Needham just before or on Thanksgiving, it would be used against them. Cops were portrayed as heartless and intrusive anyway. But the day after Thanksgiving was fair game.

He decided to take his own advice. Go home. Enjoy the day he truly could give thanks for. He'd been engaged for twenty-four hours and had spent most of that time at work. What a great start.

Chapter 33

The ringing came from far away. It was persistent and annoying. It stopped only to start again. Jack woke and remembered he'd left his cell phone downstairs in the kitchen. It was just after midnight per the bedside alarm clock. *Happy Thanksgiving, Jack.*

He disentangled his legs from Katie's and she rolled onto her side, still sleeping soundly. Jack got out of bed and quietly went down the steps to find the intruding sound. The ringing was coming from the couch where Cinderella lay sprawled out like the Queen of Sheba. Cinderella bared her teeth as he reached behind her and found the phone stuffed down in the cushion. The caller ID didn't display a number he was familiar with.

He answered anyway. "Who the hell is this?"

The voice was male. It was older and slurred. Drunk. "You need to get over here. I got something for you, Murphy."

The cobwebs were clearing from Jack's mind. "Olson?"

"You said call if I 'membered anything. I 'membered plen'y. I'm not waiting."

"Call me at a decent hour. Preferably when you're sober. I'm hanging up now."

"No. You gotta come now…" his voice trailed off and he mumbled some things. Jack caught the last word: *Sugar.*

Drunk and crazy and talking out of his ass. "I'll come tomorrow—sugar," Jack said, but the line was dead.

He debated going back to his warm bed and warmer bed partner. Curiosity got the better of him. Olson was paranoid and lonely and wanted to feel important again, so he'd fixated on Jack because he had taken the time to talk to him. He didn't want to encourage Olson to bend his ear every time he wanted company. He didn't like the man. But what if he really had something to tell him?

Jack muttered a profanity and padded back up the stairs to get dressed.

* * * *

Jack dressed as quietly as possible and as he passed by the room that would soon be occupied by a little Murphy, his heart swelled. He was going to be a father. It scared him shitless. The thought of going through all that again.

When he and Katie had gotten engaged the first time, they had talked about children. He'd teased her that he wanted sons. Plural. He was Catholic and so was Katie and he expected no less than seven children. All boys. When Katie became pregnant they were told the baby was a girl and unexpectedly, he'd felt his heart skip a beat. He wanted a girl after all.

And now history had repeated itself. They'd just gotten engaged and Katie was pregnant again. He wondered what the baby would be this time around. Another girl and they would name her Caitlyn and that thought made his throat tighten. No. Not Caitlyn. Caitlyn had died during birth. Katie had come close to dying too. He was overwhelmed with the possibility of losing everyone he loved.

He pushed the horrible idea away. This baby would live. He'd finish the nursery, spend more time at home with Katie and the baby—boy or girl—and quit his job, if that's what it took to make this work. He thought if he got mad enough he could do anything. And he was mad enough now. He'd take it out on Olson.

He left Katie a note on the kitchen table, closed the back door quietly, went to the garage, got in his Crown Vic, and said, "Olson. I'm going to kick your ass if you lied to me."

Chapter 34

He'd been told the old detective had gone downhill after retiring, but the six-foot fence and security system were extremely paranoid. Olson was surprised to see him, but invited him in and offered him a drink of some brand of rotgut whiskey, but didn't get out of his recliner to get an extra glass. They talked—or at least he asked questions and Olson remained silent. He seemed nervous, but he was relatively calm until he saw the Desert Eagle. He reached for the .45 in a holster attached to the chair's arm. But he was slow. Drunk and slow. Even drunk, Olson decided going for a gun wasn't such a good idea with a .50 caliber Desert Eagle stuck in his face. Now that he had Olson's attention, he'd asked what he told the detectives. He wasn't convinced it was nothing. Olson didn't have to play dumb. It came naturally.

To his credit, the old detective didn't beg for his life. He just smiled and picked up the television remote and pointed it at the TV. It didn't make sense that he would do that until he saw Olson's eyes cut toward the partially open front door. That's when it struck him as odd that a man so security conscious would leave the front door ajar. He was waiting for someone. Olson hit another button and floodlights bathed the front yard in light.

The butt of the Desert Eagle came down on Olson's head and he slumped in the recliner.

Outside, Murphy was caught in the middle of the yard like a deer in the headlights of a car. Murphy's arrival had taken him by surprise. More importantly, it had interrupted his getting information from Olson. He knew Olson had kept in touch with Dennis James. Olson had admitted as much when they'd talked on the phone earlier in the day. If Olson had only given up where James had gone to earth, cooperated a little, he might have lived a few more painful minutes.

He didn't want to kill Murphy. Not just yet. He could sense Murphy moving out in the yard. Then Olson moaned and cried out for help and had to be dispatched. The shark dart did so quietly, or as quietly as a head can explode when it was filled with CO_2.

Olson was of no further use. Murphy was just outside the door. He had to make a decision. Flee or kill Murphy. Murphy's shadow crossed the opening in the doorway and he made his decision. He fired a hail of bullets through the door just as Murphy was kicking it open. Murphy's idea of stealthy moves sucked.

* * * *

Jack pulled off on the grit shoulder a few houses down from Olson's. It was 1:00 in the morning. He would have called Bigfoot to go with him, but he didn't want to ruin his partner's holiday. Olson sounded plastered on the phone and was most likely going to read Jack the riot act for digging into the old cases or he wanted someone to reminisce about the old days or he wanted to shoot him because Olson was a paranoid asshole. There was a police saying that went, "Better tried by twelve than carried by six." If he had to shoot Olson he could always have his telephone records subpoenaed to show Olson had called him. He could defend himself in court. He didn't want to have to shoot someone in their own house on Thanksgiving morning.

Olson would be armed, so he would be too. He pulled his Glock, chambered a round, and kept it down by his side. In this neighborhood a gun wouldn't be out of place. It was better to be prepared than not.

Olson's gate wasn't shut. Jack thought, "Maybe it's a trap." Then he thought, "Maybe he's just really shit-faced and sat down on his remote." The lights were all off and Jack thought about calling for backup, but that would be hard to explain and he was trying to keep this quiet. He debated with himself. Pull the gate shut and go home. Go to the door and risk getting shot. In for a penny, in for a pound. He walked through the gate.

As he approached the front of the house he had another thought. He wasn't wearing a ballistic vest. Olson had an arsenal and was drunk. All he had were his balls and his Glock.

The temperature had dropped ten degrees and the neighborhood was eerily quiet. Not a creature was stirring. Not even an armed louse. There was a loud click and halogen security lights mounted over the gutters came to life, blinding him while he was still halfway between the gate and the front door.

He ran like hell, half-crouched, zigzagging toward the house. He pressed up against the wall, hoping not to get picked off like a duck in a shooting gallery. So far, so bad. He slid along the wall and reached the front door. It was cracked open a few inches. He squinted in an effort to blink the spots away that were clouding his vision. Still no sound from inside the house.

In the distance he heard a car radio pounding out a beat in time with his heart pounding in his ears. He checked all around: the street, both sides of the house, the door, and there was no movement, no sound, but he could feel a presence close to him.

Olson hadn't called out when the floodlights lit him up. He should be glad he hadn't been shot, but instead he felt a tightness in his chest that spread all the way to his crotch. He wondered what his dad would do. The answer was his dad would slap the crap out of him right now for being so stupid as to come to the house in the dark, knowing Olson was drunk and armed.

He reached for the door and heard a soft moan coming from inside. He pulled his cell phone out and hit the button for 911. He heard the operator say, "Nine-one-one. What is your emergency?" and at the same time a weak voice from inside was calling out, "Help me."

He left the line open and dropped the phone in his pocket. Holding the .45 in both hands, he put his back against the side of the door frame. Using his left leg, he kicked his heel back into the door, throwing it open. And then the fun began.

Splinters of wood exploded outward inches from his face, his arm and ribs felt a dozen bee stings, and thunderous explosions came from inside. Jack's eardrums felt the pressure of the blasts even with a wall between him and whatever cannon Olson was shooting. It sounded like a small howitzer.

Jack proned out on the ground facing the door, gun up, finger tight on the trigger, and yelled, "Olson! It's Jack Murphy. Stop shooting." The wall provided some cover, but if Olson stood in the darkness just inside the doorway, Jack could kiss his ass good-bye.

The shooting stopped. Jack yelled again. "Olson, it's Jack Murphy. Stop shooting." No response. He heard a door at the back of the house slam and feet pounding away from the house toward the alley. Jack came off the ground and cleared the side of the house when he saw a figure in black leap, cat-like, onto the roof of the small wooden shed at the back of the house. The hooded figure scrabbled for purchase on the sloped shingles for just an instant, caught hold and disappeared over the top. It definitely wasn't Olson.

Jack didn't pursue. He couldn't jump over the damn shed before the guy would be long gone. He went to the storm door. It was open against the wall; the glass was shattered and the door hung from one hinge. The steel entry door was wide open and it was pitch-black inside.

He backed against the side of the door and yelled, "Olson. It's me. Murphy. Don't shoot. I'm coming in." He quickly entered the room, moved to the side in a crouch, his gun sweeping the room, left to right and back. "Olson? It's Detective Murphy." Nothing.

The only light came from the streetlights and it was just enough for Jack to make out a doorway across from him. He felt a table's edge and a chair. He was in the kitchen. He moved toward the door opening and his foot hit something that clattered across the floor. He froze and breathed out slowly, quietly. Nothing happened. He moved on and felt around the wall, on the other side of the doorway and felt a light switch.

The house had an empty feel now. The intruder had left and he was alone, unless Olson was still inside somewhere. Maybe injured. Maybe waiting for Jack to show himself.

He flipped the switch and a light illuminated a short hallway. On the left was a smooth, bare wall. On the right were two closed doors. One undoubtedly a bedroom, the other a bathroom. He could see into the living room where he and Liddell had interviewed Olson yesterday morning. A loud clatter in the kitchen made him jump, gun pointed toward the noise. The refrigerator ice maker had dropped a load. On top of the refrigerator was a ceramic canister set. Papa Bear, Mama Bear, and on the floor was what was left of Baby Bear. The kitchen was neat and tidy, like nothing had been touched or broken, which would indicate a burglar. Except for Baby Bear.

Jack eased down the hallway and checked each room as he passed. Both were unoccupied. He made it to the front room and peeked around the opening. He could see the back of the leather recliner Olson had sat in. Nothing moved. He could hear the ticking of the ice maker as it reset itself.

Jack felt for a light switch, found it, flipped it, and saw an arm dangling from the side of the easy chair. Jack knew what he'd find when he walked around the recliner. He was right. Olson was in striped pajamas, slumped down, legs crossed at the ankles, an empty whiskey bottle lying at his bare feet. Olson's handgun was still in the holster on the chair's arm. Most of his face and the side of his head was gone. Not missing. Just blown across the back of the chair and across the man's shoulders. Brain tissue and goo dripped down the arm. The smell of burned gunpowder was mixed with the smell of human excrement and urine.

Olson's favored phrase came to Jack's mind. *Am I right? You know I am.* Only Jack changed the words. *Am I dead? You know I am.*

He pulled his cell phone out of his pocket. The line was still open and he could hear the dispatcher calling him. He heard sirens. Headlights washed over the walls of the room. Tires screeched outside. He put the phone to his ear and told dispatch his backup had arrived. He put the phone back in his pocket, held his gun over his head in one hand, badge in the other, and went out the front door, blinking into the glare of headlights and flashlights and shouts.

Chapter 35

A tired Sergeant Walker arrived and found Jack sitting in the back of an ambulance while a paramedic examined his face and top of his head with a small, powerful flashlight.

"Do I need to call the coroner for you?" Walker asked.

"Beat you to it," Jack said. "Little Casket's on her way."

"I was talking to the paramedic, Jack," Walker said. To the paramedic, he asked, "Will he live?"

The paramedic grinned. "He's got splinters in his face and if he'll hold still I'll try to wash the paint chips out of his eyes. The one in the house, though, may not make it. Most of his head is gone."

Everyone's a comic.

The medic irrigated Jack's eyes and in the background were floodlights with red, white, and blue emergency lights flashing across the front of the house. It resembled a tragic Christmas light show. All that was missing was a bloody blow-up Santa and the three wise reindeer.

"Olson?" Walker asked.

"Yeah. He was dead when I got here."

"Why were you here?" Walker asked, pulling on latex gloves.

"Olson called me. He was drunk and said he remembered something. I got here and the gate wasn't locked and his front door was open, like he was waiting for me. He's got a remote-controlled lock on the gate."

Seeing the security Olson had installed around the house, Walker asked, "He had a mental problem, didn't he?"

"Not anymore," Jack answered.

"How long ago?" Walker asked.

Jack thought about it. "He called me about thirty minutes ago and I came right over. The killer was in the house when I got here."

"Maybe he was forced to call you? Get you here."

"Maybe. He sounded drunk, but he didn't sound like he was being forced, or scared."

Walker shrugged. "Little Casket's on her way. Are you okay?"

"If this guy doesn't drown me," Jack said and Walker headed toward the house.

The medic shined a penlight in Jack's eyes, declared them clear of debris, and handed him a dry towel. Jack dabbed at his face and squinted down the street at a dark vehicle approaching. He was expecting to see the coroner's black Chevy Suburban, but it was a small SUV. When it came even with the ambulance, Jack could see it was a Suzuki Samurai. The driver leaned out the window.

Sergeant Mattingly was in street clothes. "Isn't that Dan Olson's house?"

Jack said, "Yeah. Olson's inside. Dead. Where'd you get that car? In an antique store?"

"Yeah. It was on the shelf right next to your sex life."

"You got me. Not that I'm knocking your dedication to duty, but what the hell are you doing here?" Jack asked. This was the fourth crime scene involving the murders where Mattingly had shown up, albeit he wasn't first to arrive this time.

Mattingly ignored the question. "Was he shot with a .50 caliber?"

"I don't know what he was killed with," Jack said truthfully. "But someone tried to kill me."

"Did you see the shooter?"

"Yeah," Jack lied.

"Good. Good. I guess he got away, then?"

"Yeah. He went over a shed and a six-foot fence like a hurdle jumper." A memory came to Jack. Mattingly was in his late fifties, but he was still competing in triathlons. Liddell had said something about that earlier. Jack had teased Liddell that if there was food at stake Liddell would be competing too.

"He must have had a car nearby," Mattingly said. "Do you have an alert out yet? I don't suppose you saw the vehicle?"

"Sarge, you're off duty. I've got this. Go home and get some sleep. I'll catch up with you tomorrow. You work this morning—right?"

"I can help," Mattingly offered.

"Thanks, but no," Jack said. "You should stay out of this unless we need to pick your brain some more." He could use an extra pair of eyes on this, but Mattingly had too much history with this case. That and Jack didn't want to see another good man get fired for daring to investigate the Dickster.

Mattingly gripped the steering wheel and said nothing.

Jack said, "Listen, Sarge. This could be a conflict for you. You're a prominent figure in several of these cases. I'm telling you this for your own good. Stay out of it unless I need you."

"Yeah. Okay." Another pause. "I just want to catch this bastard. Did Olson tell you anything on the phone?"

"I want to catch him too." His scalp smarted from the place where the paramedic had removed a huge sliver of wood. Luckily, it wouldn't require stitches.

"I hope the bastard comes after me," Mattingly said, grimly, did a U-turn, and sped down Fulton Avenue at top speed, which for a Suzuki was about twenty miles per hour, depending on the grade of the road.

A familiar Crown Vic came from the opposite direction and pulled up behind Jack's car.

Liddell got out and he was none too happy.

"You tell me to go home and then you go and get yourself shot at. You should have called me, pod'na."

"It was one o'clock in the morning, Bigfoot. We were supposed to be off today."

"You still should have called me."

Jack said, "I don't think this guy was trying to kill me."

"So those bloody spots on your face were an accident?"

"I think he meant to slow me down. We need to get in Olson's house."

"You said *we*. Does this mean you're going to include me now? How kind of you."

"Would you drop it?"

"Don't ever do that again."

"I promise," Jack lied.

"I forgive you. Now tell me what the hell you're doing here in the first place."

Jack told him the important parts.

"So, tell me. When Olson called you, what exactly did he say?" Liddell asked.

Jack recounted the conversation the way he remembered it and ended by saying, "He sounded like he was shit-faced drunk. Walker thought maybe Olson was forced to call me to come over, but he didn't sound like he was being forced. And like I said, if the guy wanted to kill me, he would have done a better job. He definitely had me outgunned and at a disadvantage."

"Who was that in the Suzuki?" Liddell asked.

"Mattingly. He must have heard the dispatch. He needs to stay away from this. We don't need the shit storm."

"The man gets around, doesn't he?" Liddell said thoughtfully. "I wonder what Olson was going to tell you. Any idea?"

Jack said, "We'd asked him about keeping any notes from the murders. Maybe he was going to give us his notes."

"You said the front gate was unlocked and the door was ajar. When we were here earlier he was locked up like Fort Knox," Liddell said and raised an eyebrow.

They were both thinking it might have been a setup. It could have been a lot of things. He was alive and Olson was dead. That's what was important.

Jack said, "He called me *sugar*."

"So that's why you were here. You sly old dog," Liddell said. "Wait. What about Katie?"

"I'm not going to even address the levels of wrong that statement makes. And I have an idea," Jack said. "Let's go inside."

They signed in with the crime scene log officer and met Sergeant Walker in the front room where Olson's body was slumped in the recliner. Jack told Walker the idea that had come to him.

"We're still working in the kitchen, but I'll take you in. Don't touch anything."

"Too late," Jack said. "I've been all through the house. And you're going to find Yeti footprints and body hair all over the couch in there."

"Where were you exactly?" Walker asked.

"As you know, we were here yesterday morning, but only in the living room, or the front room or whatever. I was in the front yard tonight and I heard the back door, so I came around. The guy was jetting. I came in the back door and walked through the hallway. I touched the light switch in the hallway. I opened the two doors down there and touched the light switch in this room. I didn't touch anything else and the troops arrived, and now here we are."

They followed Walker into the kitchen. The back door was still open and the storm door was bent outward.

"Nothing's disturbed much in here," Walker said. "What are we looking for, Jack?"

"Those," Jack said and pointed to the ceramic canisters on top of the refrigerator. "The baby bear one is broken on the floor, but that could have fallen off the table when he fled. Olson called me *sugar*. What if he meant sugar? The sugar canister."

Walker got one of his techs to take pictures of the refrigerator and the counters. He carefully took the two remaining canisters down from the top of the refrigerator and put them on the counter. Walker took the lid from the mama bear canister and it was filled with sugar.

Jack took an ink pen from Walker's pocket and stuck it in the sugar until he felt it hit something. Walker took a gallon-size evidence bag from a pocket and said, "Hold this open."

Jack did. Walker slowly poured the sugar from the container into the bag and stopped when something metallic poured out. Walker dug in the crystals and lifted a flat metal key with a number—111—stamped on both sides.

Walker said, "That's a locker key from the YMCA."

Jack took out his own keys and found one similar to the one they had just found. The City of Evansville offered the police department a membership at the YMCA at a highly discounted rate and suggested they use it. Most did. Jack did. But he didn't think he'd ever seen Olson there.

He called dispatch, got the emergency contact number for the YMCA, and called. The phone was answered by a woman who was none too happy to be awakened, but she agreed to meet the detectives at the YMCA in half an hour.

Little Casket said from the doorway, "I heard Liddell was here, so I thought I'd find you in the kitchen. You making cookies?"

"We didn't know you had arrived," Jack said.

"The body is in the front room," Walker said.

"I know. I walked past him to see what was so interesting back here. If you're done playing with the sugar, I got something to show you."

The men followed her to the front room and she stood close to where the victim was still slumped sideways in the recliner. "See anything familiar?" she asked them.

"A dead body," Liddell said.

Jack asked her, "Are you saying this is like Max's injury, Lilly?"

"You're supposed to be the detective," she said. "I'm just a lowly government employee. What would I know?"

He said, "Lilly, I was shot at a half-dozen times. There are .50 caliber shell casings all over the room." He motioned toward the silver shell casings crime scene had circled in chalk.

Walker bent over to examine the entry wound on what was left of Olson's head. After a few seconds he said, "She may be right, Jack."

Liddell shook his head and said, "As my daddy used to say, 'Shit fire and save the matches.'"

Chapter 36

An older gentleman wearing a gray work jacket with a cloth name tag that identified him as Lonnie unlocked the doors of the YMCA. Lonnie was even grumpier than the woman Jack had talked to on the phone. There was no small talk or introducing himself, just a scowl at being called in. Apparently, the manager had delegated this task to Lonnie.

"Lonnie, thanks for letting us in," Jack said. "We need to go to the locker room." Jack held the key out where Lonnie could read the number.

Without a word, Lonnie turned and walked toward the stairs.

"I guess we follow him," Liddell said.

They caught up with the man and walked up the stairs, through a fire door on the second floor, down a hall, past the elevator, and into the locker room. The middle of the locker room had been arranged as a mini-gym with an exercise bike, treadmill, universal weight station, and hand weights. This was for the members too lazy to go downstairs. There was a big-screen TV with comfortable couches and padded chairs. This was where the over-eighty crowd of old men sat around in their underwear—or not—arguing, comparing their various medical problems, and discussing the recently departed.

The remainder of the room was composed of rows of gym lockers with wooden benches bolted to the floors. Jack checked the number plates and stopped at locker number 111. He inserted the key.

"I can't let you do that," Lonnie said, and stood with his arms crossed, as if he'd just caught a kid stealing candy.

"Why is that, Lonnie?" Jack asked and turned the key. The door unlocked.

"Need a warrant," Lonnie said. "Beverly said I had to see a warrant before I let you *into* a locker. She said you could *see* the locker, not what's inside. We got a policy here that says—"

Jack opened the locker. "Lonnie. I assume Beverly is the lady I talked to on the telephone. The one who couldn't be bothered to come down here herself. Am I right?"

Lonnie's scowl deepened until Jack thought his face would implode or his head would melt.

Jack said, "Beverly didn't know that the owner of the contents of this locker was murdered a little while ago. Not her fault. We didn't tell her because she didn't get her lazy ass down here. So I'm telling you. We're investigating the murder. The victim can't object to our searching his locker because he's dead. Ergo, no warrant is needed. Now, unless you or Beverly are attorneys, or you want to need one, I suggest you sit down and stop interfering."

Lonnie sat down and muttered, "Beverly should have come herself."

"If it makes you feel better, Lonnie, tell her I threatened you."

Lonnie smiled and Jack saw why the man appeared to be scowling. Most of his teeth were missing or were blackened stumps. He had what Liddell called "summer teeth," so called because sum'r there n' sum' ain't.

Jack opened the locker. Black running pants were folded neatly on top of a small stack of *Playboy* magazines. On top of this were white running shoes. A black Grateful Dead T-shirt was on a hanger. Jack doubted Olson was grateful. Jack pulled latex gloves on and knelt down to go through the clothes when he saw the legal-size mailing envelope taped to the ceiling of the locker.

"What's this?" Jack pulled it loose. The envelope was sealed. He handed it to Liddell and stood up, taking a folding knife from his pocket.

Liddell turned the envelope to the other side and saw a name had been written on it in Magic Marker. "Captain D."

Lonnie was straining to see around Liddell's bulk and gave up, saying, "I was supposed to get his locker cleaned out if he died."

"Do you know what's in it?" Jack asked.

"Naw. Only that I'm to give it to the name on the envelope. I never saw what he'd written on it before. He made me swear I'd give it to the man and not open it or tell anyone."

Jack had no doubt Lonnie had been paid somehow for this little favor. Or Olson had something over Lonnie to force him to do so.

"Let's see what this is," Jack said and slipped the knife blade under the flap.

"You can't do that!" Lonnie said with anger and fear in his voice. "Now you need a warrant. That don't belong to Detective Olson. It was supposed to go to me and I ain't giving you permission."

Liddell muttered, "Everyone's a lawyer."

Jack opened the envelope. "Have a seat, Lonnie, or I'll handcuff you."

Lonnie sat on the benches where he could watch what Jack was doing. "You never read me my rights, you know. You can't arrest me."

Both Liddell and Jack said, "Shut up, Lonnie." He did and his shoulders dropped when Jack pulled a gallon-sized Ziploc bag filled with photos from the envelope. Jack opened the baggie and began going through the photos one by one and handing them to Liddell. One of the pictures was of a provocatively posed naked young lady. Jack turned the photo over and written on the back was *To my darling Lonnie*.

Jack held the picture up where Lonnie and Liddell could see it. "How old do you think she is?"

Liddell said, "She's what? Thirteen? Fourteen? Who is she, Lonnie?"

Lonnie came off the bench and made a grab for the picture, but Jack held it above his head. "Sit down, Lonnie."

Liddell put a hand on the man's chest and pushed him gently but firmly back onto the bench. "You got an office here, Lonnie?"

Tears welled in Lonnie's eyes and his breathing was unsteady.

"I'm just messing with you, Lonnie," Liddell said. "I won't get a warrant for your office, computer, or your home because you're going to tell us everything you know about Dan Olson and Captain Dick and about this envelope. Right?"

Lonnie wiped his nose on the sleeve of his jacket, snuffled, and wiped his nose again. He said, "We all called him Detective Dan. Came in here every Tuesday and Friday. He was a character. Kept us all in tears with war stories. Cop stories. I never believed he done all the stuff he claimed, but they was good stories. Car chases, shoot-outs, pinching hookers for information, pinching 'em in other ways, if you know what I'm saying. It was the kind of stuff you see in them old detective shows."

"He was a real character," Jack agreed.

Lonnie said, "I didn't want you getting in there because of that picture. I never met that girl. I swear. An' if there's any more pictures with me in 'em, they been doctored up. Photoshopped, they call it."

Jack waited.

"He said if I messed with the envelope he'd give Beverly the copies he had at home. She's a real bitch. She would cut me loose without a second thought. I'm not a prevert."

"Pervert," Liddell corrected.

"I'm not that, either," Lonnie said. "I mean, I ain't one a' them."

"We know you're not," Jack lied. "What else can you tell us? Were you and Detective Dan friends?"

"Well, we're not good friends now. We was, but you can see how he treated me. I suspected he had a good reason to need my cooperation. You know? But I didn't get in that envelope."

"Cooperation for what?" Jack asked and Lonnie explained. He seemed to be warming up to talking now that the threat of being exposed was over.

Lonnie sat with his hands in his lap, head down as he spoke. "Olson was divorced five times before he retired from the police. Then the fool up and got married again. It lasted all of five minutes. I asked him why he'd do such a thing and you know what he said?"

Jack shook his head.

"He said he needed one more ex-wife so he'd have pallbearers." Lonnie grinned. "He thought it was funny. You ever hear such stupid crap? I never believed him. I told him he was suicidal. Who'd want to have that many ex-wives?"

Unless they were under the age of thirteen. "So, getting back to what you know about Olson and Captain Dick," Jack prompted.

"Yeah, okay. Well, Olson lived alone for the last fifteen years. I've known him for nigh on thirty years and that's how I know what I'm telling you. Anyway, he was convinced the police department and the city government were conspiring against him. He said he was being watched and 'they' were listening to his every word. The only place he felt a little safe was here and that was because he knew everyone of us old guys. He said he wasn't worried about us because we'd forget what we heard or saw before we took the next piss."

Lonnie was right. Most of the guys Jack had seen hanging out in the locker room at the Y needed a bib and a call button.

Jack said, "You were his friend."

"I was his only real friend," Lonnie admitted. "I think he was just messing with me. He wasn't going to show that picture to no one, but it gave him a laugh. He was kind of cruel that way. He said if he ever disappeared, or was dead, I should give that envelope to Captain Dick. Dan trusted him and said that envelope should go to him and only him."

"Why is that?"

"Dan was always talking. Captain Dick this and Captain Dick that and telling stories about what they done together. I guess they went through some stuff together."

"What kind of stuff?" Jack asked.

"Police stuff. You know? Things ordinary people like me would never do. Never understand. They had their own code of honor. They had to, because they had to do some bad things. Make tough decisions. And he said the government was watching all the time."

Jack felt the envelope and something hard was near the bottom. He found a key taped to the inside, took it out with a gloved hand, and showed it to Lonnie.

"Know what this goes to, Lonnie?" Jack asked.

Lonnie didn't.

"I love snipe hunts," Liddell said.

"Call Walker and tell him what we have," Jack said to his partner.

"Hold the envelope open wider," Liddell said. Jack did and Liddell took a close-up photo of the key with his cell phone. "I just sent it to Walker and Angelina. See how easy that is, pod'na?"

"That's why I have you," Jack replied. "Maybe one of them can trace the key from the shape. There's a number on this one too. It's not to a locker here, is it, Lonnie?"

"I never seen one like that," Lonnie said.

"Did Olson talk about someone he trusted besides you? Could he have given anything or said anything to the other old-timers up here?"

Lonnie didn't have to think about it. "Nah. He never talked about other policemen if that's what you mean. Not in a good way, at least. And he only told the guys here war stories about him and Captain Dick. He wouldn't have given them a handful of shit if he had diarrhea. When his ex-wife died last month, it hit him hard. He got more paranoid."

"Have you been to his house?"

"Don't know where he lives. Lived, I mean. He never said. But he talked about how his neighbors were scum of the earth. He talked about everyone like that, though."

Liddell pulled a notepad from his pocket, made out a receipt for the envelope, pictures, and key. He had Lonnie sign it. "I'll give your boss a copy if she comes downtown to get it."

"I don't care what she does or doesn't do. I'll just tell her you went through the locker, if that's all right?" He showed Jack and Liddell out of the building and locked the doors.

Outside, Liddell asked, "Do you think the key goes to anything important? Maybe Olson has his porn collection locked away. You think he was blackmailing other people than Lonnie?"

Jack thought Olson was mixed up in all of this. He wouldn't know what the dead man's role was until he untangled the mess. Maybe what Jack had at first thought of as incompetence was really shrewd calculation. Time would tell. And that reminded him they were on the clock. Who knew what damaging stories Claudine was digging up. He almost wished he'd brought her on board. At least he would have had some control. But that was like trusting a snake not to bite. It was in her nature.

"We going to work Olson's murder or let third shift take it?" Liddell asked.

A new detective named Adamson had shown up at Olson's and seemed put off that Jack wouldn't stay and give him a taped statement. Imagine that. He was even more put off that Jack wouldn't tell him why he was there in the first place. Jack had said, "It's a matter of national security." Adamson didn't get the joke.

"I think we have enough going on," Jack said. "I'll go to headquarters and talk to Adamson. Then I'm going home. You should go get some rest too. Little Casket said Olson's autopsy would be around eight this morning. She's going to get Dr. Schirmer to come in with Dr. John on the autopsy to confirm the weapon."

"If it's what we think this means, the killings are all by the same person," Liddell said.

"It's time we talk to Dick's father, Bigfoot. I'd like to get to Dick Sr. this morning before he gets his coffee. Can you be back in a couple of hours?"

"I guess so. I'll meet you at Two Jakes about five."

Jack said, "I've got to give Adamson a quick statement and then I'm going to get an hour of two of shut-eye. Then we go see the big Dick."

"And the war begins," Liddell said.

Chapter 37

Jack gave a taped statement to Detective Rick Adamson at police headquarters. The statement included Olson's cryptic call and Jack's involvement at the scene. He left out the details of finding the key to the YMCA locker and the pictures and key they found there. Adamson asked if Olson was killed by the same gunman responsible for the assault on Reina Day. Jack didn't commit to a yes or no.

"I'm not allowed to make speculation as to who killed him, but I can tell you that I'm close to getting some answers. As soon as I do I'll try to pass them on to you. Sorry. I wish I could help you more, but you'll have to ask Captain Franklin if you want more information than what I've given you," Jack said.

"Not a chance the cases are related then, huh? Just blink once for yes and twice for no."

Jack blinked three times. "Talk to Captain Franklin. He's a reasonable guy. Do you have his cell phone number?"

"Oh yeah. Like I'm going to call a Captain of detectives at two-thirty in the morning. I'll stay and talk to him when he comes to work. I don't have any other leads here."

"If the Captain gives the green light I'll tell you what I can," Jack said. "And now, since I gave you nothing, I need you to do something for me."

"You know Jack, since you started working for the FBI you're starting to pick up their bad habits. You tell me nothing, I give you everything, and now you need a favor. What else is new? Shoot."

Jack asked Adamson to call if they turned up anything with the neighborhood checks. They both didn't think that likely, but Adamson said he would and thanked Jack for nothing.

Jack got in his car and headed home with the key from the sugar jar and the one from the envelope in Olson's locker. About halfway home his cell phone chirped. It was Walker.

"Jack, the key is to a U-Haul storage unit. I saw one like it a week or so ago. I'll be tied up here for a few hours. I take it you're not working Olson's murder?"

"No," Jack said, although he knew Captain Franklin would assign it to them eventually. "But call me if you or Angelina get anything else on the key." There were dozens of U-Haul businesses around the area.

Walker agreed. Jack's phone rang again before he could disconnect. It was Angelina.

"U-Haul in Mt. Vernon," she said and gave him the address. "Anyone ever tell you your timing sucks, Jack? I'm going back to sleep. Mark says hi. I sent the U-Haul after-hours contact info to your phone." The line went dead.

Jack saw he had a message. He didn't want to bother with it tonight, but curiosity got the better of him. He'd call the after-hours contact if he needed them. The address was in Mt. Vernon. It took him three attempts to get Siri to give him directions. "Bitch."

* * * *

It was 2:30 in the morning, he was tired, his face and scalp hurt, and his eyes watered. His mind shifted from one thought to another as he drove the deserted highway between Evansville and Mt. Vernon.

Shift

He remembered driving this stretch of road at the beginning of the year to view the handiwork of a serial killer. The victim was tied to a strut on a grain bin and set on fire.

Shift

He was going to get married. Remarried. He was going to be a father. Second time was always a charm. Wasn't it?

Shift

A father. The words melted his heart.

Shift

Why did Olson get a storage unit in Mt. Vernon? If he wanted to give something to his old Captain, why didn't he just leave it in his house? Why not call Dick to come and get it? Why not just give it to Dick? Why call Jack? Did he have a falling-out with Captain D?

Shift

He wondered how this marriage and fatherhood thing would turn out. The good as well as the bad. Cops were always in protect mode. Everything that happened was their doing.

Shift

Just north of here was a camp of freedom fighters. A farm was turned into an armed camp by a woman with a grudge against the government and a hatred for illegal immigrants. Her son had been killed by an illegal immigrant. Her husband died never seeing the justice he wanted for his son's death. The camp's founder was Karen Stenger. Aggrieved widow. Was she just working out her grief? Or was she someone to be reckoned with?

Jack compartmented that concern. ICE was aware of them. Not his problem. Yet.

Shift

What could Olson have left for the retired Captain that would merit a secret storage unit? Olson had given Jack a cryptic hint about the sugar jar. Did he know he was going to die? Did he intend for Jack to die? Did he leave the gate unlocked and the door open for him? Did he let someone in who he trusted and forgot to shut the door? Or did he want to put an end to thirty-seven years of paranoia?

Olson hadn't told his killer about the key in Mama Bear or it would have been gone. Was Olson blackmailing someone? The retired Captain? In any case, he hoped whatever was in storage was related to the investigations. He knew Olson had lied earlier, held back. He was pretty sure the autopsy finding would be death by CO_2 cartridge injected inside the skull. Didn't really matter if it was a shark dart or a .50 caliber. Dead was dead, and Olson was out of the picture.

Jack was rolling into Mt. Vernon before he was aware of it. It was late and there was no traffic. No police patrol. Good. He'd need them eventually. But not now.

He parked in the gravel shoulder next to the U-Haul and mulled over what he was going to do. He hadn't called the after-hours person because he wasn't sure the key even fit a storage unit there. He'd check first. If it did fit, he'd back off and get a warrant. If not, he'd go home and crawl back in bed for two hours.

He got out of the car, climbed the fence, and went in search of unit number 23. That was the number on the key. He didn't have to go far.

Chapter 38

The good news was that U-Haul in Mt. Vernon didn't have operational, CCTV so it wouldn't show Jack scaling the fence and wandering. The bad news: U-Haul didn't have a CCTV, so he wouldn't be able to see if anyone accessed the unit to deposit items.

He'd found the storage unit, the key fit; he'd opened it and saw what it contained. He locked up, climbed back over the fence, went to his car, and called the after-hours number and the Mt. Vernon PD. A nineteen-year-old zit-faced kid came out and wanted to see a warrant. Jack showed his FBI badge and his gun and was about to show him the bottom of his foot, but the Mt. Vernon cop arrived, so he decided to get the warrant.

The Mt. Vernon cop helped Jack get a judge out of bed and get him on the phone. Jack talked to the judge and told him what they were doing. The judge said there was no reason for a search warrant if the owner of the unit was dead. Jack half-heartedly argued there might be a chain of custody issue, but the judge was tired, Jack was tired, and the kid asked too damn many questions. He got verbal permission from the judge, who also spoke to Mt. Vernon PD, and it was a fait accompli. The judge said if he needed something in writing not to call him.

When the unit was opened it revealed a surprising number of photos, police files, letters, documents, and some pieces of physical evidence, such as five rifles, three handguns, and reloading equipment. Two of the rifles still had a price tag tied to the barrel that identified the weapons were from Harry's gun shop. The prices were at least thirty-seven-year-old prices for such weapons. One of the handguns was a .50 caliber Desert Eagle in a wooden presentation case. It was immaculate, as if it had never been fired. Jack called Walker and apologized, but Walker was up anyway, or so he said.

He hadn't gone through the photos they found in a box in the storage unit yet. Most were Polaroids, but some were 35mm. One showed Max's body slumped toward the driver's window of the Camaro with most of his head missing. One showed Harry Day's body laid out on the floor, facedown in the gun shop, just like Sergeant Mattingly had said. There were two photos of the safe at the gun shop. One with the door closed. One with it open and full of ledgers, a stack of cash, a silver revolver of some caliber, and other papers.

He found Harry's ledgers and notebook in the box with the pictures. The cash wasn't there, or the revolver.

In one corner of the storage bin a tire iron leaned against the wall. Walker found a paper grocery sack containing pieces of broken beer bottles. Jack wondered again if Olson was keeping all of this as insurance. But if he was, why would he have addressed the envelope at the YMCA to Dick Sr.? So far Jack had only considered Thomas Dick as a witness to a cover-up, but maybe he had a bigger part in this. He dismissed the idea. Dick Sr. was in his late seventies. He wasn't the person Jack had witnessed fleeing from Olson's house.

Olson would only be keeping this stuff hidden for two reasons: Either he was blackmailing someone, or he was afraid of someone. They might have been the same person. The obvious people were Double Dick, Needham, and James. If Olson left the message to give the key to Dick Sr., he didn't think Sr. was the person Olson was blackmailing. It was complicated. Like the old joke. Who did it was on first. Why they did it was on second. What they did it with was on third. Jack still didn't have the answers he needed, but he was very close.

He left the scene in Walker's hands and drove back to headquarters, intending to type a report. It was still dark. He would have an hour before he had to be at Two Jakes to meet with Elkins and Liddell. Few third shift people would be in the detectives' office. He'd sneak in, get his notes in order, check his mail, and then go to the war room.

When he got to headquarters he could barely keep his eyes open.

He parked in Double Dick's parking spot and shut the engine and lights off.

"Screw the notes," he said, and laid his seat back, closed his eyes, and immediately fell asleep.

* * * *

Jack was awakened by a tapping on the glass and sat up with a start. Liddell's big face was just outside the window. "Wakey, wakey, eggs and bakey," Liddell said. "Wipe your mouth, pod'na."

Jack wiped drool from the side of his mouth and exited the car. He pointed at Liddell's face. "You've got something stuck there."

"What?" Liddell wiped at the corner of his mouth.

"I think it was the back end of a gazelle, but you got it, Bigfoot."

"Oh, ha-ha. I didn't see your car at your house or at the war room, so I checked here. You should thank me for finding you before the Dickster came to work and had your car towed—with you in it."

"I need some coffee," Jack said and checked the time. "I've got to call Katie."

"I already had Marcie call her, pod'na. She won't yell at Marcie."

"Thanks. Get in. You drive."

Jack got out and let Liddell in the driver's seat.

"Where we going?"

"Thomas Dick's."

Jack laid his head back and closed his eyes. He was running on low burner and hoped it was enough to get this case heated up as Liddell headed down Sycamore Street to the Lloyd Expressway toward Warrick County.

"I don't know whether to thank you or punch you," Liddell said.

"Now what?"

"You. U-Haul. Evidence. Am I making sense?" Liddell said. "I should be pissed at you, pod'na, but I really needed some sleep."

"Yeah. Tell me about it," Jack said, rubbing his eyes. "Tell me when we get there." Jack fell back asleep.

The sun was just peeking over the horizon when Liddell found what might have been the right property. He pulled off on the gravel at the opening of the wide driveway and nudged Jack awake. In front of them stood a massive iron double gate with a stacked stone wall running off in either direction. The gate was open. There was no mailbox or number affixed to the stone or gate.

"I hope we're at the right house, pod'na."

"Is it the right address?"

"Yeah, it must be, but there's no number or mailbox. The GPS says we have arrived."

"Siri lies, Bigfoot. You can't trust a word that bitch says."

"So, should we go in? I mean, he was a Captain. Maybe we should call first," Liddell said.

"I'll protect you. You big sissy."

"Am not."

"Yeah. You are. Where's your sense of adventure?"

"I keep it with the Constitution and the Fourth Amendment."

"We've got guns and badges. Federal badges. You're a fed now. We make the Constitution up as we go."

Liddell pulled through. The gravel turned to a narrow asphalt driveway that had seen better days. Sugar maple trees grew on each side, creating a canopy, the leaves a dazzling arbor of reds and yellows and orange.

Liddell said. "It's like a tunnel. Marcie and Janie would love to see this."

The driveway curved to the left and a hundred yards or so in the distance they could see the house—more of a small mansion—with its sweeping lawn. The property was dotted with trees and created a park-like setting. In the diffused morning light an impressive display of color seemed to backlight the property.

Liddell pointed off to the east. "Those are cottonwoods. They grow close to water. The Ohio River must be close."

Jack saw the mass of gold foliage. "Yeah. Pretty. But aren't those trees responsible for all that white fluffy mess floating around in the air?"

"You just don't appreciate nature, pod'na. Cottonwood trees were important to the settlers. They told the pioneers they were near water."

"Talking trees," Jack said.

"You can eat parts of the cottonwood."

"Well, Bucky Beaver," Jack said. "You go eat a tree and I'll talk to Dick's daddy."

"Maybe we should name them Big Dick and Little Dick? Or—"

"Stop. Just stop."

Liddell picked up the pace and they passed a falling-down wooden structure that might have been an Army barracks during one of the great wars. "Those were slave quarters," Liddell said.

"What?"

"Slave quarters," Liddell said. "This place resembles Uncle Sam's mansion in St. James Parish back home. It was a working cotton plantation, but it's gone now. Just about all of the plantation mansions were built in that *Gone with the Wind* style and close to water transportation. All the land along the waterways grew cotton or sugar. This might have been a working plantation back in the day."

"Frankly, my dear, I don't give a damn," Jack said. They parked in front of the Greek Revival two-story home with wraparound verandas on the first and upper levels, and ornately framed gables and front entrance. The verandas were held up by massive octagonal columns.

Jack had seen many plantation mansions during their recent case in Plaquemine—pronounced *plak-uh-min*—where they had nearly been killed while rescuing Liddell's kidnapped niece. They'd even burned one to the ground. He didn't know about Uncle Sam's, but this structure was definitely out of time and place here in Hoosier-land.

There were moneyed people residing in Warrick County but, even given that, the Dick family home was a little too rich for a cop's blood.

"I wonder how Double Dick was able to go to Rex Mundi if they lived in Warrick County?" Jack said. "Marcie and I have been considering schools for Janie and there's only two in our school district."

"Aren't you pushing things a bit, Bigfoot? She's only eleven months."

"You can never be too prepared, pod'na. You should start thinking about that—and colleges."

Jack and Liddell got out and walked up the marble steps onto the lower veranda and rang a doorbell beside the ten-foot-tall, eight-foot-wide double doors. They waited long enough for an older gent to wake up, take a pee, put pants on, and come to the door. Nothing. A heavy iron lion's-head door knocker was attached to the center of each door. Jack used one to rap several times against the door. No answer. Jack rang the doorbell again and held the button down. Still nothing.

"Maybe we should come back?"

"Yeah," Jack agreed. "Maybe we should have Angelina find out how a retired police captain can afford a place like this. There's got to be a couple of hundred acres of land. I wonder if he's a historic landmark?"

"Three hundred and twenty acres actually and no, I'm not quite that old," a voice said from behind them.

Retired Detective Captain Thomas Dick was standing on the side veranda in paint-stained overalls. He wasn't holding a paintbrush. Instead he held a wicked pair of pointed hedge loppers. He walked over and stood facing them. "How I can afford this place is that this monstrosity has been in the family since the mid-1800s."

"We were just admiring your property," Liddell said.

"It's something, isn't it? This house is over two hundred years old. Built in 1811. The same year Captain Jacob Warrick was killed in the Battle of Tippecanoe. My great-great-grandfather bought it from his family after Jacob died. We originally owned over five hundred acres," Dick said. "And that was only a modest cotton farm back in the day. Over the years some of the land has been sold off for repairs and upkeep, but I still have enough. I'm restoring it. Maybe I'll open it as a museum. Maybe a bed-

and-breakfast. I could turn the old slave quarters into shops. Sell all that smell-good crap women like."

He took his gardening gloves off and wiped his hands on the front of his overalls. "You can scream at the top of your lungs and no one would hear you. My closest neighbor is a half mile away. We value our privacy out here."

"Lucky for us you were nearby and we didn't have to scream," Jack said and smiled.

Dick Sr. didn't return the smile. "You're not here for the tour at this hour. What do you think I'm going to tell you?"

"We're investigating the murder of—" Jack said before Dick interrupted.

"I know what you're investigating." Dick turned and gazed out over the pristine lawn to the tree line, the Ohio River hidden behind them. When he came out of his reverie he launched into tour guide mode, or history teacher mode, or—and Jack voted for this one—Captain Dick was just killing time, trying to decide how much they knew and what he should tell them.

"The only original part of the mansion still standing are these stone pillars." He said this and placed a palm against the surface of one of the pillars in a proud caress. "Everything dies and goes away with age. This was once a grand place, but now I only keep up the ten acres you see surrounding the house. Someday Richard will get all of this. The family legacy will live on after I'm gone. But not too soon. I hope."

Jack said, "I've got an eight-hundred-square-foot cabin on the Ohio that I inherited from my dad. I put in a hot tub, a dock, a boat, and a refrigerator."

Dick ignored the sarcastic comparison. "I knew Jake Murphy. He was a good cop. A cop's cop," Captain Dick said. "Is that partner of his still the chief cook and bottle washer at the million-dollar property you have on the river?"

Touché.

Jack said, "Jake Brady's my business partner and he does more than the dishes. He runs Two Jakes. I just collect the checks, drink just the right amount, and live a life of sin."

That got a chuckle out of old farmer Dick. "You sound just like your old man. You've earned quite the reputation. You both have. I still go to the retirees' meetings and they call you two the 'serial killer hunters'."

"That's not what the killers call us," Liddell said and Dick chuckled again.

"No. I guess not." He shifted his gardening gloves, a move meant to let them know he was busy and to get on with it. "What can I do for you at this hour of the morning?"

Jack felt his neck turning red. He wasn't going to get the drop on this old detective. He knew exactly why Jack was there at sunup. "Captain, we're going to need the help of any detective or uniform officer that worked the case. That would include you."

"*Captain*, huh. Showing respect. That's good," Dick said, but he didn't invite them to sit on the porch and drink mint juleps or bourbon and smoke cigars while the crop was being worked.

Jack said, "It would help if we could get some background on this case, Captain. Not much of the file survived the years, it seems." *But a lot more turned up in Olson's locker.*

Captain Dick raised an eyebrow. "I've been retired for quite some time and have no control over what is or isn't in the files anymore."

Jack switched tactics. "Captain Franklin said some of the detectives back then kept their own files. This is such an old case I'm assuming more detectives than Detective Olson have taken a crack at it over the years. Maybe you know someone I can talk to."

"I heard about Dan. That's too bad. He was a good detective in his day, but his mind started failing him after he retired. Was he able to help you?"

Jack said, "My dad kept notes on unsolved cases. He always made copies of paperwork he thought might be needed if a suspect was ever identified. I found some of his paperwork on this case. Yes, Olson was very helpful. Good thing we interviewed him before he was murdered. He had a storage locker full of evidence."

Dick's veneer slipped for just an instant. His expression said he didn't believe Jack had any such evidence, because he'd caused all the evidence to disappear long ago. Little did he know his minion, Olson, had kept all of it. Jack had thought it might be for blackmail, but Angelina had sifted through everything Olson had. If he was blackmailing anyone, he got squat.

Dick said, "I'm sorry for that family's losses—the Days, I mean. However, I unconditionally and categorically refuse to help you with a political witch hunt concerning my son. He's done nothing wrong. You can take my word for that."

Jack kept eye contact with Dick and both men were silent. Jack wanted badly to tell him that his son, Double Dick, had done so many things wrong there was no place to start listing them. But it wouldn't help the case to cause this old man, now a retired cop, a world of grief. At least not until he could put Double Dick in handcuffs and frog-march him around the Civic Center for the cameras.

Dick put the garden gloves back on and hefted the hedge trimmers. "We're done here, gentlemen."

"I think you should see this, sir." Jack reached in a pocket and brought the locker keys out. He dangled them in front of the retired Captain's face.

Dick reached for the keys but Jack closed his hand around them and put the keys back in his pocket.

"You know what these are," Jack said, not a question. "Do you want to know what we found?"

Red crept up Dick's neck like a slow burn. When it reached his cheeks he said, "Get the hell off my property. Get off and don't come back without a warrant." He pushed Jack and Liddell toward the steps, went in the front door, and slammed it shut behind him.

Liddell said, "Do you think he doesn't want to talk to us?"

"He's a lot stronger than he seems, Bigfoot. I think we'd better get off his property. He may be going for a .50 caliber."

"Or a shark dart thingy," Liddell said. They walked the long driveway, got back in the Crown Vic, and drove back onto Highway 62.

"Did you see his face when I told him I'd found my dad's notes on Max's murder?"

"I think he knew you were lying, pod'na, but those keys really spooked him. He definitely didn't know about them. Good thing you had Walker collect the contents of the U-Haul locker last night."

"Good thing one of the Posey County judges answered the phone." Jack yawned. "I need a nap, Bigfoot. Wake me when we get to Two Jakes."

"So now I'm your driver *and* your alarm clock. Power naps don't work, pod'na. What you need is coffee and a good breakfast."

"You mean *you* need a breakfast," Jack said sarcastically.

Liddell turned toward Highway 66, also known as Newburgh Road, and headed west toward Evansville and Two Jakes.

Jack said, "I want to listen to the tapes and go over the photos from last night. Is Walker bringing the stuff to us after he's finished processing it?"

Walker had found several cassette tapes in the storage bin, along with typed statements.

Liddell called Two Jakes and Vinnie answered.

* * * *

Sergeant Walker met them in the war room. Laid out on the table were four cassette tapes, eleven photos, Polaroids and 35mm photos, and complete case files for Max and Harry Day's murders.

Walker said, "There are crime scene photos from both murders. The cassette tapes have been processed for prints and DNA. There are typed statements from Double Dick, Carl Needham, Dennis James, and one from

Ginger Purdie. I haven't played the tapes to see if that's what's on them, but the names are on each one. You've got autopsy reports too."

Jack dug through the box with the files and found three typed statements. He started reading Richard Dick's, stopped, and flipped through the pages. The first page was just the identification and the legal warnings. There were two pages following that. Maybe a dozen questions in all. He read the entire statement and then read Carl Needham's statement. They could be the same statement, word for word from a script. He wondered if all three boys were in the room listening to what the other said. Dennis James's statement was longer because Dennis gave more than a yes or no answer. In fact, there were some interesting tidbits of detail in that statement. Near the end of Dennis's statement, the interviewer had instructed him to listen closely to the question and just answer the question that was asked. Jack read the questions again more carefully and they didn't sound like they came from Dan Olson, although Det. Dan Olson's name was listed as the one taking the statements. The questions and voice sounded like Captain Dick.

"Read these and tell me what you think, Bigfoot."

Liddell read through the statements and when he was done he said, "Dick and Needham's statements are identical. Olson just about told Dennis James to shut up."

"Did you notice anything unusual about the questions?" Jack asked.

"Just that they were very direct. Yes or no questions."

Jack thought he would wait to play the tapes before he told them who he thought had actually taken the statements.

"There's three typed statements, but four cassettes. Did you see a fourth typed statement?" Jack asked.

"It's Ginger Purdie," Walker answered. "The cheerleader. I was curious and played it. Her statement is even shorter than the others. Basically, she says Max started a fight with Richard Dick at Rex Mundi during football practice and broke Dick's nose. He supposedly beat Needham and James up too. Then Max stormed off, unchallenged. The boys didn't follow him and they were with her during the rest of practice. Sounded to me like someone was coaching her. Olson took that statement as well as the others."

Jack knew Walker hadn't talked to Olson or retired Captain Dick. He wouldn't know what either man's voice sounded like.

"I'd like to play the recorded statements, but we don't have a cassette player here," Jack said.

Walker reached in another box and pulled out a cassette player/recorder. He punched the *play* button and it worked. "Will this do?"

Jack put the recorded statement marked *Richard Dick* in the dock and hit *play*. The voice that came out was Detective Olson's and Jack was disappointed. The wording of the typed statement was too precise for Olson. But when Olson's narration ended a different voice asked the questions. "That's what I suspected," Jack said. "These were taken by Thomas Dick. He let Olson put his name on them as the investigator."

Jack let the tape play a few minutes. Thomas Dick asked the questions in such a way that Richard had to answer yes or no or give a brief statement. "I think they were all reading off a piece of paper," Jack said. "The typed statements are word for word when they talk about the fight at Rex Mundi."

No one was surprised. This confirmed there was a cover-up going on. The statements were never to see light of day unless a witness came forward and this had to be kicked upstairs to the prosecutor. Then the police would say they had done a complete investigation and produce taped statements. No one came forward, and Harry Dick's pleas to the police didn't merit a more thorough investigation. Case closed. But Olson had still held onto the statements and tapes and everything else he'd collected from Max and Harry's cases.

"I wonder if retired Captain Dick knew that Olson kept all this stuff?" Liddell asked.

"Olson can't tell us anymore," Jack said. "I don't think I need to hear the rest of the tapes."

"Dennis James's typed statement said they all went to the hospital. Dick's nose was broken and they all had bruises or cuts. He said he was going to have a black eye. He claimed Max started the fight and they defended themselves. Olson never asked any of them the details of the fight. He never asked if the three of them followed Max to his car, or if they pursued him to the cemetery. He never asked how Max could beat the three of them up. And get this: There's a date the statements were taken, but not a time started and ended. Not even on the taped statement we just heard. Purdie was talked to about a week after the event."

"Okay. Leave all this stuff with me, Tony," Jack said.

"Yep. You'll need to sign a chain of custody form." Walker had one already filled out, minus Jack's signature. "Do you really want to keep all this stuff here?"

Jack was already on shaky ground because of his hate/hate relationship with Double Dick, and the even shakier verbal warrant in Mt. Vernon. "I guess you'd better keep it all. Lock it up somewhere only you can get to. Don't put it in the property room."

"Thanks, Tony. Sorry you were called in." He knew Walker had worked the whole night.

"Are you kidding?" Walker said and grinned. "This is getting interesting and I want to be in on the kill. So to speak."

Jack said, "Time to see Double Dick."

Chapter 39

The address Jack had for Double Dick was in Oak Meadows, a gated golf cart community in the McCutchanville area of Vanderburgh County. Jack had been inside Oak Meadows two times: Once to a wedding at the country club, the second time at the scene of a murder. In summertime, as you drove past stately homes, an abundance of golf carts would be zipping around on the streets. It was like the Indy 500 for geriatrics. In winter and fall the traffic, both Lexus and golf cart, thinned out while residents stayed in front of their fireplaces sipping fine wines and cognacs.

The stone guard booth at the entrance to the community was sometimes occupied by a lone security officer/pensioner whose job seemed to be sitting in front of a small television and waving at every car that came in or out. You got what you paid for. The guard shack was unoccupied today and Liddell drove through the open gates and past a lone golf cart operated by an older gentleman with a golf bag in the empty seat. There was a six-pack of Guinness on the floorboard and an open one held between his legs. Jack gave the man a thumbs-up. The man scowled and slowed to let them go ahead.

"So much for community policing," Jack said.

"Maybe he thought you were going to arrest him for the open container law?"

"I should confiscate his beer," Jack muttered. "That's the street coming up. Take a right."

Liddell turned. The homes here were plus-sized, with bigger lots that backed up directly onto the golf course. Dick's house was at the ninth hole and built in a manner as arrogant as the man himself. The brick and stone structure sported at least three covered or enclosed decks. Parking included two double-bay garages. That gave him two spaces for cars and two spaces for his ego. Next to these was a smaller overhead door, most likely for the HOA—home owner's agreement—required golf cart. The landscaping was pristine, and Jack thought, a little prissy for a guy living alone.

Double Dick was at a glass patio table on a second-floor covered deck with a paper—*Wall Street Journal*—and a steaming mug of something—*skinny vanilla soy latte with whipped cream and sprinkles.* Dick's attention fixed on the Crown Vic pulling into his unstained driveway.

"Well, the element of surprise is gone," Liddell said as they walked to the front door.

"He's probably been up for hours trying on uniforms," Jack said.

Two short sets of steps led up the lawn to a spacious iron-railed porch. They went to the door and waited. Nothing. Liddell rang the doorbell and, of course, it played "Hail to the Chief." Still no answer. Liddell reached for the doorbell again when they heard a garage door going up. Jack started down the stairs and watched Double Dick drive past in a new black SUV without acknowledging their presence.

Jack and Liddell double-timed it back to the Crown Vic. Liddell backed out and headed for the cross street, but the SUV was gone.

"Should we have a police car pull him over, pod'na?"

"We can beard the lion in his den."

"What does that even mean?" Liddell asked and slowed down. "I mean, I've heard it lots of times. Are we going to put a beard on him if we catch him watching sports on television? Does he even watch sports? What kind of beard?"

"Would you just shut up and drive?"

"Ooh, that stings."

"Shut up, shuttin' up," Jack said and smiled.

"I'll bet you don't tell Katie to shut up and drive."

Liddell turned north toward town. They made it to Martin Luther King Boulevard coming up on the Civic Center and were slowed by the traffic.

"Can I talk now?" Liddell asked.

"Can I stop you?"

"No. I agree with you that Dick Senior warned him."

"Did I say that?"

"You were thinking it."

Jack had thought it. "Did you notice he was already in his uniform? I mean, come on. Who dresses like that out in public to have coffee?"

Liddell said with a grin, "Those might have been his pajamas."

Jack said nothing. Liddell didn't need encouragement. He needed an *off* switch.

Liddell again. "Nah, he wouldn't wear those. I think he wears Thor jammies. He is a god, after all."

"Let's get in there and talk to Dick while he's still in a defensive mode. You do the questioning, Bigfoot. He might talk to you."

"Can we stop by the office and make coffee? He's not going anywhere but to his office. A few minutes won't make a difference. Really."

"You have an emergency stash of doughnuts in your desk. Don't you?"

"Hey, I haven't had breakfast yet," Liddell said. "We haven't even had coffee. How am I supposed to put on my thinking cap when I'm too tired to even find it?"

Liddell pulled through the Chief's parking area and spotted Dick's black SUV. He drove on and parked behind the detectives' office.

"Five minutes," Jack said, getting out of the car. "Let's get some coffee and check our messages. Let him sweat a little, but we don't want to give him time to barricade the door. He knows we're coming."

"With two Dicks involved in this case, maybe we should number them. Dick one and Dick two."

Jack said nothing, but that didn't stop Liddell. "That reminds me of a joke. Two dicks walk into a bar and—"

"Maybe we should skip the office and go see Double Dick first if you're not hungry?" Jack said and Liddell became silent.

Chapter 40

Deputy Chief of Police Richard Dick swiveled his office chair sideways, facing the framed photos behind his desk. One photo on the credenza showed him in his Rex Mundi Monarchs football uniform, arm cocked, football in hand. He had been the starting quarterback in his junior and senior years. Next to that one was a picture of the entire team. Another with him, Needham, and James hanging out after a practice. Dick and Needham were wearing their football gear, but James had changed into pegged-leg jeans and a white T-shirt with the short sleeves rolled up, a cigarette stuck behind his ear, hair greased back, making him resemble a young James Dean.

The three had gravitated toward each other in their freshman year. Dick was friendless until he met Carl. Carl never met a person who didn't like him. Dennis was into alcohol, marijuana, and thefts, but the girls flocked to him because he was a bad boy. Dennis was the one who introduced him to Ginger. Dick wondered what had happened to Ginger. But he knew the answer: Max was what happened. Things were never the same after that night.

Another picture was of Dick in full diving gear, hood pulled back, a serious expression on his face, posing for the camera. Standing beside him was his best friend, Carl Needham. While they were in their junior year, Needham had taken diving lessons and was certified for deepwater exploration. Dick thought it would be cool. He remembered telling his father he wanted to join the Navy. His father's answer was, "You already have a fine career ahead of you. You're going to college. I'm not having any of your sass." He'd finally convinced his father to let him take diving lessons. He was certified in his senior year and made a few cave dives with Needham.

Carl developed a passion for politics and the law. It suited him. He'd risen through the ranks quickly and was an Ohio state senator. He still practiced law, but politics was his passion. He'd exceeded Dick in all ways, but they remained best of friends.

Dick was proud of where he was now, but those days in high school were his fondest memories. The three of them had all been so tight. And then life happened. They had all gone separate ways. He wondered where he would be, what he would be doing, if his father hadn't insisted he become a policeman. He might have gone on to play college football, joined the Navy, and played for Navy Midshipmen. Who knows where that would have led?

But he hadn't played college football. He'd gone to Notre Dame at his dad's insistence with no time to attend many Fighting Irish games, much less try out for the team. His time was spent earning a dual degree in criminal justice and business administration, then on to an MBA. Even back then his father had been grooming him to become Chief of Police. That had been his father's dream. Over time, he had to admit, it had become his dream too.

He hadn't slept well. He hadn't been allowed to finish his cinnamon roll and coffee this morning due to the intrusion of Murphy and that backwater partner of his. Thankfully, he had an espresso machine in his office and had brought the remainder of the Cinnabon with him. His office was bigger than any in the police department, but he still felt cramped. His was a creative mind and a creative mind needed space, and encouragement, and yes, sometimes praise. How else would a creative person know that their ideas had hit their mark? But this Chief of Police didn't hand out praise. He demanded loyalty, but gave nothing in return. He didn't trust that Dick knew the right things to do, or to say, and held him back as if Dick was someone to be ashamed of.

Pope wasn't the only problem he had right now. He was in a spot. He had always feared the past would come back to haunt him. It had come back with a vengeance and at precisely the wrong time. The persecution inflicted on him by the Day family and the news media was Chief Pope's doing. Of that he was sure, because it's exactly what he would have done himself if he had that kind of dirt on Pope. To be fair, Max Day had to share part of the blame. If Max hadn't tried to steal Ginger, if he'd stayed down, if he hadn't broken Dick's nose in front of everyone, if he hadn't humiliated him, none of this would have happened.

But it had happened. Max was dead. Harry Day was dead. Amelia Day was dead. Reina Day was hospitalized and all of it was so unnecessary.

They kept stirring the pot until it had boiled over. One good thing had come out of all this: The persecution by the Day family had ceased.

He felt no pity for that family. They'd damaged his reputation and did their best to keep him from his well-earned promotion. But they hadn't stopped him. He'd spoken with the incoming mayor. Cato assured him it was going to happen. He would be Chief. And then Murphy and all of that ilk would be forced out of the department. He demanded loyalty and their loyalties would never lie with him. He recognized that. But, unlike Pope, he wouldn't allow anyone with questionable loyalty to keep their job. It was like leaving a sharp stone in your shoe. You had to remove the stone. Permanently. Murphy would get what he had coming. Just like the rest.

Mayor Cato would let him run the department the way he thought best. A much-needed change in leadership would bring new police policies. No more waste of equipment and manpower within the lower ranks. They didn't deserve take-home police vehicles, free gas, and free meals and coffee. He would institute a strict policy of no gratuities, take their free rides away, then see how they liked that. And if they rebelled he would replace them until they fell into line. The police department was no place for a democracy.

The news media would be kept abreast of every change. In fact, he intended to create a place within the department for a new liaison. A civilian. A journalist. His would be the first police department in the country with an embedded reporter. He was sure that would get the attention of the national networks. The public could watch him clean house. The first thing he'd do was—

His thoughts were interrupted when he heard the outer door to the personnel office open and the *whoosh* sound of the hydraulic-assisted closing. He didn't need to check the clock. He knew exactly who it was.

He hadn't realized he'd slumped down in his chair until the knock on his door. He straightened up and brushed a piece of lint from the front of his shirtsleeve. He considered not answering, but that would appear that he was avoiding them. It exuded weakness. Murphy would use that to spread his poison among the rank and file and it would cast more suspicion on him. Murphy already knew about the fight at Rex Mundi and suspected there was a second fight that night at the cemetery. Probably thanks to Mattingly, who had always been jealous of his meteoric rise to power. Mattingly was just as bad in his own way as the Day family. Always watching for a place to stick the knife in. Well, not for much longer. Mattingly would be unemployed with the rest of them.

"Come," he said and the door opened.

* * * *

Liddell had scarfed down a half-dozen doughnuts, finished what remained of the coffee, belched, and was ready to go upstairs and confront Dick.

Jack put a tiny digital recorder in his suit pocket, along with the high school yearbook photos of Max, Dick, Carl, and Dennis. They went upstairs to the personnel office. Lieutenant Brandsasse's desk was vacant. A scribbled note lay on the desktop. It read, *You're late. Again. See me when you get in.* It was unsigned.

"Uh-oh. Someone's getting a spanking," Liddell said.

"Yeah, us," Jack said.

They knocked on the door and the voice of doom said, "Come." They came. Jack Murphy and Liddell Blanchard stood in front of Dick's oversized desk.

"Can we sit, sir?" Liddell asked.

Dick said nothing. Jack pulled a chair up to Dick's desk and sat. Liddell selected a chair and pushed it against the wall in the far corner.

Jack began. "As you know, we're investigating the murders of Maximillian Day and Harry Day. I'm sorry to have to bring all this up again since it happened so long ago and was investigated thoroughly," he lied. "You were a detective. You know we're starting at a disadvantage. We could really use your help. Where do you think we should start?"

Jack waited for a response. Nothing came.

"Okay, then. I'll start. What do you remember about your fight with Max Day at Rex Mundi the evening Max died?"

Dick's eyes bored in on Jack's when he spoke. "You will address me by my rank, Detective Murphy. I'm a Deputy Chief of Police. Your attitude is inexcusable and bordering on insubordination. You will *not* read me the Miranda warnings. I promise you."

The *promise* in that sounded like a threat.

"You're right—Deputy Chief. Sir. I won't read you the Miranda rights statement because it's not necessary. You're a witness at this time, sir. I mean Deputy Chief. Sir."

Dick's jaw tightened. "I'm warning you, Murphy…"

Jack jumped in. "We have a common interest in solving these cases, don't you agree? You want to clear your name and reputation. We want to find the murderer or murderers. Or at the very least, to find the truth and get some justice for the Day family. You were a detective. Right? You know the procedure. We can really use your help. Without that, I'm afraid of what will happen."

Jack hoped he wasn't laying on the praise too thick, but he didn't think it would ever be too thick with an arrogant ass like Dick.

"I know exactly what you're doing, Murphy. I know what you and Blanchard want to ask me and I'll save you the time and trouble. I don't know anything. I have nothing to say. You're wasting your time here. You can't trick me. You *can* try to humiliate me. *Try.* But you will fail. Watching you two running around desperately trying to hold onto your careers is…is pathetic. That's what it is. This is one case the great Jack Murphy won't solve. It will be your swan song."

"Are you threatening us?" Jack asked.

"Take it however you want, Murphy. Now get the hell out of my office. I have important work and we're done here." Dick shooed them toward the door.

Jack said, "That's the exact words your dad used this morning. Did he tell you that we were there? Wow, what a house. I mean, someone could get lost in that place."

Jack didn't get up. He put his hands on the edge of the desk and leaned toward Dick. "I'm going to pretend you didn't just threaten me." He added, "Deputy Chief."

"Get out, Murphy! Leave. Now!"

Jack said, "I didn't think of you as a real suspect, but your refusal to talk to us makes me think differently. Let me promise *you*, Deputy Chief Dick. If you do—or say—anything to harm me or my partner's careers *or* interfere in our investigation in any way, I'll be coming for you. You can take that any way you want."

Jack stood up and headed for the door. Liddell was frozen to his seat for a beat and then followed Jack.

Dick said to their backs, "I have an attorney. You'll be talking to him."

Jack turned around and approached the desk so quickly Dick drew back.

"Have your attorney contact me today, sir. This morning, if you please. You know my number," Jack said. "Better yet, give me the attorney's number. I'll contact him."

Dick smirked. "Senator Carl Needham. I assume you have his number. If you don't, I'm sure that little girl of yours, Angie, can get it for you. She seems adept at getting things. Illegally, I would guess. Maybe someone should investigate her?"

"You're right. We are done here. For now."

Jack and Liddell left the office and went down the hall to the elevator. Jack said, "Let's take the stairs. I need to burn off some steam."

"Do you think it was wise to threaten Double Dick? I mean, he *is* a Deputy Chief. He's proud."

"I just wanted to wind him up. An angry man is a foolish man." Jack called Angelina and asked her to check local hospital records for Double Dick, Carl, and Dennis. He was particularly interested in the dates around Max's murder. He told her Dick had called her "that little girl, Angie" and she responded appropriately before the line went dead.

"Let's get breakfast at the war room," Jack said.

"Now you're talking, pod'na. "My stomach's talking to me."

"It's talking to me too," Jack said and patted Liddell's stomach.

They rode the elevator in silence and left headquarters by the back entrance. Outside, Jack asked, "Did you notice the photos in Dick's office?"

"The walls were full of awards from kindergarten. Why?"

"There were several photos on the credenza. Dick's a diver."

"Dick Diver." Liddell chuckled and repeated, "Dick Diver. Get it?"

"He hates me enough as it is."

"Deputy Chief Dick Diver," Liddell said again. "I like it."

"Would you stop?" Jack got in the passenger side of the Crown Vic.

"Dick Diver," Liddell said and sniggered. "Dick—Diver." He turned south toward the river. "So. What next?"

"I'm going to do something I've never done before," Jack said. "I'm going to take Double Dick's advice. We'll call Needham and set up an appointment for later today. It's about a five-hour drive to Columbus."

"Aqua Dick," Liddell said. "The comic book action figure will be a phallus in a Speedo. What do you think?"

Chapter 41

Carl Needham dialed the number Richard Dick had provided. The phone was answered after several rings. "Yeah."

"Detective Jack Murphy?" Needham asked. It annoyed him when someone didn't use proper phone etiquette. He didn't like to have to ask who he was talking to. Evidently, Jack Murphy thought he was above introducing himself in any official capacity.

"You got me. Who is this?" Jack asked.

"This is Ohio State Senator Carl Needham, Detective Murphy." He said this distinctly, officiously, putting Murphy in his proper social status. Putting the man on notice.

"Carl," Jack said merrily. "I was just getting ready to call you, man. You must be psychic, but I guess that's what makes you a good congressman. You're Dick's attorney, right?"

"Senator," Needham corrected Jack.

"You're Dick's senator?"

"I am a senator for the State of Ohio," Needham said, his annoyance rising.

"That's what I meant. What can I do for you, Carl?"

The senator had been warned Murphy was a disrespectful smart-ass. But a dangerous smart-ass, he reminded himself.

"I was advised you were told to contact me. I wanted to make sure we spoke sooner rather than later to prevent you from further harassing my client."

"Just to be clear, Carl, I assume by *your client* you mean Dick, the son; not Dick, the father." Jack motioned at Liddell to record the call. He put the call on speakerphone.

"Yes, I'm referring to Richard. Your Deputy Chief. Richard Dick. I also received a call from his father. I understand you trespassed onto the father's private property this morning and created quite a disturbance."

Jack said, "Hey, what's the father's name? I forgot to get it."

"Retired Captain Thomas Dick. Were you at his home extremely early this morning?"

"He was up, but, yeah. We were there early because Dick Sr. wasn't answering his phone." Needham probably wouldn't check phone records.

"Why were you calling him?"

"Well, I'm not supposed to talk about an open investigation, but since you're a state representative, I guess I can make an exception." Jack heard a sigh on the line. "I guess Dick—the son, my Deputy Chief—didn't tell you that a buddy of his old man was killed early this morning. The victim had some things that belonged to...Tom Dick. Did I get that right?"

Needham didn't answer.

"Anyway, we wanted to be sure Tom Dick wasn't dead also. But he's not. I assume you're representing him too?"

"You know what they say about assuming things, Detective Murphy. It will make an ass out of you and me. In this case you assumed right. However, you could have sent a Warrick County sheriff's deputy to make the welfare check."

"I think you're confused, Carl," Jack said. "It had nothing to do with a welfare check. We were just trying to ascertain the health of the gentleman."

"Why did you feel the need to drive all the way to Thomas Dick's house?"

"We're also federal agents, Carl. Hey, that means we both work for the federal government. How about that. I mean, you're more important than I am, but what a coincidence."

"Detective Murphy..."

"So anyway, we got there and we had to walk all the way up to the house because he didn't have a doorbell out there at the road. Right? Have you seen that place? Holy cow!"

"Detective Murphy, I don't see—"

"We were there on police business. We knock and he comes around the side of the house holding a big pair of loppers that I thought was a machete at first. We felt threatened and when he told us to leave we got out of there. If he told you any different, he's lying. Maybe he wasn't lying because he's old. He might have just had—a moment. You know? If he's calmed down now we'll go back out there and apologize."

Needham said, "You will *absolutely not* bother Mr. Dick again!"

"Excuse me, Senator, but which Dick are you referring to now? My boss or the older one?"

"Detective Murphy, I'm speaking on behalf of both Dicks, Richard and Thomas. They are both my clients. I'll have to take your word for it that no harm was done. Do I need to remind you of the Fourth Amendment? The U.S. Constitution says…"

Liddell snickered and said, "Did he just say 'both Dicks'?"

Jack interrupted again. "Senator, we're aware of all those rules. And let me assure you the Dicks are not prime suspects," he lied.

"Excellent," Needham said. "You were directed by my client—Richard Dick—to speak to me in future about any questions you may have for him concerning the case you're investigating. That goes for his father as well. May I ask what case you're investigating?"

"Let me ask you a question first, Senator. You're a possible witness in the case in question. Doesn't that create a conflict of interest? I mean with you representing both Dicks?"

"I wasn't aware that you've had legal training, Detective. Where did you go to law school?"

"Just street training," Jack replied. "You know. Cop 101 and 102. A murder here, a murder there."

"No offense, Detective Murphy. Maybe you should let people who *have* had legal training make the legal decisions? I have every right to know why you want to question my client. You're fishing, Detective Murphy, and in dangerous waters."

He's the one fishing, Jack thought. "Okay. You got me there. We've been assigned to investigate the murder of an old friend and classmate of yours, Maximillian Day, and the murder of his father, Harry Day. And since we started digging into this, Max's sister was beat up and shot at, and the mother was shot and killed. Can you believe that? And then the original detective on the cases was murdered last night. I mean, it's crazy. Right?"

The silence stretched out.

Murphy's Law said: *He who talks first loses.* Jack was good at the game too.

Just when it seemed neither would speak again, Needham folded.

"If that's true," Needham said and repeated it for emphasis: "If that's true, you will get very few helpful answers from my client. He was not a friend of Max, as you suggested, nor an acquaintance of his father. Dick and I were very close. And before you ask, I'm referring to Richard. I assume you know that Maximillian Day was a transfer student from Central High School where he was on track to be expelled. Just what are you after, Detective Murphy?"

"Senator, this is a murder investigation. Scorched-earth type. No stone unturned. You understand that, right? And your client, my boss, is a stone that needs to be turned. It's in his best interest to be eliminated from our investigation. Isn't that what we both want? Truth. And justice for Max and Harry. The CIA motto is *the truth will set you free*." The CIA were professional liars.

"I agree that Richard should be eliminated from your inquiry. However, if you do your job correctly he can be eliminated without being interrogated. In my experience, anything you say *will* be used against you."

"Let's cut to the chase, Senator. This case is as old as I am. I'm at a real disadvantage here and it may take years to get ahead of this thing." Or not. "We need to interview everyone involved. The people that were in Max's world at the time in particular. Both of the Dicks' cooperation will speed this up considerably. Yours too. You agree?"

"I appreciate your candidness, Detective."

Jack said, "I don't know what that word means. Was that an insult, because I didn't insult you, did I?"

"Detective Murphy, don't play stupid with me."

"Then don't play stupid with me, Carl. You knew Max. You were involved in those fights with him the night he was killed."

"Okay, Detective Murphy. Like you said, we'll cut to the chase. I personally have nothing to hide," Needham said. "I have it on good authority that you know about the little spat at Rex Mundi during football practice, so there's little more I can tell you about that. It was a nonevent. Two teenage boys squaring off. That's practically a rite of passage in high school."

Jack knew he was right about that. He'd come home many times scraped up, torn clothes, bloody lips. The difference was he'd kicked the other kids' ass and after the fight they were friends. They respected, not killed, each other. Getting a gun and killing after a fight was more of a millennial thing. Sad but true.

"I also have it on good authority that you are in possession of certain items that make you believe there was a fight at the location where Maximillian Day's body was found. I know you will be checking phone records for everyone you think knows anything. For the purpose of ending this witch hunt, I'll admit that Richard and I went to high school together and have remained friends over the years. As such, we talk on the phone. There is nothing suspicious about old friends talking. You might research me or my client's financial records, although I must warn you to tread carefully. You're aware the Fourth Amendment to the Constitution forbids any search or seizure without a warrant. That would include trolling the internet in places where you don't have legal access."

Jack didn't interrupt. Needham was similar to Double Dick. He liked the sound of his own voice.

"I also have been informed of Mrs. Day's recent death, the death of her husband, and the assault on the sister, Reina. Believe me, Detective Murphy, talking to Richard or myself will gain you nothing. If we knew anything we would tell you. Richard is, after all, a policeman, like yourself. I'm an officer of the court. We have a duty just like you. But my duty as a lawyer is to protect my client's reputation as well as his freedom. If you're releasing damaging or untrue information to the news media, we will take action."

Jack said, "I'm confused, Senator. Did you just say *you* are willing to speak to us, or are you invoking your rights now? Or maybe you just told me in legalese to stuff myself?"

Needham chuckled. "Richard said you were quite the smart aleck. A throwback to police days of old. The world has moved on since the days of *Dragnet*, Jack. You are putting yourself in a precarious position," Needham continued.

"I'm hurt, Senator. I think very highly of both Dicks," Jack lied for the recording. "This is the second time I've been threatened over this case. That tells the detective in me that I'm on to something."

Needham laughed outright this time. "Under different circumstances, I think you and I would get along just fine."

"However?" Jack asked.

"However, circumstances preclude us from bonding, so to speak. I'm not one of your drinking buddies. Neither I, nor my clients, will speak to you. If you have a search or arrest warrant, we will cooperate, but we will *not* speak to you."

"Do you like to fish?" Jack asked, catching Needham off guard.

"Why do you ask?"

"Listen, I have a cabin on the Ohio River. I love fishing. I love the water. When this is all over and I catch the asshole that's been killing people, maybe we could go fishing. Just you and me. You know. Do guy things that take us back to our grade school days. It's only a four- or five-hour drive from Columbus. Why don't you come and visit and I'll show you my cabin and we'll settle things."

"I'd be wasting a lot of gas, Detective Murphy. I'm already in Evansville. In fact, I'm at Two Jakes Restaurant having breakfast. Nice place. It would be too bad if you had to sell it to settle a lawsuit."

"And here I thought we were getting along swell, Carl."

"I think we're done here," Needham said and the call disconnected.

Jack dialed a number. "Angelina?"

"We need to talk, Jack," Angelina said. "Where are you?"

"On our way there. What's going on?"

"Carl Needham is in here right now. He asked Jake what a place like this is worth. Then he asked about me. He knows my name and a lot of personal stuff, Jack."

"Get a picture of him, Angelina. We may need it later to show a pattern of threats."

"You think I've been doing my nails?"

Jack said, "I just got off the phone with him. Get me everything on him you can."

"What an asshole. He knew my name, Jack. He knew who I was married to and about my business and where I live."

"Keep him there. We're less than ten minutes out."

"Hang on." Jack heard a door open and she said, "He just left. He's driving a black SUV. A new Lexus. You want me to stop him? Cut his tires? Smash his face? Please say yes."

"He's a senator, Angelina. They have a thick hide. And he is an attorney, so he has no feelings. Besides, he's the Dicks' family attorney. He warned us off and said we were harassing them." Jack thought the senator from the State of Ohio would just love it if he was detained by a civilian. "No. Let him go. Turds never go far from the toilet bowl."

"Jack, he was wearing dark jeans and a black hoodie jacket. Who's that sound like?"

"It could be coincidental," Jack said, although the idea of a senator in his early sixties dressing like antifa didn't sound normal. "It's not enough to hold him. We can't even question him. Let it go, Angelina." *I'll see him later.*

"This is the guy. I just know it."

"We'll talk when we get there. Stay away from Needham."

Chapter 42

Dennis James knew he had always been different. When he met Carl and Richard in high school they hit it off right away, but he was still a little bit of an outsider. He always felt they'd let him hang around because girls liked him. All kinds of girls from all walks of life and even some of the female teachers. He'd gotten it on with Mrs. Hungate in the tenth grade. Bent her over the teacher's desk and made her howl. He got all A's that year. Then in eleventh grade he got some 900-year-old nun who was built like a gorilla and smelled like one too. He'd almost failed school that year. Even he couldn't get his sailor to come to attention with the mug on that woman.

He was a below-average student but he was a natural athlete. In any case, he'd wasted his talents and life on drugs and drink. Richard Dick was smart, devious, quick on his feet, good with his hands, all of which made him a helluva quarterback. Dick was being scouted by some heavy colleges, but he had opted to go to Notre Dame and get a couple of lame-ass degrees. He'd gone on to become a police officer like his old man and had done okay for himself. Dick had helped him out a time or two over the years.

Carl Needham: Rich kid, charming, fit in with every crowd, had every advantage in life and made the most of it. His mom and dad were surgeons. Very high-class snobs. Carl had gone to Harvard, contributed articles to scholarly legal tomes, graduated top of his class, was hired by a prestigious firm in Ohio, then on to private practice, taking some of the bigger clients of the firm with him. Smart move. He ran for the Ohio Senate and was elected. He was a big deal.

He, Dennis James, was a different story altogether. Instead of excelling after high school, starting a career or running for office, he spiraled into a nightmare life, frequently tapping his more fortunate high school friends for favors or money or both. The only thing he and his old buddies had in common now was that they had followed in their fathers' footsteps. His old man was an addict who died in prison.

He'd only maintained a shred of his dignity by attending the church his mother had insisted he grow up with. His dad was whatever drug he was worshipping at the moment. His mother was a devout Catholic and he had been brought up to believe that any sin he committed would be expunged when he went to church and confessed his sins to God. He was there now. Front pew, kneeling, hands folded in prayer, beseeching help from a God he'd never truly believed in.

A priest came from the sacristy dressed in the vestments for the confessional, saw Dennis James and smiled. "Are you here for confession?"

Dennis didn't recognize this man and his gut reaction was to glance around nervously. He'd heard those same words from cops so often he almost laughed, but the humor was short-lived. Long ago he'd been an altar boy at this church. Today the place felt alien to him. He didn't like it when things were different than he expected and he'd been expecting Father Davis, his regular man of God.

"Where's Father Davis?" Dennis asked, his eyes constantly roving around the church.

"I'm Father Carrell. Father Davis had an accident and I'm helping out from St. Agnes Parish until he's back on his feet." He asked, "Are you a friend of Father Davis?"

"He's been here since I can remember. What happened to him?"

Father Carrell took a step forward but stopped when Dennis drew back. "He was on a ladder. Changing a light bulb. He fell and I'm afraid it was the last straw for that bad knee of his."

Dennis relaxed. He knew Father Davis, even though he was of nursing home age, was a jogger, and had seen him limping around many times over the years. His mother always taught him to be nice. That was mostly beat out of him by his father, but he was in church now. "Name's Dennis." He put his hand out.

"Dennis. I'm glad to see you here." Father Carrell shook his hand. "Are you here for confession?"

Dennis said, "No, Father Carrell. I only got a second. Just came by to say hello to Father Davis, but I got to get to work," he lied and got up.

"You seem troubled, Dennis. Can I help? We can talk here, or back in the rectory if you would feel more comfortable. Maybe you could talk to Father Davis. He's in bed, but I'm sure he wouldn't mind. He would welcome the company."

Father Carrell's face was sincere, but he hadn't come to see anyone, or go to confession. He just wanted to sit somewhere safe and think. It was a mistake coming here.

"Gotta go, but thank you, Father," Dennis said, got up and hurried out the back door of the church without noticing the black SUV parked on the street.

Chapter 43

Jack and Liddell entered the war room. Angelina sat in front of a bank of computer screens and didn't acknowledge them.

"Angelina," Jack said.

"What?"

"I'm sorry if he scared you."

Angelina bristled. "Who says I'm scared? I'm too pissed to be scared. This guy doesn't know who he's messing with. I'll bring hellfire down on his ass. Credit rating—gone. I'll put him on the no-fly list. Load child porn on his office computer and tip off the Ohio authorities. A few rumors in the right ears—he'll be on his knees begging to talk to you."

"I believe you," Jack said, "but I need you to focus."

"What do you think I'm doing?" she said. "I've got Deaconess Hospital records."

She had everyone's interest.

"Double Dick went to the hospital around three hours after the fight at Rex Mundi, give or take."

"And that was two hours after Max's time of death from the coroner's report," Jack said.

Angelina said, "Right. Dick was treated for a broken nose, various bruises, and a minor cut on his left hand. He told them he was in a vehicle accident. Dennis James was treated at Deaconess about the same time as Dick. He was complaining of a headache from the same accident. He didn't have any obvious injuries. They came in on their own. No ambulance. Carl Needham wasn't with them."

"Did you check accident reports?" Jack asked.

"The police department doesn't keep vehicle accident records from that far back, and there's a possibility Dick never reported it. Do you want me to chase down the cars he might have owned in 1980? I might be able to check with body shops, but it'll take a while. I'll have to do most of that on the telephone."

It had been so long ago. Chances of finding Dick and/or his friends' cars was slim and even if they did, there would be little of evidentiary value left. "If we don't get anywhere soon, we might revisit that idea. There was no mention of Carl Needham at Deaconess Hospital?"

She shook her head.

"That doesn't mean he wasn't with them," Liddell suggested.

Angelina said, "And I can see another problem if you're going to bring criminal charges against any of the three boys."

"What's that?" Liddell asked.

"They were all seventeen."

She was right, of course, but Jack wasn't concerned with charging them. That was the prosecutor's responsibility. If these seventeen-year-olds had continued to cover up their involvement in Max's murder all this time, they were adults now and guilty of conspiracy at least.

"We catch them and let the courts sort it out. When Harry Day was killed they were all twenty-one. And one of them has killed twice recently. And an attempted murder, aggravated battery, and theft on Reina." *Their convictions might belong to a jury, but their asses are mine.*

"I'll track down the Dick Diver information, pod'na."

"Am I missing something here?" Angelina asked.

"Liddell thinks he's being funny again," Jack said. "You know Dr. Schirmer thinks the weapon that killed Max was a shark dart that injects compressed air. Double Dick had some pictures in his office of him and Carl Needham in scuba gear. And at Olson's house, Little Casket thought the weapon that killed him might have been injected CO_2."

Liddell added, "Schirmer said we should talk to someone in Special Forces, Navy divers, or cave divers."

Angelina tapped at the keyboard while Jack said his piece. She turned the laptop around for them to see. "Come see what I found."

Jack and Liddell huddled around the screen. The picture was of a wicked knife in a padded gun case. The blade was as big as a bowie knife in length, ten to twelve inches. Fitted in the case next to the knife were three CO_2 cartridges.

"It's called a WASP," Angelina said. "The air cartridge is inserted into the handle and is activated by a button on the hasp of the knife. You stab and inject the compressed air."

"Max had other injuries," Jack said. "We think he'd been in a fight with Dick, Needham, and James at the cemetery. Max against the three of them. They all got in some licks. One of them had a tire tool and-or beer bottles. We just recovered a tire iron and broken bottles from Olson's secret U-Haul bin."

Liddell said, "I'm going old-school. All the scuba suppliers here should be listed. I need to find out if any of these guys bought a shark dart or a WASP."

"Beat you to it," Angelina said. "There's one dive shop in Evansville. Perry's PADI Shop, Professional Association of Diving Instructors, specializing in everything aquatic. Let me call them." She did.

"Bingo," she said when she hung up. "They've been in business for fifty years. It's a family business. Best of all, they kept records on everyone they trained. Listen to this: 1978—Carl Needham completed advanced open water, nitrox certification, night dive, cave dives, and rescue. Richard Dick followed suit in 1979. No mention of Dennis James." With a wicked grin, she said, "So Dick really *is* a diver." She and Liddell bumped knuckles.

"Don't encourage him, Angelina. I've got to put up with him all day. I don't suppose Perry's dive shop has a knife like the WASP?"

"Not for sale. But they said we can borrow one for testing. You're thinking about Olson's murder, aren't you?"

"I'll get the knife," Walker said. "We can run some forensic tests and see if that's what killed Olson."

"Who are you going to test it on?" Liddell asked.

"I would suggest he try it out on you, Bigfoot, but your skull is too thick to penetrate," Jack answered.

"Oww!"

"We have some ballistic gel dummies. I'll film it," Walker said.

"What have you got on Harry Day?" Jack asked Angelina.

"I've got financials, bank records, firearms license, registrations of gun purchases, tax records. There's nothing there. He had a comfortable life, but he wasn't pulling in big money from anywhere. Unless he was buying and selling guns from street people, he's clean as a whistle."

Liddell posited, "Robbers don't always go after big money."

Chapter 44

Dennis James was predictable due to two habits in his routine. He was still a practicing Catholic who attended the same church his parents had taken him to during his formative years *and* he had an addictive personality. Smoking, drinking, sex, gambling, drugs, stealing, drinking, drugs, and from there on it was mostly about drugs.

Dennis left St. Anthony's Church and, true to his nature, his head swiveled around, checking out the street before walking south and circling back behind the school that had been turned into a homeless shelter. He skirted the homeless shelter and continued walking west toward Fulton Avenue, occasionally casting a glance back over his shoulder. Twice now Dennis had looked directly at the black SUV parked on the street across from the Econo Lodge and not reacted. He couldn't see through the smoked glass windshield or he would have run.

Dennis picked up the pace and the driver of the SUV was tempted to follow, but he knew exactly where Dennis was going. There was a little store on Columbia Street, not two blocks from where they were, that sold various and sundry tobacco products. It sold other things too, like LSD and crack cocaine. It had done so when they were all in grade school together. All the kids knew. The adults were clueless. They had even scored cough syrup laced with morphine. It was a rite of passage. A way to numb the boredom of listening to the nuns all day.

The SUV circled the church in the other direction from which Dennis had walked. It pulled to the curb on a side street facing Sam Day's Market. Dennis didn't disappoint. His head darted around before he went in the shop and swiveled like a tank turret on his shoulders when he came outside, eyes never pausing once on the black SUV.

Dennis walked west on Columbia Street and jumped when he was honked at as he stepped into traffic to cross onto Third Avenue. He gave the offending horn the double bird and continued north on Third Avenue. The SUV driver lost sight of Dennis, who cut in between two houses, but he picked him up again as he cruised past the alley entrance. He slowed and watched Dennis climb the outside stairway at the back of a house. He settled in and waited for Dennis to come out. Thirty minutes later, he left the Desert Eagle and the WASP in the car and put a small tactical knife in the pocket of his hoodie jacket. He pulled the hood up, slipped on sunglasses, and walked down the alley.

He climbed the rickety stairs to the second floor, where a door had been pried open. He listened. No noise came from inside. He looked through the door's window and saw Dennis sitting on the peeling linoleum floor in the corner of the kitchen, legs drawn up with a shard of glass from a broken window propped on his knees. On the glass was a teaspoon-sized mound of white powder, and several lines of the stuff he'd bought at Sam Day's Market. Dennis's eyes were unfocused and his head was lolled back against the wall. He turned his face toward the dark figure standing near him.

"Waa'chu wan'." Dennis slurred the words and drew the piece of window glass closer, cutting himself and not noticing, protecting his skag.

"That's China white, Dennis. Pure. Uncut. It must have cost you a chunk of the money I gave you."

Dennis's head nodded and bobbed on his neck like a bobblehead doll. "'S mine."

"I don't want your heroin, Dennis. Want a cigarette?"

The man pulled a Bic lighter and a pack of unfiltered Camel cigarettes from a pocket of the hoodie. He wasn't worried about fingerprints or DNA. The good thing about tobacco was that it destroyed itself. Just like the tobacco smoke destroyed your lungs. He didn't have the smoking habit himself, but he remembered Dennis smoking these coffin sticks in high school. Dennis thought it made him cool.

"You still smoke Camels, Denny?"

Dennis's head bobbled on his shoulders.

"I guess that's a yes." He clicked the Bic and burned the end of the cigarette until it glowed. He stuck the other end up to Dennis's lips. Dennis seemed to be too tired or too weak to raise his arms.

He laid the pack of Camels on the floor a few feet away from the almost-unconscious Dennis James. He pushed some paper rubbish against the bottom cuff of the dirty blue jeans and lit it with the Bic. The pants caught fire, but the wearer didn't seem to notice as the flames climbed his leg like a tree branch. There would be no need for the knife.

He could imagine the police report. *Known drug addict found burned to death. Pure heroin found in his system.*

"I always told you those things would kill you, Denny."

He watched until Dennis's clothes burst into flames, the man wearing them barely reacting. There were curtains hanging from the kitchen windows. He lit these and backed out of the door. He saw some movement. There were other junkies inside. No matter. They were as good as dead anyway.

He stood on the stoop outside and left the door halfway open, allowing the air to feed the fire. The wallpaper caught and burning curls fell to the floor in the kitchen. The linoleum began to blister and then roll up like the Fruit Roll-Ups he'd had when he was a youngster.

He hurried down the steps, across the street, and between houses to the alley. If anyone had noticed him, it would appear he was escaping the fire. Just another druggie running from a shooting gallery; a drug den.

In the alley behind the houses he took the hoodie jacket off and circled to the block. returning to his SUV. He drove slowly away and watched smoke rise from the fire.

Chapter 45

Jack and Liddell talked through the evidence again, description of both scenes, autopsy reports, hospital records, and statement from James, Needham, and Dick, plus the recorded statement of Ginger Purdie. They still needed to talk to her, but said her taped statement was just more cover-up for Dick. The prosecutor would be hard-pressed to convince a jury that a fight that led to Max's death had ever taken place. And there was no definite proof in Harry's case, except for Olson's thievery of guns, money, and business papers and Olson was dead. They were no closer to an arrest than the original investigation.

Jake Brady stuck his head in the door of the war room. "Someone here to see you, gentlemen, and I use that term loosely."

"Who is it?" Jack asked.

"I'm not your secretary," Jake said. "You want to see him or not? He stinks and I want him gone. I made him stay out front."

"Okay. I'll be right out."

"I'll get him," Liddell said. "I need to get away from this stuff for a bit. My mind is reeling."

Jack went back to reading the case file documents on Max Day's murder. He hoped he'd see something he'd missed.

Liddell came back in the war room with an old derelict in tow. The man smelled like burned hair and fresh manure. Liddell said, "Jack Murphy, meet Dennis James."

* * * *

The smell of smoke and body odor and other unpleasant things was overwhelming in the small room. Over Jake Brady's protests, Liddell and Jack led James through the kitchen and out the back door.

Dennis James was wearing a thin button-down shirt out over soot-covered blue jeans. The sides of his tennis shoes were blackened. One leg of his jeans had holes burned out of it. The sleeve of his shirt was singed. His hair stuck out at angles. His eyes were wild and constantly moving.

"I came to you," James said. "Remember that when I get to court. I know you two are the cops on Max Day's murder. I want to be locked up. You got to arrest me."

"Why? What have you done?" Jack asked. The man's pupils were pinpoints, but he was frightened, manic.

James stuffed a hand deep in one of his pockets and came out with a baggie of something resembling raw sugar and handed it to Jack.

"That there is pure H. China white. Heroin. I ain't saying no more."

Jack was temporarily speechless. This wasn't exactly how he'd expected it to go once they located Dennis James.

"Are you hurt?" Jack asked. "Have you been in a fire?"

Dennis chuckled. "You could say that. I've been *on fire*. That's why you gotta arrest me."

"Why are you in such a hurry to go to prison, Dennis?" Jack asked.

"I don't want a lawyer. I'm guilty of drug possession with intent to sell." He emptied his pockets and a wad of rolled-up fifty-dollar bills hit the floor. "That's five grand, Detective Murphy. All proceeds of selling drugs. Arrest me."

"That's not what I asked."

"I want you guys to book me. No one else. Just you two."

Before Jack could respond, James said, "And I want guarantees. First off, I don't want to be put in a cell with anyone. Anyone. I want to go in lockdown. Suicide watch. And I don't have to say nothing else, cause that's my God-given right. You got the evidence. I'm making it easy for you."

Jack could now smell the fear underneath the stink. He examined Dennis James to determine if the man was in need of medical facilities. He decided it could wait until he finished talking.

"I don't think I can do that," Jack said. "In fact, I don't think I'm going to arrest you. This is a drug unit case. I don't have any way of testing this crap. For all I know, it's sugar and you're some nut that's wandered away from a psych facility. You're free to leave."

Liddell stood back to let the man leave, but Dennis James made no move to go. His face twisted up and he broke down, sobbing and shaking.

"Please arrest me, you guys. I don't want to go to jail, but it's either that or I'm a dead man. They're gonna kill my ass."

"We can protect you," Jack said, "if you tell us everything you know about Max Day's murder."

James rubbed snot dripping from his nose and wiped it on his pants, smearing soot down his pant leg and across his hand. "You can't protect me. You have no idea who these guys are. I'm telling you. They won't quit until I'm dead."

"Who won't quit?"

He seemed to get some steel back in his spine and said, "I'm not telling you anything until you give me what I'm asking for. I got some real good stuff for you."

Jack was getting tired of being jerked around. He had no doubt Dennis James knew something about Max's murder, but he wasn't about to make a deal with this piece of human scum.

"You *are* going to tell me," Jack said. "Or I'll stick your ass back on the street and jump for joy when you get picked off. You tell me what you know about Max's murder and then I'll tell you what I might—just might—do. No guarantees. No deals."

"I know who killed Max Day," James said.

"Who?" Jack asked. When Dennis didn't answer, Jack took him by the shoulders and pointed him toward the parking lot.

"Carl Needham's trying to kill me. It was Carl, man!"

Chapter 46

Jack went to the restroom and washed his arms up to his elbows. Twice. Jake borrowed some of Vinnie's spare clothes for Dennis James. Liddell stood watch while James showered with a garden hose and dish soap beside the outside trash bin. It was chilly, but he didn't seem to mind. He didn't have any blisters on his legs, but they were red and Jack had no doubt the burns would hurt like hell once the China white wore off. Vinnie's spare pants were a little short, but the tie-dyed sweatshirt fit him fine. Vinnie's shoes wouldn't fit, so James put the half-melted sneakers back on.

After he was somewhat clean, Jack led him through the back and into the war room. Jake brought food and strong black coffee. James was destroying all of it.

When Jack thought James had sobered a little, he said, "This isn't a food kitchen, Dennis. You tell us what you know or out you go."

"I know lots of things," James said, noshing on a hard-boiled egg he'd wrapped with several strips of bacon.

Jack took the plate away and leaned forward, staring at him.

"You want me to start with the fight?"

"That's a good place," Jack said.

"Okay. Max and Richard Dick hated each other's guts."

Jack leaned back and remained silent.

"There was a football practice before the championship game. Did you know that?"

Jack rolled a finger in the air.

"Well, Dick was sweet on Ginger Purdie. Truth is, most of the team was sweet on her. You know what I'm saying? Max was trying to make time with her. Dick caught him watching Ginger. Truth is, I think Ginger had a thing for Max too. Or she was just trying to make Dick jealous."

"The fight?" Jack asked, his patience running very thin.

"So anyway, we was with Dick and he smacked Max in the back of the head with his football helmet. Max went down, but when he got up he was smiling-like, and he punched Dick in the nose and knocked him down. Some things were said back and forth and then Max left."

Jack said, "Go on."

"Dick wasn't done, man. Max was leaving but Dick went after him."

"Did you go with Dick? Did Needham?"

"Yeah. But we weren't part of this. At least, not then."

"This?"

"There was a feud going on between them. Dick and Max. It wasn't just over that cheerleader. They was like two alpha dogs. Max played for Central High School before he come to Rex Mundi. He sacked Dick—hard—every time the two teams played each other. Then when Max played for Rex Mundi he started tackling Dick extra-hard during practices. That night Max was out near the field flirting with Ginger and Dick wasn't gonna have it no more."

"What else?" Jack asked.

James coughed up a wad of black goo into his palm and wiped it on the borrowed pants.

"Dick was top dog until Max came to Rex Mundi. Afterwards, it was like Dick was always being knocked down a peg or two. People were scared of Max. It was like Mad Max was invincible. That's what we called him. Mad Max. You couldn't hurt him, man. I mean, Dick hit him hard enough to knock him out. I'm telling you, the guy didn't feel pain. It was scary. He was like Superman, you know."

"Okay. Max left, but Dick went after him. You and Needham went with Dick. What happened after that?"

"Well, Dick calmed down a little before we got to the car. Then he saw Ginger fawning over Max. Out by Max's Camaro. That's when Dick went nuclear. Man, I never seen him like that, not in all the years I'd known him."

"Was anyone else with Max?"

"Yeah, Reina was there too. Anyway, we was all coming at Max. I wasn't going to fight, but I think Carl and Dick were gonna bust his head. But Max got in his car, peeled out. Then we got in Dick's car—he had a Cadillac."

Of course it was a Cadillac.

"Dick took off down First Avenue, trying to find Max."

"Where was Reina Day?"

"Reina was standing there at Max's car. We just blew past her and Ginger. Carl was mad at Max because of an earlier fight. Carl had told some people that Reina was pregnant and he'd made her get an abortion. Max heard about it and beat the crap out of him after school one day."

Now Jack was surprised. "When was that?"

"I don't remember, but it was early in the school year. I think it was," James said.

"Was this reported to the school police?"

"It wasn't on school property. Dick was there and Carl didn't want anyone to know. He didn't come to school for about a week because of the black eyes. He looked like a racoon, man."

"Did you see the beating?" Jack asked.

"I wasn't there, but Carl was pissed that Dick didn't help him out."

"Dennis, you need to focus. Did Carl ever threaten to kill Max?"

"That's what I'm getting at," James said. "It wasn't just Dick that had a dog in that fight at the cemetery. Needham wanted a piece of Max too. Maybe more than Dick. Carl was a spoiled rich kid. He was used to being untouchable. Well, I can tell you, Max touched him. Everyone heard about Carl getting his ass handed to him by Max and after that his reputation was in the toilet. His girl dumped him over it, is what I heard."

"Tell me about the second fight. You caught up to Max, didn't you?" Jack asked. He could feel his adrenaline kicking in. Here, at last, was confirmation of the second fight by a witness.

"Yeah. Well, we chased Max around over by Gloria's Corral Club. Where Gloria's used to be, I mean. It's been torn down now."

Jack said nothing.

"And Max pulled a fast one on Dick. Dick was right on Max's bumper, but Max slammed on the brakes when we was coming up on the double dipper and Dick had to swerve around him to keep from rear-ending him. By then we were going so fast we went airborne on the double dipper."

Jack knew the place on Allens Lane that was called "double dipper." Even when he was a kid, the double dipper was well known. In high school they would dare each other to see who could cross the tracks the fastest and not total their cars. Later in life, he'd bottomed a police car out on that exact location during a car pursuit.

"You're talking about the double set of railroad tracks on Allens Lane near Kratzville Road?" Jack asked, just to be clear.

Dennis's head bobbled up and down and his eyes grew wide.

"Damn near killed us," Dennis said. "We was off the side of the road in a ditch. Smoke was coming from under the hood, we all got banged around, my head hit the ceiling twice, and the engine was dead. Dick tried to get back on the road, but we was out of control and went airborne off the other side of the road and damn near flipped.

"And then here came Max, tooling by in that souped-up Camaro, waving and smiling. Dick went crazy, man. He was throwing big rocks at Max's car. I got the Caddy started and we got back on the road. Dick's car was messed up, man. If it was me, I would have called it a night. But Dick was gone. He said he was going to kill Max. We drove around some and saw some taillights in that cemetery where the second fight happened. Max's car was parked in there and Dick told me to block it in. So I pulled in behind the Camaro and we all got out."

James rubbed his throat. "I'm getting real dry, man. You got any whiskey?"

Liddell went to find Jake and came back with a partial bottle and one glass. James took a swig from the bottle, ran an arm across his mouth, and said, "Max didn't try to run. Like I said, he was invincible. I guess he thought he could take us all on. And he kind of did. He took what we threw at him, I mean, what Dick and Carl did to him, and he just stood there, grinning. And then we left."

"You just left. All of you?"

"Yeah. I mean *we*—they got tired cause Max wouldn't stay down. One of his arms was hurt, but he punched Needham out with the other arm. That boy could fight. Then Max got ahold of the tire iron Needham was using and we—they backed off. Dick told Max it wasn't over and we all left in Dick's car and went home."

"Max was still alive when you left? He was outside the car?"

"Yeah. Like I said, he was standing there and grinning when we left. Holding that damn tire iron. He would've hurt someone real bad. I seen a fight once with a guy and he got his head caved in. I wasn't fighting. It was two of my friends. Other friends, I mean."

"You're lying," Jack said. "We know you're lying because we have hospital records from that night."

Dennis held the bottle in his lap, twisting his hand around the top.

"I'm starting to get pissed off here, Dennis. You're wearing me out—*man*." He took the bottle out of Dennis's hands and gave it to Liddell. "You said you knew who killed Max Day. Do you or don't you know? Last chance."

"Okay, okay. I just don't want you putting it on me. I'll tell you the truth. The God's truth this time. Everyone got hurt a little more than I let on, but I swear, Max was alive when we took off."

"They were a little more than hurt, Dennis. You told us Needham killed Max and that he's trying to kill you. Now you're saying Max was alive when the three of you left him at the cemetery. Needham's not trying to kill you, is he?"

"He did. I mean, Carl's the only one that could have killed Max. I didn't see it, but I swear he did. He was whaling on Max with that tire iron, and Dick was swinging with a beer bottle. You got the hospital records. We all went to the hospital."

"Carl too?" Jack asked.

"Yeah. Carl drove us to the hospital, but I don't remember him coming inside. He kind of disappeared. I guess the nurse called Dick's father. When Captain Dick got there no one could find Carl. Me and Dick were there at the emergency room, but Carl wasn't nowhere to be found."

"What did Captain Dick do at the hospital?" Jack asked.

"You probably know all this."

Jack shook his head. "I want you to tell me, Dennis."

"Okay. When Dick's father found out what had happened he asked about Carl because he knew we hung out together and he knew Carl wasn't at the hospital with us. He told us to stay put and took off. When he came back he took us to the police station and asked us some questions."

"When did you next see Carl? I'm verifying your honesty, Dennis. I'll know if you lie. Continue."

"Well, we was taken to the police station by Captain Dick and he stuck us in his office. Carl was in there when we got there."

"Why didn't Carl stay at Deaconess to be treated?" Jack asked.

"He had some lumps. Max popped him a bunch of times in the face and head. I can guess."

"Then guess," Jack told him.

"I think he went back to the cemetery. To get even," Dennis said. "He got beat up pretty good that night and he was mad, but he was real quiet. Dick had a broken nose, some cuts under his eye, and his nose was bleeding again and we was all hurt, so Carl drove. Carl had the car keys at the hospital."

"Let me ask you something, Dennis, and I want a truthful answer. Did you see Carl kill Max?" Jack asked.

"No, sir. I didn't see that. But it had to be him. We couldn't find Carl and the next thing we know, Carl's in the Captain's office and the Captain's telling us Max is dead and we have to get our stories straight."

"Is that the first time you knew Max was dead? Did you know before Captain Dick told you?" Jack asked.

"I didn't know until right then. I can't say for Richard or Carl, but like I said, Richard was at the hospital with me until his dad came and got us, so he probably didn't know, either."

Jack would get back to that. "And Carl was already in the Captain's office when you and Richard got there? Is that the right order of things? Think hard."

Dennis thought and said, "Yeah. Just like I told you."

Jack said, "Let's go back to the hospital when Captain Dick arrived. Tell me again what he did?"

"He wanted to know what happened. Richard tried telling him we'd been in an accident, but he didn't believe it. I told him what really happened. He asked where Carl was and we told him we didn't know. I guess that's about the first time I'd noticed Carl was gone. Then the Captain said we was to stay put. He'd take care of the hospital stuff and he'd be back. He left and was gone about an hour or so. When he came back he made us get in his car and took us to the police station. Like I said, Carl was in the Captain's office."

Jack asked, "Did any other detective or police officer see you or talk to you?"

"Yeah. A Detective Olson. He was in the Captain's office about an hour after we got there."

"What happened when Captain Dick had you in the office? Before Olson arrived."

"He told us that Max was dead. He asked us if we knew who killed him. We all said we didn't know. When we last saw him at the cemetery, he was alive. The Captain was taking notes. He wrote down some things and made us read it. He told us to repeat what we'd read. I guess that's when we got our stories straight. He said we had to say exactly what he wrote or we'd go to prison. And that's about when the other guy came into the office."

"What did the Captain say had happened?"

"He said Max started a fight with us at Rex Mundi. Max hit Dick in the nose and Dick might have hit him back, but it was a reflex, kind of. We yelled at each other and that was it. Max left and we didn't go after him. And if anyone saw us leaving we were to say we were on our way to the hospital to get Dick's nose fixed."

"And the fight at the cemetery...?"

"He said there wasn't a fight at the cemetery because we were never there."

"What was your story about going to the hospital if someone asked?"

"He told us that his son's nose was bleeding and he ran his car off the road on the way to the hospital because he couldn't see. That's where me and Carl got our injuries."

"Did anyone interview you and record a statement?" Jack asked.

"Yeah. Captain Dick and the other detective gave us each a copy of his notes about what happened and then they both recorded us."

"They both asked questions on the tape?"

"Sort of. Yeah. Dick went first, then Carl, and then me."

"You were all together in the Captain's office when you gave your statements. When the recordings were made?" Jack asked.

"Isn't that in your files there?"

"Just answer the damn question, Dennis."

"Can I have some more to drink? I'm starting to hurt a little."

"Not until we're done," Jack said.

"Yeah. We was all still in Captain Dick's office. Olson and the Captain came in and they locked the door."

"Were there any other detectives or uniformed policemen around when you entered the police station? Did anyone see you?" Jack asked.

"I remember one old guy—a detective, I guess—he was in the hallway and Captain Dick told him to make himself scarce."

"Okay, Dennis. Did you tell the truth to Captain Dick at the hospital?"

"Yes."

"Did Richard tell his father the truth at the hospital about the fight at the cemetery?"

"Yes."

"Was Max still alive when you left the cemetery?"

"Yes. He was standing by his car."

Liddell had been standing behind Dennis the entire time. Liddell held up a recorder and gave Jack the thumbs-up.

"Dennis James, did you kill Maximillian Day?" Jack asked.

The answer was immediate. "Hell no, I didn't. I never killed anyone. I know I been in all kinds of trouble, but I'm not a killer. Are we done here? I want to eat and get tucked in. I haven't been sleeping too good. And I need to see the nurse at the jail. I'm not feeling too good."

Jack could see Dennis had broken out in a cold sweat and was trembling. Signs of withdrawal.

"Just a couple more questions, Dennis, and then we'll book you."

Jack slid the plate of food back to Dennis, but he didn't seem to notice. His knees were pulled up to his chest, arms wrapped around his knees.

"How did Captain Dick react when he came to the hospital that night?"

"He was cool as a cucumber, man. I could tell he was out of sorts with his boy, but he never lost it like my old man woulda done."

"Did he find Carl?" Jack asked.

"He must have," Dennis answered and his trembling worsened.

"Did Carl say where he'd been or did you ever find out?"

"We never found out. The Captain never asked him about that while we were in that office and afterward when we'd talk to him he wouldn't tell us. Or at least he didn't tell me. Him and Dick—Richard—were besties, so he might have told him."

"Do you own a gun, Dennis? And don't say, 'Who, me?'"

"Who—No, I don't have one. I guess you saw that criminal reckless charge. That was a long time ago and I found that gun."

"You found it in the house you were burgling," Jack said. "Have you ever seen Carl or Richard with a handgun or any type of deepwater diver's weapon?"

"You know about that?" Dennis hugged himself tighter, but the question had gotten his attention.

Jack asked the question again. "Have you ever seen Carl Needham or Richard Dick with a handgun or any other type of weapon used by divers?"

"Both of 'em was gun nuts and then Carl got Dick into deep-sea diving or was it cave exploring? They were always talking about guns. Richard brought one to school one time, but the principal called Captain Dick and that was the end of that. We was sophomores when that happened."

"Did you see what kind of gun?"

"Yeah. Him and Carl called it a Dirty Harry gun. After those Clint Eastwood movies. I don't remember much else, but it was one big badassed gun."

"Do you know the difference between a revolver and a semiautomatic, Dennis?" Jack asked.

"It was like the ones you guys carry, but way bigger."

"You said they were both into diving. Did either of them have any weapons they would dive with?"

Like a shark dart or a WASP.

"I didn't never see any weapons, but I heard about them all through our senior year. I guess they didn't show me cause I'm not crazy enough to get in the water with a tank strapped to my ass. I heard stories from Richard and Carl about seeing sharks up close and them man-of-wars… and what do you call them big snake things with teeth?"

"Moray eel," Liddell said.

"Yeah. Eels. Carl and Dick got their rocks off stabbing them things and anything else when they was diving. They used a shark stick like you see on that one James Bond movie. You stick a shark and it explodes. They particularly liked blowing up those electric eels and some big fish. Carl said it was better than sex." He shook his head disbelievingly and said, "Nothing's better than sex, man."

"Why is Carl Needham trying to kill you, Dennis?" Jack asked finally.

"He's cleaning house, man!"

"What do you mean?"

"Getting rid of anyone that's a threat to him. Knows about what he's done. I swear to you, Max Day was alive when we left that cemetery. Carl was the only one that didn't stay at the hospital and next thing we hear, Max is killed. Head blown off. Only one of us capable of doing something like that and that's Carl, man."

"You said Carl Needham tried to kill you. When was this, Dennis?"

"That's what I'm telling you, man. He's after me. He set me on fire and… I don't want to say no more. He's crazy. You got to get me somewhere safe."

"What do you mean? Is that why your shoes are melted, Dennis? Did you see who it was?"

"It was Carl, man."

"Did you see his face?"

"Look, I was zoned. But I seen Carl. He was like a dark shadow. He asked me if I still smoked Camels. And he called me Denny. And then he lit me, man."

"Have you heard about a company called Monarch Investments?" Jack asked.

"Nah, man. I don't know nothing about investing."

"I warned you, Dennis. Out you go." He grabbed Dennis's arm to pull him out of the chair.

Dennis pulled away and said, "I've been getting money to keep my mouth shut."

Chapter 47

Every time Jack thought he had squeezed Dennis James dry, the man came up with another surprise, another avenue of investigation into other murders. If Dennis was telling the truth and if he knew what he was talking about, Carl Needham and/or Richard Dick had systematically killed three members of the Day family, and an ex-detective and attempted to kill Reina Day and Jack.

He and Liddell left Dennis James happily eating and finishing the fifth of whiskey in one corner of the war room, while Jack called Captain Franklin and explained what Dennis James told them.

Captain Franklin had a surprise of his own.

"Jack, there was a house fire two hours ago. Three dead. Arson suspected. It was a drug den in the upstairs of an abandoned house. I'll call narcotics and then bring the Chief up to speed. Sounds like your boy was in the house when the fire was started," Captain Franklin said. "Good job. Sounds like we're on the way to wrapping this up."

"Captain, do me a favor and hold off on telling anyone besides the Chief about Dennis James." Dennis had given them a description of the vehicle he'd thought was following him, and of the shadow man who called him Denny and then set fire to him. "I'll take care of Dennis James. The less people that know he didn't die in the fire…"

"Got it," Franklin said. "You should know Channel Six is all over the fire. It won't be long before they come snooping around here for a statement. I swear, we should hire Claudine Setera as an investigator."

"I don't think she would keep her own name out of the news. She's a camera hound just like the Deputy Chief. Sir."

"Do we have enough for warrants for Richard and Needham, Jack?"

"I have a witness that's not too credible. I also have hospital records to back up Dennis's account of the events that night. And, if the autopsy report is accurate on the time of death, Max died while Richard and Dennis were at the hospital. Dennis James said Carl Needham drove them to the hospital and disappeared. The thing with retired Captain Dick is pretty much verified now with the crappy statements that have Olson's name as the interviewer and the Captain's voice asking the questions. I can't narrow the timing down with the statements because the only solid times are the hospital records."

"What about the shell company in Minnesota? Dennis told you he's been getting money to keep quiet," Captain Franklin said.

"Dennis James is a silent partner in the company, but he didn't know it. He believes he's just getting hush money from Carl and Richard. The bank said the earlier small deposits in Dennis's account were from a different source than Monarch, and I'm guessing that money came directly from Carl Needham, but Angelina's still tracking that down. I guess if Dennis ever told someone what he knew, or if we started researching that twenty-grand deposit, Dick and Needham could say that was Dennis's share of the company."

"But Dennis didn't get that large amount until right after Richard talked to Mrs. Day and things started getting heated up again. Right?" Captain Franklin asked.

"Right. The company was nonexistent until the day of the big deposit. To a reasonable man, it would appear Needham and Dick had opened a shell company to hide what the money was really for. I think we need more, Captain," Jack said.

"Do you have any leads on where Needham is? I think I can run down Richard's location if you want to pick them both up for questioning," Captain Franklin offered.

Just follow a news van and you'll find Double Dick.

Jack said, "I need more time, Captain. What about Reina Day?"

"I had two experienced plainclothes guys guarding her, but she threatened to file charges for police harassment. She called Chief Pope and told him she would get a restraining order if any of us bothered her. I posted a uniform car with two officers on her street. What is she playing at?" Franklin asked.

Jack thought he knew, but he didn't want to rain on her parade. If she wanted to kill Needham herself, who was he to stop her? Her whole family had been killed. He thought she was using herself as bait. Maybe she thought she could get the drop on the killer before he got her. Maybe she just didn't care anymore. On the other hand, what if she just went after Dick or Needham and gunned them down? He had a duty to enforce and uphold the law. Right?

Franklin misunderstood Jack's silence for concern. He said, "The ones watching her are good. They won't lose her, Jack."

Murphy's Law said: *The degree of experience you have doing something is directly proportional to the chances of a screwup.* In this case, a screwup could cost a life or two or three.

"Captain, can you call the Posey County sheriff and arrange for James to go into isolation at their jail? They should put him on suicide watch. And make sure the sheriff knows he's a target. We can house him as a John Doe. I don't want anyone talking to him."

"We can't keep him without charging him indefinitely, Jack. But I'll do what I can. Do you need a uniform car to transport?"

Jack said, "We'll take him. If they need a charge, we can charge him with dealing narcotics. He gave us a bag of heroin when he turned himself in."

Jack ended the call and turned to Liddell. "Let's get him in the car."

* * * *

The trip to Posey County lockup took longer than the booking procedure. The sheriff was all too happy to help out, since Jack and Liddell had solved a murder for him and gave his department all the credit last year.

They even agreed to skip the usual routine of entering anything in the computer before putting James in isolation. A note was stuck to his cell door that said *quarantine*. That would keep all but the medical officer away for a while, and the sheriff assured them there would be no visitors of any kind. Especially attorneys. He laughed and said, "We don't even have a Dennis James in custody, so how can anyone visit him?"

They thanked the sheriff and left. Liddell said, "We can't put a BOLO on Needham without him getting wind we're after him," Liddell said. "We can't talk to Double Dick because Needham has invoked his rights. But since Needham is now a suspect in a conspiracy, does he still have the right to represent someone?"

"Yes. He can represent himself and Double Dick can represent himself—twice. Besides, they both told us to piss up a tree. The only way we'll get them to talk is drive a wedge between them. Dennis might be the wedge," Jack said.

Liddell said, "Double Dick is in this up to his spiked Prussian helmet. We have him and Needham as prime suspects in Max Day's murder. I don't think we can build a case for the other murders. Do you think James was involved in Max's murder?" Liddell asked.

"He had a part in it even if he only conspired to hide the truth," Jack said. "He's got reason to be scared. Someone wants to kill him. Hell, they set him on fire. It had to be Carl or Dick. We might be able to see where they were when the house fire was called in. Maybe Angelina can trace their credit card use and give us some times. We might be able to get Needham for the other three arson deaths."

Liddell said, "I don't want to be a Debbie Downer, but the fire could have been started by one of the druggies. It might not have anything to do with our guy."

"That's possible, Bigfoot, but Dennis gave the same description of a black SUV that Reina and Angelina did. We know Dick owns such a vehicle. Needham was taunting us this morning. He's a little too cocksure we won't get anywhere. When Angelina gets what we need, let's put a BOLO out on both of them. We'll get the Captain to tighten security on Reina. If I'm right about Needham, he'll enjoy the challenge."

A text came up on Liddell's phone with the make and license plates of Needham's Lexus SUV and Dick's Cadillac SUV. Liddell called dispatch to put the BOLOs out and said, "He did what? Are you sure you got the right name?" Pause. "Okay, take it easy, I was just asking because I was surprised. I'm sure you're good at your job." He hung up.

"You won't believe this, pod'na."

"Needham wants to meet with us?" Jack said.

"He told dispatch he'll meet us at Milano's on Main Street."

Jack pushed the Crown Vic harder.

Chapter 48

Milano's was an old-world Italian family-owned restaurant, minus a bar. A wine list would get you some fermented grapes, but there was no hard liquor. Jack and Liddell were frequent fliers for lunch when they were working and as they entered, they were greeted at the door by the owner, Tough Tony. His real name was Tony Bella, a transplant from Queens. He'd been in Evansville so long that no one called him anything other than Tough Tony. It had a nice ring to it and the customers loved it.

"Hey, Jack. Who's the little guy with you, huh?" Tough Tony said. Standing on tiptoes, Tough Tony could just make eye contact with Liddell's nipples. "You here to eat? I got something special from Mama in the back. It's to die for. Whoops. I almost forgot what you guys do for a living." He walked away laughing at his lame humor.

Mama was almost one hundred years old and had cataracts and rheumatism so bad she was twisted like a bonsai tree. But the old woman still cooked.

"That's tough, Tony," Jack threw back a pun of his own. "We don't have time."

Tough Tony surprised them and said, "You here for that guy over by the window?"

From what Angelina had said, Jack was expecting a guy dressed in black with a black hoodie. He recognized the face from the pictures Angelina had given them. Ohio State Senator Carl Needham had changed from the hoodie into a slick politician-go-to-meeting suit: charcoal gray with a thin gray stripe, starched white shirt with a bright red tie and red suspenders. His hair was dark gray with lighter gray streaks around the temples. Needham was sipping from a coffee mug, his eyes taking Jack and Liddell in.

"I never seen him before, Jack," Tough Tony said, not hiding his interest. "Oscar said he sounded uppity. But hey, business is business, right? If I threw every suspected asshole out, I'd go broke. Right? You want Oscar to see what he wants?"

Oscar was the busboy, dishwasher, part-time cook, and nurse's aide when Mama needed help. He was an ex-boxer who kept in shape, but his face was in bad need of plastic surgery to hide the cuts, bulges, and smashed nose. Oscar didn't talk much. He didn't have to. And he didn't like uppity white guys. He didn't have to.

Jack spotted Oscar standing in the kitchen doorway, watching them watch Needham.

"Not necessary," Jack said.

"I'll get a to-go box ready, Jack," Tough Tony said with a grin, and he and Oscar went into the kitchen.

Jack and Liddell approached Needham's table and Jack visually checked for telltale signs of weapons: a Desert Eagle, or a knife equipped with a CO2 cartridge.

"There you are. Jack Murphy and Liddell Blanchard. I'm honored to meet you," Needham said. "Please join me." His smile was all bleached white teeth and as showy as a shark inspecting a meal.

"Thanks for the offer, but we won't be here that long. You won't, either," Jack said.

Oscar brought a Styrofoam container.

"Don't waste a good container. He won't be able to bring that with him," Jack said. Oscar gave Needham a dark glare and left.

Needham dabbed at the corners of his mouth with a napkin. "The rigatoni carbonara is to die for. Tough Tony's mama made it special. Did he tell you? And the garlic rolls are heavenly. You sure you don't want to eat before you falsely arrest me?"

"We're not arresting you, Carl," Jack said and smiled. "We're just holding you for questioning. You've heard of investigative detention. Right? It doesn't violate the Fourth Amendment." *Unless we hold you up by your feet and shake you until your white teeth fall out.*

Needham got to his feet. "I'll come along quietly, gentlemen." He giggled and said, "I've always wanted to say that. No need for drama."

"I prefer drama," Jack said. In fact, he wanted to stuff the rest of the meal in Needham's face.

The smile again. "Richard said you would be entertaining, Jack. You don't disappoint. Lead on, detectives."

Needham removed a crisp fifty-dollar bill from his wallet and left it on the table. One or two customers watched Jack and Liddell lead Needham out of the restaurant, but lost interest quickly. Not enough drama. Nothing to post on YouTube.

On the sidewalk, Needham said, "I take it I'm a suspect in something, Detective Murphy?"

"You are."

"Please enlighten me."

"If I tell you, I have to kill you. No, wait—I mean I have to Mirandize you and you have to tell me you understand your rights. So, before I go any further... I want to be clear," Jack said. He read Needham the Miranda warnings and watched his expression closely. The man was made of ice.

"You're good. I understand my rights, Detective Murphy, and you did an excellent job of reciting them without a Miranda card to read from. Most law enforcement officers leave one or two things out that result in charges being dismissed."

"Why, thank you," Jack said. "I've had a lot of practice." *Arresting scumbags.*

"Now, will you tell me what I'm being suspected of and taken into custody for?"

"The murder of Maximillian Day in 1980, for starters," Jack said. He didn't want to bring Dennis James's accusations into the conversation just yet. A little rope was always best.

Needham stopped walking and turned toward Jack and Liddell. "You're serious? I mean, of course you're serious. But..." He let the word trail off before finishing. "Are you sure you want to do this?"

"Keep walking," Jack said and took Needham by the arm.

Chapter 49

Jack and Liddell marched Needham through the front lobby doors at the police station and walked smack into a media orgy. A temporary podium bristling with microphones had been set up against a wall directly in front of the police department seal. Mayor Thatcher Hensley stood behind the podium. Chief of Police Marlin Pope stood on one side of the mayor and Deputy Chief of Police Richard Dick stood on the other side. Pope's expression was unreadable, but Dick smiled like a teen discovering masturbation for the first time—delighted, surprised, and wondering if anyone was watching.

Three of the local television stations and a gaggle of other TV and radio stations formed a semicircle in the front row. The newspaper and rag reporters were squeezing in between the television cameras, notebooks or recorders in hand. Filling the remainder of the lobby were uniformed officers, detectives, civilian personnel. There were one or two street people who were angry at having their safe zone invaded.

The news conference was obviously starring Double Dick's favorite person, himself. Thatcher Hensley was giving a good effort to appear excited and happy and optimistic. He wasn't pulling it off.

One reporter in the crowd noticed Jack and yelled, "Detective Murphy. Detective Murphy." That caused clumps of two, three, and four reporters to turn in Jack's direction and soon it was a domino effect. The dignitaries behind the podium were forgotten as the newspeople began peppering Jack with questions.

"Detective Murphy, have you made an arrest?"

"Is this the suspect?"

"Who is he?"

"Is this connected to the assault on Reina Day?"

"Is he the murderer?"

Jack's speech professor in college said, "If you feel nervous speaking in front of people, imagine them in their underwear." Or maybe it was "Imagine them naked." He settled for imagining them gone.

Mayor Hensley raised his voice. "Detectives Murphy and Blanchard are in the middle of an investigation and are unable to answer your questions at this time. You can refer your questions to the new Chief of Police."

New Chief? Jack felt his legs weaken. When he first saw this fiasco, he'd hoped the Chief was giving an update. Or that Double Dick had confessed and was going to be publicly hanged.

"Richard Dick, our new Chief of Police, will take questions," Mayor Hensley said.

Needham gave them his shark's smile again. "I did ask if you were sure you wanted to do this."

Jack realized they'd been set up: Dennis comes in and confesses. Gives them a story that leads them to Needham and Dick. Then Needham calls and wants to meet. It was a little too convenient. "You planned this."

Needham said, "You should've eaten with me and I would have told you all about this. I think Richard will make an excellent Chief of Police, don't you? Oh, right. You two hate each other. Well, I'm sure Richard will find a part for you both to play in the revamped police department. I made a few suggestions of my own while Richard and I were having dinner last night with the mayor."

Double Dick stood tall and resplendent in his dress blues, to which he'd added extra medals and ribbons. He also was wearing the five-star epaulet and collar dogs of the Chief of Police.

New Chief of Police Richard Dick raised his hands as if directing an orchestra. "Settle down. Settle down. One thing at a time, ladies and gentlemen. I can promise you we will keep you all updated on the progress of these cases, but as Mayor Hensley pointed out, we can't comment on an active investigation yet. I'll tell you what I can if you will."

Jack ignored Dick's speech and continued leading Needham toward the door to the detectives' corridor and interrogation rooms. Jack had put a hand on Needham's back to hurry him along, just as Claudine Setera stepped in front of them with her cameraman in tow.

"Claudine Setera, Channel Six news live," she said.

They were doing this live?

"Are you Senator Needham?" she asked.

Needham feigned surprise at being recognized and Claudine's cameraman moved in for a close-up of Needham, then of Claudine. "Senator Needham, are you under arrest?" she asked. The cameraman panned from face to face, from Jack to Liddell, and stopped on Needham's serious expression.

"Miss Setera, I am not under arrest," he said. "Just the opposite. I contacted these detectives to assist them in their investigation. They were kind enough to let me watch my good friend Richard Dick receive his richly deserved and long overdue promotion before our discussion."

Needham waggled his fingers at Double Dick.

"I guess we've been triple-dicked now," Liddell muttered in Jack's ear.

Claudine's microphone jerked toward Liddell and she said, "Detective Blanchard, did you have something to add?"

Liddell smiled and said, "I was just saying, I guess we'll have to work three times as hard now. Dick is a hard man."

The pun wasn't lost on Claudine and she had to swallow a smile. She kept the microphone in Liddell's face until she realized he wasn't going to say more. She then turned to Jack.

"Detective Murphy, without compromising the investigation, can you just tell us how the Deputy Chief's promotion will affect your ability to investigate him as a suspect in the murder of Maximillian Day or these other murders?"

"No comment," Jack said, but she wasn't done.

"Detective Murphy, you've heard the taped conversation between Chief Dick and the recent murder victim, Amelia Day, that was aired exclusively by Channel Six television. Isn't it unusual for Richard Dick, a suspect in a thirty-seven-year-old murder, to be appointed as Chief of Police?"

Jack couldn't have said it better. "No comment, Miss Setera. Excuse us. I'm sure Mr. Needham has other things to do." *Until I book him, that is.*

Jack took Needham through a locked door, leaving the news crews behind. He put Needham in a chair in the interview room, when there was a knock on the door.

"I think my parole has just come through, Detective Murphy," Needham said and made a frowny face at Jack.

Jack opened the door to find Captain Franklin slightly pale. Franklin motioned Jack to step into the hall. Jack did and shut the door behind.

"We have Carl Needham, Captain. Dennis James is safely housed and I think we're a go for arresting Needham based on the new evidence and statements."

Jack knew his probable cause was weak as soon as he said this. James was as good of a suspect as any of the others. He admitted to blackmailing

Needham for the last thirty years with what he knew about the fight at the cemetery. With Needham's social station, he could be paying just to keep any tarnish from his profile. And James might have been the one who tried to kill Jack at Olson's house. As far as using James as a witness against Needham, Dennis James had the credibility of a pissant. There were too many suspects and too little physical evidence. The items in Olson's storage bin were basically stolen.

"Jack. Liddell. Your jobs are on the line here. Neither I nor the Chief—I mean ex-Chief—can protect you. Your parading of a senator past a news conference won't go well for you with the press. Blood is in the water, Jack."

"All I can do is what I do, Captain. Are we still good to go?"

Captain Franklin gave a sigh. "I'd tell you to tread lightly, Jack, but you'd ignore me, wouldn't you?"

"Thanks for your concern, Captain. Promise me you'll throw your weight behind Liddell. He's got a new baby."

"What about you, Jack? I hear Katie's pregnant."

"I've got a gun," Jack said and patted his .45. "They'll never take me alive. Sir."

Captain Franklin walked away, shaking his head, and Jack reentered the interview room.

Carl said, "Am I free to go now?"

Jack took a seat close enough to Needham to make the man turn his chair. "You told Claudine you were here to cooperate. Let's begin."

"Do your best, Detective Murphy."

Jack had to admit that if Needham was in the hot seat, he wasn't showing it.

"Tell us about the fight at the cemetery the night Max died," Jack said.

"Not much of a fight," Needham said. "We were just boys then. You know how boys have to show their toughness. It was all bravado."

"Max's head blown all over the inside of his car. Is that what you mean by bravado?"

"Let me ask you something, Detective Murphy. Why would we want to kill Max? What would we have to gain? He was one of our best tackles. Everyone knew it. Sure, he and Richard had some competition going, but it was over nothing. Richard was a team player. He would do nothing to harm the team's chances of winning the championship game. And I suppose you heard about the cheerleader. She was disposable. Richard wasn't serious about her."

"How did the game end?" Jack asked.

"I know you know that we won that game. The trophy is somewhere. Rex Mundi closed its doors and a lot of things went missing from the trophy cases. Are you investigating that too?"

"Tell me about the fight at Rex Mundi." Jack knew he was running out of time to question this arrogant turd, but this all went to motive and opportunity and Needham was a firsthand witness.

"Richard caught Max flirting with Ginger. Ginger was Richard's girlfriend. Richard had warned Max to stay away from her. When he caught Max out by the football field flirting with her, he confronted Max. Max punched Richard in the nose. End of fight."

"And that was it?"

"No. It should have ended there, but Max made some threats toward Richard. Richard wouldn't let it go. It was a matter of honor, you see, because a small crowd had gathered by that time and they were making fun of Richard's bloody nose."

"It took the three of you to pursue Max and soothe Dick's ego."

"Richard was going to have it out with Max. We—Dennis and I—were Richard's closest friends and naturally we went with him. I only tagged along so there wouldn't be any violence. But I'll admit, Dennis was wired, high, and ready to go. Before or maybe afterwards—it's been a long time ago and my memory isn't what it used to be, sorry—but I think it was during the scuffle between Richard and Max and Denny that Denny made some threats and said awful things. Stuff about Max's mother and sister; you know the sort of things. Denny threatened to kill Max but we didn't believe he meant it. Of course, Denny was under the influence of the latest pharmaceuticals. You do know that Denny had a drug problem?"

"Denny?" Jack said.

"Dennis James. We called him Denny."

"Are you suggesting Dennis James killed Max?" Jack asked.

"You're the detectives. I'm only telling you what I remember."

"Do you agree that one of the three of you killed Max?" Jack asked.

"If you say so."

"You said Dennis *had* a drug problem. Does he have one now?" Jack asked.

"I haven't had contact with Dennis James for quite a long time. I wouldn't be surprised if he didn't give himself a hot shot."

Jack knew a hot shot was what druggies called dying from an overdose. But that wasn't what Needham meant by the remark.

Needham leaned forward, speaking in an arrogant tone, a tone Jack had heard coming from Dick's mouth many times. "Both Richard and I have respectable, responsible, *powerful* careers. On the other hand, Dennis

James, by all accounts, was a career criminal, an alcoholic and drug addict. If he's not careful, his habit will be the end of him."

"Dennis James *was* a career criminal. Is that what you said?"

"I simply meant he has always been a criminal. A thief. A drug addict. A liar. But he was still our friend, for all that. We tried to help him all we could. He was pathetic, really."

"Dennis James was killed in a fire this morning," Jack advised.

Needham forced a shocked expression, and said, "That's what I predicted. His drug addiction finally got the better of him."

"Are you familiar with Monarch?" Jack asked. This got the first unprepared reaction from Needham.

Needham said, "Well, yes. We played for the Rex Mundi football team. The Monarchs."

"Are you partnered with Richard Dick and Dennis James in a company called Monarch Investments?"

Needham said sheepishly, "You got me, Detective. You are as good as Richard said you were. He hates you for it, but then, Richard never did like to be outdone."

"Monarch," Jack said.

"Monarch is the name of a company—a start-up, really—that Richard and I are building for our retirement. We had the idea to name it Monarch after the football team, and then at the last minute decided to bring Dennis in on the deal. Of course, he had no money to invest, so we made him a silent partner and paid his share. We were going to share the profits with him to keep him alive. I guess that won't happen now."

"You weren't telling the truth when you said you hadn't been in contact with James for a long time."

"Old habits die hard, Detective Murphy. I was trying to protect our reputations and the reputation of our fledgling company."

"Have you been in touch with James recently?" Jack asked.

"We were close friends in high school. I kept in touch with him for a few years and then… well, I got involved with law school and the tedious climb to where I am now. I have to say, after the earlier contacts during college, it was Dennis who maintained contact with me. In fact, he called me only a few days ago. Needing money."

"You didn't want him to contact you?"

"It's complicated," Needham said, and settled comfortably back in his chair. "I'm a loyal friend. So is Richard. Once a friend, always a friend. We were teammates. When a friend is down, you don't abandon them. I gave Dennis money from time to time. I knew he was putting it up his nose or in his veins or whatever junkies do. But I also encouraged him to get counseling or into rehabilitation. So, no. I didn't particularly relish his calls."

"Did you meet him recently?"

Needham hesitated. It was almost unnoticeable, but it was enough.

"As I told you, I spoke to him on the telephone a few days ago. He called my office and insisted he talk to me. He was rather abrasive, with my secretary and I could tell he was losing it. He wasn't making a lot of sense. Rambling. Making accusations about conspiracies and the like. He said he knew who killed Max Day, but when asked he would start rambling again. I put a rather large deposit in his bank account and told him there would be no more money. That he was on his own. I suggested he get help. I threatened to kick him out of the company if he didn't."

"Why didn't you tell us this right off?" Jack asked.

"Because I know how the police mind works. You would focus on Dennis as a killer and with his record and his mental state, he would be locked up. I'm still his friend and I'm still an attorney."

"How noble of you, Carl," Jack said.

"Anything else you need to know?" Needham asked.

"Yeah. Did you kill Maximillian Day?"

"No. I did not."

"Did you kill Amelia Day?"

"Who?"

"Amelia Day. Max's mother," Jack said.

"Oh. Right. No. I did not kill Amelia Day."

"Did you kill Harry Day?"

"No. I did not kill Harry Day or any other Day, and I hope you're not going to run through all of your unsolved homicides."

"Are you acquainted with Thomas Dick. Richard's father?" Jack asked.

"Where are you going with this now, Jack?"

"Did you know Dan Olson?"

"I think you're fishing without bait now, Jack."

"Well, I think that about does it, Carl. Thanks for answering my questions. We'll show you out. I'm sure you're anxious to meet with the new Chief of Police. Give him my best," Jack said.

Jack and Liddell walked Needham to the door and Jack shook his hand. "I hope to see you again, Mr. Needham. Real soon. We'll take that fishing trip I talked about."

Needham didn't smile. He turned and walked toward the Chief's complex.

Jack let the door shut and Liddell asked, "What do you think?"

"He's our guy," Jack said.

Chapter 50

Reina made a pot of strong coffee and sat at her table, sipping it black. She thought about taking a couple of cups of coffee down the street and knocking on the damn police car's window to let them know she was aware of them. But she didn't do that. She thought about calling the Chief of Police, but that wasn't going to happen, either. She had Detective Murphy to thank, or rather to blame, for this invasion of her privacy. Detective Murphy hadn't struck her as a man who gave up easily. She knew she should feel grateful, but she only felt pissed off. She had a right to make her own decisions and go about her day without being followed by the police. Just the thought of being watched made her skin crawl after the ordeal she'd endured.

She'd just watched Channel 6 television. Richard Dick had been appointed as Chief of Police. She saw Murphy bringing Carl Needham through the reporters, but not in handcuffs.

She could no longer call the police to complain about the harassment. Any complaint made by her would fall on deaf ears. But maybe Dick would call off the dogs. He didn't care if she was killed. In fact, she suspected very strongly that Dick was the one doing all this and she intended to prove it. That was when she came up with an idea.

She searched her contacts in her iPhone and found the number for the Chief of Police. She hesitated only a moment and punched the *send* button. The phone was answered almost immediately by a male voice. She recognized it from the taped conversation.

"Chief of Police Richard Dick. Who is this?"

"You know who this is, don't you?"

Dick was silent and she could almost see the gears in the bastard's head turning.

"I think you've gotten the wrong number," Dick said. "If you want the Evansville Police Department you need to hang up and dial 9-1-1 for an emergency dispatcher."

"Oh, I've got your number, Richard. This isn't an emergency. At least not for me. I have all the time in the world. I've waited thirty-seven years to make this call."

"What do you want, Reina?"

She cringed at the sound of her name coming from that twisted bastard, but it was good that he knew who she was.

"What I want, Dick, is for you to feel what my family has felt all these years. No more television. No more reporters. No more investigation. The next time I talk to you will be face-to-face. Do you understand?"

Dick's voice came down the line; strong, angry. "It has been thirty-seven years, Miss Day. Your family suffered an injustice, but I am not to blame. I promise you: If you continue to besmirch my name, I will sue you for every dime you and your family have. This news campaign you've run to keep me from becoming Chief of Police didn't work. Your threats mean nothing to me. I'm sorry you are angry, but this is the last time we'll speak. Do *you* understand?" He said this last in a threatening voice.

"You were always a dick. Even in high school. I can see why Max hated your guts. If you're such a coward, I guess you'll be seeing me on television. My next call is to the major television stations. FOX, CBS, NBC—I'm sure one of them will want to hear how you victimized and murdered an entire family for three decades."

"I'm warning you…"

"No. I'm warning you. I want you to listen close, or maybe you should write this down. I want you to meet me. If you don't, I go straight to the news media and I'll accuse you of being the one who shot at me. I'll tell them I saw you. That we spoke. That you threatened me to stop talking to the news. I'll put your face on Twitter and Snapchat and Facebook and anywhere I can humiliate you. Then I'll swear out charges and have you arrested. We'll see who a jury believes."

The line was silent for a long time. Reina's hand was shaking when his voice came back.

"Tell me where and when. And then this is the end of it."

Chapter 51

Jack and Liddell were sitting at the table in the war room at Two Jakes Restaurant with Angelina, Captain Franklin, and a new member of the team, exiled Chief Marlin Pope.

"So, this is the famous—or should I say 'infamous'—war room? Impressive, Jack," Marlin Pope said.

Jake Brady came in and set a tray of pastries on the table. Vinnie brought two carafes of coffee with mugs, creamer, sugar, and spoons.

Liddell poured a mug for himself and said, "Want some fresh, Angelina?"

"None for me. I'm trying to keep that stuff out of my body for a while. It makes me feel sick to my stomach, anyway."

Liddell asked, "Are you… you know?"

Angelina saw that Jack, Captain Franklin, Pope, and Liddell were all staring at her.

"Okay. I wasn't going to tell you until I started showing. I know how you guys are and I don't want you to treat me any different. Mark is already buying things for a boy. What is it with you men?"

"Are you going to name her Wonder Woman?" Liddell asked.

Angelina came right back at him. "Yeah. And she'll kick your Cajun ass back to the swamp you came out of."

"Oh, yeah. She's pregnant," Liddell said.

Pope said, "I guess our little band of misfits is growing. I hear congratulations are in order, Jack. Give Katie my best wishes."

"I will, Chief," Jack said.

"Marlin will do for now," Pope said. "I'm not the Chief after midnight tonight."

Angelina said, "I'm sorry, Chief Pope. That was a dirty move by the mayor."

"Yeah," Liddell said. "What made him do this now?"

"That's not important," Pope said. "I'm a Deputy Chief by merit rank and Charles is still a Captain. They can't fire either of us without just cause. But I'm afraid I've painted a target on your backs, given what I've asked you to do. The mayor has given me a little time to clean up any open business."

It was silent around the table and eyes were cast down as Pope continued. "My last act as Chief of Police is to relieve Jack and Liddell of the responsibility to investigate any of these cases. I'll reassign you to homicide. I'll try to protect your job, Charles, but even I'm not sure what's coming. I'm sorry, Angelina, but you should expect to be fired by Richard first thing in the morning."

"We have until midnight," Liddell said.

"I think we have enough to charge Needham. Do you agree, Captain?" Jack asked.

Franklin said, "Maybe we should call the prosecutor's office first."

"While you're doing that, Captain, Liddell and I will go find Needham before he disappears or gets Dennis James sprung and kills him," Jack said. He and Liddell got up to go.

"I'll call the Posey County lockup and make sure they don't release James to anyone for a while," Chief Pope said. "But wait to hear from us before you take Needham into custody, Jack."

"You bet," Jack said.

Chief Pope muttered, "When have we been able to stop you?" as Jack and Liddell left the war room.

They got to Jack's car. Liddell's phone dinged. "Angelina just sent the files."

Jack tossed the keys to him. "You drive. I don't trust myself right this minute."

Chapter 52

Liddell drove past the Civic Center and turned north on Sycamore Street. He pulled into the private parking area by the Chief's complex.

"Double Dick's parking spot is empty," Jack said. He'd seen Dick's black SUV at his house earlier, but nothing was parked in the Chief's or the Deputy Chief's parking spaces. He couldn't believe Dick would miss a chance to park in the big dog's parking spot.

"Maybe he's getting five gold stars painted on the hood," Liddell suggested. "Or tattooed on his forehead."

"Let's go inside and see where they've gone," Jack said. "Park in the Chief's spot. He won't mind and Dick's not Chief Dick until after midnight."

Liddell pulled into the space. "We're getting fired anyway."

Jack used a master key he'd talked the building super out of a few months ago to open a door that led directly into the Chief's complex. Judy Mangold was busy putting things from her desk into a Bankers Box.

"Going somewhere, Judy?" Liddell asked.

"Does the Pope shit in the woods?" she said in a deadpan voice.

"Hey, that's my line."

"As Jack would say: Bite me."

"Is he gone?" Jack asked.

"You mean Attila the Dick? Yes. He and that smarmy friend of his took off about fifteen minutes ago. I'm hoping to be gone before they get back. I've put in a lot of years here, but I refuse to work for that grade-A asshole. I'll get a job at Walmart first."

"Did they say where they were going, Judy?" Jack asked.

"Why? Are you going to arrest them? Tell me you're going to arrest them, Jack. Or that you're going to shoot the bastard."

"Okay, Judy. I'm going to arrest one of the assholes. Maybe shoot the other one. Feel better now?"

She dropped her stapler into the box, her arms fell to her sides, and she sat like that, stunned. "Not really. Chapman and Wolf turned in their retirement papers just now. They're up in personnel signing their pension papers. There will be a lineup there before the day's out. Oh Jack! I never thought I'd see this."

"Judy, did you see which way they left? Out the front? Through to the garage?"

"What difference does it make now, Jack? Who knows where they went or how they left?" Her eyes widened. "Or are you really going to arrest them?" She drew in a breath and covered her mouth. "You are, aren't you! Well, I'll be damned."

"Judy. Please don't say anything," Jack said.

"Okay. I think they were going to eat somewhere down the walkway. That 'friend' of Dick's was talking about how you had interrupted his meal."

"Thanks, Judy. If Chief Pope calls, tell him where I'm headed."

"Where *are* you headed, Jack?"

"Into trouble, Judy."

She pushed the buzzer and Jack and Liddell entered the lobby. Jack wondered what she would do. If she had savings. Family. He wasn't sure if city employees were on some type of pension plan like law enforcement officers. He'd never thought about it until now. And for the first time he thought about what he would do if worse came to worse He couldn't just think about himself anymore. He was going to be married. Be a father. And he felt responsible for Bigfoot's family. He'd just have to do what he thought was right, as he'd always done.

They were on foot on the Main Street walkway two blocks from the restaurant where they'd been two hours ago. Jack felt for his handcuffs. He'd forgotten them again.

"Did you bring handcuffs, Bigfoot?"

"Are we going to need them?"

"We might. Depends."

"Well, I only have one set. You sure you want to do it this way, pod'na?"

They were half a block from Milano's when Liddell's cell phone chirped. The screen read *Urgent. Call me.* The text was from Chief Pope.

They stopped on the sidewalk and Liddell dialed and punched the *speaker* button.

"Detective Blanchard," Chief Pope said in a relieved voice. "Is Detective Murphy with you?"

"I'm right here, Chief," Jack said. He didn't like the sound of the Chief's voice. It was flat. Defeated.

"Our prosecutor says we have no case against Carl Needham," Pope said.

"He always says that, Chief. We'll take him into custody and get more evidence."

"Jack. You can't arrest a senator from Ohio based on someone illegally entering his office in another state and videotaping the room. You know that would never be admitted as evidence. Dennis James is not a credible person, Jack. It's over, Jack. We're beaten."

Jack clamped his lips together so he wouldn't respond too quickly, say something he'd regret. He'd never expected Chief Marlin Pope to give up. Liddell's face was unreadable, but Jack knew from years of experience with this man that he'd go to the wall for him.

"Jack," Chief Pope said.

"Yes, Chief. I agree with you. We'll be at Two Jakes soon."

"The Captain and I will be waiting for you. We'll talk."

"Will do, Chief," Jack said and the call was disconnected. The time for talk was over.

Liddell put the phone in his pocket and turned to head back to their car.

"Where are you going?" Jack asked.

"But you said we'd be there soon."

Jack said, "I didn't say how soon. Give me the handcuffs, Bigfoot. You head back to the war room. Tell the Chief you couldn't stop me. Tell him I threatened you."

"I'm bigger. No one would believe you made me." Liddell took the handcuffs off his belt and handed them to Jack. "You can have the pleasure of putting these on him, but it doesn't matter who locks Needham up. We're both going down. Too bad we can't hook Double Dick up too."

Jack felt both relief and concern at Liddell's support. Maybe with Liddell there at least he wouldn't punch Dick in the face. Too many times.

As they walked in Milano's doors, Tough Tony greeted them with a nod toward the table by the front window where Needham had been sitting earlier. There were two glasses of iced tea sitting on the table in front of two chairs that had been pushed out. Chief Richard Dick sat alone at the table. He saw the handcuffs in Jack's hand and smiled.

"Have a seat," Dick said to them.

"Do you want something to eat?" Tough Tony asked them, his angry glare focused on Double Dick.

Jack said, as he'd said to Needham earlier, "I don't think we'll be here that long."

Chapter 53

"Thanks for doing this, Jenny," Reina Day said. "I'll owe you one."

"You'll owe me more than one. Are you sure you don't want me to come along? The cops are only trying to protect you," Jenny had said, but finally gave in and agreed to what Reina had planned.

Reina waited by the phone for the text message signal that the car was there and when it came, she sent Aldo down the street. He'd been dying to confront the establishment about invasion of rights and curbing freedom—his terms for any police action. She watched Aldo approach the police officers. He would be her distraction.

She climbed out a side window of her house and snuck through backyards to get to the rental car Jenny had arranged. This took her back to her high school days, when she would sneak out of the house and go to a girlfriend's house—usually Jenny's—to drink beer and smoke cigarettes. Max would come along with her sometimes so that they had something on each other and wouldn't rat each other out to their parents. The car was right where Jenny said it would be. Reina felt on top of the left front wheel and found the car keys. She got in and found the items she'd requested Jenny purchase. It was all hooked up and ready to go.

She drove to the corner so she could see that the police car was still there and she hadn't been discovered. Satisfied, she headed toward the meeting place. When she gave Dick the time and place she wanted to meet, she'd lied and told him that after she had her say she'd drop this. She'd waited all of her adult life to tell him what she thought of his cowardly attack on her brother. She had no intention of letting him off the hook.

Dick had demanded that in return for meeting her that she turn over all the documents the family had saved relating to Max's death. He made her promise they would be quits after this. She lied again and agreed.

She entered Hillcrest Cemetery and parked near the back once again. She synced the small camera to her cell phone and attached it to the rearview mirror. The screen on her phone showed the entire front seat. She hit the *record* key on the phone and said, "Testing. Testing." She played it back and saw and heard herself clearly. She tapped the *record* button again and put the phone over the visor. She would be able to record Dick arriving.

She'd found the camera using the internet and had downloaded the app that would sync the camera and phone. Jenny had gone to Best Buy and the salesman had been more than happy to sell her the right Wi-Fi camera for the job. She wanted to record what happened here and it would all be stored in the cloud. She sent an email to Jack Murphy giving him a sign-in and password to the program on her phone. She needed someone to know what had happened here and why, just in case something went wrong. She planned to kill Richard Dick.

Her father had kept a .357 magnum Smith & Wesson revolver hidden at home. Reina only knew about it because she had watched him hide it. She took the fully loaded gun out of her purse, held it on her lap. It was fitting she finish this in the place where it all began. She felt goose bumps rise on her arms when she thought of nearly being killed here, but she was sure it was Richard Dick who was the killer. Who else could it be? She would kill him for her brother. For her father. Her mother. And for herself. Then she would end it. No more Days. Dick would never be king.

She turned her head toward the row of grave markers where her brother and father were laid to rest. Her mother was to be buried beside them tomorrow. Soon they would be burying her there. Her family, all gone by the violence of an arrogant bastard.

She heard tires crunching on gravel and looked in the rearview mirror. The black SUV stopped close to her trunk and the driver's door opened. The man who got out wasn't wearing a police uniform. He wasn't wearing the black hoodie jacket she'd seen before, either. He was in a dark striped suit and she recognized him immediately.

She cursed under her breath. "The coward didn't come himself. He sent his footman instead. I should have known." She rolled her window down. "Hello, Carl. Where's Richard? Are you still doing his dirty work?"

Needham leaned in the window, one hand on the sill, the other behind his back. "I really didn't want this, Reina."

She felt a sting on the side of her neck. She wanted to lift the gun, but her arm wouldn't obey. She could move her head. He'd shot her with a paralytic agent. Maybe succinylcholine, a powerful anesthesia used in surgeries.

She felt the car shift, the door open, and she was aware he was lifting her from the seat. Her vision jostled as she was carried. A door opened and she was slung onto a backseat. She was in his car. She saw the gray felt ceiling and the back of his seat. He stuffed her legs in and pushed her further across the seat. She wanted to scream out, but knew it was futile. The medicine would wear off in an hour or so. Would she still be alive in an hour or so?

Needham's face was over hers again and it wore no expression. That was the most frightening thing of all.

"Comfy?" he asked. "I forgot. You can't answer. Well, don't worry. I'm taking you somewhere safe. I'm not going to kill you. You have to answer some questions and then I'll take you home. We have so much catching up to do, Reina. I always favored you, you know? You were hot in high school and I have to tell you, you've gotten better with age."

She could feel his hand under her skirt, touching her, entering her, and she screamed inside her head.

"Maybe we'll have time for that later," he said and took his hand away. His face disappeared and the door shut with a *thud* of finality.

Chapter 54

Dick pushed his plate of half-eaten food away, stood, and brushed at his shirtfront. He straightened his medals and ribbons and asked, "Are you here to try to arrest me?"

"Not you," Jack answered and gave Liddell the handcuffs.

Dick smirked and said, "I told you that you'd never read the Miranda rights to me. We need to talk. We can either do it here or in the Chief's office." Dick stressed the word *chief.*

"Where's Needham?" Jack asked.

Dick's chuckle was short. "You won't be seeing him again—Detective Murphy. Nor you, Detective Blanchard. In fact, I have a job for you. Let's go to my office."

"We'll meet you there," Jack said. Without waiting for a response, he and Liddell walked out of the restaurant.

Outside, Liddell put the handcuffs back on his belt and they began the trek back to their car. Jack was uncharacteristically silent.

"I could sure have used something to eat, pod'na. A last meal."

Jack was silent.

"I think he was going to buy, pod'na."

"It'll be *his* last meal as Chief of Police," Jack said. "We're going to find Needham."

They walked into the lobby of the Chief's complex and Judy Mangold held the door open for them.

"You should carry a radio, Jack," she said.

"Why? What's going on?"

"Reina Day's gone missing," Mangold said.

"Are they sure she's not in the house?"

Mangold stood with her hands on her hips. "Her detail called Chief Pope and he told them to make entry. She's not home, Jack, and her car is undrivable."

The Bankers Box sat on the floor beside Judy's desk. He hated to admit it, but he was running out of moves—and time. She picked up the box and walked to the exit door. "Oh, and Sergeant Mattingly called for Chief Pope. I didn't want to tell him where the Chief was, so I said I'd pass it on. Well, I passed it on."

"Did he say what he was calling about?" Jack asked.

"No one tells me anything. I just step 'n fetch. I better get to stepping. I'm afraid of what I'll do if I have to talk to that insufferable prick one more time."

"Thanks, Judy. Good luck." He and Liddell made their way to the parking area and got in Jack's car. Liddell drove while Jack called Sergeant Mattingly.

* * * *

Five minutes later, Liddell was pulling into the service road at Locust Hill Cemetery and stopped behind Sergeant Mattingly's police car. A blue Ford Focus was sitting in front of the police car. The driver's door of the Focus stood open.

Mattingly came to their window. "She's gone. Reina's gone."

Jack and Liddell got out, walking close enough to the abandoned car to see a big revolver laying on the front seat.

"We heard she slipped past her guardians," Jack said. "Was she driving this?"

Mattingly was wearing latex gloves and holding something in his hand. He showed it to them.

"I found her phone. He took her."

"Back up a minute. Who took her?" Jack asked.

"Dick's buddy. Needham," Mattingly said and began pacing. "This car was rented by some woman by the name of Jenny Taylor, but this phone is Reina's. She recorded the whole thing. It's on the phone."

"Recorded what, Sarge?" Jack said.

"You can see Needham snatching her from the car. She had the phone on *record*. He must not have noticed it because you can see him plain as day."

Jack slipped gloves on, took the phone, hit the key to rewind, and then hit *play*. He watched Reina talking into a camera. The camera angle was wrong unless she was holding the phone up near the ceiling. He stopped the video, stooped down, and the little black hump stuck on top of the rearview mirror. *A pinhole camera.*

"How long has she been gone from her house?" Jack asked.

"Half hour. Maybe more. Who knows? The car was rented two hours ago. The team that were supposed to be watching her found a side window open on her house. She could have been gone for a couple of hours before Needham grabbed her."

"Was she meeting someone here?"

"She was going to meet Dick," Mattingly said. "Watch the video, Jack. She set this up with Dick. She says so on the video. Then Needham showed up, drugged her, and took her. You can see him doing something to her and she just goes limp. If she's dead, I'm going to kill that bastard."

Jack held the phone so they could all see the screen and hit *play* again. Reina Day was in the driver's seat with the phone propped on her leg. She hit a button on the phone and said, "Testing, testing." The screen went blank for a moment and then came back on. She said, "I'm meeting with Richard Dick here at Hillcrest Cemetery in a few minutes. Richard Dick killed my brother, Maximillian Day. Richard Dick killed my father, Harry Day. Richard Dick killed my mother, Amelia Day. And he tried to kill me."

Mattingly said, "See what's on her lap now?"

Reina removed a large stainless-steel revolver from her purse and held it between her legs.

She took a breath and said, "For that, I'm going to kill him. I'm making this recording so you'll know exactly what happened and why. This is me getting justice for my family. The police wouldn't help and it doesn't take a rocket scientist to see they aren't going to be able to get him now. I'm recording this on the internet cloud and I've sent an email to Detective Jack Murphy with instructions on how to retrieve this video in case something goes wrong."

She turned the gun over in her hands, checked that it was loaded, and rested it on her leg before she continued talking.

"I want whoever sees this to know that I'm not a violent person. I'm not. I'm a doctor. I became a doctor to help people. To fix them. But Richard Dick can't be fixed with medicine or surgery or counseling. He's a disease that has to be destroyed. My father would—"

A crunching sound could be heard on the recording. A car was coming up behind her. On the video you could see a part of a dark black vehicle stop behind her car.

Reina muttered something Jack couldn't make out, but she was unhappy. She powered her window down as a figure approached her door. "Hello, Carl. Where's Richard? Are you still doing his dirty work?"

She gripped the gun and held it close beside her right leg. A man leaned in the window and said, "I really didn't want this, Reina."

The gun was still in her hand, but his hand punched or pushed on the side of her neck and she went limp. The man leaned over her. The video caught a perfect shot of Carl Needham, still dressed in the expensive suit from earlier. He lifted her limp form easily from the car.

There was a sound of crunching again and the video showed the back of Needham's legs and then they were gone. A car door could be heard opening and closing and the car backed away. The picture was now of an empty front seat.

"Is that all that's on there?" Jack asked.

"That's it. There's no time/date stamp on the video."

Jack checked his cell phone. There was an email from Reina Day. It had come in while they were on their way to arrest Needham at the restaurant. "Have you called crime scene?"

"I was waiting for you. You said you wanted this kept on the low and—"

"And with Dick in charge now, there would be little chance of getting a manhunt underway for his best buddy," Jack finished the thought. "Well, screw Dick and the mayor he rode in on. Put out a BOLO on Carl Needham. He's driving a black SUV with Ohio license plates. He's wearing a dark pinstripe suit and is possibly armed and dangerous. Strike that. He's to be considered armed and dangerous. And you can add that he's kidnapped Reina Day."

"Will do, but I want to get out there."

Jack put a hand on Mattingly's shoulder. "I'll keep you involved, but you have to stay here for now and make sure the scene is done right. Call crime scene. We can't all lose our jobs today."

Mattingly turned away and called dispatch. He gave them the BOLO and asked them to run Needham for license and registration. Jack and Liddell turned their car around and drove down the narrow service road.

"What are we going to do now?" Liddell asked.

"I know where he's taking her," Jack said and peeled out as he turned onto Kratzville Road.

Chapter 55

It was just getting dark as Jack drove past the iron gates and found a place to pull off the road. They were far enough from the house to conceal an approach on foot.

Jack checked his .45 and made sure a round was chambered. He put two extra magazines of ammo in his back pocket. Liddell went through the same routine.

"You don't have to go in with me, Bigfoot. I'm just going to see if Needham's car is there and come right back. Give me five minutes, then call the state police and the sheriff and all the king's horses and men."

"You're so full of it, pod'na," Liddell said and got out of the car.

Jack felt his mouth go dry. They were crossing a big, bright line here and Jack would never be able to talk his way out of. If Needham was in there, Reina Day was in there as well. Alive or dead. And that's how he'd take Needham. He gave one last thought to Katie and the baby growing inside her. He thought about Marcie and little Janie. They were risking their families. They both knew that, but you had to protect the world your loved ones lived in.

"Did you bring your handcuffs?" Liddell asked.

"No."

"Good," Liddell said. "I don't think Needham will come out without a fight."

"My thoughts exactly."

The two detectives slipped into the woods. Jack set a course for what he hoped was the mansion. They had to work around wild blackberry bushes and thick undergrowth, snagging pants on thorns and stepping into mole burrows. They reached the edge of the woods and saw the mansion dead ahead. A black Lexus SUV was parked on the grass near the front of the house. Needham's. The lights inside the mansion were on. There was no movement inside or around the house.

"What's the plan?" Liddell said in a whisper.

"Kill the bad guys, save the young maiden, have a scotch."

"Okay."

Jack said, "If Needham surrenders and Reina's undamaged, we don't shoot him. If he even points a finger at us, we blow him away."

"Why did you think Needham came to Dick's dad's house?"

Jack couldn't really say why he knew. He just did. "We go in hard and fast, get Reina out, and you take her to the car while I sort some things out."

Floodlights on the lawn and on both sides of the house came to life.

"No way to get across the yard now without being seen," Liddell said. "I'll circle around and see if there's a way in the back."

"Wait here and cover me." Jack stood and began walking across the lawn, gun held down by his side.

Liddell started to tell Jack to come back, but he knew it was like talking to the back end of a donkey. He caught up with Jack, keeping ten feet between them so as not to make an easy target. As they neared the veranda, they saw two more black SUVs parked beside the house. Jack recognized one as Double Dick's tricked-out Cadillac Escalade with smoke-black windows and gold-plated wire wheels. The other was a BMW, dark color, low profile, expensive even to look at, the kind of personal vehicle that would require CPR for your wallet. *That one must be Daddy's.*

"That's far enough," a voice called out from the left side of the mansion.

Jack turned in the direction the voice came from and was almost blinded by the bright lights. He could make out the shape of a tall man, and as the shape came forward he recognized the expensive suit and shiny take-me-to-the-White-House shoes.

"Carl," Jack said, shielding his eyes with the hand not holding the gun. "Is Dick here with you?"

Jack heard a snicker and Carl said, "Which Dick do you want? Pun intended."

"Considering you're all dicks, I don't particularly care."

Jack heard a handgun slide ratchet on the other side, the right side of the house.

"Is that you, Deputy Chief?" Jack called out. It wasn't.

"Carl, put the gun down. I don't want to shoot you, son." Retired Captain Thomas Dick walked onto the veranda.

Needham's face froze in surprise and he turned slightly toward Thomas Dick. It was the first time Jack saw the weapon in Needham's hand. Big. Very big. A Desert Eagle for sure. Maybe the same one that shot at him at Olson's house. The one that shot Reina's car to hell. The one that killed Amelia Day and maybe Harry.

Thomas's voice commanded, "The gun, Carl. Put it down. Now."

Carl's gun didn't move. The Desert Eagle was pointed roughly in the direction of Jack's chest, but was inching toward Captain Dick's position. Needham's eyes moved to the left and back to Jack. To the left and back to Jack, as if he was watching a tennis match.

"I don't mean to get in the middle of this hormonal exchange," Jack said. "But where is Richard? Thomas, where's your son? Is he hiding in the dark with a gun like the coward he is?"

Liddell said, "I think we interrupted a party, pod'na. We weren't invited, so let's go."

"Stay where you are," Needham said. The Desert Eagle shifted positions, pointing now at Liddell.

"I won't ask again, Carl," the older Dick said. "There's been enough killing, son. You're finished. I'm turning you in."

Needham's uncertainty was replaced by fear.

Jack said, "This is the part of the movie where someone confesses to being the third gunman on the grassy knoll. You can all put your guns down and I'll accept your surrender."

"Shut up, Jack!" Double Dick said, coming into the light from behind his father. He too was holding a Desert Eagle.

"Did they have a special at Guns R Us?" Liddell asked.

Needham said, "Lay your weapons on the ground."

"I'm confused, Carl. There are so many guns here," Jack said. "You three lay your weapons down and kick them away. And *then* things will be hunky-dory."

Thomas again: "That's not going to happen, Murphy." There was a tremendous blast. The muzzle flash was blinding and Needham folded inward at the waist. His body drew up into a fetal position on the veranda and he was still.

"I told him not to move," Thomas Dick said.

Jack said, "You two, Dick and Dick, put the guns down. Do it now." Jack had drawn his Glock. Liddell moved up beside Jack, gun in hand.

Double Dick immediately dropped his gun and put his hands on the back of his head. Thomas wasn't quite as fast to obey and Jack began putting pressure on the Glock's trigger.

Thomas lowered his weapon, until the business end pointed at the ground. He said, "He's the one who killed Max. He's the murderer. He killed Harry Day and Amelia Day. He admitted it when he brought that woman here. He's a murderer and a kidnapper. I couldn't let him kill you. It's over."

Jack kept his gun trained on Thomas. "It's over when you give me that gun, Mr. Dick. You've saved lives tonight. Don't make things worse."

Thomas backed up a step, but held onto the gun. He said, "Richard, call the authorities."

To Jack, he said, "You have no jurisdiction here. You're witnesses that Needham was an immediate threat to our lives and yours. It was a justifiable shooting. Stand down, detectives, and wait for the troops."

Double Dick looked from Jack to his father and back to Jack, trying to decide what to do.

Jack said, "Go on. Call an ambulance and the cops. Let them sort this out, so no one else gets shot."

That seemed to break Double Dick's spell and he started to pick up his gun, but Jack stopped him. "Leave the gun, Chief."

Double Dick did as told and disappeared down the side of the house into the dark. Jack didn't think Richard Dick was responsible for any of the killings. He didn't have the guts for it. He didn't think Richard Dick had been in a fight since Max Day whipped his ass thirty-seven years ago. He wasn't so sure about Thomas, though. Not that Jack wasn't grateful that Needham was dead, but Needham seemed to think Dick wouldn't do it. In fact, it seemed like Needham was totally surprised. Why would Needham bring Reina here? And how had Double Dick gotten here ahead of them? He must have just arrived. He must have known about Reina.

Jack thought he could easily overpower the older Dick, but the Desert Eagle made him think twice about trying it. "Mr. Dick. You can put the weapon down now. The danger is over. Needham's dead."

"You first," Thomas said.

Jack nodded to Liddell and they holstered their weapons. "Now put the gun down and tell us where Reina Day is. Is she safe?"

At the mention of Reina Day, the older man's demeanor changed and the Desert Eagle pointed in Jack's direction. "You know, don't you?"

"Know what?" Jack asked, but he did know—now. He'd suspected Dick Sr. played a part in Max's murder, but until now he thought the man was merely covering up for his son.

"Don't play games with me," Thomas said and yelled for his son. "Richard. Get back out here, son." No response.

"Richard! I said get out here."

Double Dick hadn't gone in the house. He was standing just out of sight. He stepped up onto the veranda.

"Pick up your gun," Thomas said. Richard hesitated. "Damn it, boy, pick it up. This mess is partly your fault. If you had just kept your mouth shut and stayed away from that family, none of this would have happened. You made this mess, now you'll help clean it up."

Dick leaned down stiffly and picked the Desert Eagle off the ground, holding it with thumb and forefinger.

Thomas said, "Richard. Listen to me. This is what really happened: Needham is a killer. He kidnapped that woman. He was going to kill her here in our house and frame us for all of the murders. He attempted to murder Murphy once at Olson's. We can fix this. All the evidence will point to him. Needham is the killer."

"That's not what happened, Dad," Dick said. "When I got here, you were with Carl. Carl wasn't threatening—"

"Shut up, boy!"

"But Murphy and Blanchard know none of that's true," Dick said. "Reina's tied up inside, but she was conscious the entire time. She heard everything. She'll tell a different story. It's too late."

"Stop your damn whining. I can't believe I raised such a pussy," Thomas said. "You got your stupid from your mom. I thought when she was gone you'd grow up, but I guess I was wrong."

"I'm not stupid. I just—"

"Shut up and listen for once in your life. Just listen. That woman won't be telling anyone anything. Carl killed her. I'll fix this like I've fixed everything in your life that you screwed up."

"What are you going to do with Reina?" Double Dick asked.

Thomas Dick answered, "I'm not going to do anything. You are." Thomas nodded toward Needham's body and said, "Now go get his gun. He killed that girl. We tried to stop him."

"Kill her," Richard Dick said quietly.

"Yes. Kill her. And then bring the gun back out here. After he killed her, these two showed up and Needham killed them. I was able to get to my gun and shot him."

Dick was motionless and expressionless.

"Listen to me, Richard. These men hate your guts. They detest you. You said so yourself. And now that you're the Chief, they came after you to stop you from running that police department the way it should have been run for the last thirty years. With my help, you'll put it in shape in no time. You would have had to get rid of these two anyway and they aren't the type to go quietly. Can't you see that?"

"Can't we just let them all go? Carl was the killer, like you said. He killed Max. Everyone will believe us."

Thomas barked at his son, "What did you think, boy? That they would just go along with us? Hell, if you let them go now, they'll destroy you. Destroy us. Destroy everything I've built for you."

"But kill them?" Richard Dick asked incredulously and stood, mouth hanging open.

"Oh, for God's sake! If we don't kill that bitch she'll back up anything they say. She wants revenge. She blackmailed you into meeting with her. You heard what Needham said. She was waiting for you with a gun. She was going to kill you."

Jack said, "So your son didn't kill Max Day. If he didn't, who did? You? Needham? James?"

Thomas sneered at Jack. "Dennis James? An idiot. A junkie. Not worth wiping my ass on, but he won't be talking to anyone again. Carl killed him too."

He addressed his son. "You're pathetic. Do you realize what I've done for you? I risked everything. All of this. I did things you could never do. I've kept you clean all these years for one reason: For you to rise to the top. Something I never could do because of the politics. But now you're where I always dreamed I'd be. You're the Chief of Police. You can write your own ticket in a few years. Get any job you want. Be important for once in your life, Richard."

Richard Dick's grip tightened on his gun. He stared at his father as if seeing him for the first time. The barrel of his gun rose. Thomas saw the move. His face turned red in a mask of rage. Thomas's gun was still trained on Jack and Liddell, but his eyes were on his son.

"You said Carl was the killer. But it was you all this time." His eyes teared up and his mouth turned down at the corners. "I know he killed Max. He told me. And he told me you fixed things so we'd never have to answer questions. And then Harry. Why, Dad? Because he wanted to punish his son's killer?"

"Yeah. That's right. I did everything I could to shut Harry Day up. And I'll tell you someone else that needs to be dealt with: That Mattingly fellow. He kept Harry stirred up and it was going to ruin your chances of becoming a policeman. I had to do it. He had to die. You can see that. I had to."

Richard's eyes welled with tears, but his expression was one of anger. "Don't say you did it for me. You did it for you. *You* wanted me to be

Chief. I never wanted this. I didn't know what I wanted. I was just a kid and *you* kept pushing me. I wanted to be just like you, but now I can't stand the sight of you."

"You're weak. If your mom could have had another kid, I would have strangled you in your crib. Get out of my sight. I'll do this myself."

Richard didn't move and Thomas said, "Go on! Get out of here! Get in your damn car and leave. I'll talk to the cops. You were never here."

Jack's hand was moving toward his waistband. Thomas caught the movement and lifted the Desert Eagle toward his face. It was as if time itself slowed down and Jack could see and hear everything clearly; had all the time in the world to think about what he was going to do. He could see the bore of the Desert Eagle pointing directly as his face and Thomas's finger tighten on the trigger. Jack tugged impotently at the baby Glock in the back of his waistband. His knees tensed to propel him out of the path of the .50 caliber projectile and he dropped and rolled, tugging at the baby Glock, and dragged it from underneath him to get off one clean shot. Time caught up. The Desert Eagle screamed. He knew he was dead.

But there was nothing except the fading echo of the blast. Jack rolled onto his side, gun thrust forward, but there was no need. Thomas Dick stood with the Desert Eagle hanging from his trigger finger. His face was slack, eyes staring straight ahead. A hole had opened in one side of his throat just below his jaw; the other side ruptured open like someone had put their fist through a screen door.

Retired Police Captain Thomas Dick stood swaying, mouth gaping, gun in hand, and then dropped like a sack of potatoes. Carl Needham had been struck by Thomas's bullet, but he wasn't dead. He had rolled onto his stomach, both arms stretched out in front, holding the Desert Eagle. He struggled to lift the heavy weapon again, this time targeting Richard Dick, and Jack sprinted across the end of the veranda and drove his shoulder into Dick's chest, propelling them both out into the yard. At the same time, there were two loud reports. Definitely not from a Desert Eagle.

Richard Dick got his breath back. "Get off me, Murphy." He shoved Jack away and got to his knees. He brushed some of the dirt away from his shirt and stood up, ignoring the dirt ground into his knees. He picked up his gun from the ground and ran to his father.

Liddell had leaned Needham against one of the pillars and was handcuffing him. Needham seemed to be having trouble getting his breath. He was lucky to be drawing a breath.

"Just in case no one heard the racket, I'll call 9-1-1," Jack said and made the call. Warrick County dispatch acted quickly and the sound of sirens started up in the far distance.

Liddell found a very large knife when he patted Needham down. "It's a WASP," Liddell said to Jack and held it up. "You're under arrest for murder. You know your rights, so let's pretend I read them to you."

Liddell said, "He was wearing body armor, pod'na. I shot him twice when I saw him shooting. All of the bullets hit the vest or he'd be dead."

Jack nodded and flexed his elbow. It hurt like hell.

Sirens were closer now. Jack thought about taking Richard's gun, but it was on the ground and the man didn't seem to have any fight left in him. Dick was sitting in a pool of his father's blood, hugging the body in his lap, oblivious of the sirens, or Jack or Liddell. Jack didn't like the man, but he was still a human being. Maybe.

"I'm not weak, Daddy. I won't let you down," Dick said and before Jack could make a move, Dick grabbed the Desert Eagle from the ground. The blast was deafening.

Chapter 56

Uniformed and plainclothes officers milled around inside the small visitation room at Alexander Funeral Home. More of them stood outside in the parking area or leaned against the police cars that would make up the procession to the crematorium.

Almost a week had passed since the carnage at the Dick mansion in Warrick County. Statements were taken, fingerprints of the corpses taken, forensic evidence collected, weapons test-fired for ballistics, and the questioning of everyone had continued ad nauseam. The incoming mayor, Benet Cato, had fired her abrasive assistant, the one Liddell had rightly dubbed Tilly the Hun, and consequently had stopped giving the current mayor a load of grief. He was getting enough grief from everyone. The news media—Claudine Setera—were blaming Cato for the cock-ups. She'd been labeled as a heartless bully. Her ratings were down and somehow her credit score had tanked along with her popularity.

The cold cases hadn't turned out like Jack or Liddell or Chief Pope had hoped, or even imagined. But it was a result. Marlin Pope had resumed duties as Chief of Police, while Richard Dick made arrangements for his father's cremation, although, in truth, Dick would not ascend the throne under either mayor. The case was closed, the dragons slain, the fair maiden—Reina—saved. Jack found her inside the mansion, tied in a chair and gagged. She had heard everything.

Richard Dick was never charged with any of the crimes Jack was investigating. He would never be Chief, but he was the next highest merit rank, which meant he could only be demoted for good cause. Like being charged with using a shell company to pay off a murder witness. But Jack would never be able to prove that Richard Dick knew Monarch Investments was used as hush money to cover up Max's murder. Richard Dick's weapon didn't match the ballistics evidence of any of the murders. Dennis James had testified that Richard wasn't directly involved in anything other than the fight at the cemetery and even then, the man apparently received worse injuries than he gave. The statute of limitations had run out on simple assault. If stupidity was a criminal charge, Richard would spend the rest of his life in some kind of institution. He had skated on criminal charges, but was still undergoing an internal affairs investigation for his role in the shoot-out at his father's house. Richard had, in a fit of grief, blown Carl Needham's head into the next county. Jack and Liddell hadn't actually witnessed this, but they were standing right there when they heard a cannon boom and the next thing that you knew, Carl's head was gone. Jack and Liddell would swear it was self-defense.

The only one left to be held accountable was Dennis James. He had taken part in covering up the murder of Maximillian Day, which was charged as conspiracy to commit murder after the fact because of his admitted conspiracy with Carl Needham. The difference between Richard and Dennis, as far as conspiracy went, is that James knew Needham had committed the murder. It wasn't proven that Richard knew who had killed Max. After a few days in jail, Dennis James gave everyone up, including himself and his drug supplier. He would also clear up the arson and murders by giving a statement against Carl Needham, who was deceased. So no one was arrested.

Ballistics confirmed Thomas Dick's gun was the weapon that killed Harry Day. Max's murder—and later, Olson's murder—was attributed to the WASP belonging to Carl Needham, or a weapon of the same nature. Carl's Desert Eagle was confirmed as the weapon that killed Mrs. Day, Dan Olson, shot at Jack, and shot up Reina's vehicle. Jack got a warrant for the senator's office and home and his desk calendar confirmed he was in Evansville when Mrs. Day and Olson were killed, and Reina Day was attacked. Crime scene collected hair, fingerprints, a syringe of SUX, and DNA evidence from Carl's SUV that confirmed Reina had been in the backseat of Needham's SUV.

Reina Day was treated by AMR at the scene and spent another night in Deaconess for a second concussion. Here was the happy ending. Sergeant Mattingly spent the night at Deaconess, watching over Reina after hearing what she'd been through. The fact that she'd had a loaded gun and had recorded her plan of killing Richard Dick was beside the point. No one had watched the video on Reina's phone, or saw the handgun found in the car except Jack, Liddell, and Sergeant Mattingly. In fact, Mattingly had kept both of these items and it wouldn't surprise Jack if they never made it into evidence. He didn't care. Dick was alive and... well, still a dick. The bad guys were dead. Reina had, in some small part, brought about the avenging of the murders of her family. It was win-win. The really happy ending to this case was that Sergeant Mattingly and Reina Day had become close. Mattingly was divorced, Reina Day was divorced; maybe they would get married and then divorced like half of all America.

EPILOGUE

Three weeks after the shoot-out at the Not-Okay Dick Corral, as Liddell liked to call it, Jack and Katie sat on the covered deck at the back of the Blanchard homestead. Jack sipped Glenmorangie and Katie had a Diet Coke. She was already watching her diet. Marcie Blanchard prepared the picnic table with napkins, silverware, water glasses, side dishes, and a carafe of strong coffee. Bigfoot was playing the steaks on the grill like a concert pianist.

Jack's mind was still working out the moral implications of his and Liddell's part in all that had happened. He still didn't feel that in good conscience he could have brought charges against Double Dick, and that was in direct conflict with his hatred for the man. Right was right and wrong was—whatever. In the end, no one died except the ones who deserved to. The killers had become the killed. He had scotch. Katie was beside him. Liddell, Marcie, and Janie were happy and healthy. Double Dick was leaving him be. What more could a man ask for?

Mattingly and Reina Day had already taken their relationship to the next step and Mattingly moved in with her. That meant Aldo had to pack up his happy-face Speedos and move out.

Jack was pulled out of his thoughts by Marcie nudging his arm. "I'm sorry, Marcie. I was in la-la land."

Marcie smiled. "I swear, you two are in la-la land most of the time. I was asking how the new mayor is working out for you?"

"Same old, same old," Jack said.

"I second that," Liddell said from the grill.

"Is Cato going to order the Chief to release all of the case file to Channel Six?"

Channel 6's legal department was claiming the case files were public record and under the Freedom of Information Act, they were taking legal action against the police department and specifically Chief Pope, Liddell Blanchard, and Jack Murphy. Jack was proud of Chief Pope when he told Channel 6 to "Bite me."

"I don't think we can find the case files," Jack answered. In fact, he knew all of the files and all of the evidence were still in the war room. It had been lost for thirty-seven years. It could stay lost.

Liddell came onto the covered deck with a platter full of steaming New York strip steaks.

"It's on the news, pod'na. Chief Pope is having a news conference tomorrow morning and Reina will be there. She'll get her day in front of the cameras after all."

"I know. Claudine Setera hasn't stopped calling me all week," Jack said.

"She's writing a book," Liddell said.

"Who is?"

"Reina is cowriting a book with Claudine. Everyone writes books these days. She's going to expose the corruption in the police department and trash the city government for allowing it to continue," Liddell said.

"Continue?" Jack said. "Jesus!" *And after we took pity on her.* Murphy's Law said: *No good deed will go unpunished.* He just hoped it wouldn't come back to bite them.

Katie asked, "What will the book say about you two?"

"You can ask her yourself," Liddell said and nodded toward the back door of the house.

"I knocked and no one answered," Claudine said. "I hope you don't mind."

"You didn't tell me she was invited, or I would have worn my knife-proof vest," Jack said.

Claudine was wearing a red dress with a slit up the side to her thigh and the neckline plunged to her navel. She was the only person Jack knew who would dress like she was at the Academy Awards to attend a backyard barbecue. Well, maybe Captain Franklin would as well. He imagined when the man was born he was given a little black suit and a birth certificate. And speaking of the devil, the man who came through the door right behind Claudine bore a suspicious resemblance to—

"Hello, Captain," Jack said. "Want some scotch?"

Claudine said, "I'm sorry, I just came from another event downtown. Mayor Cato is taking bows for the case your husbands just solved."

"Of course she is," Marcie said. "That weasel."

Jack poured a paper cup with scotch and was handing it to Captain Franklin when Chief Pope came out of the door.

Pope asked, "So what are your plans, Jack?"

"I plan to get drunk, Chief," Jack said.

"You got another glass?" Pope asked.

"Real men drink from paper cups," Jack said. He'd already had two doubles. He filled another cup and handed it to Pope. Jack took a swig of his scotch and held the paper cup out in a toast. "Here's to the new weasel. May she be as bad as the last one."

Marcie handed Claudine a Solo cup of Diet Coke. Liddell picked up a beer. They all toasted.

Claudine downed her Coke and said, "Can I have some of that scotch, Jack?"

"You don't have to try and buddy up any more, Claudine. You got the whole damn exclusive story." Jack tipped a quarter-inch of amber liquid in her Solo cup.

"That's just like you," Claudine said. She took the bottle from him and poured another two fingers in her cup, took a hefty sip, and said, "You drink this rotgut?" She surprised him with her knowledge of single-malt Scotch whiskey and they argued which was the best.

Liddell interrupted and said, "Dig in, folks."

He made a plate for Marcie and a smaller bowl of mac and cheese for little Janie, who was getting sleepy. She stuck her hands in the bowl and rubbed the sticky cheese in her hair.

Marcie said, "I think someone needs changing and a nap."

Jack held his steak up on a fork. "My steak's still walking, Bigfoot. Did you kill it first?"

"Bite me, pod'na."

"I'm just kidding. I'd rather bite this," Jack said and cut into the steak, which was perfect, as usual. "If Marcie comes to her senses and divorces you, Bigfoot, you can come live with us."

"Are you hitting on me, pod'na? That's sexual harassment."

The back door opened again and Jack almost choked on his drink.

"Sorry I'm late," Deputy Chief Richard Dick said and everyone's attention turned to Jack.

Jack could tell Liddell wasn't surprised at all. This was a setup.

Dick was wearing blue jeans and a knit shirt with his shiny Corfam dress shoes. He was holding out a brown paper bag, twisted around the top of what could only be a bottle of liquor.

"Macallan twenty-five-year-old," Dick said, holding the bag out to Jack. "I heard this is your preference."

Jack opened the bag and indeed it was Macallan, twenty-five-year-old, thousand-dollar-a-bottle scotch. He said, "You don't drink this stuff, Deputy Chief. You bow down and worship it. You didn't have to do this."

"You're right," Dick said, straight-faced. "I really can't stay. I have a meeting with Benet Cato."

Jack could see the man was as uncomfortable as he was.

Katie quickly came over and held a hand out. "I'm Katie. Jack's wife."

Dick shook her hand and said, "I hear congratulations are in order, Mrs. Murphy?"

"Please call me Katie. Yes. That goes double," she said, and immediately realized she'd maybe put her foot in her mouth. "I mean we're getting married and I'm pregnant."

Dick was silent a moment and said, "You may call me Richard and I'll call you Katie."

Chief Pope chimed in: "Katie, if you have a boy, don't let him grow up to be like Jack."

Dick actually smiled and Jack could swear Dick's eye's glowed red. But maybe that was the scotch.

Katie said, "We've picked out names: Little Jack for a boy, Jackie for a girl."

We did what? "Little Jack"? Over my dead body.

"And I hope the baby will be exactly like my husband."

Jack smiled at her. *That's my girl.*

"Brave, honest, loyal, stubborn as a mule and ever-so modest. Well, maybe not exactly like Jack," she said teasingly and everyone got a laugh, especially Devil Dick.

Traitor.

Without further ado, Dick said, "I'd better go. This meeting with the mayor is very important. Budget concerns and such." He locked eyes with Jack and said, "Perhaps some policy changes. Transfers."

That's it for me. "Thanks for coming by. And thanks for this, Deputy Chief. Call me Jack."

"Detective Murphy, mind where you park or you'll pay a towing fee," Dick said, but Jack thought he heard a note of playfulness. Or deep, rumbling laughter and the roar of flames.

With that said, Dick turned and left.

"Chief, I think he's due for a psych evaluation," Jack said. "I can't be bribed." *I can.*

"Never look a gift horse in the mouth, Jack," Captain Franklin said.

Katie added, "Or a bottle of Macallan. I thought that was very nice of Richard."

Richard? WTF?

Claudine interrupted the tender moment. "Open it and pass it around, Jack."

Jack held the bottle against his chest. "Not by the hair of your chinny chin chin. This is a drink for adults."

Captain Franklin said, "Ladies, I hate to be a buzzkill, but I need to talk to Jack and Liddell. Can we go into the kitchen?"

Jack put his empty Dixie Cup down, but held onto the Macallan and got up. They went in the kitchen and Franklin shut the door. He said, "I got a call from your FBI boss. You need to meet the director in my office first thing tomorrow morning."

Franklin was referring to Assistant Deputy Director Toomey, FBI Joint Task Force—USOC—Unsolved Serial and Organized Crimes. The last case he and Liddell had been assigned to had taken Jack across the West to Arizona. Well, he went on his own authority, but Toomey had eventually approved it.

"What are we getting into this time, Captain?" Liddell asked.

"Are either of you claustrophobic?"

Don't miss the next exciting Jack Murphy thriller by Rick Reed

THE FIERCEST ENEMY

Coming soon from Lyrical Underground, an imprint of Kensington Publishing Corp.

Keep reading to enjoy an excerpt...

Chapter 1

He jerked awake in a pitch-black world. He pushed himself up to a sitting position and slid downward until his lower legs plunged into ice-cold water. He dug his elbows into the hard surface, pulled his knees up, and used the soles of his bare feet flat to stop. He was on his butt on an incline on a surface that was like sandpaper; grit and small sharp cinders. A headache pounded behind his eyes and he felt his grip on consciousness was tenuous at best. He lay still until the pounding eased up and he could think.

The skin on his elbows, palms of his hands, and soles of his feet felt raw, like he'd slid down a cheese shredder. But at least he was now on a surface that was warmer than the water below.

"Where the hell am I?" he muttered and twisted his head right and left. It was beyond pitch-black. He could see nothing. The effort made him nauseous and pain exploded behind his eyes and in the back of his skull. *Must have fallen.*

He vaguely remembered being in a bar, drinking tequila. "What have I done?" he asked aloud and his words reverberated, not quite an echo.

He was cold, but not freezing. He must be inside—somewhere. It was early February, bitterly cold, sometimes dipping into the single digits at night. He tried to think, but his skull ached, particularly behind his left ear. He gently touched the spot, felt a lump, and his fingers came away sticky. *Did someone hit me?*

He scooted away from the water and felt the cinders cutting into his feet and arms and palms, but the incline eased to more of a level surface. He tried to stand, but the nauseating dizziness washed over him and his legs buckled. He slid until he plunged into the icy water up to his thighs. The incline was even steeper in the pool of water. He put his heels down to push himself out, but it was slippery. He used his arms and elbows to drag himself back far enough to get out of the water. When he gained some traction, he crab-walked up the slope a short distance before his strength gave out. He lay on his back, panting with the effort. Fear hammered through him, matching the beat of his heart.

He spread his arms like a snow angel and felt the ground to each side. It was hard and slick and peppered with grit-like cinders. He realized he wasn't wearing anything but his boxer shorts. He wrapped his arms across his chest and rubbed and shivered. He was wet, he was cold, his feet and legs were numb. He wanted to remember how he'd gotten here, but his head hurt too much to think.

"What the hell?" he said loudly. His voice bounced back to him. He'd been taking shallow breaths, but the effort of dragging himself had made him breathe more deeply. His nose tickled each time he inhaled and he felt a familiar itch begin in his lungs. He suddenly was sure he knew where he was, or at least what this place was. A cave. It had to be. He could smell the moisture, the earthy smell of undisturbed soil, the pool of water.

He tried not to breathe deep, fearing the tickle he felt was from spores or mold on the cave walls and he had a breathing condition. Not COPD, but close. His inhaler was in the pants he wasn't wearing. To make matters worse, he had a touch of claustrophobia and that feeling of dread was beginning to kick in. He had to find his clothes and get out. Or just get out.

The tickle in his nose grew worse. He slid his boxer shorts off and held them over his mouth and nose. If he could filter the musty stuff, calm himself, take slow breaths, he would be okay.

He sat still, concentrating on each breath, feeling his lungs expand and contract, expand and contract. The cave was dead quiet, except for a steady drip. The water must be coming from the rocks. He could feel it beneath him, a steady drizzle. Not a flow. He would be safe if he could find a way out. His breathing became more regular and his panic subsided. He would work on one problem at a time. He wouldn't drown. Now he just had to find a way out of here.

He rolled carefully onto his side. His head pounded, but the nausea was gone. He pushed up into a kneeling-squatting position. Still good.

"Hey!" he yelled. "Can you hear me?" His words flattened, bounced off the ceiling and walls of his dark prison. "Where am I?" The steady drip answered him.

He crawled four or five feet further away from the water and his hand struck a smooth vertical wall. It was rock, the same as the floor, but there was something wrong with this rock if this was a cave. The rock was smooth, slick, damp. He turned and crawled carefully to his left, planting his hands and knees carefully to lessen the sharp cuts from the cinders.

His hand hit something metal. He ran his hand over it. It was hard and shaped like a train track rail. But the gauge of the steel wasn't heavy enough for a train. *Not a cave. Not a tunnel. A shaft. An underground mine shaft.*

He sniffed his hand. It smelled of charred wood. Charcoal. He *was* in an underground coal mine. He remembered that the machinery used to grind through the coal seam threw off cinders of burned coal. His throat threatened to clench shut and he fought off a wave of panic. He crawled over the track and found another running the same direction. It was a steel track for a railcar. He sat back on his buttocks, thinking, calming himself; taking slow, steady breaths.

The pain in his head was forgotten. To hell with his clothes. If he followed the tracks they would lead to an exit. He couldn't be that deep in a mine. He must have been blitzed last night, but still, he couldn't imagine how he'd even found a mine. Couldn't imagine that he—someone who grew up in mining country and was deathly afraid of the dark spaces underground—would go into a mine. Some of his high school buddies had gone to work for Peabody Coal, but not him. Hell no! He'd been in one mine in his whole life and that was on a dare at a graduation party.

He stood up and reached above his head. He was six-feet-tall and the ceiling was just above his head. The water at the bottom of the shaft must have been rain runoff. The dripping sound was steady. He remembered hearing the pools were sometimes so deep the shaft required constant pumping or it had to be abandoned. He couldn't hear a pump, so this one was abandoned. He was lucky he hadn't staggered into the water and drowned.

He followed the tracks, one foot touching the rail. He covered several feet and stumbled, went down hard, and landed smack on his face. His reflexes were too slow to throw his arms out to break his fall. He heard his nose crunch and felt the cinders grind into his lips and teeth and cheek.

He pushed himself up on his knees and examined himself. He could taste the blood running from his nose. He held his head back and pinched the bridge of his nose to stem the flow, knowing it would do no good. He'd played football in school and had a little experience with broken noses. It would hurt like hell, but would eventually stop bleeding. He wanted out of here. He put the meat of his palms on each side of his nose and popped it back in place. He got to his feet and moved forward, feeling in front, shuffling his feet, feeling for other obstacles.

From somewhere in front of him he heard hinges squeak and a bolt slide into place.

"Hey, I'm in here!" he yelled. "Help me!"

Nothing. He yelled again. "Help! Help me! There's someone in here! I'm in here!"

Still nothing. He moved forward faster, hands feeling out in the darkness. His hand came in contact with another wall. This one felt like wood. *A door.* His heart pounded and he frantically scrabbled for a handle, but found none. The boards making the wall up were wide and fitted together closely, but he found a seam and ran his fingers along it, up to where it intersected with another wider seam. It *was* a door, but there was no handle. He felt the entire surface and felt a smaller door set into the door roughly in the center near the top. It was closed too. He beat on the door, then the smaller one. It felt like it was heavy, thick, and neither one budged.

He put his face against the seam and felt cool air coming through. *At least I'll have air. And water. If the water is drinkable. But I'll get out of here before any of that happens. Someone will come.* He remembered meeting a bunch of friends in the bar. They had gotten him rip-roaring drunk. They were probably having him on. *It's a joke. A not-very-funny practical joke. Right?*

He pounded the sides of his fists on the wood and yelled until he became hoarse. The wood was solid. Probably to keep anyone from going down in that shaft. It was thick enough that he couldn't hear a sound, except for his pounding and yelling and the steady drip of water from below.

He stopped pounding, put his back against the door, and kicked his heels into the wood and screamed until his throat hurt and his head pounded. He sat down against the door, legs straight out, his breath coming in pants. The wound on his head was forgotten. He had bigger problems. He was trapped.

He let his arms drop to his sides and he felt something on the ground. He picked it up. It felt like an empty plastic bottle. He tossed it and listened to it rattle across the ground. The sound was eerie in this small space.

He was angry and scared. Mostly scared. What if none of this was real? What if he'd had an accident, a concussion? He was unconscious and imagined all of this? He'd imagined the sounds. Maybe he was hallucinating the whole thing. The last thing he could remember was going to a bar in Linton and running into a couple of old friends from high school. Maybe someone there had slipped acid or roofies in his drink. Was it even last night? He had no way of judging time.

He'd grown up in a mining town, but he'd only been in a mine once after graduation from high school. His friends had pressured him into going to a by-invitation-only graduation party. His father was a minister and would never have allowed him to go to a party where there would be drinking and drugs and sex. He snuck out and met them near the old Sunflower mine number 2. The Sunflower was on the edge of the hustling metropolis of Dugger, population eight hundred. He didn't have a serious girlfriend all the way through high school and his friends knew it. They also knew he was claustrophobic. They'd taken care of both of his problems, or so they said. That was where he lost his virginity.

He'd hated the shadowy entrance that grew bleaker as it retreated into nothingness. If he hadn't been afraid of his friends calling him a pussy he would never have gone with them. But he was more afraid of what they'd think than being scared of the dark. He'd done a little acid that night too, but he justified it because they all had. He regretted it to this day.

He had to wonder if his father had been right. If this was his punishment for mistakes made. Being here. Reliving that experience. Doing penance in hell. A fist of emotion seemed to swell in his chest and tears streamed down his face.

A hinge squeaked and he caught a glimpse of movement above him. Something hit the ground a few feet in front. The hinges squeaked, the bolt slid shut, and he heard a loud hissing noise coming from nearby. His reflex was to jump up and bang on the door again, but caution told him he should find remain still, find out what had been thrown into his cell. It sounded like a snake.

The hissing continued and his eyes stung, his nose clogged, he couldn't breathe. It was gas. Tear gas. The fumes were filling the shaft. He lay on the floor, where he thought the gas might not be as strong, but he was wrong. It was worse near the ground. Gas was heavier than air.

He scooted back to the door and stood against it, trying to find the seam where he'd felt the air coming in. For one panicked moment he couldn't find it, but when he did he put his mouth against the crack. He succeeded in drawing in a large lungful of the gas.

He rubbed at his eyes and coughed and spat, but everything he tried made it burn deeper. He hacked and gagged until his throat closed. He laid back against the door, unable to even cry out. Soon, he slumped to the floor, eyes open and swollen, nose running, hands on his own throat. His body spasmed, one leg kicked out, and he lay still.

Acknowledgments

I would like to acknowledge some special people who have allowed me the use their names as characters in this story: Tony Walker, Tim Morris, Penny "Jackie" Pepper, Karen Stenger Walker, Ginger Purdie, and Bennet Cato.

I would also like to acknowledge the men and women of the Evansville Police Department and the civilian employees. I can't imagine a world without law enforcement. Be safe. Thank you.

The existence of this eighth book in the Jack Murphy thriller series is due in no small part to Michaela Hamilton, my editor, who believed in me and gave me a chance. I consider her my friend and mentor. And kudos to my excellent team at Kensington, who are experts at publicity, marketing, proofing, editing, legalese, cover design, distribution, and so many other things. Without all of you this book would still be a file on my computer.

If I have not mentioned you, I hope I have thanked you in some way and you will forgive my omission.

Last, but not least, I thank my beautiful wife, Jennifer, for giving me space and understanding, not to mention reminding me it's time to eat or go to bed, and bringing me a scotch from time to time.

This novel is a work of fiction and is not intended to reflect negatively on any law enforcement agency or person. Any resemblance to people, groups of people, businesses, or agencies is purely coincidental. I sincerely hope readers will understand my taking poetic license. If there are any errors in this book, they are all mine.

USOC, or Unsolved Serial and Organized Crimes, is not a real FBI task force and is solely my creation.

About the Author

Author photo, by George Routt

Sergeant Rick Reed (Ret.), author of the Jack Murphy thriller series, is a twenty-plus-year veteran police detective. During his career, he successfully investigated numerous high-profile criminal cases, including a serial killer who claimed thirteen lives before strangling and dismembering his fourteenth and last victim. He recounted that story in his acclaimed true-crime book, *Blood Trail*. Rick spent his last three years on the force as the commander of the police department's internal affairs section. He has two master's degrees and upon retiring from the police force, took a full-time teaching position at a community college. He currently teaches criminal justice at Volunteer State Community College in Tennessee and writes thrillers. He lives near Nashville with his wife and two furry friends, Lexie and Luther. Please visit him on Facebook, Goodreads, or at his website, www.rickreedbooks.com.

Don't miss these other thrilling books by Rick Reed!

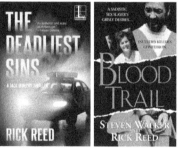

ɪ can be obtained
.ng.com
JSA
05070420
V00001B/78